"*T*ell me your name," the marquis demanded gently.

Heart throbbing in the base of her throat, Lily shook her head.

"Is it Diana? Anna? Am I even close?"

"No."

His jaw tightened. "Well, then, since you insist upon leaving me with nothing more of yourself than a memory, I suppose I had best make that memory one neither of us shall ever forget."

Before she could draw her next breath, his lips claimed hers, moving over her own with a skill and passion that sent her thoughts whirling away at the speed of a shooting star. Dark and demanding, his kiss sizzled through her, firing her blood and leaving her dizzy and trembling in his arms. . . .

Also by Tracy Anne Warren

*My Fair Mistress*

*The Husband Trap*
*The Wife Trap*
*The Wedding Trap*

# THE ACCIDENTAL MISTRESS

A NOVEL

## TRACY ANNE WARREN

BALLANTINE BOOKS • NEW YORK

*The Accidental Mistress* is a work of fiction. Names, characters, places, and incidents are the products of the author's imagination or are used fictitiously. Any resemblance to actual events, locales, or persons, living or dead, is entirely coincidental.

A Ballantine Books Mass Market Original

Copyright © 2007 by Tracy Anne Warren
Excerpt from *His Favorite Mistress* copyright © 2007 by Tracy Anne Warren

Published in the United States by Ballantine Books, an imprint of The Random House Publishing Group, a division of Random House, Inc., New York.

BALLANTINE and colophon are registered trademarks of Random House, Inc.

This book contains an excerpt from the forthcoming mass market edition of *His Favorite Mistress* by Tracy Anne Warren. This excerpt has been set for this edition only and may not reflect the final content of the forthcoming edition.

ISBN 978-0-345-49540-2

Cover illustration: Chris Cocozza

Printed in the United States of America

www.ballantinebooks.com

OPM  9  8  7  6  5  4  3  2  1

For my sister, Victoria.
Talented chef, avid romance reader,
and devoted lover of dogs

# Acknowledgments

MY SINCERE GRATITUDE to the entire team at Ballantine—I appreciate everything you do!

A special mention to my friends at DCAA—thanks for your warm wishes and support.

And hugs to Lannette and Gus Moutos, who knew me years ago when being an author was nothing but a far-off dream.

# Chapter One

### April 1814
### Cornwall, England

*O*NLY A FEW *more yards,* Lily Bainbridge told herself. *Only a little while longer and I will be safe. I will be free.*

An icy wave struck her dead in the face. Gasping for breath, she pushed on, arm over arm, as she fought the unrelenting drag of the rough, rolling sea. Above her, lightning flashed against a viscous gray sky, slashes of rain hurtling downward to sting her skin like a barrage of tiny needles.

Arms quivering from the strain, she put the discomfort out of her mind and kept swimming, knowing it was either that or drown. And despite the suicide note she'd left back in her bedroom at the house, she had no intention of dying, certainly not today.

Many would call her insane to plunge into the sea during a storm, but regardless of the danger, she'd known she had to act without fear or hesitation. Delay would mean marriage to Squire Edgar Faylor, and as she'd told her stepfather, she would rather be dead than bound for life to such a loathsome brute. But her stepfather cared naught for her wishes, since marriage to Faylor would mean a profitable business deal for him.

Slowing, she scanned the jagged shoreline, and the waves that crashed in thunderous percussion against the rocks and shoals. Although she'd swum these waters for nearly the whole of her twenty years, she'd never done so during such a seething tempest. Alarmingly, nothing looked quite the same, familiar vantage points distorted by the dim light and the churning spray of the surf.

Treading fast, she fought the clinging weight of her gown, the sodden muslin coiling around her legs like iron shackles. Doubtless she would have been better off stripping down to her shift before taking to the sea, but her "death" had to look convincing, enough so that her stepfather would not suspect the truth. If she lived through this and he discovered she was still alive, he would hunt her down without an ounce of mercy.

With her heart drumming in her chest, she swam harder, knowing she dare not let herself drift and be swept out to sea. A knot formed in the base of her throat at the disquieting thought, a shiver rippling through her tired limbs. *What if I've miscalculated?* she worried. *What if the storm has already carried me out too far?*

Her apprehensions evaporated when a familiar sight came into view: a narrow fissure, black as coal, that cut its way into the towering cliffs that lined the shore. To the casual eye, the opening appeared no different from any of the other sea caves in the area, but Lily knew otherwise. For beyond its foreboding exterior lay protection and escape.

Giving an exuberant pair of kicks, she continued forward, crossing at an angle through the waves. With the tide now at her back, the surf pushed her fast. For a moment, she feared she might be dashed to pieces against the rocks, but at the last second the current shifted and washed her inside with a gentle, guiding hand.

Darkness engulfed her. Tamping down a momentary sense of disorientation, she swam ahead, knowing better than to be afraid. The cave was an old smuggler's pass that had fallen into disuse, a secret retreat that had once provided a perfect hideaway for inquisitive children, and now for a truant would-be bride.

With seawater eddying around her at a placid lap, she glided forward until she brushed up against the cave's perimeter wall. A small search soon revealed a ledge that told her she was in the right place. Dripping and shivering, she hoisted herself up onto its surface, then paused for a moment to gain her breath before rising to her feet. Careful of each step, she followed the cave's gentle bell shape until the interior gradually widened to provide a pocket of natural warmth and dryness. When her foot struck a large, solid object, she knew she had arrived at her ultimate destination.

Teeth chattering, she leaned over and felt for a wooden lid, opening the trunk. Her fingers trembled as they curved around the lantern she knew lay inside and the metal matchbox set carefully to one side. With the strike of a match, light filled the space, flickering eerily off the rough walls and low stone ceiling. Stiff with chill, she stripped off her clothes, then reached again into the trunk for a large woolen blanket, wrapping herself inside it.

Thank heavens she'd had the foresight to secret away these supplies! After her mother's death six months ago, she'd known she would eventually have to flee, aware that as soon as the mourning period ended, her stepfather, Gordon Chaulk, would likely decide "to do something about her," as he'd been threatening to for years.

And so, while out on her regular daily walk, she had slowly filled the smuggler's chest with necessities, including money, food, and a set of men's clothes she'd altered from old ones of her father's. As for boots, she'd had no choice but to steal a pair from one of the smaller stable boys. Not wanting the lad to suffer for his loss, she'd anonymously left him enough coin to purchase new ones. He'd grinned about the odd theft and his propitious windfall for weeks.

To her knowledge, no one but a few old-time smugglers knew about this hideout, despite the thriving business of sneaking contraband tea and French brandy past the noses of the local excise men. Certainly her stepfather wasn't aware of the caves. To most Cornishmen, he was still considered an outsider, despite having lived here for five years—ever since marrying her mother and taking up residence at Bainbridge Manor.

*Five years,* Lily sighed. *Five years to wear the life out of a good woman who'd deserved far, far better than she'd received.*

A familiar lump swelled in her throat, a single tear sliding down her cheek. Ruthlessly, she dashed it away, telling herself that now was not the time to dwell upon her mother's untimely demise. If only she'd been able to convince Mama to leave years ago. If only she'd been able to keep her from falling prey to the blandishments of a handsome charmer, who'd turned out to have the heart of a poisonous viper. But having been a child at the time, her opinion had not been sought, nor would it have been heeded.

Toweling dry the worst drips from her hair, Lily crossed to a pile of kindling stacked against the far wall. Using some of the wood, she built a small fire. Blessed heat soon warmed the space, calming the worst of the shivers that continued to rack her body. Returning to the trunk, she dressed in a shirt, trousers, and coat, the masculine attire feeling strange against her skin. *At least the clothing is warm, and—even better—dry,* she mused. *And until I reach London, I had best get used to being dressed like a boy.*

She wasn't so foolish as to imagine she could journey to London on her own, at least not dressed as a woman. A female traveling without escort would invite comment, but worse, she would be subject to all manner of predators wishing to make her their prey—out to steal her reticule or, shudder the thought, her virtue. And in addition to providing her some measure of safety, the ruse would allow her to leave the area without detection. Rather than accept help of any kind, she planned to make the long walk to the coaching inn at Penzance. That way, should her stepfather question anyone later, they would have no cause to remember a redheaded girl matching her description.

Nerves made her wish she could leave now, but until the worst of the storm subsided, she knew she would be better off staying here inside the cave. Pulling on a pair of long woolen socks that eased the cold from her toes, she reached once more into the trunk for a cloth-covered wedge of cheese. Belly growling, she broke off a chunk and ate, enjoying the sharp, satisfying flavor.

Minutes later, her meal finished, she prepared to complete one last task—an act she had been dreading. Just the thought of proceeding made her cringe. *But the deed must be done.*

Locating her ivory comb, she drew the teeth through her damp, waist-length hair, careful to remove every last tangle before tying it back with a thin, black silk ribbon. Drawing a deep, fortifying breath, she lifted a pair of scissors and began to cut.

Three days later, Ethan Andarton, Fifth Marquis of Vessey, swallowed a last bite of shepherd's pie, then set his knife and fork at an angle on his plate and pushed it away. Reaching for the wine bottle, he refilled his glass with a dry red of questionable vintage—apparently the best The Ox and Owl in Hungerford could provide.

Crowded full of men come to town for a nearby boxing mill, the public room hummed with noise and the occasional raucous burst of laughter. Drifting in spirals near the ceiling lay an acrid blue cloud of pipe smoke, combined with the yeasty scent of ale and the heavy aroma of fried meat. With the inn's only private parlor already occupied, Ethan had decided to sit among the locals, tucking himself into a surprisingly comfortable corner table. From his vantage point, he could see all the boisterous goings-ons. But such matters were not on his mind as he quaffed another mouthful of wine.

*It will be good to get back to London,* he mused. *Good to return to my usual amusements and haunts now that I've taken the necessary first steps to see my future arranged.*

Not that he was eager to *have* his future arranged, but a long span of serious reflection on the matter had convinced him he could no longer afford to put off his duty. At thirty-five, he knew he must wed. He had a responsibility to his lineage, an obligation to sire sons who would carry on the family name and title. And in order to do so he must have a bride—whether he truly desired one or not.

Of course, were his older brothers, Arthur and Frederick, alive, he wouldn't be facing this particular dilemma. Arthur would be marquis now, no doubt long since married with children of his own. But by some cruel twist of fate, both of his brothers had lost their lives during an attempt to save a tenant's child from drowning in a storm-swollen river. Frederick had dived in first; then, when his brother failed to emerge, Arthur had followed. In the end, all three had perished, both men and the child.

Ethan had often wondered what might have happened had he been home that fateful day instead of traveling on the Continent. Would he have been able to save them? Or would he, too, have lost his life? He knew he would gladly have traded places, gladly have died in order to save the life of even one of his brothers. Instead, in an instant, he'd gone from third in line to being marquis, a position he had never once craved for himself.

After the accident, he'd arrived home raw with grief over the loss of his brothers only to find every eye upon him—family, servants, and tenants, all looking to him for guidance and reassurance. Feeling his old, carefree life slip like sand from his grasp, he'd done his best to step into Arthur's shoes and honor what his older brother had left behind.

In the twelve years since, Ethan had risen to the challenge, learning what he must, meeting each expectation and every demand with determination and fortitude. There was one obligation, however, upon which he had long turned his back, stubbornly retaining that last bit of independence—until now.

He remembered his friend the Duke of Wyvern's reaction when he'd mentioned his decision last week.

"You cannot mean it," Anthony Black had said, his brandy snifter frozen halfway to his mouth. "Why on earth do you want to go and get leg-shackled? Especially when you've a surfeit of beautiful, willing women climbing in and out of your bed. Women, I might add, who have no expectations of achieving a ring out of the deal."

Leaning back in his chair at Brooks's Club, Ethan met his friend's midnight-blue gaze. "Because it's time, Tony, whether I want it to be or not. I can't put this off forever. I need to think to my future, the family's future. It's my duty to set up my nursery and father an heir or two to assure the title."

Tony waved a dismissive hand, his ruby signet ring winking red as a prime Bordeaux in the mellow candlelight. "That's what cousins are for—to continue the line when the present titleholder doesn't wish to be bound for life."

"So you are as set against marriage as ever, then?"

Ethan said, already knowing Tony's answer. "But won't you regret not having sons? Do you truly not mind the idea of letting your cousin Reggie inherit the dukedom?"

Tony produced a quiet snort. "Reggie is a bit of a dandified fool, I'll grant, but he'll do well enough. Besides, I don't plan on dying anytime soon. If I have my way, I'll outlive Reggie, and one of his sons or grandsons will take the title. As for sons of my own, well, one can't have everything in life."

The duke rubbed a fingertip over one of the understated gold buttons on his white Marcella waistcoat. "Besides, just think if I swore off my bachelor state and married some vapid miss. We'd likely end up at each other's throats and she'd give me nothing but daughters, just to be spiteful. No, my friend, I prefer to remain single."

*I wish I could be so sanguine,* Ethan had mused at the time. *How much simpler everything would be.*

"If you are determined to pursue this folly," Tony said, "which I can see by your face that you are, then I assume you will be dancing attendance on this year's crop of eligible debutantes."

Ethan grimaced. "I've already viewed this year's crop and last year's as well—the past decade's worth, come to think, and there's none who strike my fancy. Each girl is just like the next, all of them silly, giggling misses who think of nothing but acquiring a fine title and enough money to keep them in fancy silks, grand carriages, and extravagant parties for the rest of their natural lives." He shook his head. "No, courting one would be grim work indeed, especially since any girl I chose would undoubtedly expect me to profess undying love for her, despite us both knowing such devotion to be a lie."

"If not the marriage mart, then what? I fail to see how you plan to accomplish your goal otherwise."

Ethan set a fist beneath his chin. "Have I ever told you about my neighbor, the Earl of Sutleigh? When my brothers and I were all just babes, my mother apparently made a pact with the earl, the pair of them deciding that one of her sons would someday marry one of his daughters. A tacit understanding has existed between our families ever since, though it is not widely known.

"Arthur, of course, was expected to marry Sutleigh's eldest girl Matilda, but that idea ended with his death, and Frederick's. If Mother could have managed it, she would have pushed the match for me, but I wasn't about to wed then no matter Mama's protestations. The following spring Matilda married another and I was off the hook."

"So what has changed?"

"Sutleigh's youngest daughter, who just turned seventeen. After a great deal of consideration, I've decided to offer for her. Not only is she eminently suitable to be my marchioness, marrying her will honor the old agreement between her family and mine."

"Good God, Ethan, have you even met the chit?"

"Yes, for a few minutes at last year's family yuletide celebration. She's a pretty child, well-bred and biddable. What more do I need to know?"

"That you are insane to bind yourself to her. You'll be bored in a fortnight."

"If I am, what will it matter? She will provide me heirs, and in return I will allow her to go her own way so long as she is discreet. The arrangement is sure to suit us both."

*So why does it already seem so hollow and dissatisfying?* he wondered.

Perhaps he'd spent too much time around his friends Rafe and Julianna Pendragon. Of all the couples he knew, their marriage was one of the few based on genuine, lasting love, the relationship made even more special by its uniqueness. But such unions were rare, particularly for those of their class.

"So when is the felicitous event?" Tony questioned with a cynical twist to his lips.

"Not for some months yet, since Amelia is still in the schoolroom. I've sent a letter asking to call upon her father and he has agreed. I have no doubt he will greet my offer with felicity. So I am off to Bath, where the earl is taking the waters. I don't expect the two of us to arrive at anything more than a casual understanding for now. Next year, after Amelia has enjoyed a bit of the Season, will be soon enough to discuss a settlement and make the engagement official."

And so everything had gone—his assumptions proving true a couple of days later over glasses of the foul-smelling water served at Bath's Pump Room. The earl expressed great pleasure at Ethan's proposal, granting him the right to seek his daughter's hand in marriage. Nothing would be said to Amelia for now, they agreed, but the earl assured him she would accept his offer without hesitation when the time arrived.

With that settled, Ethan had headed back toward London.

Tired and hungry from the journey, he'd stopped here at The Ox and Owl to change teams and break his fast. Raising a hand now, he signaled for the serving girl, sending her off for a bottle of brandy.

Hips swaying, she soon returned, an open bottle and a snifter in hand. Setting the glass on the table, she leaned forward to pour, making sure he had a keen view of her very healthy breasts, her bodice straining wildly to contain them.

Once his beverage was poured, he handed her a coin. "Thank you, love."

The girl giggled, then made a little cooing noise before slipping the sovereign between her breasts. "Is there anything else I can be gettin' fer you, my lord? Anything at all?"

For a second, he debated the offer. "The brandy will do."

Bobbing a curtsey, she sighed out her disappointment. "If you change your mind, you've only to say."

Forgetting her the moment she'd gone, he removed a cheroot from his inner coat pocket and used his silver cutter to snip off the end. He was withdrawing a match when a new group of people entered the room.

By the weary look of them, he assumed they were travelers fresh off one of the mail coaches that made regular stops along this route. As he watched, three men and a woman shouldered their way forward, leaving a boy to stand alone in the doorway.

Top hat pulled low across his eyes, the youth was a curious figure. Slight as a wisp, the child's out-of-date clothing hung a bit too large on his lean frame. Just as antiquated was the thick rope of fire-colored hair he'd gathered into a queue along the back his neck. Possessed of a soft chin and rounded jaw, his smooth cheeks were years away from whiskers.

*What a babe-in-the-woods!* Ethan mused. *Not a day above fourteen, if I don't miss my guess.* Looking again, he noted the boy's delicate heart-shaped face, fair skin, and pretty pink lips that formed a perfect cupid's bow.

As he watched, the child scanned the room, clearly seeking a place to sit. After a long moment, the youth spied an empty spot along the far wall and crossed to slide onto the end of a bench seat. Ethan couldn't help but smile at the obvious gap the boy left between himself and the burly laborer to his side.

The servant girl arrived moments later to take the

youth's order, a teasing grin on her lips that the boy was clearly too young to appreciate. With a laugh and a shimmy of her hips that drew suggestive remarks from a pair of men at another table, she soon retreated into the kitchen.

Pouring more brandy into his glass, Ethan quaffed a slow mouthful, then lighted his cigar and took a leisurely pull. As he did, his eyes went again to the child, watching as the serving girl returned to set a steaming cup of tea and a plate of biscuits and jam before him.

Laying a napkin across his lap, the boy took up a knife and cut open one of the biscuits, his movements delicate, with none of the usual ham-fisted carelessness of a child still learning to control his developing body. When the youth reached for his tea, his movements betrayed him once more, as he lifted the cup between a pair of slender, elegantly balanced fingers.

Poised fingers.

Dainty fingers.

The kind that clasped "just so," employing a hold no male—man or boy—could ever hope to achieve.

A burst of knowledge suddenly sizzled in Ethan's brain. Staring harder, his eyes narrowed as he more closely studied the shape of the youth's face—the soft sensuality of his lips, the almost porcelain smoothness of his translucent skin.

*That's no boy,* Ethan realized. *That's a woman!*

A wide smile tilted Ethan's lips, together with a great deal of intrigued speculation. *Who in the world is she,* he wondered, *and what does she think she's about, masquerading in masculine garb?* Unable to look away, he watched again as she sipped her tea, her gaze finally lifting to briefly survey the room. And in that instant, he finally got a glimpse of her eyes.

Green and gorgeous, they were as intense as a cat's

and just as full of curiosity, trimmed with a fringe of long, fire-colored lashes that were as luxurious as they were feminine.

He sucked in a breath at the sight, a hard pull of desire springing to life beneath his trousers. Now that he'd deduced the truth about her gender, he couldn't believe he'd been fooled for so much as an instant. With the possible exception of her cropped hair, there was nothing remotely masculine about her—not her features nor her figure nor the manner in which she held herself, each gesture of her hand and face announcing her innate femininity.

Glancing around, he checked to see if anyone else had noticed, but none of the other patrons were paying her the least heed, busy with their own conversations and concerns.

*Amazing,* he mused, *that I am the only person in this room who has guessed that we have an imposter in our midst, and a lovely little imposter at that.*

He supposed the reaction was normal enough. As a rule, people often saw what they expected to see, not pausing long enough to question, not even when the truth was literally staring them in the face.

Perhaps the success of her disguise was for the best, though, he decided. A woman without escort took great chances—especially a female daring enough to portray herself as a man. Not only did she hazard social censure, she ran the risk of inviting unwanted attention from all sorts of dangerous individuals. Some men would interpret such a provocative act as license to do as they pleased with her—anything they pleased, regardless of gaining her consent.

Whoever the minx was, she clearly had no notion of the potential jeopardy in which she'd placed herself. Continuing his contemplation of her over another swallow of brandy, he estimated her age. Twenty or twenty-one, he suspected. Young enough to make mistakes, but old enough to know better than to have made this particular one.

Filling her cup with the last of the hot tea left to her in a small teapot, the young woman took a single, restrained sip, then returned her cup to the saucer.

Scant moments later, she jumped and turned her head, clearly startled by whatever the hefty man on her other side had barked out. Leaping up with surprising speed, the young woman flattened her back against the wall to let the man pass.

As willowy as she might be, there simply wasn't room for them both. Nonetheless, the man made an attempt to shuffle by, jarring the table and tipping over the cup of tea on his way.

Hot liquid flowed outward in a quick rush and splashed onto his trousers. Beating frantically at the spreading stain, he knocked into the table again, huffing out a bellow worthy of an enraged bull.

Ethan surged to his feet and started across the room.

The man turned on the girl. "Look what you've done! Ruined me duds and damn near scalded me jewels besides. You'll have to answer for this, boy."

"I am sorry, but I . . ." The girl broke off, obviously realizing her voice was high enough to give her away had anyone cared to listen.

"But I *what*?" the big man repeated with menacing intent.

"Was not at fault," Ethan answered in a firm tone as he stepped forward and inserted himself into the fray. "Or at least that's what I assume the young man planned to say. If he wasn't, he should have done."

Her back still pressed against the rough plastered wall, Lily looked up and into the face of an avenging angel. Breath flowed from her lungs at the sight of him—indisputably the most dynamic male she had ever glimpsed in her life.

With hair the color of sun-ripened wheat and eyes as luminous as polished amber, he exuded masculinity and an undeniable aura of easy, confident power. She allowed herself a second longer to explore, letting her gaze roam over his strong, square jaw and refined nose, across the sculpted contours of his high forehead and angular cheeks. Last, she traced the shape of his sensuous mouth, lips that promised the kind of exquisite pleasure even a girl as innocent as she could sense.

Her heart thudded faster, though not from fear this time.

Doing her utmost to shake off her instant and completely uncharacteristic attraction to the man, she shifted her gaze and tugged her hat lower on her head.

*So much for traveling to London without incident!* she mused. *Yet thank heavens this man has come to my aid.*

Her savior gave the brute a smile that didn't quite reach his eyes. "You were in the process of leaving, were you not?"

Silence descended, the burly laborer staring as if he didn't fully understand.

"Move along, then," the tall stranger said. In the next instant, his gaze lowered, glancing over the rather large wet patch on the other man's trousers. "I suspect a few minutes in the sunshine will set that to rights, though you may have to field some rather uncomfortable questions in the interim."

Ruddy color flashed in the brute's cheeks, his embarrassment and frustration clear. Giving them both a fearsome glare, he shoved the table and sent the teacup and what remained of her biscuit toppling to the floor. On a growl, the man strode from the room.

Lily looked at her ruined meal and the broken crockery, wondering how she was going to pay for the damage if they insisted she do so. Despite starting the journey with what had seemed an adequate sum of money, she'd soon discovered her error. Due to inflation from the war, everything cost more—coach fare, food, and especially lodgings. Of course, once she reached London and claimed her grandfather's bequest, her financial worries would cease, but until then, every shilling counted.

Her stomach grumbled with hunger, making her wish she'd been a lot faster when it came to finishing her repast.

Noticing the commotion, the innkeeper hurried toward them. "My lord, what has happened? Is this boy bothering you?"

The golden-haired gentleman shook his head. "Not at all. It was the other fellow, the one who just departed, who caused all the difficulty."

Peering downward, the stranger met her gaze, a curious twinkle in his amber eyes, as if he held some secret. "Are you all right, lad?"

Lily started to answer, remembering only at the last second to lower her voice to its deepest baritone. As a result, her words cracked, high to low, as if she were indeed a boy going through puberty. "Fine. I'm fine. Thank you, my lord. It was most kind of you to intercede."

An amused expression crossed his face before he waved off her gratitude with a hand. "It was my pleasure, lad. And where are you headed, if I might inquire? I could not help but notice that you are here alone."

She opened her mouth to say *London,* then realized that perhaps she oughtn't. True, she would never see this man again, but she would be wise not to underestimate the resourcefulness of her stepfather. Chances were slim, but if someone did come snooping, she wanted no potential trail left to follow.

"Bristol," she improvised. "I . . . um . . . have cousins there who are expecting me."

"I am relieved to hear you will soon be in the care of family." The nobleman cast his gaze over the ruined remnants of her snack. "Your meal has met a sad fate. Shall we see it replaced?"

She shook her head, thinking again of the meager contents of her coin purse. "Oh no, I've had all I want."

He arched a brow. "Half a biscuit hardly seems sufficient fare."

Her stomach chose that moment to prove him right by emitting a mortifying rumble that left no one in doubt as to the emptiness of her belly.

The man smiled again and turned to the innkeeper. "Is the private parlor still occupied?"

"No, my lord, the gentlemen departed only a few minutes ago."

"Good. Then I shall take it for the young man so he might enjoy a hearty repast—at my expense, of course."

Lily moved to object. "It is most kind of you to offer, my lord, but I cannot allow you to buy nuncheon for me." She straightened her shoulders with pride. "I do quite well on my own."

"Oh, I'm sure you do, but a good meal never comes amiss." The nobleman met her gaze, his expression reassuringly honest as he bent closer to her. "You have naught to fear, you know," he promised in a hushed tone meant only for her. "I expect nothing in return save your company and a bit of conversation."

*So he means to join me?* she thought. Allowing him to purchase a meal for her was unseemly enough, but to actually dine with him . . . well, no proper young lady would dare. Then again, what proper young lady would fake her own death, run away from home, and journey to London disguised as a boy? When she considered the situation from that perspective, sharing a meal with a stranger didn't seem so dreadful.

*And what a gorgeous stranger he is!* She sighed inwardly, peering up at him from beneath her lashes. *A veritable blond Adonis.* What harm could come from spending an hour in his company while she waited for the coach to resume its journey? After all, it was *only* nuncheon and a bit of talk, as he suggested. Once she'd eaten, she would thank him and be on her way, the two of them destined to never meet again.

Hunger pangs jabbed like a sharpened pick inside her belly, urging her to accept. Since her mad flight from home three days ago, she hadn't eaten a single satisfying meal. Between the less-than-stellar fare to be found at some of the coaching inns and her need for frugality, she'd mostly made due with biscuits, tea, and soup, grateful if the broth contained a few small chunks of meat or vegetables. How wonderful it would be to eat a decent meal. And all she had to do was agree to converse for a brief time with an attractive lord, who didn't even know she was a young lady.

"Very well, you have convinced me," she said, ignoring the little voice that reminded her that she had just agreed to be alone in a private parlor with a man. "Thank you, my lord."

*My lord what?* she wondered, suddenly realizing she didn't even know his name.

"I am Vessey, by the way," he stated in answer to her unspoken question. "The Marquis of Vessey. And you are?"

*A marquis! Good gracious! But more to the point, he has asked who I am. Well, I can't very well tell him Lily Bainbridge, now can I?*

She cudgeled her brain. "Uh . . . I'm Jack. Jack Bain."

Another slow, half-amused smile crossed his face as if he were enjoying a private joke. "Well, Jack, Jack Bain, I am pleased to make your acquaintance. Now, if you are ready, shall we adjourn upstairs?"

She gulped down a breath, nerves crashing like cymbals inside her chest. Meeting the marquis's leonine gaze, she paused for one long, last moment, then sealed her fate with a nod.

# Chapter Two

❦

"ARE YOU NOT having anything?" asked the young woman known to Ethan only as "Jack Bain," her knife and fork poised over a plate of roast chicken and vegetables.

Seated across from her at the private parlor's round oak table, he shook his head. "I find I am not terribly hungry. This brandy will do quite well." Raising the snifter, he took a swallow. "Go ahead, eat. No need to stand on ceremony."

After a momentary pause she dug in, not at all missish about enjoying her food. Despite her enthusiasm, and obvious hunger, there was nothing lacking in her table manners. They were excellent, as were her manners in general—all testament to her having been raised a member of the Quality. Her diction was exceptional as well, in spite of the amusing baritone voice she struggled to maintain. He'd forced down a laugh on more than one occasion during the past twenty minutes, enjoying her act far more than he knew he ought.

*Who is she?* he wondered, not for the first time. *And why is she perpetrating this charade?*

Rather than simply demand the truth from her, he'd decided it would be more fun to play along for a while and see just how far she was willing to take her deception.

He poured another inch of brandy into his snifter, sunlight from the room's trio of windows refracting through the glass to turn the alcohol a shade reminiscent of warm honey. Swirling the liquor, he watched the rivulets pool at the bottom before taking another drink.

When she'd eaten nearly every bite on her plate and was about to lay down her utensils, he gave in to the impulse to tease her a bit.

"More chicken?" he asked, reaching for the knife to cut a large slice of breast meat. Considering the substantial helping she had already consumed, it was doubtful she would be in want of seconds. "When I was your age," he continued, "I could never seem to eat enough. I am sure it must be the same for you, a growing young man and all."

Her brows knitted into a V on her forehead, her gaze focused in obvious consternation on the thick slice of chicken he was cutting.

After a long hesitation, she showed her mettle by extending her plate.

"How about potatoes?" he dared, scooping a pair of tender, golden halves onto a pewter serving spoon. "I hate to see good food go to waste, don't you?"

With determination, she accepted the offering.

"Creamed onions?" he suggested next. "You commented you thought them particularly delicious."

Her nostrils flared around the edges.

He waited for her to refuse. Instead she held steady despite a faint quiver of her hand.

Disguising a smile, he relented, setting down the serving utensil, then leaning back in his chair.

With a deep breath, she began eating what he'd heaped onto her plate.

*She has pluck*, he mused as he observed her effort to maintain her guise as a boy and do justice to the food.

"So Bristol, is it?" he commented, drinking another mouthful of spirits.

She paused in her eating. "What?"

"Bristol. That is where you are headed, are you not? To your cousins?"

Her jewel-toned eyes grew round for a faint instant before relaxing again. "Yes, that's right."

*He wondered if she'd ever even been to Bristol.*

"Tell me of these cousins, then."

He watched as she lay down her knife and fork and used the delay to concoct an answer, leaving several un-eaten bites of food on her plate—much to her relief, he was sure.

"There is little to tell," she replied. "They own a house and some land."

"They've tenants, do they?"

She lifted her fork again to slide an onion to a new lo-cation on her plate. "Yes."

"And will you be staying with them long?"

She paused, then shook her head. "No, not long."

*Not at all,* he thought.

A minute later, a knock sounded at the door, a differ-ent serving girl from the one who'd waited on him downstairs coming in to clear. Once the dishes had been removed, the innkeeper returned with a round pewter plate containing a selection of apples, dried figs, and a wedge of blue-veined cheese.

"Help yourself," Ethan suggested once the others had departed.

"Thank you, but I am well satisfied."

Taking up a knife, Ethan sliced a fig in half, then added a sliver of cheese on top. He washed the combina-tion down with a swallow of brandy. "Delicious."

She said nothing.

"Do you mind if I smoke?" He drew a fresh cheroot from his coat pocket.

"No, not at all," she replied in her mock baritone, the husky quality beginning to make his blood hum.

After lighting the cigar, he enjoyed a drawing puff, exhaling an elegant stream of smoke at a sideways angle, away from her.

He couldn't help but notice her interest in the process. Likely she was used to withdrawing from the room with the ladies in order to allow the gentlemen to partake of a pipe or cheroot. But as he reminded himself, she was currently in the guise of a young man, an adolescent male who would be inclined to enjoy the camaraderie of such an exclusively masculine act.

*Which gives me a rather naughty idea,* he mused.

Sending another plume of smoke toward the ceiling, he met her gaze. "Care for a try?"

The V formed again on her brow. "Oh, I don't know—"

"I can see your curiosity; nothing wrong with that. Most young men your age sneak the occasional puff when they know they won't be caught." He extended the cigar lengthwise for her to take. "Don't worry. I won't say a word."

Clearly she was tempted, this woman who played at being a boy. What else might she be tempted to try if given the proper incentive? Just the right sensual provocation?

A long moment later, Ethan was wondering if he might have overestimated the extent of her daring after all when she reached out and took the cheroot from his hand. Balancing the rolled tobacco between her fingertips the way one might hold an extremely delicate, rather volatile weapon, she slowly raised it to her lips.

"A shallow puff only," he warned. But his admonition came too late, "Jack" drawing in a robust inhale that made the tip glow red.

For an instant, the world hung motionless on its axis

as each of them took in the magnitude of her act. Expelling a cloud of smoke from her mouth and nostrils in a rapid gust, she fell into a violent paroxysm of coughing, gagging and gasping for air, a faintly green cast tingeing her skin.

*Good God, she isn't going to cast up her accounts, is she?* he thought, suddenly worried he oughtn't to have prodded her into eating such a large nuncheon.

But as she continued to cough and wheeze, struggling desperately for her next breath, her normal pink color returned. More than returned, he noticed, color ripening over her cheeks and forehead as though she'd stood face-first in front of a blazing kitchen spit.

Locating a pitcher of water, he poured a glass and came to her side. "Here, drink this."

Waving him away, she shook her head and continued to cough.

Catching her hand in his own, he set the glass inside. "Drink," he ordered.

Still coughing, she obeyed, taking small, hesitant sips of the water, then longer, deeper gulps.

"More," she begged, her voice raspy with strain.

He poured another glass for her, then stood back and watched as she swallowed it all.

*"Augh!"* she exclaimed, smacking her lips against what she clearly considered to be a disgusting taste.

Then, as if only just realizing she was still holding the cheroot, she flung it onto the table, uncaring whether or not the tip continued to burn.

Acting fast, he caught the cigar before it could roll onto the floor and cause damage.

"No need to treat a fine smoke in such a disrespectful manner," he stated, tamping out the end on a nearby dish.

"Fine smoke! That . . . thing . . . is utterly vile."

"That 'thing' is an imported Cuban all the way from

the islands. I take it that was your first time trying a cheroot?" he drawled, a smile turning up the corners of his mouth.

"First and last," she declared in a lovely, very feminine contralto, having obviously forgotten her ruse in the midst of her distress.

"Then you won't be wishing to acquire the habit?"

"No, most definitely not. I cannot fathom why you, or anyone else, would want to." She smacked her lips again. "*Ugh,* awful!"

"It is a nasty predilection, I agree, but then I suppose that is why women do not generally take up the pastime."

She froze, the color fading from her cheeks. "What?" she squeaked before forcing her voice to drop low into the old baritone. "I'm . . . I mean, what?"

Tossing back his head, he let out a laugh. "You might as well give up the charade. Although I must confess you've put on a bravura performance. Had everyone fooled, I believe. Except me."

Her vivid eyes grew round as marbles as she stared at him in obvious consternation, the internal battle she waged clearly visible on her face. Abruptly her shoulders drooped as she gave up the fight.

"How long have you known?" she asked.

"Since about ten minutes after you first walked into the public room downstairs."

Her lips parted. "All that time and you didn't say a word?"

He gave her a grin. "No, I did not."

The frown returned. "Then you put me through all that misery for nothing?"

"I don't recall any surfeit of misery. You ate a generous meal and enjoyed your very first cheroot—an admirable way to pass the time, in my estimation."

"For you, by amusing yourself at my expense, you mean?"

"By letting you spin out your game a bit longer. I was intrigued to see how long you would persist, and I must say you held steady to the very last. Now, why don't you tell me who you really are and why you're dressed in those clothes?"

Lily stared at him another long minute, then straightened her shoulders.

*He knows,* she cursed inwardly. *Damn and blast, he knows! Now what am I to do?*

Bluster her way through the best she could, she realized, and hope she could repair the mess. Telling him the truth was out of the question. Despite his generosity to this point and the undeniable magnetism of his charm, she really knew nothing about the man. Confiding in him and hoping she could count on his discretion was not an option, at least not one she was willing to take. After all, her whole future depended upon keeping her secrets intact. Anything less could spell doom for her, or worse, marriage to her stepfather's brute of a business associate.

Luckily there was no chance of the marquis and her stepfather ever meeting. For one, Gordon Chaulk didn't go to London—he considered such visits an expensive waste of time. For another, her stepfather could only dream of moving in the same exalted social circles as those in which the marquis must dwell. Despite her respectable lineage, she could hardly imagine such a thing herself. But that was neither here nor there. Right now she needed to find a way to extract herself from her current predicament.

*Do not panic,* she told herself. *Use your brain and all will be well.*

"If you must know," she declared a minute later, "I am dressed in this fashion as a lark."

Her audacious statement wiped the lazy grin from his mouth. "A lark?"

Next to her hip, she crossed her fingers. "That's right. A friend of mine and I wagered that I could travel in male attire and no one would suspect a thing. You, my lord, have just cost me two guineas."

Emotions chased over his sculpted features, running the gambit from amazement and incredulity to irritation. He waved a hand toward her. "So this disguise is nothing more than a silly prank?"

"I don't think it's silly, but yes, I am having a bit of fun. After all, why should men be the only ones who can play adventurous games?"

He shot her a scowl, his golden brows scrunched up in a way that didn't lessen his attractiveness one iota. "A foolhardy way to entertain yourself, if you ask me. Do you have any idea the sort of trouble in which you could have landed?"

Her heart warmed at his outrage on her behalf. She thought again of how he'd stepped in to save her from the burly oaf downstairs and realized that he really was quite gallant.

"I am perfectly well, as you can see."

He scowled harder. "You might not be well were I another sort of man, were I the variety given to taking advantage of lone females who put themselves at risk for a bit of pin money."

"But you said yourself my disguise fooled everyone."

"Everyone but me. And how do you know I won't importune your favors? I could lock that door right now and ravish you on this very table."

Her breath caught in her lungs at the lurid idea, her pulse skittering wildly beneath her skin. "Will you?"

He pinned her with a smoldering look, leaning over her so that she could feel his size and sheer male power.

"I could, but luckily for you, I would never force myself upon a woman."

Lily didn't know whether to be relieved or disappointed. "Then I have nothing of which to be afraid."

Stepping back, he resumed his seat. "You might at least have a care for your reputation, since it is obvious you come from good family."

"I do care, which is why I haven't told you my name."

A faint twinkle gleamed in his amber eyes. "You mean your name isn't really Jack?"

She laughed.

"So you won't divulge the truth?"

Tipping her head to one side, she pretended to consider his offer. "Alas, I don't believe I shall."

"I didn't realize before that you possess a cruel streak. At least tell me your first name."

Another laugh bubbled past her lips as she shook her head.

He crossed his arms over his chest. "So who is Jack? Your father or your brother?"

"Neither, since I don't have a brother and that wasn't my father's name. Actually, Jack was my dog when I was eight. And now, if I am not mistaken, I must say my farewells or I will miss my coach. Thank you for the meal and the company, even if you were wicked to lead me on the way you did."

"I believe that makes two of us," he remarked. "As for the coach, I fear you have missed it."

"What!"

Leaping to her feet, she raced to the window and peered down into the inn yard below, finding it bustling with hostlers and horses, carriages and patrons. Scanning the fray, she easily located the mail coach with its distinctive maroon and black panels.

She sighed in relief that the coach had not left without

her after all. "But you are wrong. The coach is still here."

Strolling up behind her, Vessey stretched out an arm, planting a hand onto the window near her head. "Strange, but I don't see a coach to Bristol, though perhaps that is because there *is* no coach to Bristol, at least not one due for several hours yet. Before I came upstairs to dine, I asked my man to check on the matter. He informed me there have been two mail coaches here since your arrival. One headed to Exeter and another to London."

Too late she realized her careless mistake.

"So which is it?" he murmured near her ear. "Exeter or London? Methinks London the more likely choice."

Shivering, she closed her eyes for a moment.

"Very well," she admitted. "You are correct."

"Since London is my destination as well, I will give you a ride."

She whirled, stopping short as she found herself standing practically inside his arms, his body so near she could smell a delicious hint of cloves and musk on his skin and feel the warmth that radiated like a small furnace from his large, male body.

Tipping back her head, she met his gaze. "I cannot ride in your coach."

He bent closer. "And I cannot allow you to journey unaccompanied to London. We have already discussed how dangerous it would be."

*It will be dangerous with you,* she thought. *But not for the same reasons.*

"I will be fine in the mail coach. No one will suspect."

"You did not think *I* would suspect. Now, I really must insist," he stated in a low rumble that trailed like silken fingers over her spine. "I wouldn't be able to live with myself if something untoward were to occur to you."

"But we shall not see each other again. You would never know."

Something darkened in his eyes. "A circumstance that would trouble me greatly."

And in that moment, both of them knew he was not merely talking about her safety.

Her heart beat like a bird in her throat. She knew she should refuse, find the strength to slip away and return to traveling on her own. But she sensed he would not let her escape quite so easily, that he might even follow her onto the mail coach and make sure she had an escort, whether she wished one or not.

Besides, it might be fun traveling with him. Given the elegant cut and quality of his garments and the fact that he was a marquis, she knew his coach would be far more comfortable than anything provided by the Royal Mail Service. And she had to admit she enjoyed his company and would be far safer with him than alone. What could it hurt to pass a few more hours together before they parted for good?

"Go on, Jack," he urged. "Say yes."

She hesitated a few seconds longer, knowing she ought to say no. "All right, yes."

# Chapter Three

"**P**ENELOPE."

Lily relaxed more fully against the dark-blue velvet coach seat across from Lord Vessey and shook her head. "No."

"Margaret."

His vehicle, which was every bit as luxurious as she had suspected it would be, raced along the turnpike toward London. Fitted with polished brass fixtures, supple tan leather appointments, and springs so lithe even large ruts in the road could barely be felt, the coach was one of the finest she had ever seen. Certainly the finest in which she had ever ridden.

"Afraid not," she said, reveling in her present comfort.

He stroked a thumb against his chin in a moment of silent consideration. "Jane."

She sent him a sympathetic little half-smile. "Come now, my lord, do I really look like a Jane to you?"

"What you look like is a vexing minx who thinks herself quite clever. Come on, now, let's have it. What is your name?"

"Oh no, you won't worm it out of me so easily. It is my secret to keep and yours to find out."

"I've been making guesses this past hour and I assure

you there is nothing remotely easy about it." He pinned her with an assessing stare. "Bertha."

"Bertha!" A laugh shot past her lips. "You are growing desperate, I can see."

"Not at all. Believe it or not, I've known a few Berthas and none of them ever likes to admit to their name. Brunhilde, then."

"Now you are just being ridiculous. Who in the world is named Brunhilde?"

"I feel certain Prinny has at least one Cousin Brunhilde tucked away in some remote Hanoverian principality. Good God, I never thought! You don't have one of those impossibly tongue-twisting Latin names like Agrippina or Domitilla? Now *that* I would wish to hide."

"No, my name is really quite ordinary and very easy to pronounce."

"*Aha!* Finally a clue. Perhaps I'll figure it out after all."

*Perhaps he will,* she thought, wondering why she had divulged even that amount of information. She barely knew him and yet felt comfortable in his presence in a way she could not before recall ever feeling with a man. He set her at ease, enough so that if she was not careful, she might make another unfortunate error like the one she'd made about the London-bound coach.

*How easy to fall victim to his charm,* she thought, *something against which I must guard and guard well!*

Nonetheless, she could hardly deny her attraction, not when the very sight of him left her jittery, pulse stuttering, her breath shallow as if she couldn't quite draw in enough air. She might be innocent, but she recognized her desire for what it was.

Being confined in the coach with him barely two feet away left her insides as warm and gooey as a melted marshmallow. Though she tried not to notice, she couldn't help but be aware of his long, powerful frame as he sprawled in negligent grace against the seat across from her.

Wide and strong as an ancient oak, his shoulders filled his chocolate-hued coat to perfection, leaving him without a need to resort to the padding some men used to conceal their flaws. The rest of him was every inch as delicious—strong arms, solid chest, muscular legs encased in a pair of buckskin pantaloons that hugged every inch of his taut thighs and calves with glovelike perfection.

In fact, as far as she could tell, Lord Vessey had no imperfections, none that were visible, anyway. From his wavy golden hair to his Hessian-clad feet, he was masculinity personified.

She swallowed against the sudden knot lodged at the base of her throat, wondering how many miles yet they were from London.

"Rose."

His voice, silky and robust as a tot of heated rum, interrupted her musings.

"What?" she murmured.

"Your name. Is it Rose? You said it was ordinary and easy to pronounce and yet I am sure it is lovely as well. As lovely as you."

Her heart thudded.

*What a providential guess,* she thought, *and one far too close for comfort.* If he proceeded along the logical path and continued listing flower names, he would surely come across her own.

"It is not Rose," she stated in a dismissive voice. "Good try, however. And now, if you would not mind terribly, I find myself rather tired and would like to sleep for a while."

He inclined his head. "Of course, please rest. I promise to wake you when we reach the city."

Giving him a shallow smile, she angled her shoulder into the nearest corner and closed her eyes.

Five minutes later, though, she was still awake, unable to find just the right spot despite the plush accommodations.

"Why don't you stretch out?" he suggested, obviously aware of her dilemma. "If you lie on your side, you should fit quite comfortably across the seat."

Had she been in a dress, she would never have even considered the idea, forcing herself to sleep upright regardless of the circumstances. But over the past few days she had come to enjoy the freedom of wearing trousers, understanding the unique range of motion they could provide.

*Why not take advantage of my male attire?* she reasoned.

Tomorrow, after she settled into a hotel, she would be forced to make her transformation back into a woman. No more tailcoat and trousers for her.

Deciding she had long since passed the point of attempting any sort of formality with the marquis, she nodded her thanks. Sliding to the middle of the seat, she leaned over and curled onto her side. An instant sensation of relaxation enveloped her, the swaying motion of the coach rocking away her every concern.

Scant seconds later, she fell asleep.

Ethan watched her, tracing the fine bones of her face and the sprinkling of tiny freckles that dotted the bridge of her nose. *Adorable freckles,* he thought, *for an equally adorable young woman.* How she had been able to travel in the guise of a man still had the power to amaze him.

People, he decided, were obviously blind.

He wished he knew who she was. So far she'd been doing an excellent job refusing to tell him much of anything about herself, although he had to confess he'd been enjoying their name-guessing game despite its probable futility. When she awakened, he might try one more time. After all, how could he allow her to leave without at least knowing her name?

The thought troubled him, as did the idea of letting her vanish totally from his life. Was he content to let her go, satisfied to remember her as nothing more than an outrageously bold and lovely young woman? An amusing adventuress who had come briefly into his life, then passed just as quickly out again? The notion rankled—far more, he realized, than it ought.

Slumbering deeply, she released a breathy little sigh, a sound that shot directly to his groin. Beneath his snug-fitting pantaloons, he grew stiff with arousal, aching as though she'd actually touched him rather than merely caressed his ears with the music of her sigh.

Deciding to ignore his blatant physical reaction, he gazed out the window at the passing countryside. The ploy did him no good. Soon his eyes were drawn back to her just as they had been at the inn, when he'd first spied her and had been helpless to look away.

He didn't fully understand the attraction, especially since her most obvious physical assets were concealed in men's clothing. Though not all of them, he had to confess, her legs displayed in what many would have deemed a shockingly salacious manner, the shape of her rounded derrière revealed by the snug woolen cloth of her trousers.

As if her body read his thoughts and appreciated the attention, she shifted, rolling over onto her other side to expose that very portion of her anatomy to his view.

Under his breath, he groaned.

His erection stiffened further at the sight of her lush bottom, which his hands were itching to touch.

*And this,* he thought, *is why women should not wear trousers. Far too much temptation for any man's sanity.*

Leaning his head back against the upholstered seat, Ethan closed his eyes and willed himself to think boring thoughts. Crop rotation. Latin declensions. Golf.

Nearly an hour later, the city gates appeared on the horizon, traffic steadily increasing as the metropolis began to rise around them. The noise level increased as well, people filling the streets, horses' hooves ringing out against the cobbles, with an occasional shout or the bark of a dog punctuating the fray. Time to wake his still slumbering companion, he decided. She'd moved again in her sleep and was now lying on her back, one leg angled beneath her at the knee, the other dangling half off the seat in yet another unknowingly provocative pose.

"Jack," he called.

No response.

"Jack," he repeated, raising the volume of his voice.

She gave no sign of having heard. *And why should she,* he thought, *since "Jack" is not her name.*

Rather than shout and possibly frighten her half to death, he climbed to his feet, balancing himself against the sway of the vehicle as he bent over her recumbent form. Reaching out a hand, he touched her shoulder, giving it a light shake.

"Miss Bain," he said, doubtful her last name was any more honest than her first. "It is time to wake up."

She groaned and muttered something under her breath, her eyelids fluttering faintly.

"We are almost there. Awaken, my unconventional sleeping beauty."

Rich and steamy as a cup of simmering chocolate, a deep male voice cut into Lily's slumber. Opening her eyes, she looked up into the arresting face of the man with whom she'd just been dream-dancing, his eyes even more brilliantly hued than they'd been in her imagination. Her lips parted on a silent gasp, her breasts rising and falling beneath the finely woven cotton of her shirt.

A gleam darkened his eyes, his lids drooping as his gaze slid over her face, pausing at her lips before moving lower.

Suddenly realizing how disheveled she must appear, she drew the edges of her coat closer and slowly sat up, the last of her sleepy haze falling away. "Have we arrived?"

"Very nearly," he said, retaking his seat across from her. "I suppose the answer depends upon our destination. Where does your friend live? Shall I take you there?"

For a second she stared, not immediately understanding. Then it came to her. The supposed bet and her "friend."

"No," she retorted. "That is, it would look most odd if I arrived on her front step in my present attire, especially accompanied by you, my lord. Anyway, you must realize I cannot reveal her address."

"Nor your own, I suppose, though it would be a great deal simpler if you just told me where you live. To protect your reputation, I would be willing to have my driver stop a block or two distant and let you walk the rest of the way."

"If I am unwilling to give you my name, my lord, I am hardly likely to share my address."

*Even if I had one,* she thought, *which I presently do not.*

"You could remedy that, you know," he said in a warm tone. "I do not know the particulars of your situation, but I should like to see you again. Why do you not tell me who you are?"

His statement seemed to surprise him as much as it did her.

Longing beat in tandem with panic inside her breast. "That is impossible."

"Why?"

*Because I already know you are too much.* Too dangerous. Too debonair. And far too intelligent to be satisfied with the half-answers she would be forced to provide.

Besides, she couldn't afford to let down her guard. She had a plan for her future—her *independent* future— and that plan had no room in it for a roguish nobleman who made her pulse flutter like the last leaf on a windswept branch. Besides, he couldn't really be serious. Likely he was merely intrigued by her evasions and only wanted to have his curiosity satisfied.

She shook her head. "Giving you my address is out of the question. You had best tell your coachman to stop ahead and set me down."

A frown collected like storm clouds on his brow. "I cannot just drop you off on the odd street corner. We are hardly in a part of town were I would leave anyone, not even a man."

"A hackney, then, once we reach a more amenable location. I will be fine from there."

She could tell he wanted to argue, knew by the martial gleam in his gaze that his temper was frayed. After a long minute, he gave a curt nod and leaned up to rap against the wall above her head. A small hatch that connected the coach interior with the driver's seat slid open.

"Hyde Park," the marquis ordered, the coachman murmuring his confirmation. With a click, the hatch closed again.

Vessey had just taken his seat when the coach jerked hard, sending her forward so that she nearly toppled to the floor. Instead, he caught her, tugging her into his arms.

A pair of shouts erupted in the street, obviously the

result of an accident that had stopped traffic in its path. Yet Lily barely heard the commotion, every sense focused on the strong pair of arms at her back, the hard muscled thighs tangled with her own. Shifting, he lifted her up and set her onto his lap. She gasped at the novel sensation and gazed into his eyes.

He gazed back, tightening his hold. "It appears we are stuck."

"Yes."

"But nothing stands still in London for long. We shall be on our way soon, leaving us little time together. Tell me your name."

Heart throbbing in the base of her throat, she shook her head.

"Is it Diana?"

Her lips parted on a shivery sigh. "No."

"What about Anna?"

"That name is lovely, but not mine."

"Mary, then. Am I even close?"

"No."

His jaw tightened. "Well, then, since you insist upon leaving me with nothing more of yourself than a memory, I suppose I had best make that memory one neither of us shall ever forget."

Before she could draw her next breath, his lips claimed hers, moving over her own with a skill and passion that sent her thoughts whirling away at the speed of a shooting star. Dark and demanding, his kiss sizzled through her, firing her blood and leaving her dizzy and trembling in his arms.

She had been kissed once before at sixteen, and had quite enjoyed the brief interlude with the visiting cousin of a neighbor. To his clear disappointment, she'd never asked for a repetition, however, and now she knew why. If that boy had been able to kiss like the marquis, she wouldn't have been able to keep herself from him.

Then again, Lord Vessey was a man—debonair and experienced, his every touch speaking of a confident mastery and an elegance of persuasion. Even in her naïveté, she could sense his innate abilities, recognizing he had a talent for pleasure that few men possessed, a deftness in the amorous arts that could very possibly make a woman beg.

Suddenly the coach began to move forward again.

Had he not been holding her, she knew she surely would have toppled to the floor in a heap. But she had no fear of such a fate, not when he slid her closer and angled his mouth more fully across hers.

She gasped as he ran the tip of his tongue over her bottom lip, then again as he slipped inside, filling her mouth in a way she would never have imagined she could like. But she did, the sensations both hot and sweet, delicious as candy. Letting instinct lead, she licked him back, swirling her tongue around his before stroking over his teeth and the velvety smoothness of his inner cheeks.

A growl of pleasure rumbled low in his throat, his fingers tunneling into her short hair to cradle her head. Holding her steady, he took her deeper, making her toes curl inside her boots as she whimpered with delight.

Utterly adrift, she felt his hand slip inside her coat to stroke over her chest. With unerring dexterity, he found one breast, cupping her inside his palm through the cloth of her shirt. The rapid pace of her breathing pushed her more fully into his clasp, a wild shiver rippling through her as he stroked a thumb over her nipple. Once, then twice, then yet again until she lost count, too drowned in the pleasure to think.

An ache settled between her thighs, along with a disturbing restlessness. Claiming her mouth with ardent intent, he urged her to match him, to surrender herself to each of his kisses and return them with ever more passionate ones of her own.

In thrall, she lay trembling as his fingers went to work on the buttons of her shirt, cool air wafting faintly over her flesh as he peeled away the layer of cloth to expose her naked breast to his sight.

His eyes glittered with hunger as he arched her back over one arm and buried his face against the curve of her neck. Stringing a line of kisses along the column of her throat, he played there for a brief time, tormenting her with a series of drawing, openmouthed kisses that made her skin throb as if she had more than one pulse. Continuing across her collarbone, then over her sternum, he trailed lower.

A jolt as fierce as lightning arced through her when he fastened his lips to one of her breasts. Never in her life had she felt a sensation that even came close, his mouth warm and wet, his tongue like a sweep of fire against her tightly beaded nipple.

She swallowed, unable to contain the moan that rose from deep inside her throat. Barely recognizing her own actions, she threaded her fingers into the wavy silk of his hair, caressing the strong shape of his head as she silently urged him on.

Just then he nipped her, a light scrape of his teeth that sent her winging upward. He soothed her with a lick, then another, until she thought she might go quite mad.

He was turning his head, presumably to lavish the same devilish torture upon her other breast, when the connecting hatch suddenly opened.

"Hyde Park, my lord," the coachman announced before he just as quickly slid the little door closed once again.

The marquis grew still against her, a muffled groan resonating softly from between his lips.

She groaned as well, only then realizing the coach was

no longer moving. A gentle darkness engulfed the interior, the sun having begun to set without either of them taking the slightest notice.

*And thank heavens for the concealing shadows,* she mused, imagining the shockingly improper sight the pair of them would have presented to both his servants and any casual passersby who happened to glance inside the coach.

Still dazed from a surfeit of passion, Lily struggled to free herself, sliding ignominiously off his lap onto the seat. With a hasty tug, she pulled her shirt closed, fingers shaking as she worked to fasten the buttons.

The marquis brushed her hands away. "Let me."

She hesitated briefly before acquiescing to his demand.

Efficient as a valet, he fastened her shirt, tucking the loosened tails in a bit at her waist before straightening the rumpled lines of her coat.

The casual intimacy stunned her, but considering what they had been doing not two minutes ago, she supposed she had little cause to act the outraged maiden.

Surveying her in the dim light, he reached out and slid the tie from her hair.

"Oh," she gasped as her straight, thick locks fell forward across her cheeks, the ends just brushing the tops of her shoulders.

"Your hair is mussed," he explained. Without awaiting her permission, he combed his fingers through her tresses, his touch sending a fresh rush of pleasure through her already awakened senses. She could tell he liked it as well, and thought for a moment that he was about to kiss her again.

Instead, he gathered her hair at her nape inside his fist, then tied the thin strip of black silk in place. Once he'd finished, he didn't immediately release her. "Are you sure you won't allow me to see you home? I do not like the idea of leaving you here, even if you plan to travel the rest of the way by hackney."

"Do not worry, my lord. I shall be fine. And now, I really must be going. Thank you for the meal and the ride and . . ." She broke off, feeling her cheeks ignite with heat. "Well, thank you."

"Will you go and not even tell me your name?"

She paused, reading the need in his gaze.

*What does it matter?* she mused. *Once we part, I shall never see him again.*

Her lips turned up in a bittersweet smile. "It's Lily."

Then, before she could stop herself, she laid a palm against his cheek and brought his head down for one last impulsive kiss. She savored the sweetness of his lips, wanting to memorize the sensation so she would remember just as he'd promised she would.

Ending their embrace as quickly as it had begun, she turned, opened the door, and leapt to the ground.

As she hurried toward a cab, she sensed him following. Yet he did not try to stop her as she climbed into the nearest hackney and gave the driver the name of a hotel, careful to keep her voice lowered so only the man could hear.

With a nod and the flick of his whip, the driver set his horses into motion.

Turning her head, she gazed over her shoulder and saw Vessey watching, his golden hair glinting in the lamplight. She stared for a long minute more, then forced herself to put him from her sight. As for putting him from her mind, well, that she feared was going to take a good deal longer.

# Chapter Four

❧❦❧

TWO DAYS LATER, Lily sat in the law offices of
Pennyroyal and Sons, Mr. Eustace Pennyroyal himself at her service.

"Well then," the solicitor told her, "it will only be another minute or two for my clerk to locate the file containing your grandfather's bequest. In the meantime,
may I offer you a cup of tea? The water should be hot by
now."

Glancing at the room's small fireplace and the kettle
resting on its metal hob grate, Lily nodded her agreement. "Thank you, Mr. Pennyroyal, that would be most
welcome."

As the solicitor crossed to prepare the beverage, she
glanced around the office, the walls lined four-square in
heavy leather-bound books, most of which she assumed
dealt with the law. Resting one of her black-gloved
hands against the skirt of her black muslin gown, she
tried to relax. For the first time in nearly a week, she felt
fully herself, dressed once more in feminine attire.

Yesterday's trip to the secondhand clothing stalls that
lined Petticoat Lane had provided her with a new gown
and accessories, items she hadn't been able to carry with
her from home. A few extra pence in the stall owner's
palm had convinced the woman to keep her silence
about the "boy" who'd purchased the garments, and the

young woman who had emerged from the dressing area afterward.

Although her new attire wasn't as fashionable as her own clothing would have been, the gown had once belonged to a gentlewoman, and more important, had been all Lily could afford. Once she had her inheritance in hand, she would see about locating a proper modiste and having a new wardrobe created. She also planned to locate a better hotel—her third since arriving in London—after she left the solicitor's office today.

She'd checked out of the first hotel after only one night, deciding she had better not chance returning to "Jack Bain's" room dressed as a woman after her return from Petticoat Lane. And although last night's new lodging had proven adequate, she'd felt distinctly uncomfortable at breakfast this morning when a pair of male lodgers decided to join her at table over plates of toast and eggs. She'd paid her tab with relief and departed.

"Here we are," Mr. Pennyroyal declared. Smiling at her over the pair of half-glasses perched on the end of his long nose, he passed her a cup and saucer, the Darjeeling's sweet fragrance drifting upward like a rare perfume.

Taking a sip, she gave herself a moment to enjoy the small luxury after days of privation. Of course, there had been a few bright spots during her journey to London. The delicious meal at the inn with Lord Vessey and the ride in his luxuriously appointed coach. And, of course, his kisses and the dangerous yet glorious touch of his hands.

Warmth shot into her cheeks, turning them an incriminating shade of pink she hoped the solicitor would ascribe to the temperature of her tea.

*I must stop thinking about the marquis,* she warned herself. *He is out of my life and I have to forget him.* An objective that had so far proven impossible, her dreams filled with nothing but the man.

Silently she ordered herself *to concentrate on her future*. To focus on the freedom that was so nearly at hand, courtesy of her mother's last loving gift.

Lily would never know why, but when her mother married Gordon Chaulk, she had failed to inform him of the inheritance her own father had set aside for Lily. Ten thousand pounds, or so her mother had told her only five months ago. Perhaps even then, her mother had realized she would not survive the year, and that she'd kept the secret as long as she dared.

After one of Chaulk's far too frequent beatings, Lily had tended to her mother's wounds as she always did, cleaning the blood from her swollen face, binding the broken ribs she'd received from crashing into a wall when he'd hit her. Lily had imagined her asleep, and was about to tiptoe from the room, when her mother reached up and grasped her wrist.

"There's money from your grandfather," she had whispered. "It's in London at Pennyroyal and Sons. Use it and get away while there's still time. Go now. Save yourself, Lily."

Of course she hadn't left. How could she while her mother was alive and in need of her? But as fiercely as Lily had fought to convince her mother to live, Louisa Bainbridge Chaulk had withered away. A winter pneumonia, the doctor said, but Lily knew the truth. Her mother had given up on life, her heart crushed by the two men who should have cherished her the most.

Without question, Chaulk was a vile human being, but at least his brand of cruelty was straightforward, predictable even, in a horrific kind of way. The misery inflicted by Lily's father, however, had been of a far more insidious nature. Although he'd never laid a rough hand upon his wife, he'd done far worse—taking her love and devotion, then using it, however unintentionally, to slowly break her heart one piece at a time.

As dashing and handsome as the prince in a fairy story, Timothy Bainbridge was the fourth son of an earl. A devil-may-care sort, he could charm the gold from a leprechaun and leave him smiling for his loss. When her father set you in his sights, his focus was absolute, his attention mesmerizing in a way that left you feeling, for that brief span of time, as if you were the most special person on earth.

Lily remembered the feeling, knew the giddy, almost druglike rush of having his unique and undivided attention—yet knew as well the soul-crushing agony of wanting his love and approbation so badly she would have given anything in order to attain it.

But as she and her mother had discovered, Timothy Bainbridge bored easily, needing constant novelty in his life, as well as ever-increasing doses of excitement and adventure in order to be happy.

Instead of settling him down as many had imagined marriage would, the commitment had only driven him to take more chances, to chase more unknowns, to face bigger, ever greater dangers and risks. And in the meantime, while he'd been off hunting tigers in India, climbing mountain peaks in the Alps, and sailing the wide China seas, she and her mother had been left to fend for themselves.

Money would arrive, but only when he remembered to send it, which was sometimes as often as every month but at others as seldom as once a year. There would be a flurry of letters and gifts, strange and beautiful objects that arrived from all over the world, then suddenly all communication would cease.

And occasionally—usually when life at home had taken on an almost normal rhythm—he would appear on the doorstep unannounced. Once again he would dazzle them with his charm, making them want him to stay when, of course, they both knew he never would.

Lily had hated him. She'd been resentful of his absences, angry at him for causing her mother to sob hysterically each time he left, and then to grow pale with worry when he failed to write and let them know he was alive and well.

His death had been almost a relief when it had come—the letter from an official in one of the Canadian colonial provinces explaining that Mr. Bainbridge had met his end after being severely mauled by a bear. Yet despite her animosity toward her father, Lily had wept just as hard as her mother, an emptiness and grief lodging inside her that she knew would never completely go away.

Unlike other girls, who dreamt of a perfect man who would one day arrive to sweep them off their feet, she'd known that spring of her thirteenth year that she never wished to love, never wished to marry. When a woman wed, she became the property of her husband, her physical and emotional safety his to decide. Better to be alone, she reasoned, than to risk the promise of betrayal and pain. Better a lonely heart than one shattered by despair.

Her father had taught her one lesson: never trust a man. Her mother's second husband had only reinforced that belief.

"How is the tea, Mrs. Smythe?"

Lily startled, frowning as she took a moment to remember that *she* was Mrs. Smythe. At least that's what she had decided to inform the solicitor upon her arrival.

As an unmarried woman of only twenty years of age, Lily knew it would be greatly frowned upon for her to apply for use of her inheritance, even for funds legally set aside for her use. Custom called for her guardian to make the request—in her case, Gordon Chaulk. Obviously, that option was out of the question.

And although she didn't believe Mr. Pennyroyal knew anything about her mother's remarriage, she couldn't take the chance of him contacting her stepfather about the transaction. So, to give herself a measure of credible autonomy, she had decided to invent a husband. Then, in a subsequent flash of inspiration, she had just as quickly killed him off.

She smiled to herself, still rather proud of having thought of the ploy. Now she had only to act the part of a young, grieving widow and let matters play out as they would.

"The tea is delicious, thank you." She took another sip, then sent him a demure smile.

He set his own cup aside. "My sincere condolences on your losses. What a dreadful time you must have had, with first the death of your husband and then your mother. The passing of loved ones is never an easy matter."

"No, indeed." Thinking of her mother, she had no difficulty coaxing an expression of genuine sorrow. "It is one of the reasons I decided to come to London. Too many sad memories at home."

"Where did he fall, if I might ask?"

For a second she didn't know what he meant. *Where did who fall?*

She nearly blurted out the question before realizing he meant her "husband."

*Dear heavens,* she mused, *I am going to have to do better than this if I am not to be caught! And gracious, I suppose he expects me to name a battle. Think, Lily, and be quick about it.*

Taking another sip of her tea, she gave herself a minute to compose her answer. Her cup clinked as she set it onto its saucer.

"Vittoria," she said in a somber tone, "not quite a year ago." She was glad now that she had always made time to read the news reports about the war.

"Ah, Vittoria. A great victory for the British and Portuguese. Helped us topple the little emperor off his throne and put him on a tiny one in Elba, where he belongs. Seems fitting, I think. You must be very proud of your husband's noble sacrifice."

She nodded. "Of course, and relieved to be at peace once again."

*Will that clerk never return?*

As if he'd heard her wish, a tap came at the door only moments later, one of Mr. Pennyroyal's four assistants rushing in to place a thick set of bound papers before his employer. Once the young man had departed and closed the door, the solicitor reached out and untied the ribbon that held the file shut. He shuffled through a couple of pages before pulling one free.

"Ah, here we are. Already drawn up in anticipation of your one day claiming the funds." He paused briefly to scan the document. "Everything seems in order, although your maiden name is still listed for the signature." His gray brows drew together. "Perhaps I should have this redrawn?"

A lump tightened in her stomach. "Is that strictly necessary?"

*Good heavens, what will I do if he insists that I sign my "married name"?*

He placed a finger against his lower lip in consideration before pulling it away. "No, I suppose not strictly."

Her stomach pitched like a small boat on a high sea. "You see, I would much rather sign today. As indelicate as it is to say, my . . . um . . . husband was an infantry officer, and as much as such things do not matter when one is in love, I must confess that we were never financially well off. Can we not proceed now? I am in rather urgent need of funds, if you must know."

The older man pursed his lips and scowled. "Hmm? There is no question that you are the rightful beneficiary, maiden name or married. Yes, I believe it will be all right." Sliding the paper forward, he handed her a pen. "Sign at the bottom."

Fingers trembling, she steadied herself before dipping the nib in ink and affixing her name. Only when the solicitor blotted the ink from the paper and placed it back in the file did the tension ease from her stiff muscles.

He smiled. "If you do not mind waiting, I will have a voucher drawn for you. We have the funds invested in a very reputable bank. I assume you will not wish to withdraw the entire amount from their accounts?"

"No, I do not suppose I will have immediate need of all ten thousand pounds."

"Ten thousand? Oh, I believe it is far more than that." Shuffling some more papers, he pulled another one from the stack. "Here is the latest statement of account. Yes, just as I thought. The current balance is forty-eight thousand nine hundred seventy-three pounds, eleven shillings, and six pence. Your grandfather set this money aside nearly two decades ago. It has since grown considerably in value."

Lily's heart thumped. *Forty-eight thousand pounds. Stars above, I am rich!*

"Will five hundred do for today?" Mr. Pennyroyal asked.

Lily couldn't help the smile that spread like a sunrise over her face. "Mercy, yes!"

The solicitor laughed, and called again for his clerk.

"One more thing," he said, once he'd sent a different young man than the first off to draft Lily's check. "You said you are new to London. I know of an excellent townhouse that might be of interest to you. Shall I tell you about it?"

*A townhouse?* She hadn't thought that far into the future, but she certainly didn't wish to continue living in a hotel, even if she could now afford to stay somewhere as elegant as Grillons or Claridge's.

A townhouse might indeed be just the thing.

"Yes," she agreed, "please do."

Conversation and laughter flowed like a meandering river through the Bascoms' drawing room, the elegant chamber set aside for those who preferred not to dance in the crowded ballroom nor congregate around its equally noisy perimeter.

"Your play, Vessey," Tony Black, Duke of Wyvern, said.

Ethan glanced up to find the other three men at the card table waiting, expectant expressions on their faces.

"What?" he murmured.

"It is your turn," prompted Viscount Howard, an amiable Corinthian who had sought out the card room earlier and agreed to make up a fourth.

"Oh, right." Ethan nodded and scowled down at his cards. Relying on instinct alone, he chose a jack of clubs and tossed it down.

The other men gave soft grunts of dissatisfaction.

"Count on Ethan to take the trick, even when he's not paying attention," Rafe, Baron Pendragon, commented as he reached for his glass of port.

"Lucky in cards, as they say," Tony quipped as he waited for Ethan to lead out the next hand.

Ethan laid down another club. The others played in turn, Ethan again taking the trick. On the next hand, though, his thoughts began to drift once more. By the third, he had to be reminded yet again when his turn came around.

Tony quirked a brow. "So, who is she?"

"Who is who?" he countered in a nonchalant tone as he considered which card to play.

"The woman who has your mind tied up in knots, that's who."

Ethan laid down a heart, the only suit left in his hand. "I don't know what you mean."

The duke rolled his eyes. "Of course you do. Distraction such as yours can only come from two sources, money or women. You'd be drunk and ready to shoot yourself by now had you wagered your massive fortune at some gaming hell last night and lost. Meaning that the source of your current lack of attention is a female. So, who is she?"

"Yes, divulge all, Vessey," Lord Howard encouraged. "Is she a lady or a light o' love? I'm rather hoping for the latter, since Cyprians provide far more interesting tales."

"There is no one and nothing to tell."

"Hmm, I wonder what this *nothing*'s name could be?" Tony mused.

*Lily.*

Her lovely heart-shaped face appeared before his mind's eye just as it had with regular frequency since he'd watched her drive away three nights ago.

"Camilla," Tony suggested.

"Aurora," Howard offered, playing a card.

Rafe took a sip of wine. "Joan, mayhap."

Their teasing antics reminded him of his own recent guessing game in the coach, his loins stirring at the heated memory of what had happened between him and Lily. "Her name is of no importance," he said.

*Especially since that is all of her I know.*

"Ah-ha!" Tony declared. "So there *is* a woman."

"Ignore them," Rafe said. "Though if you are in a confiding mood, you know you can always tell me," he added with a good-humored smile.

Ethan shook his head. "Thank you, but no."

Although maybe he should tell Rafe, since the man had a knack for knowing everything worth learning and a little more besides. A wealthy financier who had ascended to the ranks of the aristocracy only last year, Rafe had ways of locating information and people that none of the rest of them could even hope to rival. If anyone could locate Lily, it would be Rafe. *Lord knows I've certainly had no luck,* Ethan mused.

As soon as her hackney had departed, he'd sent one of his footmen to trail her. When his man returned later that evening, he reported, much to Ethan's surprise, that the cab had let her out at a hotel, and not a private residence as Ethan had assumed.

Up at first light the next morning, he'd skipped breakfast and gone to the hotel to inquire after her. The desk clerk said a Jack Bain had stayed the night but had departed less than an hour earlier, leaving no forwarding address.

Ethan spent the next hour driving his phaeton around the area in the dim hope he might spot her, but to no avail. What he had planned to say or do if he'd found her, he didn't know.

Returning to his townhouse, he'd told himself to forget her. Their chance meeting had provided an interesting interlude, but now it was over. She would go on with her life and he with his own.

Still, he couldn't stop thinking about her, puzzling over her real identity, worrying about her welfare.

*Is she safe?* he kept wondering. *Is she well?*

Perhaps he should not have allowed her to leave in that hack, insisting instead that he take her to her home regardless of her wishes. Why had she gone to a hotel? Had it been yet another part of what she'd termed "a lark"? Or was there another explanation? Did she even have a home in London? Or a female friend who made outrageous, irresponsible wagers?

When it came to Lily, he couldn't be sure of much. All he knew for certain was that he'd never met a more vibrant, intelligent, independent young woman in all his years. She alternately exasperated, amused, and amazed him. She also made his blood burn like fire, leaving his body stiff and aching with the kind of arousal he hadn't felt since he'd been a randy youth just discovering the glorious delights to be found inside a woman's soft embrace.

Try as he might, he couldn't get her out of his head— or his senses, it would seem. Three days later and he could still taste the delectable sweetness of her kiss, smell the clean vanilla scent of her skin, feel the beauty of her gentle touch that was both bold and remarkably innocent.

*How could I have lost her already when I barely had her to start?*

"There he goes again. She must indeed be unique."

He heard Tony's remark and glanced up to meet his friend's interested gaze.

"Whatever she may or may not be, it scarcely signifies since I will not be seeing her again." Ethan fanned out the cards in his hand. "Now, are we going to play or not?"

Three weeks later, Lily alighted from her brand-new landau, her footmen assisting her to the sidewalk while her coachman held her new team of matched bays steady. Subtly adjusting the skirts of her elegantly made black silk day dress, she gazed upward at the townhouse of her friend Davina Finch—or rather Davina Coates since she was now a married woman.

Despite a friendly exchange of letters over the past week, Lily wasn't certain what to expect. After all, what did you say to a friend you haven't seen nor spoken with in the last eight years?

She certainly had fond memories of Davina, the pair of them best friends the entire two years they had been boarding students at Miss Tweedmont's Academy for Genteel Young Ladies. From the moment of their introduction, she and Davina had bonded, drawn together by their mutual apprehension and misery over having been sent away from home.

As Lily realized now, her mother had only wanted to provide her with a better education. Over the years, the succession of governesses hired had proven a dismal failure—particularly given Lily's propensity to spend her time running wild over the rocks and cliffs that lined Cornwall's majestic shoreline.

Davina, on the other hand, had studied to be a lady practically from the moment of her birth. Her father, a wealthy wool merchant from Leeds, had always harbored grand aspirations for his daughter. Davina, he had promised, would marry well—no less than an aristocrat if he had his way.

And it would seem her father had achieved his aim, Lily mused as she ascended the front steps and crossed into the refined Mayfair residence of Lord and Lady Coates. Their butler greeted her, then showed her into a drawing room to wait while he informed his mistress she had arrived.

Glancing around, Lily admired the red-and-blue flocked wallpaper and dark mahogany furnishings carved in the Egyptian style. Although the room was attractive, Lily found she preferred the cleaner, simpler lines that graced her own townhouse, as well as the more soothing pastel shades adorning its walls.

Located in an affluent section of Bloomsbury, her residence had everything she could want and more, boasting four stories and many comfortable, spacious rooms.

She'd had no difficulty locating staff, a majority of the former owner's servants eager to remain in her service. The house even boasted a friendly feline resident—a large brown-and-black-striped tabby cat named Mouser.

Not long after moving in, however, Lily became aware of a growing problem—she was lonely. When she'd run away to London, her focus had been fixed solely on escape and gaining her freedom. But once she'd reached the city and achieved her initial goals, the reality of her new circumstances had quickly become apparent.

Just as she'd wished, she was living a self-sufficient life. But that did not mean she wanted to live a solitary one. After all, she wasn't a recluse. Yet without the support of family or friends, she had no links to Society and no easy means of gaining entrée.

To her dismay, her thoughts had flown first to the Marquis of Vessey, her body growing warm at the mere notion of the man. In spite of the weeks that had passed since their meeting, he still crowded into her mind, especially her dreams.

What irony, she admitted to herself, that he was the only person she knew in London! But turning to him was completely out of the question. For one, no respectable woman would ask favors of a gentleman who was not a member of her own family. For another, she and Lord Vessey shared a brief but significant history that she would much prefer stay secret. She planned never to see him again, and that was the way circumstances must remain.

Then last week she'd happened upon a small *on-dit* in *The Morning Post*'s society column that made mention of a party attended by several ladies including a "Davina Coates." With such an unusual first name, Lily couldn't help but wonder if that Davina might be *her* Davina, memories of her friend returning in a nostalgic wave.

Never one to hesitate, Lily had dashed off an inquiry. To her delight, she received a prompt reply from Davina saying she was the same girl and that of course she would be most pleased to renew their acquaintance.

Now, filled with too much anticipation to take a seat on the drawing-room couch, Lily waited to meet her old friend, wondering what she would do if Davina was not as she recalled. But the moment Davina entered the room, she realized her fears had been for naught, the years falling away as if they had never passed.

*"Lily!"* exclaimed the ethereal blond. Hurrying across the room she enveloped Lily in an enthusiastic hug, one Lily returned with alacrity.

"Davina!" She laughed as she pulled away. "How wonderful it is to see you again!"

"I know. I could not believe my eyes when your note arrived, I was so glad." Davina, who was even more improbably beautiful than she'd been as a girl, pulled Lily over to the sofa and drew her down. "So, tell me everything."

Lily laughed again, a last coil of tension relaxing from her shoulders. "All eight years?"

"Yes, every one. I couldn't help but notice you signed your name 'Smythe.' Are you married now as well?"

Lily paused, guilt crawling over her skin like a small army of ants. She didn't want to lie. In fact, she hated the prospect. But if the adult Davina was like the child had been, she would never be able to do a credible job of maintaining Lily's fabrication. Not that Davina couldn't be trusted with such a secret—she could—but if she knew the truth, she would never be able to lie to others. Sweet and trusting, Davina was the type who simply could not tell an untruth, even to protect a greater good.

Silently begging her friend's forgiveness, Lily started telling her tale.

By the end of the story, the smile had fallen from

Davina's lovely mouth. "You poor dear, losing both your mother and your husband so close together, how utterly dreadful! Well, you are not alone anymore. You are with friends and are not to worry further."

Lily shared a heartfelt smile with the other woman.

"And though your grief is only natural," Davina continued, "you cannot hide yourself away. You need to be around people, and I have just the solution. I am hosting a dinner party this Thursday evening and I insist you come. I shall not take no for an answer."

Lily chuckled, feeling brighter than she had in days. "Well then, I suppose I had better say yes."

# Chapter Five

ETHAN ACCEPTED A glass of whisky from the butler. Taking a swallow, he listened to the conversation of the small group of men with whom he stood.

"We have too many soldiers returning from the war with no prospects of employment," stated Lord Pomfrey. "It's a foregone conclusion there will be unrest unless something is done."

"Yes, but what? There are no simple solutions, particularly with prices so exorbitantly high," replied another lord.

"Just the reason we need to change the obstinate attitudes of Liverpool and the rest of the Tories," their host, Lord Geoffrey Coates, declared with righteous zeal. "Surely there are ways to convince them to compromise."

"Now that, my lord," Ethan said, "is an effort that will last you a lifetime. Haven't you heard the old chestnut about why Tories can't ride donkeys? Because the donkey will be too stubborn to move and the Tory too stubborn to get off."

The men laughed, including Coates, though Ethan could tell his reformer's enthusiasm remained undaunted.

Ethan barely knew Lord Coates, he and the other man tending to run in different social circles. But in order to help the passage of a bill that would aid the laborers and farmers in Ethan's home district, he had accepted tonight's invitation to dinner.

The men were diving into another burning political debate when a radiant blond threaded her way through the guests and stopped next to Coates.

"Geoffrey, gentleman, your pardon for the interruption, but as some of you may know, there are ladies present."

Lord Pomfrey nodded his balding head and smiled. "Yes, madam, I believe you are quite correct."

"Then take pity upon us poor females and mingle a bit. There will be time aplenty for all of you to rail against injustice once the port and cigars have been served."

"Duly noted, my lady," Pomfrey agreed, sharing genial smiles with the others.

As the men began to disburse, Davina Coates laid a gentle hand on Ethan's sleeve to stop him. "My lord, if you would indulge me, there is someone I should like you to meet. She is a dear friend of long acquaintance who is newly arrived in London. Shall I make you known to each other?"

"Of course, your ladyship," he agreed, setting down his whisky tumbler. "Please lead the way."

He wondered about the identity of this friend and hoped his hostess wasn't trying to play matchmaker. If so, she was destined to be disappointed. Preparing himself to be polite, he followed Lady Coates.

As they walked, he couldn't help but notice a slender woman standing with another pair of ladies on the far side of the drawing room. Vibrant as a flame, her tresses were pinned in an upsweep, a few short tendrils left to curl against the graceful length of her neck. With her back turned to the room, he couldn't see her face, but was left instead to admire the willowy beauty of her figure, draped in a gown of rich emerald silk.

His body tightened of its own accord, reacting as it seemed to do these days to every redheaded female he encountered. Weeks may have passed, but he still couldn't seem to shake from his mind or senses the recollection of one particular auburn-haired minx. To his surprise, his hostess led him past a number of other guests on a path that drew him closer and closer to the redhead.

Could *she* possibly be the friend? he wondered.

Apparently so, he realized, when Lady Coates stopped at the woman's side and leaned forward to murmur something in her ear. After a quiet excuse to the other women with whom the redhead had been conversing, Lady Coates turned back, a wide smile on her lips. "Pray allow me the pleasure of introducing my dear friend to you. My lord, Mrs. Smythe. Lily, Ethan Andarton, the Marquis of Vessey."

As if the earth were suddenly shifting on its axis, he watched as the woman he'd never thought to see again spun slowly around. Air whooshed from his lungs, the sight of her catching him like a fist to the belly.

*Lily! His* Lily. And yet not her at all. At least not the version of her he remembered. For one thing, she looked stunningly soft and feminine. Gone were the trousers and coat, together with all the other little masculine details she'd tried to mimic, including the snug queue of hair she'd worn against her neck.

Gone, too, was the sight of her comely legs and taut little buttocks, hidden now beneath the folds of her dress. However, as regretful a loss as that might be, he could not complain about the view of her breasts—the lovely rounded shape of them delineated by her bodice, a tantalizing strip of flesh revealed to his appreciative eyes.

Yet as markedly different as she appeared now in her female attire, there was no mistaking her face. The same adorable nose with its delicate sprinkling of freckles.

The same jewel-tone eyes, her green irises nearly a match for her elegant evening gown. The same mouth, her lush, sultry lips the very ones he'd plundered with a series of hot, passionate kisses, kisses he imagined he could taste even now.

He struggled to quash his instant rush of desire, his loins aching in a way that he knew might prove embarrassing if he didn't get himself under firm control. Catching her gaze with his own, he read the astonishment shining in her eyes.

Her lashes swept downward just before she dropped into a deep curtsey. "An honor, my lord."

He bowed, only then recalling the name by which Lady Coates had introduced her.

"Mrs. Smythe." Even to his own ears, his words sounded harsh, reverberating in a graveled rumble. *Mrs. Smythe!* His brows drew together, sharp as a set of daggers.

*Hell and damnation, is she married?* Unable to voice the appalling question, he stared.

Davina Coates, about whom he'd very nearly forgotten, glanced between them, an expression of puzzled inquiry on her face. "Perhaps it is my imagination, but do the two of you know each other?"

"No," Lily shot back.

"Yes," he said at the same time, their voices crossing over each other's.

Lady Coates laughed. "Goodness, which is it? Yes or no?"

He waited, allowing Lily to speak first.

"No," she said. "At least not really. Lord Vessey and I have . . . seen each other, I believe, but have never been formally introduced."

"Yes," he drawled. "We have *seen* each other." *And kissed each other, and touched each other as well.*

"Oh," their hostess said, looking even more curious

than before. "Perhaps you were acquainted with Mrs. Smythe's late husband, your lordship? Could that be where you met?"

*Late husband? Ah, so she is a widow!* A rush of coiled tension eased from his shoulders.

"Hmm," he said, "I do not believe so, but perhaps. Wherever it was our paths crossed, I am glad they have done so again."

Lady Coates cast them another bemused smile. "Well, good. It pleases me that I could introduce you properly this time. If you will excuse me, I see I am needed across the room. Something about dinner, I expect."

Lily tossed her friend a narrowed look as though she wished to protest the desertion. Instead, she held her tongue as the other woman smiled once more, then glided away.

For a long moment, neither he nor the beautiful adventuress before him spoke. And she was indeed beautiful, more radiant and bewitching than he remembered. A part of him was irritated with her—for what he didn't entirely know—but another, far stronger part of him was pleased, happy and relieved to have suddenly discovered her once again.

*This time,* he mused, *I will not be letting her get away.*

Angling his body forward, Ethan crowded closer in the hopes of their conversing without being overheard. When she took two steps back into a nearby corner, he followed. As he did, a hint of the rose-and-vanilla scent perfuming her skin drifted upward to his nostrils.

Desire thickened in his blood. Had they not been in company, he wasn't sure whether or not he would have been able to restrain the wild urge to press his face against her neck—or better yet, her breasts—for a deeper inhalation.

Instead, he forced himself to meet her gaze. "So, how

are you, Lily? I presume I may call you Lily, or would you prefer Mrs. Smythe?"

She played her fingers over a button on the wrist of one of her long, white evening gloves. "Mrs. Smythe, I think. And I am quite well as you can see, my lord. Yourself?"

He quirked a brow and smiled, more amused than annoyed by her somewhat prickly reply.

"I enjoy robust health as well. And you may relax, Lily," he said, ignoring her request to maintain formality. "I have no intention of telling anyone where it is we actually met, nor more importantly, how you were garbed at the time."

Her delicate brows moved across her forehead like two small slashes of fire. "I certainly hope not. Should you decide otherwise, I shall deny it most emphatically."

"Yes, I am sure you would. But pray do not overset yourself. What passed between us shall be our own little secret, including what happened in the coach. You have my word as a gentleman."

His statement seemed to reassure her, anxiety visibly draining from Lily's body as though she had been waiting for him to unmask her before one and all.

"I must admit, however," he continued in a low voice meant only for her ears, "that I am surprised to learn you are a widow. You certainly gave no intimation that such might be the case."

"There were a great many things I did not mention on that occasion, if you will recall. Introducing such a topic did not seem germane."

"I am sure it did not. Permit me to extend my sympathy for your loss, however."

Her lashes swept downward, lowering to fix in the vicinity of his waistcoat. "Thank you."

"You must have married young. You cannot be a day above nineteen."

Pale pink spread across her cheeks as her gaze returned to meet his own. "I am twenty, which is not so young, considering that many women marry at sixteen."

"Yes, but most of them do not lose their husbands. How did he perish?"

At first she said nothing, worrying her fingertips over her glove buttons once more. "He died a soldier's death on the battlefield. And now, if you do not mind, I would rather not discuss any more of the particulars."

"Of course." He paused for a moment. "So is that why you do it, to distract yourself from the grief?"

Puzzlement filled her eyes. "Do what?"

"Indulge in risky and thoroughly outrageous wagers with friends."

Surprise flared inside her gaze for an instant before an expression of thoughtful introspection replaced it. "I had never thought of it as such, but perhaps you are correct. One can sometimes find oneself running quite literally from one's troubles."

"Then might I suggest exploring alternate outlets for exorcising such needs."

She arched a brow. "Like what, my lord?"

He was about to tell her when the Coateses' liveried butler called for everyone's attention to inform them that dinner was now served.

Around the room, as ladies and gentlemen began to pair up according to rank, Lily leaned toward him, her voice a whisper. "And in case you are wondering, Davina is not the friend involved, so please leave Lady Coates out of this. She has no idea about my little excursion, and would be distressed if she did."

He dipped his head toward hers. "I told you before, this is our secret and no one else's."

Just then, a slender gentleman appeared at Lily's side, bowing to them both. "Your pardon, but I believe I am to escort Mrs. Smythe into dinner."

Ethan wanted to flick the other man off like a pesky fly. Instead he restrained the urge, faced Lily, and executed a perfect bow. "Until later, madam."

She curtseyed. "Of course, my lord."

Forcing himself to turn, he went in search of his own partner, wishing the woman were Lily.

*He really needs to stop gazing at me,* Lily thought nearly an hour later.

Dinner was proceeding apace, wine and conversation flowing liberally as a small multitude of voices mixed with the quiet background click of silver utensils scraping against fine bone china and the occasional ringing tap of delicate cut-crystal glassware. Beautifully wrought silver candelabra were positioned throughout the room, the lighted beeswax tapers adding a honeyed sweetness to the air. Footmen served and cleared with nearly invisible precision, every course more delicious than the last.

Yet Lily barely noticed the food or the conversation, far too aware of a certain golden-haired gentleman and his watchful gaze.

The marquis was seated several feet down and opposite, relaxing back in his chair with the graceful assurance of a lion. With candlelight burnishing his hair to a gleaming gold, he reminded her of some ancient god of Nordic myth. Or a warrior perhaps, since she was coming to realize he possessed a wild intensity that belied his veneer of quiet sophistication. Added to that was the fact that he was, without question, the handsomest man in the room. Of course, given his undeniable masculine beauty, he was likely to be the handsomest man in *any* room.

And he was looking at her. *Again.*

Glancing down at her plate, she struggled to slow the rapid pace of her heartbeat, aware of him as if he were seated only inches away instead of feet. *He really ought to stop,* Lily thought, silently chiding him as she cut a tiny piece of the roast venison with cherry port sauce and lifted the bite to her lips. Despite the buttery tenderness of the meat, she had difficulty swallowing, knowing if she glanced up she would find those mesmerizing amber eyes still upon her.

Luckily she didn't think anyone else in the room had noticed Lord Vessey's attentions toward her, despite the fact that he'd been playing his little game through the entirety of the meal. Even while he ate his dinner and chatted with the guests to his right and left, he had kept her in his sights, his gaze stroking over her like a sleek, velvety glove. His visual caresses set her body atingle as memories of his talented hands and glorious kisses replayed themselves in her mind.

Of all the unlikely coincidences, she still couldn't believe she had encountered him here tonight, particularly when she'd thought never to see him again!

Shock was the only word to describe her earlier reaction when she'd turned around at Davina's urging and found him standing before her. She'd very nearly died on the spot. He had been equally surprised, she could tell, his eyes mirroring the astonishment she had felt. At least he had given his promise not to reveal how they had really met, nor the way she had been attired at the time— behavior many would consider scandalous were it to become generally known.

No, on that score at least, she knew she could relax. Lord Vessey had given his word as a gentleman, and she believed him. But what did he think he was about, gazing at her with such rapt attention? Was he simply "punishing" her for her so-called wild behavior, or was that really desire she saw gleaming in his eyes? And if it was, how should she react?

Soon the main course was cleared, dessert and coffee served, along with a sweet wine for the ladies and a fortified vintage for the gentlemen. Lily was trying to make polite conversation with the man on her left when she once again caught the marquis's eye.

Meeting his gaze directly this time, she watched as he gave her a slow smile. Raising his wineglass, he took a drink, his strong throat working beneath his cravat. Her mouth grew dry, her pulse pounding as his tongue slid out to catch an errant drop of wine—the act leaving his own mouth moist and gleaming as if he'd just indulged in a heated kiss.

Her nipples hardened beneath the fabric of her bodice.

*Good God,* she realized, *he's seducing me without so much as a touch! Dangerous. That's what he is. Far too dangerous for me.*

Relief swept through her when Davina called for the ladies to withdraw, Lily's legs shaking slightly as she rose and walked from the room. Entering the drawing room, she accepted a cup of tea, then crossed to take a seat on one of the sofas. As she sipped the gently steaming beverage, she considered the marquis.

*Some men a woman can handle,* she mused, *and some men a woman cannot.* Ethan Andarton was unquestionably one of the latter variety. She might not know him well, but already she could tell he was strong-willed and persistent, the kind of man who would never allow himself to be manipulated or persuaded from his chosen course.

What she found herself wondering was whether or not his "chosen course" currently included pursuing her. His behavior at dinner would certainly seem to suggest the possibility—the mere recollection of his gaze enough to provoke a full-body flush.

Her intuition told her to flee.

Her head told her not to be a silly goose.

True, he made her tingle in ways and places she'd

never realized a woman might crave a man, but it was just as true that she had no intention of doing anything about the attraction. For one, she had no wish to marry. And as for an illicit affair, she knew nothing of such matters, only that it would be in her best interest to steer well clear of such a tangle of complications and intimacies. Nonetheless, she'd never been one to back away from a challenge. *So,* she decided, *whatever Lord Vessey's game might be, I will match him and win.*

Her confidence faltered a bit, though, when he strode into the room with the rest of the gentlemen nearly an hour later. Yet instead of crossing to her, he continued a discussion with his host, the pair of them apparently involved in some weighty matters given the serious expressions on their faces. Once he'd finished his talk with Lord Coates, he allowed himself to be drawn into conversation with a pair of ladies, who flirted and laughed, making every effort to display their more-than-ample feminine assets to his apparently appreciative eyes.

More irritated than she cared to admit even to herself, Lily drew her shawl around her shoulders and stood. Turning her back in his direction, she decided she would make her excuses to her hosts and call for her coach.

"Hello again, Mrs. Smythe," rumbled a familiar male voice from over her shoulder. "And how have you been enjoying the evening?"

Turning to face him, she found herself far too close—a faint trace of the bay rum on his neck pleasuring her senses, the subtle rows of white-on-white acanthus leaves that were intricately embroidered on his waistcoat near enough to be easily visible to her eyes.

Refusing to retreat, she tipped back her head and met his keen gaze. "Quite well, though I am just on my way to say my good-evenings to Davina."

"Surely you aren't leaving? The night is entirely too young for you to depart yet."

"Nonetheless, I believe I shall take my leave."

"But there is to be music, or so I am given to understand. Both singing and playing."

"I assume you heard that from the young ladies with whom you were so recently conversing," she retorted, her words sounding far more tart than they ought.

He lifted a brow, amusement curving his sensual mouth. "Actually, our hostess is the one who mentioned tonight's auditory entertainment, but Miss Chartman and her cousin will no doubt be eager to participate. You must do so as well. And at which talent are you more proficient, ma'am, singing or playing?"

A delicate guffaw escaped her lips. "Neither, my lord. I am a sad hand at both. Lady Coates and I were in school together years ago and she can attest to my failings in those disciplines. If she has any care for her guests, she will spare them such tortures."

"Come now, it cannot be as bad as all that."

"No, it is worse."

Quite without knowing how, she found herself sharing a mutual smile with him, one that was oddly conspiratorial in nature.

The merry twinkle that danced in his gaze gradually faded, deepening to something else entirely.

"Well, I am sure you possess many other exceptional talents," he drawled, his eyes lowering slowly to her lips.

Her breasts rose and fell on a quick inhalation, an electrified shiver traveling through her system.

*Mercy, there he goes again,* she thought, *threatening to turn me into a puddle!* Quite likely he employed the technique—one of his exceptional talents—on a regular basis. She imagined women were forever casting themselves at his feet. And how many, she wondered, did he accept?

"Why do we not take a turn in the garden?" he suggested. "So you can tell me more about yourself."

"I thought you wanted to hear the music."

"I would rather hear about you."

His words snapped her out of her haze. If there was anything about which she did *not* want to talk it was herself. Already, he knew far too much for comfort.

"Thank you, my lord, but I must decline," she said, fighting to keep her tone light and even. "As I told you before, I really need to leave."

"Very well, then, if you insist, madam. But know that I shall see you again and we will have that walk." He bent closer, lowering his voice to a whisper. "You will not be able to run and hide from me this time. No erroneous dead-end trails for me to follow without success."

She bit the corner of her lip and stared in dawning wonder. "Whatever do you mean? Did you follow me that first evening?"

"One of my footmen did, actually, though I went to your hotel the next morning only minutes after you'd left. I am glad to know you will not be disappearing again."

*Gracious, he tried to find me! I am in even deeper straits than I had imagined.*

"Good evening, my lord."

One corner of his mouth tipped up in a sensual smile. "Good evening, Jack."

# Chapter Six

❧

"**Y**OUR PARDON, MADAM, but these just arrived," Lily's butler announced from the doorway of her study.

Setting down the quill pen she'd been using to write Davina a thank-you note for last night's dinner party, she motioned the servant forward, her eyes widening at the sight of a massive arrangement of flowers held inside a white porcelain vase.

"Mercy, who could have sent those?" she wondered aloud.

Yet as soon as the words left her mouth she knew the answer.

*Lord Vessey.*

*Heavens, he's sent me flowers. And not just any flowers—lilies!*

Each creamy white, saucer-sized flower bore a delicate pink center, their heavenly fragrance filling the room like an open bottle of the finest French perfume. She drew in a deep breath, unable to keep herself from savoring the magnificent scent.

"There is a card," her butler volunteered, placing the huge mass of flowers—three dozen at least—atop a nearby table. Plucking free the small paper square, he brought the card to her and offered it with a bow.

She hesitated before reaching out to take it. "Thank you, Hodges. That will be all."

Waiting until the servant withdrew, she gazed at the card and the bold yet elegant script written thereon.

*For the fairest Lily of them all.*
*Until we meet again.*
*Vessey*

A gentle sigh escaped her lips, her insides turning to the consistency of warm taffy as she gazed at the flowers.

*How lovely they are,* she mused, the buttery-yellow walls of the study a perfect complement to their beauty.

Rising to her feet, she crossed the room and stretched out a hand to stroke a single, velvety petal, noticing the stamens had been thoughtfully removed so there would be no pollen left to scatter. As before, the flowers' sweet fragrance drifted upward to delight her senses.

Clearly, Lord Vessey was not a man to waste time or hide his interest behind a series of false lures and half-veiled persuasions. Whatever this attraction was between them, he wanted to pursue it—to pursue *her.*

A quiver resonated deep within her at the knowledge.

*Gracious, even his posies turn me soft and gooey!* she thought. *Perhaps I would be wise to withdraw from the field rather than risk further temptation.* For in spite of her emboldened decision last evening to meet and match him at his own game, she wasn't certain of the strength of her willpower—not where the marquis was concerned.

Before she had time to change her mind, she rang the servant's bell.

Hodges appeared less than a minute later. "Yes, ma'am, how may I be of service?"

Casting a last soulful glance at the flowers, she forced

herself to turn her back on them. "If you would be so good, please see to it those are returned to their sender."

The middle-aged butler arched a brow but said nothing to appease his obvious curiosity. "Of course, Mrs. Smythe. Whatever you wish."

Crossing her arms, she watched out of the corner of her eye as he strode across the room to take the huge bouquet in hand. Turning, he started toward the door.

"*Wait!*" she exclaimed as he neared the threshold.

The servant stopped in his tracks and looked over his shoulder. "Yes, madam?"

Hurrying forward on the toes of her thin leather slippers, she came to a halt, then extended a hand to carefully slide a single flower free from its fellows.

"I wish to keep one," she said, realizing the defense was as much for herself as for her butler.

A half-smile hovered over his lips. "Very good, ma'am."

Clutching the single lily in one hand and Vessey's card in the other, she watched the servant depart. When he had gone, she lifted the flower to her nose, closed her eyes, and inhaled.


"Oh, I am so glad you decided to join us!" Lady Julianna Pendragon declared when Ethan entered the breakfast room two weeks later. "Rafe should be here shortly. He had some pressing matter of business that could not wait, not even for his usual morning cup of coffee."

Mid-May sunshine flooded into the space, bringing with it an atmosphere of light and cheer. The garden visible beyond the glass double doors was a virtual rainbow of color; fat, red-breasted robins hopping over the verdant grass in search of their own breakfast of worms.

Ethan paid scant attention to nature's bounty, however, as he bent to dust a friendly kiss across Julianna's smooth cheek. "I am glad too. With Rafe absent, we'll be able to steal a bit more time for ourselves," he teased with a wink. "May I say how radiant you look, even more so than usual. Carrying that newest little one must agree with you."

Julianna laughed, her dark eyes and beautiful face alive with unconcealed happiness. "He does, or should I say *she*, since I am hoping for a girl this time. Whichever sex, I cannot complain of feeling ill in even the slightest way, no queasiness or fatigue. Were it not for this," she said, laying a palm across her slightly rounded belly, "I would hardly know I am with child."

Ethan smiled and took a seat.

Ever the polite hostess and being familiar with his tastes, Julianna lifted a Sèvres teapot from the center of the linen-lined table and poured him a cup.

"My sister claims the second baby is always easier," he observed. "I am pleased it is proving so for you. And how is young master Campbell?"

"He is wonderful," she replied, refilling her own teacup before replacing the pot in its cozy. "Although testing his nurse's patience lately, ever since he learned to run. When he gets going, catching him can be the very devil. Last night, he would not settle down until Rafe came in. Of course, Cam is such a skilled negotiator at only fourteen months that he managed to wheedle an extra bedtime story out of his papa. He lasted a single page, then fell fast asleep."

Her mouth curved in a tender smile of remembrance. "But enough about me and mine; how are you?"

*Hmm,* he considered, *how am I? I would be better if a certain widow weren't doing her best to elude me, and making a damned fine job of it, too.*

Over the past two weeks, he'd expected to encounter Lily Smythe at one Ton function or another. Yet despite his efforts to seek her out, she had so far managed to avoid any of the events to which he was also invited. Assuming she was going out in the evenings—and he rather expected that to be the case—then Lily was obviously confining herself to small dinner parties and symposiums and such for ladies only.

Were it not for her rejection of the bouquet he'd sent, he might have put her elusiveness down to a circumstance of unfortunate coincidence. But he rather suspected her actions to be deliberate.

Since procuring her direction from Lady Coates on the evening of her party, he'd toyed with the idea of calling upon Lily at her townhouse. Given his brief acquaintance with her, though—at least in a public forum—he decided it might be wiser to find another method of wooing the mysterious widow Smythe.

Generally, he didn't indulge in chasing after women, especially ones who seemed reluctant to be caught. As a rule, he found women eager for his attentions, providing him with a more than ample selection from which to choose. Unfortunately, though, at the present time he had no desire for any of those women, his thoughts focused squarely upon one.

By now, he supposed he ought to have banished memories of his passionate encounter with Lily. Yet those few minutes of contact had remained lodged like an aphrodisiac in his senses, leaving him hot and hungry for more. Meeting her unexpectedly at the Coateses' had done nothing but increase his appetite.

At its base, he knew one thing for certain: he wanted Lily Smythe in his bed.

*And by God*, he thought, *I mean to have her. Now all I need to do is convince her that's what she wants, too.*

"So, tell me," Julianna inquired, intruding into his thoughts, "what feminine hearts have you been breaking lately?"

He paused, keenly aware of how close to his thoughts

she had unwittingly come. "Alas none, dear lady," he said, recovering quickly enough to send her a flirtatious smile. "Not with your own heart already spoken for, that is."

"That's right, she *is* spoken for," Rafe Pendragon announced in a growl as he strode into the breakfast room, "and I'll thank you to remember it. No poaching, even if you are one of my best friends."

Ethan smiled and sipped his tea, knowing himself safe from Rafe's wrath. Of course, the situation would have been completely different had his words been even remotely serious. Rafe, as he well knew, would tear apart any man who attempted a dalliance with his wife. Not that Julianna was interested; she had eyes for no one but her husband.

Walking up to Julianna's chair, Rafe leaned over and gave her a quick but infinitely loving and tender kiss on the lips. Straightening, he nodded a friendly hello to Ethan before taking his own seat at the table.

A servant entered the room carrying a tall silver pot. Crossing to Rafe, he poured steaming coffee into the baron's china cup. Another footman followed, bearing a platter heaped with eggs, bacon, kippers, and kidneys. A silver holder laden with golden squares of toast was next placed onto the table, along with a basket of assorted muffins and crumpets. A bowl of freshly sliced fruit came last.

After helping himself to eggs, three slices of bacon, and a single kipper, Ethan added a delicious-scented blueberry muffin, then dug into the food with enjoyment. Rafe and Julianna made their own selections, then did the same.

Over the meal, the three of them talked, sharing stories and opinions on a variety of topics. Ethan waited until the plates were cleared and fresh cups of coffee and tea had been poured before he launched into the subject foremost on his mind.

"I understand you have a new neighbor here on the square," he remarked, stirring a teaspoonful of sugar into his tea, faint tendrils of steam rising from the beverage's surface. "A young widow, is she not?"

Julianna set her own cup onto its saucer. "Oh, you must mean Mrs. Smythe. Yes, she is new to the neighborhood. I had occasion to meet her when I took Cam out for a walk last week. She seemed very pleasant and sweet."

Ethan wasn't sure he would apply the term "sweet" to Lily given her spirited ways and behavior that would shock a great many in Society if they knew, including, he suspected, Julianna. Then again, perhaps describing Lily as sweet was exactly right—she'd certainly turned sweet in his arms.

"Why do you ask? Are you acquainted with her?" Julianna inquired, arching a dark brow.

Glancing down, he rubbed a thumbnail over the starched white tablecloth. "Only slightly. We were introduced at a dinner party a couple of weeks ago. I merely found it interesting to discover she purchased a townhouse on the opposite side of the square from you."

Julianna's mouth curled upward at one corner. "Ah, is that the only thing about her you found interesting?"

"I am afraid I do not know what you mean."

She laughed this time, Rafe joining her from across the table.

"You've been fairly caught, good fellow," Rafe said. "Julianna can sniff out romantic interest a mile away."

"Well, it's not terribly difficult when he gives such broad hints, now, is it?" She cast Ethan a warm smile. "Go on. What is it about her you should like to know, although I cannot say I know much, since she and I did not speak of personal matters."

He couldn't say he knew much about Lily either—he wondered if anyone did. Her friend Davina, perhaps, though he wondered if Lily kept secrets from her as well. He suspected she very well might.

"Mrs. Smythe is extremely pretty, is she not?" Julianna observed.

Smiling, Ethan relaxed back in his chair. "She is very becoming, if you like redheads. So, is she coming to your ball next week?"

Julianna nodded. "As it would happen, I did pen her an invitation."

"And?" Ethan prompted, his pulse kicking into a faster beat.

"And she accepted. Her card arrived just yesterday, as I recall."

He fought the impulse to grin like a fool, contenting himself with a silent inner shout of triumph. "Good."

"Is that all you have to say? You remind me of a cat who just swallowed a rather delicious canary."

Shrugging, he made no reply.

"Should I happen upon Mrs. Smythe again before the ball, shall I tell her of your interest?" she inquired in a teasing voice.

"No!" He felt his eyes grow large for a second before he recovered his calm composure. "That is, I would rather you not and give me the pleasure of renewing my acquaintance with the lady on my own."

"Never fear," Julianna promised, "I shan't say a word to her."

"My thanks, my lady."

After that, the conversation moved on to less sensitive subjects.

A short while later, Julianna made her excuses. "I really should go upstairs to the nursery. Heaven only knows what sort of mischief Cam may have gotten himself into by now."

Ethan and Rafe stood as she left the room.

Knowing Rafe must have business, and having a measure of his own awaiting him at home, Ethan prepared to depart.

"This widow," Rafe inquired. "She wouldn't happen to be the same woman who had you so thoroughly distracted over cards a few weeks ago, would she?"

Having known Rafe since they were childhood friends at Harrow—the pair of them and Tony a loyal triumvirate—he knew better than to attempt a lie. "What if she is?"

"Then I would caution you to have a care. She may be a widow but she is still a lady, and from what I am given to understand, a young and perhaps vulnerable one at that."

"I am aware of her age and the fact she lost her husband only a year ago. I do not intend to harm her, if that is your concern."

"I am sure you do not plan to do so. Yet what of this understanding of yours to contract a marriage alliance with the Earl of Sutleigh's daughter?"

Ethan gave a nonchalant shrug. "What of it?"

"You see nothing contradictory in the two arrangements?"

"No, since there is no *arrangement* as of yet with either young woman. I am not engaged to Sutleigh's girl and Lily Smythe is not my mistress."

"But you intend for her to be."

"If I do, that is my business," Ethan said, his jaw tight.

"You're right, it is your business. I am simply pointing out, as a friend, that you may wish to consider the ramifications of your actions before you commit to them."

"As a friend, I appreciate the warning. But there is no need. Everything will work out to everyone's mutual satisfaction."

Rafe gave him a long stare. "I hope so. Come now, let me walk you out while you tell me about that new team of grays you bought at Tattersall's last week."

Relieved to be done with the uncomfortable topic of his romantic intentions, Ethan dove into a discussion of his newest acquisition. "They're the best pair of two-year-olds I've seen in a decade. Livermoor's loss and my gain, I have to say."

The following Tuesday, Lily entered the Pendragons' ballroom, nervous excitement whizzing through her bloodstream like tiny effervescent bubbles of wine. Tonight would be her very first Ton ball, her prior experiences having been confined to the occasional country dance held at the assembly rooms near her home in Cornwall.

And what a difference there was between the two locales, Baron and Lady Pendragon's London townhouse was every inch as beautiful and refined as the company assembled. Gentlemen and ladies were bedecked in a sea of elegant finery, the corridors and drawing rooms crowded with members of some of the best families in England. Laughter and conversation hummed inside the ballroom as she walked forward on the arm of her escort. Overhead, crystal chandeliers sparkled in the reflected glow of several hundred candles, while many tall, rose-filled Meissen vases turned the air candy-sweet.

Despite her usual confidence, Lily found herself unexpectedly grateful for Lord Ottwell's supporting arm. To be honest, she would much have preferred attending alone, but as Davina had told her in a half-appalled whisper, such things were simply *not* done, as Lily knew full well. A lady must *always* be accompanied by friends, family, or a suitable male escort.

Since Lord and Lady Coates were already promised

elsewhere for the evening, Lily had agreed to allow Lord Ottwell to take her to the ball. Although she had been introduced to him only last week at a small evening musicale, he seemed a pleasant fellow, ever eager to please, though perhaps a bit too eager, as she was coming to realize.

Having already been warmly welcomed by Rafe and Julianna upon their arrival, the two of them strolled deeper into the room to stop along its periphery. As soon as they drew to a halt, Lily withdrew her gloved hand from her escort's arm.

"The dancing has yet to begin," Lord Ottwell remarked, smiling just enough to display his set of crooked incisors. "May I be the first to request a dance?"

"Oh well, of course," Lily replied, manners requiring nothing less.

"I thought we might partake of a waltz," he suggested, gazing at her out of a pair of earnest gray eyes. "Unless you would rather not," he rushed on. "I know some ladies find the dance far too indecent and scandalous, preferring to sit out those particular sets. Not to say that you would, or wouldn't, it's just that I do not wish to offend. We shall do as you like, Mrs. Smythe." He cleared his throat. "So what do you like . . . that is, when it comes to dancing?"

She waited a moment to make sure he had finished his long trail of words, then replied. "A waltz sounds delightful. I should very much like to try it."

"Have you never waltzed before?"

"No," she answered honestly. When he looked as if he expected some further explanation, she decided she would have to improvise. "Prior to my . . . um . . . marriage I did not have the occasion, and then, well, my . . . husband died and I . . . I just could not."

His sandy brows gathered in concern. "Pray do not upset yourself, ma'am, by mentioning things that are of a far too painful nature. Tonight is meant for frivolity, and that is what you shall have. In that vein, it shall give me great happiness to introduce you to the joys of the waltz."

"Thank you, my lord."

A short pause descended, each of them gazing out upon their fellow guests.

"Lady Coates tells me you have not resided in London above a few weeks," he remarked, rocking up and down on his heels. "Have you had an opportunity yet to visit the sights?"

"Only a few. Davina . . . Lady Coates and I went to Astley's Amphitheater, and although the acts were quite exciting, I found myself feeling rather sorry for the animals."

"They seem well cared for. I am sure they must enjoy the audiences for whom they perform."

*And do they enjoy their cages afterward?* she thought. *I know a bit about how it feels to live in a cage and long to be on the other side.*

"You know what I would really like to do," she declared abruptly, throwing caution to the wind and speaking her thoughts aloud. "I would like to learn to drive a team."

"Of horses, do you mean?"

Turning her head, she met her escort's startled gaze. "Yes, of course, horses."

For although there was nothing strictly forbidden about a lady driving her own equipage, Lily realized that most women preferred to let men, quite literally, take the reins. She was not one of those women. A frown settled over Lord Ottwell's brow as he fought for a suitable reply.

Just then, she sensed someone approach from behind her. The delicate hairs on the base of her neck came to attention, heightened awareness prickling through her only seconds before a familiar velvety voice slid past her ears like a caress.

"Good evening, Mrs. Smythe. What a pleasure to find you here tonight."

A shiver that began at the base of her spine rippled outward, spreading all the way to the ends of her fingers and the tips of her toes. Slowly, she turned and gazed upward into Ethan Andarton's penetrating amber eyes.

Her breath caught at the sight of him, looking resplendent in a traditional black tailcoat and breeches, white shirt and waistcoat, his attire as impeccable as that of Beau Brummell in his prime. His starched linen cravat rivaled Beau's as well, the knot—tied in a precise *Trône d'Amour*—emphasizing the strong, square line of his jaw and setting off the golden brilliance of his neatly trimmed hair.

*So, he has found me,* she sighed, unable to decide whether to be vexed or glad.

"My lord," she replied with a curtsey. "How do you do this evening?"

"Very well, thank you." He paused, then tossed the other man a nod as if he had only just noticed him. "Ottwell."

"Vessey."

"What is this about horses, then?" the marquis asked, obviously having overheard the thread of their earlier conversation.

Lily straightened her shoulders. "I was just telling Lord Ottwell that I wish to learn to drive, and he was about to tell me whether or not he would consent to give me lessons."

Beside her, Ottwell made an odd humming noise in the base of his throat as though he were preparing to issue a refusal, but a moment later he surprised her. "Why, it would be my great honor to instruct you on how to manage the ribbons, ma'am. We must be sure to set a date."

"Splendid, my lord," she said, bestowing a smile upon him that left the man blinking as if he'd stared directly into a noonday sun.

Vessey arched a brow, one corner of his mouth turning upward in a knowing way.

Lily ignored the look. "Lord Ottwell has also agreed to teach me to waltz this evening. I am quite looking forward to our dance."

She didn't know what prompted her to make such a bold declaration, other than the fact that Lord Vessey seemed to bring out the imp in her. Instead, she knew she ought to be looking for ways to extract herself from his presence. Yet like all forbidden fruit, he was a temptation not easily denied.

"In that case, you must allow me the pleasure of claiming the second waltz of the night," he said.

Knowing herself caught in a trap of her own design, she inclined her head. "As you will, my lord. The second waltz is yours."

"We shall wait until later to see what else may yet become mine."

She quivered, readily sensing the underlying sensual implications of his remark. She only hoped Lord Ottwell didn't realize them as well.

Moments later, a quartet of musicians assembled on one side of the room and played a few notes to signal to the guests that they should take their places for the opening dance. To Lily's relief, she realized it was the waltz.

"Ma'am," Lord Ottwell said, extending his arm.

"If you will excuse us, Lord Vessey," she said, "the dancing is about to begin."

The marquis bowed and stepped aside to let them pass.

Strolling onto the dance floor, Lily restrained the urge to glance back to see if Vessey was still watching. But a full minute later as she waited for the first strains of music to begin, she gave in and turned her head to check—and discovered he was no longer there.

Her shoulders drooped.

*He's probably gone in search of a dance partner of his own,* she mused. *Just as he should. Well, no matter,* she told herself. *I am far better off without the constant attentions of Lord Vessey.*

*So why am I disappointed?*

Calling herself ridiculous to the utmost degree, she pasted a cheerful smile on her face and let her partner lead her into the dance.

From a shadowed corner of the ballroom, Ethan quaffed a mouthful of Malaga and watched Lily glide around the ballroom in Lord Ottwell's arms. The excellent flavor and body of the wine barely registered on his tongue, however, his thoughts focused almost completely upon her.

If he suspected even for an instant that she might seriously be interested in Ottwell, he would have separated him from her the way a lion drove a rival from his pride. But Ethan could tell she was merely here to enjoy herself, Ottwell being nothing more than a convenient male escort and dancing partner. Still, he was sure Ottwell did not feel the same; his usually calm expression all but enraptured as he gazed upon Lily.

*And why should it not be?* Ethan thought, considering just how lovely she was—radiant as a perfect summer day, her deep blue skirts billowing around her trim ankles, her upswept Titian locks as vibrantly, vividly alive as she herself. Simply being in the same room with her set his senses afire, reconfirming the instinctive depth of his attraction for her.

But his desire could wait for now. First he needed to exercise patience and bide his time as the two of them played their mating game to its inevitable conclusion. In his mind he thought again of their brief but invigorating verbal sparring from moments ago, cognizant of the fact that he was eagerly anticipating the next round.

Until their waltz, he supposed he ought to dance with a few other ladies instead of skulking in corners. Julianna would be demanding answers if he wasn't careful. Her interest in Lily was piqued enough already without him drawing more attention Lily's way. Neither did he wish to earn the notice of the Ton itself.

Besides, if he took to the dance floor, he would have little trouble keeping her in his sights. *Who knows, perhaps we might accidentally brush up against each other as we pass,* he thought with anticipation. Tossing back the last of his wine, he set down his glass and strode forward.

Lily discovered she had been right about Ethan seeking out other dance partners. With the exception of her first dance with Lord Ottwell, the marquis hadn't taken a pause, standing up for every set with one beautiful woman after another.

If she had cared about such matters—which of course she did not—she might have found her nose quite out of joint by the time the second waltz arrived. Not that she had lacked for partners in the interim, barely having had time to catch her breath from one set before being led out by a new man to enjoy the next. All the while, she had been aware of Lord Vessey, catching a glimpse of his tall form moving in graceful accompaniment to the music, or else hearing his deep-throated laughter ring out over some apparently amusing remark made by his latest partner.

Now her turn had arrived—or *his,* depending upon

how one wished to view the matter. Sipping a glass of cool lemonade to relieve the dryness in her throat, she waited for him to appear.

And appear he did, slipping up behind her just as she was swallowing a last mouthful.

"Lemonade, hmm?" he observed. "I would have assumed a more daring beverage would be to your liking."

Startled, she swallowed wrong, a cough erupting from her throat. As she continued coughing, his broad palm settled against her back and began to rub in wide, comforting circles.

A quiver trailed down her spine.

"Are you all right?" he queried in a low, almost intimate tone.

She nodded her head and coughed again. "You really must stop sneaking up on me," she said the moment she could draw enough breath to form the words. "Can you not find a way to approach from the front?"

Apparently reassured she was in no real danger, his lips turned upward into an easy smile. "I could, but I find I rather enjoy a back view, at least *your* back view."

She nearly choked again at the naughty remark, a fresh tingle plunging low as he moved his hand again, stroking his palm along her spine all the way to its base. He toyed there for a brief instant as if he longed to travel onward, then dropped his arm casually to his side.

Her nipples tightened, uncontrolled warmth seeping into her cheeks. She restrained the urge to cross her arms over her chest, grateful for the shift and stays that kept her reaction from being visible. Flashing him a look, she noticed he appeared utterly unrepentant.

*Lord above, what if someone has seen?* But a quick check around the room showed that no one was looking at them, the majority of people far too busy talking or making their way onto the dance floor.

With a clearly wicked light gleaming in his gorgeous eyes, he extended an arm. "Shall we?"

For an instant, she nearly refused, then decided better of the impulse. Seemingly quiescent, she laid her hand atop the luxurious black fabric of his sleeve.

She touched more of the elegant cloth a minute later as she set one gloved hand onto the firm expanse of his shoulder, her other palm clasped securely inside his own.

Once again, his other hand was at her back, positioned in a spot just south of where it ought to be. The same was true for the distance between them, their bodies a good two inches closer than those of any other couple on the dance floor.

When she tried to step back, he refused to let her, holding her in place with nothing more than a gentle tensing of his muscles.

"*Shh,* be still," he murmured. "You are exactly where you ought to be."

She was opening her mouth to contradict him when the music began. Suddenly they were gliding, her slippered feet floating across the polished wooden floor to the dulcet strains of flute, violin, and cello.

If her first waltz had been exhilarating, this second dance was sublime, as close to soaring on clouds, she suspected, as a human being could come. Her pulse fluttered as he took her sailing, his every move one of confident control and finesse.

He took advantage of a turn to draw her another inch nearer, his eyes for her alone. "So tell me, madam, why is it you have been avoiding me this past fortnight?"

Her lips parted and she felt her eyes widen faintly before she had a chance to rein in her surprise. "Pardon me, my lord, but I am afraid I do not know what you mean," she dissembled.

His eyes gleamed. "Of course you do, but we'll let the matter drop for now."

"There is no *matter*," she insisted, refusing to admit he was right. "If our paths have failed to cross lately, I am sure it is merely a case of circumstance."

"Ah. Well, that is good news indeed. I had wondered if you might have taken me in dislike for some unknown reason. I am greatly relieved to know I may be at ease on that score."

He swung her in another gliding arc. "In honor of our friendship, I must ask that you allow me to teach you to drive a carriage, if you are truly set upon such a course."

"I am. But I must decline your offer, since I have already promised Lord Ottwell that he may teach me, as you well know."

"Yes, but Ottwell only agreed in order to spare your feelings. I am sure he would not complain too loudly should you wish to withdraw."

"But I do not," she returned, giving him a polite little smile.

"I feel it my duty, then, to warn you that he's not much of a hand with the ribbons."

"I am sure he does well enough."

Vessey shrugged. "I don't generally care to tell tales, but the man is ham-fisted. You would do better to hire your local butcher for the task."

A burst of laughter escaped her lips. "Surely you exaggerate."

"I assure you, I do not," he said, his expression serious.

An inkling of real doubt crept in, but she held firm. Of all the foolish ideas she might entertain, agreeing to let Lord Vessey teach her to drive was one of the worst. Besides, after this evening, she planned to start letting circumstances keep them apart again. For her own safety, she had no other choice.

"I thank you for the warning," she said, "but Lord Ottwell and I will do fine together."

His arms tightened around her waist. "Will you? And what of Ottwell? You know you're leading the poor man around by the nose already."

She gasped. "I am doing nothing of the sort!"

Vessey rolled his eyes. "You most certainly are. The fellow is half moony over you now, and he's only known you a few hours. Just think of the damage you might cause with prolonged exposure."

"Good heavens. You make me sound like a . . . a Jezebel!"

"No, no, nothing of the kind. But you are a captivating woman, one who is perhaps unaware of the power of her own allure."

Her pulse thudded. "You astonish me, my lord, since I have no particular allure of which to speak. I do not know where you come up with such ideas."

"Why, from being around you, of course." He spun her in an intimate series of steps, locking his gaze with her own. "Have supper with me tonight."

She shivered and fought off the wish to agree. A few loose curls whispered against the nape of her neck as she shook her head. "I cannot. I have promised the supper dance to another."

"Then meet me afterward. We'll share a dish of ice cream. Lady Pendragon told me she is serving strawberry as a special treat. You like strawberries, do you not?"

His voice coiled around her, seductive as a caress. "Yes, very much."

"And Champagne. There is nothing better than ice cream and Champagne. The first, sweet on the tongue; the next, a series of little bubbles that tease your senses as they pop. Come to the garden balcony at one o'clock. I shall be waiting."

She shook her head. "I shall not."

Without her awareness, the music ceased, the dance

done. He drew her to a halt but kept her cradled inside his arms.

"One o'clock," he whispered. "Do not be late."

And then, before she could refuse again, he released her and blended away into the crowd.

# Chapter Seven

❧

*E*THAN LEANED BACK against the balustrade, the carved granite smooth and cool beneath his hands. Behind him, the darkened garden hummed with life; newly blossomed lilacs turning the air to honey while night insects sang a gentle tune. A warm evening breeze moved in a lazy rhythm, occasionally rustling tree branches filled with young green leaves. Inside the house, light shone from the windows, music drifting quietly outward now that supper was over and the dancing had resumed in the ballroom upstairs.

Near his hip, balanced atop the flat surface of the balustrade, sat two crystal flutes of Champagne and a china bowl filled with fresh strawberry ice cream. He wasn't concerned about the confection melting since he'd talked one of the kitchen maids into placing the bowl inside an open, straw-lined basket filled with ice chips.

The scene required only one more element in order to be perfect—the lady for whom all this had been arranged.

Lily.

*Will she appear or won't she?*

Earlier out on the dance floor she had rejected his offer, but he'd refused to take no for an answer, confident that she would change her mind and meet him regardless of her initial rebuff.

Still, when he'd passed through the empty rear hallway that led to the garden, the hands on the casement clock had read five minutes to one. That had been fifteen minutes ago. Maybe he should give up and admit defeat.

For this evening, anyway.

Ten minutes later he was seriously considering drinking the Champagne—both glasses—when the nearly silent whisper of slippered feet reached his ears. And suddenly she was there—the dark blue of her gown nearly black in the pale moonlight, her coppery curls gleaming with a luminous sheen. He could tell she didn't see him, her eyes still adjusting to the heavy shadows that pooled in a small lake across the ground-floor balcony.

Then, abruptly, she stopped and gazed straight at him. "Oh, you *are* still here."

"Yes, and you are late. But I shall forgive you, since I am sure you were unavoidably detained," he stated, slowly gaining his feet. Reaching out, he picked up one of the Champagne flutes and passed it to her.

Stepping closer, she accepted the wine.

Lifting his own glass, he took a sip. She joined him, swallowing a long drink as though she needed a dose of mock courage.

"Actually I was not going to come at all, as I told you earlier. But I . . . I did not like to think of you waiting out here alone."

"My thanks for your kindness." He made her an elegant bow. "Though now that I hear your tardiness was deliberate, I may decide to demand a boon."

Her lips parted. "A boon? You, my lord, are outrageous."

"So some would claim."

Putting her glass to her lips, she drank another sip.

"Not that I am in any way agreeing to your suggestion, but what sort of *boon* are you envisioning?"

"Well now, that would be for me to decide and you to grant." He held out a hand. "Come now and join me, so we may talk."

"Oh? Is that what you wish to do? Talk?"

He met her look with an expression of deliberate innocence. "Of course. What else have you in mind?"

Slowly, like a rising sun, she smiled.

A moment later, however, the reaction faded, her earlier doubts obviously having returned. Hurrying forward on a quick swirl of skirts, she set down her Champagne. "No, I am afraid I really must go."

Reaching out, he caught her wrist in his hand. "But you cannot leave, not when you have only just arrived. Stay and share a dish of ice cream. Strawberry, exactly as promised."

Her breasts rose on an indecisive inhale, her inward struggle clear. "Has it not melted by now?"

He shook his head. "No, I've had it chilling on ice so every spoonful would stay creamy and delicious. Shall we see how our dessert has fared?"

Tugging her gently forward, he positioned her on his far side so she couldn't easily flee, then reached for the dish. Resuming his seat, he took up a spoon, then dipped the utensil into the frozen confection.

"Here," he encouraged, holding the spoon steady for her. "Have a taste."

At first, Lily did not move, staring at the bite of ice cream and the large, beautiful man who was offering her the sweet.

*Whatever possessed me to come out here?* she wondered, her heart racing like a fox escaping from a hound. *'Twas an idiotic decision, risky and imprudent.* Before she'd made her way here, she'd wavered for many long minutes, turning down more than one potential dance partner as she fought a silent, internal war. All through supper, her thoughts had centered upon one man, and her decision.

Go to him in the garden, or stay where it was safe, but dull? Take the prudent course, or the one filled with excitement and danger and the devastating Lord Vessey?

As she'd made her way downstairs and through the house to the garden, she'd told herself she was only going to check on him. No more, no less. But then he spoke to her and like a moth drawn to a particularly enticing flame, she had drifted closer.

Too close.

Once more, she considered the dessert.

*Should I take the bite or walk away? Then again, it is only ice cream, is it not? Where is the harm?*

Yet when she leaned forward and placed her lips around the spoon, the act seemed forbidden somehow, almost sinful. Though perhaps that was not because of the ice cream itself but because of the man who offered it. Cold and velvety, the sweet melted over her tongue, heightening her senses in a burst of flavor and scent.

"Good?" he questioned, drawing back the spoon.

Humming with pleasure, she nodded and swallowed.

Dipping out a bite for himself, he ate.

Unable to look away, she watched as he slid the spoon past his sensual lips, taking his time as he savored the confection.

"Hmm, you are right," he said. "Here, have another."

Feeling reckless and decadent, she let him feed her another spoonful, knowing she shouldn't be enjoying the act so much.

"Champagne?" he suggested in a husky voice. Taking a moment to set down the ice-cream dish, he leaned back to retrieve her glass.

A fresh set of warning bells pealed inside her head. Ignoring them, she drank again, the wine sharp but playful as it bubbled against her tongue.

Bending toward the ground, he retrieved a bottle, then moved to refill her glass.

Just barely, she stopped him. "Enough, my lord, otherwise I might wonder if you are trying to get me foxed."

He arched one golden brow. "Do not be absurd. You've only had one glass."

Sliding her fingers off the top of her champagne flute, he poured more wine, froth racing toward the rim. With a laugh, she brought the glass to her lips, sipping just enough to keep the wine from overflowing.

"So tell me, Mrs. Smythe, how have you been occupying yourself these past two weeks? Hopefully you have not been masquerading in male attire again in an attempt to win yet another bet."

Her eyes flashed to his, momentarily taken off guard by his question. "Actually, if you must know, I am not ordinarily in the habit of making wagers. That occasion arose from an . . . unanticipated whim . . . one that shall not be repeated."

"For your continued safety, I am relieved to hear that you have decided to cease such madcap activities. I hope you haven't discarded the outfit, however." He leaned toward her as if to impart a confidence. "Since I must say I rather fancied you in those breeches. Mayhap you'll put them on for me again sometime."

Warmth surged into her cheeks like a rising tide, making her glad for the concealing darkness. "And mayhap, if you wish hard enough, a fairy will appear and sprinkle gold dust over your head, my lord."

Silence fell, making her wonder for an instant if she had gone too far. Then abruptly he tossed back his head and released a hearty laugh.

"You know, madam, I never tire of that nimble

tongue of yours, nor that pretty mouth. What—I find myself waiting to discover—shall the pair of them say or do next?"

"If you promise to behave, my lord, I just might stay long enough for you to find out."

*Dear heavens,* she thought, *listen to me flirt—when I don't even know how to flirt! Then again, I say and do things around this man I otherwise would never dream of saying or doing, all the while pretending to be a woman I am not. If only he knew who I truly am, what would he think?*

Knowing she didn't dare let him ever find out, she once again set down her glass of Champagne. "The hour grows late and Lord Ottwell is expecting to escort me home. I should be going."

A muscle tightened in his jaw. "Ottwell can wait. And if he doesn't care to do so, I shall be happy to provide you escort. I have before."

*Yes, you have,* she mused, *and I well remember what passed between us during the journey.*

She gave him a sweet smile. "Good night, my lord."

"But we haven't finished the ice cream. Surely you can stay for another bite or two."

"You want to eat dessert?" she questioned with obvious skepticism.

"Is that not what I pledged? Ice cream, Champagne, and conversation?"

He was correct, that was what he had promised and delivered—so far at least. Caution vied with temptation, sensible retreat battling once again against the opportunity to stay and spend another few minutes in the marquis's indisputably divine company. 'Twas said that Satan often assumed a pleasing shape. Was Lord Vessey the Devil? If so, then he had chosen a most excellent disguise. For what woman, she mused, would not sell her soul to have him—even for something as simple as a shared dish of ice cream?

Before she knew what she meant to do, she found herself giving her consent. "All right, but only long enough for a bite."

"Or two," he added, flashing his gorgeous white teeth in a smile that made her toes curl inside her slippers. Picking up the bowl, he dipped in the spoon.

"Come closer," he urged in a silky purr. "I cannot very well feed you from there."

Despite knowing she ought to take the spoon in hand and feed herself, she inched nearer and let him serve her the confection for yet another time that night. Sugary sweetness flooded her mouth as she accepted the bite, the combination of cream and strawberries as velvety and cold as it had been earlier.

Still, something essential had changed. For when the marquis gently eased the spoon from between her lips, he paused to rub the cool underside of the utensil against her lower lip in a movement very much like a caress. Only then did he withdraw.

Instinctively, she swallowed, her tongue darting out to lick away the sticky residue he'd painted over her mouth. His eyes followed, glittering with a hunger she could detect even in the low light—a hunger, she suspected, that had nothing whatsoever to do with food.

A deep quiver fluttered in her belly, her breath growing shallow and fast.

He extended another spoonful, the swirl of frozen cream poised for her delectation. But as she bent forward to receive the bounty, his hand shook, a few cold droplets landing on the exposed flesh of one breast.

On a gasp, she reached to brush them away, but he stopped her.

"Let me," he enjoined, quickly setting aside the dish and spoon to pull her to him. With a strong arm locked around her waist, he buried his face against her breasts. A fresh gasp escaped her throat as he set his warm tongue against her flesh to lave away the treat.

"Delicious," he murmured as he captured the first droplet and then the next, gliding from one to the other with his lips and tongue. On a shaky sigh, she let her eyes fall closed as sizzling pleasure crashed through her.

Spreading his muscled thighs apart, he drew her between them, settling her there so he could have full access to her curves. With a series of heated kisses and languorous licks, he began to rove, wandering over her breasts with the movements of a skilled explorer. Using a maneuver she had no idea how he performed, he freed one of her breasts from her stays and bodice, then closed his mouth over an already hardened nipple to suckle upon her. Her knees buckled but he caught her, clasping her buttocks inside a wide, steady hand.

She shuddered, a moan escaping her parted lips.

Bending toward him, she threaded one hand into his hair, then kissed the side of his cheek, finding it faintly rough from a full evening's growth of whiskers.

He was the one to moan this time, shivering faintly beneath her touch. Lifting his head from her breast, he sought her lips, taking them in a wild, plundering kiss that demanded everything she had to give and more.

Drowning in a dark lake of need, she yielded, returning his kisses with an urgency she would never have thought she could feel. But with this man anything seemed possible, pleasure a quotient that appeared to have limitless boundaries.

In those moments, her senses narrowed down to only the two of them, her focus locked on the warm, wet silk of his mouth, the gliding bliss of his touch, the heady richness of his clean, male scent turning her drunk and drowsy. Breathing him deeper, tasting him more, she clutched her fists into the fabric of his coat, breath panting in ragged gasps from her lips as she tangled her tongue with his own in an untamed dance. With only a vague awareness of her surroundings, she let him draw her down to perch atop one of his strong thighs, a single powerful arm nestled securely at her back. Something hard and thick prodded her hip, a something nestled right between his legs.

*Oh my,* she thought, *is that his arousal?*

From somewhere deep, her conscience warned that matters were moving much too far, much too fast—leagues beyond her ability to control. Even so, she ignored the mental alert, too lost in the sensations he was evoking to stop. She shuddered as he stroked her back and over her bottom, caressing her through her clothes as she'd sensed he'd wanted to do earlier out on the ballroom floor. Scattering kisses over her cheek and chin, he ran his lips along her throat to its base, pausing to draw upon the spot with a delicate suction that made her pulse flutter like the wings of a trapped bird.

Seconds after, his free hand slipped beneath her skirt and covered her knee. For long, long moments, he teased her there before sliding ever so slowly upward, beyond the top of her stocking, to find the bare skin of her thigh. Heat ignited inside her, spreading with the force of a wildfire, a demanding ache centering low between her legs. Shifting her slightly, he ravished her mouth anew, drawing her into an intense by-play of lips and tongues. Caught in the glory of his kiss, she didn't notice that his hand had moved again until he lay his palm over the place where she ached the most.

Her closed eyelids sprang open at the unexpected touch, pulling free of his kiss. "Oh! What are you . . ." Without thinking, her hand swept down from his shoulder and caught hold of his wrist through the cloth of her gown. "Stop."

"Stop?" he panted, meeting her gaze, barely banked passion mixing with confusion in his eyes. "Why?"

"Because I . . ." She broke off, not knowing how to answer, nor even how she truly felt. His every touch until now had been bliss and would surely continue to be. Yet she shouldn't be doing this, should she?

His eyes narrowed suddenly. "Surely he touched you here before?"

*He who?*

Reacting spontaneously, she shook her head—answering honestly, since no one had ever touched her there, especially a man. A second later, though, her thoughts focused enough for her to make sense of his question. She stiffened. *Dear Lord, he must mean my supposed husband!* Suddenly she began to struggle, trying her best to climb off his lap. Instead he kept her in place, though he did move his hand down to her thigh.

*Mercy, what have I done?* she thought, heart hammering in her chest.

"So he bedded you, but did naught else?" Vessey demanded in a hard yet gentle voice. When she said nothing, he continued. "He sounds like a lout."

"No, he wasn't, not at all," she said, leaping to the defense of her husband—even if he was fictitious. "He was very . . . kind and . . . gentle. But we . . . we were both . . ." *Yes,* she thought half panicked, *what were we?*

"Young," the marquis supplied. "Is that what you are trying to say?"

"Yes. We were young. Now, you need to let me go. I should not be doing this, nor should I have come out here with you. It was a mistake and I am sorry for it."

"Are you?" he murmured. "I am not."

But clearly knowing the mood was now irreparably shattered, he slid his hand from beneath her skirt. Taking hold of her hem, he smoothed the material down her legs to cover them properly again. Reaching up, he gently straightened her bodice, working his magic in reverse on her stays as he put her clothing to rights.

Trembling, she remembered him doing the same for her when they'd been together in his coach. *How is it,* she wondered, *that he can so scatter my every thought that I find myself at his mercy time and time again?*

When he was done, she tried again to climb off his lap, but he refused, holding her where she sat.

Meeting his beautiful amber gaze, she decided to try the unvarnished truth. "My lord, this"—she paused to wave a hand—"whatever it is between us must end. Surely you can see that. I may be a . . . widow, and I admit that perhaps I have given you cause to think I am interested in taking a . . ." Her sentence trailed off.

"Lover," he offered.

Warmth crept into her cheeks. "Yes. But I am not. Truly, in spite of tonight, I want no man in my bed."

He paused, tipping his golden head slightly to one side. "Are you sure?"

She nodded. "Quite sure."

Smiling, he lifted a palm and laid it boldly over one of her breasts, openly caressing her flesh.

Her pulse gave a hard kick, her nipple beading into a betraying point.

"Are you still sure?" he murmured, rubbing his thumb over the sensitive nub.

When she shivered and sighed, he laughed. Bending forward, he dusted a kiss across her lips, then stood her on her feet.

"Go on for tonight. We'll speak of this later."

Her brows drew together. "No, I . . . we shall not speak of this later. I do not wish to have an affair, my lord."

"Ethan. Don't you think, under the circumstances, that it is a bit late for such formality?"

"No, *my lord,* I do not."

He laughed again. "You are a delight. Now, run on and let Ottwell take you home, since I needn't worry he'll make it past your front door." Catching her hand inside his own, he brought her palm to his lips and pressed a kiss onto its center.

Her toes curled against the inside of her slippers—*traitorous toes that they are,* she thought inconsequentially.

Knowing she had better leave while she still had the strength of will to do so, Lily whirled and hurried toward the house.

Remaining seated, Ethan watched her, his eyes following until she disappeared from view. Only then did he allow himself to climb to his feet. Knowing he needed to protect her reputation, he decided to stay in the darkened garden a while longer. If he did not, he feared he might be tempted to go after her again despite having sent her on her way.

Even now, his loins throbbed, demanding a satisfaction he knew he would not be finding tonight. Nor for many more nights to come, if he didn't miss his guess.

*So she believes she doesn't want a lover?*

Her mind might tell her that, but her body clearly knew otherwise. Despite the failures of her obviously inexpert husband, she was an extremely passionate woman. He need only coax her into seeing that too, into taking pleasure in the responses of her own body, and she would be his.

Until then, he would need to be patient.

Perhaps tonight should have dissuaded him. After all, widows were supposed to be experienced, women who understood the act of physical love in all its forms and permutations. Yet Lily did not seem to possess a similar level of experience. In spite of what she had revealed—or perhaps because of it—he found himself wanting her all the more. There were many reasons he ought to do as she asked, and relinquish his pursuit of her. God knows, they would probably both be better off, since he knew these things rarely turned out well in the end.

But he had to have her. Anything less would just not do.

# Chapter Eight

❧❧❧

SEATED AT HER bedroom dressing table two mornings later, Lily let her maid, Susan, pin her thick hair into a fashionably elegant upsweep, a few short strands left to curl in becoming disarray against her temples and cheeks. With the exception of those deliberately trimmed pieces, Lily's cropped hair had grown dramatically over the past several weeks, the additional inches making Susan's efforts increasingly easier to achieve.

Forcing herself to sit still, Lily smothered a yawn, tired despite what should have been a restful night's slumber. Instead, she'd slept very little, tossing and turning against her mattress for the second night in a row. And all because of one particular man.

Lord Vessey.

*Ethan,* as he'd told her to call him, his voice a seductive whisper in her memory.

*But no,* she scolded herself, *I will not permit myself to think of him in such familiar terms. Doing so will only invite weakness, and that is something I cannot afford.*

As it stood now, she was far too susceptible to his blandishments. Thinking of him in intimate terms would only make her more so. But dear heavens, it was hard *not* to think of him, especially after the torrid embrace they'd shared in the Pendragons' moonlit garden.

Without meaning to do so, her eyelids drooped, sliding shut as memories stole into her drowsy mind. How wonderful she'd felt clasped inside his arms, her body trembling as she nearly drowned beneath the pleasure of his ardent kisses and passionate caresses.

*What would have happened if I'd let him continue? What would he have done, and how delicious might his further touches have felt?*

Her eyes popped open, her body tingling to her great mortification. Ignoring any damage such a move might cause to her coiffure, she leaned forward and picked up her cup of morning tea. Drinking deeply, she prayed the hot beverage would conceal the real reason for the sudden wash of color in her cheeks.

"Oh, ma'am, I need you to hold still a tad bit longer," Susan said. "I'll be done in a thrice."

Resuming her prior position, Lily allowed the girl to work. As she did, Lily tried to review her list of duties for the day—a meeting this morning with her housekeeper about the servants' schedule, then an hour in her study going over the household accounts. Later would be lunch with Davina, and this evening she planned to attend a musicale—a small entertainment she prayed would have no appeal to a man of Lord Vessey's interests.

*When will I see him again?* she wondered.

She knew she would not be able to avoid him for long. If she didn't miss her guess, he would seek her out soon if their paths did not cross again in the next couple of days. After all, he'd been quite open in expressing his wishes.

*He wants me as his lover.*

*And what do I want?*

She had come to London in order to live independently, free from the demands of men, unburdened by the shackles of marriage. And on that score, her wishes remained unchanged.

Not that Lord Vessey had ever mentioned the subject

of marriage. In fact, she had the distinct impression wedded bliss was not something he desired any more than she did herself. And therein lay the crux of her dilemma.

*Passion.*

Her breath grew shallow at the mere thought, her tongue suddenly dry despite the tea she had drunk only a minute ago.

Before meeting the marquis, she hadn't given any thought to the idea of engaging in an amorous relationship with a man. For one thing she was a virgin, innocent of such needs and temptations. At least that was what she had thought until *Ethan* had come into her life. Kissing him that first time in the coach had been devastating enough, but she'd put the memory aside, believing he was part of her past. Then the night of the ball he'd shaken her world again, his touches and kisses awakening her senses as though he had ignited a blazing spark inside her.

*And will that spark burn me if I let it? If I let him?*

"There you are, ma'am," Susan announced, sending Lily a cheerful smile in the mirror. "All done."

Forcing aside her inner musings, Lily studied the results. "Lovely as always. My thanks."

Satisfied that her task was now complete, the maid moved to one side of the dressing table and began tidying the items scattered across the polished rosewood surface.

Lily stood and crossed to the window, barely bothering to gaze out. "Susan, would you mind finishing that later?"

The girl paused and glanced up. "Oh, of course not. I've your gown to press for tonight anyway."

After her maid departed, Lily walked to her large bed with its pretty yellow draperies and matching counterpane. Sinking onto the soft goose-down mattress, her gaze fell upon her night table and the circular, painted miniature of her mother that rested there in a place of honor. Picking up the tiny portrait, she gazed at the beloved face, the likeness wrought when her mother had been young—not much older than Lily was now.

*I miss you, Mama,* she thought, her heart squeezing achingly inside her chest. *How I wish you were here so I could talk to you and take comfort in your counsel.*

Even as the thoughts passed through her mind, Lily realized that she would never have been able to share her present feelings of desire for Lord Vessey with her mother. Despite the unbreakable bond they had shared, her mother would not have understood, nor even countenanced the idea. Gently bred young ladies must save themselves for marriage—that would have been her mother's belief.

Yet what of a young lady who planned never to marry? Was such a woman to remain innocent and untouched all her life? Most would say yes, her mother included.

*But what do I say?*

A rumbling meow interrupted her musings as a large brown-and-black-striped cat leapt up onto the bed. Padding across the counterpane on a set of generously sized paws, he angled his body and rubbed against her side. Lifting a hand, she stroked over his silky back from head to tail, deciding to ignore the trail of cat fur she knew he must be leaving in his wake. Apparently approving her movements, he nudged his head into her hand and began to purr, kneading his paws against her thigh.

"So, Mouser," she murmured, "what do you think?"

He meowed again as if answering her query.

Lily laughed, a smile breaking over her face. "Well, thank you, sir, for your opinion. What's that? You think his lordship is right? Well, you would take his side, would you not, considering you and he are both tomcats."

She stroked Mouser again and scratched his head, eliciting an even louder round of purring. A couple of minutes later, the cat sprang off the bed and glided toward a patch of morning sunlight on the carpeted floor. Lying down, he began to groom his coat.

With a sigh, she placed her mother's miniature back on the night table, her thoughts turning toward home. By now she assumed her stepfather had ceased any efforts to search for her, concluding that she must indeed have drowned at sea. He would have had a funeral, resenting the cost she was sure but wanting to present a façade of grief to the community. He'd probably even had a grave dug and buried a coffin, empty though it might be, and erected a headstone. How peculiar to think of her name chiseled there—*Lily Bainbridge*—dead to all who had known her. She supposed she really was Lily Smythe now, her old self and her old life gone forever.

So where did that leave her with Lord Vessey?

The same place she had been before, she realized. He was a weakness she simply could not afford to indulge. And so, when next they met, she would refuse him again, making it clear that they would not be lovers. For though she might desire him, she could not allow herself to succumb to his charms. Undoubtedly such an interlude would be pleasurable—very pleasurable, she decided with a small inner shiver—but she couldn't take the risk. Clearly, he would not like her answer, but he was a gentleman and would abide by her wishes.

Now she had to steel her resolve and convince herself that *only* being his friend was what she wanted.

Early the next afternoon, Ethan secured the bouquet of flowers he carried beneath his arm, then rapped one gloved hand on the front-door knocker of Lily Smythe's townhouse.

He supposed he ought to have sent a note to let her know he planned to call, but he hadn't wanted to give her the opportunity to "miss" his visit. As it was, he was taking a chance since she might very well be out shopping or calling upon friends. He didn't think she would be with Davina Coates, however, since he had it from a very reliable source that Geoffrey Coates's notoriously difficult mother was visiting for the week. Having met the old harridan a time or two, he pitied poor Davina, who would be at her mother-in-law's constant beck and call with no time for her own personal amusements.

The door opened, a middle-aged servant—the butler, no doubt—eyeing him and his floral offering with obvious curiosity. "Good afternoon," the man said.

"Good afternoon." Ethan withdrew his card, a stiff rectangle of pristine white, and handed it to the servant.

The man's eyes widened as he read the name engraved on its surface. "My lord, please come inside."

With a nod, Ethan crossed into the foyer.

Juggling the flowers, he drew off his gloves, taking a moment to glance around at the attractive décor with its polished marble floor, warm caramel-colored walls, and select Hepplewhite furnishings. A beautiful green ground Sèvres jardinière stood as a focal point on top of a fine walnut marquetry hall table, ormolu branches of porcelain jonquils extending from its top.

*Lily has excellent taste,* he decided. Then again, he would have expected nothing less.

"Is your mistress at home?" he asked.

"If you would care to have a seat in the withdrawing room, my lord, I will inquire."

Ethan allowed himself to be placed inside the room. Yet less than a minute after the butler departed, he decided to follow, instinct urging him not to give Lily the chance to send him packing. Walking up the stairs and down a hallway, he found his way by listening for the sound of voices. Stopping at the open doorway of a sitting room, he gazed inside just as she was answering the servant.

"Tell his lordship that I am not at home today."

"Yes, ma'am, but I believe he knows that you are in residence."

"Your man is entirely correct," Ethan declared, pushing the door wider to step into the room. "Hello, madam. Don't you look radiant today!"

And indeed she did, attired in a walking dress of striped green-and-white jaconet muslin that set off her jewel-toned eyes and Titian curls to perfection.

Lily's head swung up to face him. For an instant, her lips thinned, clearly aggravated at having been caught out. Obviously aware that the servant was watching, she fashioned a smile. "I could say the same of you, my lord. Though perhaps in your case 'superior' would be a more apt description."

His lips twitched with humor at her veiled jab, but he remained silent.

"Thank you, Hodges, that will be all," she stated in a firm yet quiet voice.

Bowing, the butler exited the room.

Once the man was gone, Ethan stepped forward and offered her the bouquet of roses he held. "These are for you. I had them cut from my own hothouse not an hour since."

A long moment passed before she accepted.

Gathered inside tissue and tied with a broad white silk ribbon, the arrangement looked large inside her delicate grasp. Not wishing to stint, he'd ordered three dozen carefully selected flowers, each stem trimmed of its thorns so there would be no possibility of injury. As for color, he'd chosen red.

Red for beauty. Red for passion. Red for the glorious, fiery hue of her hair, through which he fervently hoped to be running his fingers very soon.

He watched as she slowly brought the petals up to her face and breathed in the succulent fragrance. Her expression softened, her eyelids falling to half-staff.

He smiled to see her pleasure and her loveliness.

Lowering the flowers again, she peered over at him, her brows drawing together as though she'd been caught doing something she ought not to have done.

"I hope you are not going to refuse those as you did the last ones," he remarked casually. "Lilies may not be to your liking, but I have eyes enough to see that roses do not offend."

"No, indeed they do not," she said in a mollifying tone. "The flowers are beautiful. Thank you, my lord."

"Ethan," he corrected in a low tone.

*"My lord."*

His mouth turned up at one corner. "As you prefer. For now."

Turning, she crossed to lay the bouquet on a nearby table. "And I did like the lilies. I just did not feel they were appropriate for me to keep under the circumstances."

"Why ever not? Gentlemen send flowers to ladies all the time."

"True, but I did not wish to give you false impressions, nor engender hope where none should lie." Her eyes met his with a pointed look, obviously intending for him to take her hint.

He strolled forward, leaving only a few inches between them. "Oh, but I believe I have plenty of reason to hope, especially after the time we spent together the other evening. As you get to know me better, you will see that I am possessed of a very resilient nature. I do not tend to give up easily, at least not on the things I truly want."

The freckles on her nose became more noticeable as a mild flush stained her cheeks.

*Adorable as always,* he thought, blood humming in his veins.

"Mayhap we should have that discussion now," he murmured, his gaze tracing over her face. "The one we agreed to in the garden but decided to postpone."

"There was nothing to discuss, nor postpone, my lord, as you well know. I gave you my answer then. It has not changed."

"And what answer is that? As I recall, you were conflicted." He laid a hand against her waist, stretching his long fingers upward so they settled scant inches beneath her breast. "Maybe we need to explore the situation, just us two, to help you decide."

Her rib cage expanded on a deep inhalation, moving his hand in the direction his fingers longed to go. But suddenly she pulled back and away, shaking off his touch.

"I *have* decided, and the answer is no," she said, her words throaty and breathless and unsure enough to make him grin. "Now," she declared, lifting her delicate chin, "if that is the only reason you have called upon me, I believe you should go."

Deciding he'd pressed her as far as he could for one day, he relented. "Actually, I did visit for another reason, besides the flowers, that is."

She crossed her arms over her chest, looking as though she wanted to tap her foot as well. "And what might that be, pray tell?"

"Driving. I thought you might enjoy a spin in my phaeton. If we find an open bit of road, I might even be talked into letting you take a try at the reins."

Her hands fell to her side, an eager light sparkling in

her vibrant green eyes. "Oh, that sounds diverting." The light faded a moment later though. "But I am afraid I cannot accept."

"Why not? Worried I won't be able to keep my hands on the ribbons with you so close beside me?"

Before she could respond to that salvo, the butler appeared in the doorway. "Lord Ottwell, ma'am," he announced in a carrying voice.

Ethan's jaw tightened.

"*That* is why," she murmured softly so only Ethan would hear. "Lord Ottwell has already offered to take me out in his carriage. He is giving me my first driving lesson today."

Before Ethan had a chance to remark, Ottwell strolled forward, pausing in front of Lily to execute a neat bow. "A fine good day to you, Mrs. Smythe. May I say you look as bright and inviting as a ray of sunshine after a storm."

She laughed and stepped forward to offer her hand. "You may, my lord, but I do not believe I am deserving of such an enthusiastic description."

"Oh, but you are, ma'am. All that and more."

A second laugh floated from her lips, making Ethan's jaw clench another millimeter tighter.

Ottwell pivoted as though he had only just noticed Ethan's presence. "Vessey."

"Ottwell." Ethan restrained the urge to show his teeth.

The other man met his look for a moment before glancing away, audibly clearing his throat.

"I don't mean to hurry us along," Ottwell continued, his pale gaze once again centered on Lily, "and we may remain here and converse for a while, if you would rather, but my tiger is holding my team at the ready. You have only to give your assent and we shall be on our way." He flicked a glance toward Ethan, surreptitiously straightening his shoulders and puffing out his thin chest. "I am taking Mrs. Smythe for a driving lesson."

Ethan set a fistful of knuckles against one hip. "So I am given to understand. I trust you will have a care."

"Of course. I won't allow her to attempt anything too risky."

"I wasn't talking about her."

A hint of dull color stole upward from beneath the other man's neckcloth, turning the underside of his chin a shade reminiscent of a newly made brick.

Lily turned toward Ottwell before he had a chance to reply. "Give me a moment to gather my spencer, my lord, and we shall be off." Gliding toward the doorway, she paused, then turned and made a slight detour. "I shall have my maid put these in water," she said, bending to gather the bouquet of roses into her arms.

Some of Ethan's tension eased, a smile forming when he saw her raise the petals to her nose and inhale just as she was walking from the room.

After her departure, silence fell between him and the other man. Ottwell thrust his hands into his pockets and made a remark about the weather. Ethan gave some equally innocuous response. To his relief—and Ottwell's, too—Lily soon returned, looking lovely in a white spencer and chipstraw bonnet, a green-and-white-striped ribbon tied at a jaunty angle beneath her chin.

As the three of them left the room, Ethan maneuvered matters so that Ottwell was forced to take the lead. Further slowing his step and hers, Ethan bent toward Lily. "Did you set them on your dressing table or your nightstand?" he murmured into one of her beautifully shaped ears. "I am curious to know, so I can properly envision you enjoying them."

She turned her head. "Set what?"

He met her gaze, taking her elbow as they walked

down the stairs. "The roses I gave you, of course. You did take the bouquet to your bedchamber, did you not?"

The flash in her eyes answered his query, pleasure flooding his chest to know he was correct. *Ah, Lily, you took my roses to your room,* he mused. *It is only a matter of time until you shall take me there as well.*

"I had my maid place them outside in the corridor," she prevaricated. "And how do you know I have a dressing table and a nightstand?"

"Just a guess, since those are common items for a lady's boudoir."

"A subject on which you would know much," she quipped in an undertone.

He leaned even closer. "A subject, in your case, on which I hope to know a great deal more very soon."

A nearly imperceptible tremor ran through her as they reached the marbled foyer. With a gentle tug, she removed her elbow from his grasp. "Alas, my lord, you will have to keep speculating. And now I have a driving lesson."

Stepping forward, she lifted her voice. "Lord Ottwell, shall we depart?"

The other man sprang to attention, clearly pleased to be taking her away from Vessey.

Ethan trailed them down the front steps onto the sidewalk. "Have an enjoyable drive," he called as Ottwell assisted Lily up into the curricle's elevated seat.

"We will." She sent him a little wave. "Good-bye, my lord."

"Au revoir, madam. I will not say good-bye, since I am certain we shall be seeing each other again quite soon."

## Chapter Nine

AN HOUR LATER, Lily found herself wishing she had taken the marquis's warning about Lord Ottwell's driving skills more to heart.

From her perch on the carriage's seat, she found herself in the center of sheer chaos as dogs barked and voices shouted; a small army of people gathered to watch the proceedings as his lordship attempted to calm the frayed tempers of a pair of merchants. Scattered in the street lay the remains of several spilled wooden crates—apples, onions, cabbages, and pears mixed in with loaves of bread, broken pies, and crumbled pastries. As for Lord Ottwell's carriage, the damaged vehicle sat at an awkward angle—half in, half out of the street, leaving other drivers to maneuver their horses and carriages around the wreckage however they could manage.

As if that were not bad enough, a small flock of street urchins raced into the fray, pausing to fill their empty pockets and grab whatever foodstuffs they could carry in their scrawny arms before fleeing down the street. Lily cringed as one of the merchants let loose a fresh round of invective, waving his arms and bellowing at the departing miscreants.

Lord Ottwell wrung his hands. "My apologies. I truly do not know how this could have happened."

"It 'appened because you couldn't turn a bloody corner," huffed the other man. "You drove straightways into me stand."

"Yes, well, the horses shied just as I was making the turn," his lordship defended, "and I had not the time to adjust for their course deviation."

The merchant paused, his thick gray eyebrows crowding together as he scratched his balding pate. "Adjust their *what*?"

While Ottwell continued his impassioned explanation, Lily heaved a sigh. From her vantage point, the horses hadn't appeared to shy at all, at least not until after he'd urged them into too narrow a turn, leaving the team no option but to crash the curricle into the food stands. The poor shaken animals had shied plenty after that. Ottwell's tiger had leapt down to calm the horses, the team now standing in quiet obedience despite the disorder around them.

The produce seller pointed a carrot-sized finger toward his ruined merchandise. "What I wants t'know is if I'm to be paid fer me loss?"

"Of course I shall make recompense. Both of you have only to send me a reckoning—"

"And how long will that take? Me livelihood depends upon this stand."

"It would appear Ottwell has his hands full," remarked a deep, silky male voice not far from her ear. "Quite a mess, I must say."

Lily swung her head to the left and gazed over to find Lord Vessey standing next to the carriage. Tall and impeccably attired in a chocolate-brown coat, biscuit waistcoat, and fawn trousers, he looked every inch as splendid as he had in her sitting room only a brief while ago. One difference, however, was the unmistakable gleam of amusement lighting his intense amber eyes.

"My lord, what brings you here?" she asked.

"I was driving through the area and noticed the accident. Imagine my surprise to find you and Ottwell involved."

She studied him, trying to decide if his appearance was merely a fortunate coincidence or if he had been in the area because he'd been following them. Either way, she was glad for his timely arrival. "I must confess when I left home I was not expecting to crash into a pair of street stalls."

"You are unharmed, I trust?"

"Yes, completely, not so much as a bruise."

"Good, because I would be most displeased to hear otherwise. Since you are stranded, may I offer my assistance and see you home? My carriage is parked just there." He pointed to a splendid, high-perch phaeton waiting ahead, his own tiger holding a team of precisely matched grays at the ready. Painted a glossy dark blue, the racing vehicle sported the Vessey coat of arms, emblazoned in gold on the door. Even before the accident, the marquis's equipage quite cast Lord Ottwell's into the shade. In fact, the phaeton was one of the finest Lily had ever seen, not counting the marquis's magnificent coach-and-four, of course.

Glancing toward Ottwell, she found him still engaged in negotiation with the stall owners.

"Who can tell how long he will be," Vessey remarked as though he had read her thoughts. "Even when he calms those two down, he'll still need to call for a new carriage and make arrangements to have this one taken away. You could be here for hours."

Much as she did not like on principle to abandon Lord Ottwell, Lily had to agree that Lord Vessey made several excellent points, not the least of which was the dismal prospect of spending the rest of her afternoon sitting here in this broken-down curricle. With a nod, she agreed. "Yes, thank you, I would appreciate a ride home."

"Ottwell," the marquis called, his voice carrying easily over the crowd. "Mrs. Smythe is coming with me."

Lord Ottwell paused in mid-sentence and looked over, a series of lines descending across his forehead.

Without giving her an opportunity to speak to the other man, the marquis reached up, caught her around the waist, and swung her to the ground with a confident power that made her belly flutter. Once her feet were on the ground, he tucked her hand into the curve of his elbow and led her forward. She only had time for one last glance at Lord Ottwell, who looked profoundly perturbed, before the marquis drew her to a halt in front of his phaeton and moved to help her inside.

Up, up she went, her pulse quickening as Lord Vessey caught her around the waist and lifted her off her feet. For an instant, she hung suspended inside his powerful embrace, her eyes even with his, his mouth scant inches from her own. For the faintest fraction of an instant, he paused as if he were considering drawing her nearer for a kiss. Instead, he lifted her farther upward and set her on the seat.

Steadying herself, Lily willed away a momentary sense of vertigo, telling herself the reaction was due to the lofty height of the phaeton and not from having just been held so closely inside the marquis's arms. Gazing around, she noticed that the carriage really was set high, making her feel like a bird perched on the top branch of a forest's tallest tree. A smile broke across her mouth, excitement rising as she surveyed London from an entirely new perspective.

Lord Vessey vaulted up and settled next to her on the seat, his broad shoulders nearly touching her own. Taking up the reins, he whistled softly to his horses and eased them into traffic, his every movement bespeaking competence and control.

*Now this,* she thought, *is a man who knows how to handle the ribbons.*

"Not quite the experience you were hoping for on your very first lesson, I imagine," he remarked once they were safely on their way.

Her shoulders drew back. "If you are inquiring as to whether I was driving when the accident occurred, I was not."

He tossed her a look. "I never imagined you were. If you will recall, I warned you Ottwell is as ham-fisted as they come." He paused, making a quick turn that would have set the other man on his heels. "Did he let you take the reins even once?"

Her lips tightened. "He said he was working up to it, looking for just the right spot."

Vessey barked out a laugh. "In Covent Garden? He would have been looking all day."

"So I was beginning to realize," she agreed with a sigh.

"Disappointed, hmm?"

"Yes, if you must know."

"Let me teach you, then. My offer is still good."

A wave of longing unfurled inside her chest, but she pushed it aside. "I cannot."

"Of course you can."

"No," she replied in an emphatic tone. "I cannot. And you already know the reason."

His lips turned up in a slow, sensual smile. "I thank you for the compliment, madam, but even I would find it difficult to make love to you in an open phaeton in full public view. Why else do you imagine Society so thoroughly approves of the sport?"

Her mouth parted at his bold statement, yet she knew he was right. Even girls with overly protective mamas were permitted to go driving with a single gentleman as long as the pair did so in an open carriage. Even so, had she not resolved only yesterday to see *less* of the marquis rather than more? And spending long hours with him, snuggled hip-to-hip inside a small carriage, was not the way to achieve her aim. Still, she couldn't deny the fact that letting Ethan Andarton teach her to drive would be nothing short of divine. Assuming she could keep her mind on the lessons, instead of the man.

Linking her gloved hands in her lap, she forced herself to resist. "While I concede there would be no room for impropriety, I do not think—"

"Don't think, dear lady," he murmured with silky persuasion, "just say yes." He shot her a quick glance. "I can see by your face that you're dying to learn how to handle the ribbons. And although I am not generally in the habit of lauding my own abilities, I am considered by most to be an excellent driver. I can assure you, I will never pitch us into a fruit stand, nor give you the opportunity to do so while you are in the process of learning."

A laughed escaped her lips. "No, I have no fears on that score." *And I don't,* she realized, feeling as safe with him as a babe in a cradle.

"Then give me the pleasure of teaching you," he urged. "It will be great fun, I promise."

*I am sure it shall, which is precisely the reason I ought to refuse.*

"If it will allay your concerns," he offered, "I promise to keep our lessons strictly platonic. You can think of me in the guise of a trusted cousin."

She chuckled. "A *distant* cousin, I presume, who isn't above leading his female relations astray. Now, were you to swear to act like my brother . . ."

"You do not have a brother," he replied with a growl.

"Exactly so."

He tossed her a look that was equal parts amusement and exasperation. "Just say yes, Lily."

How easy he made it sound. She wondered if Eve had felt this way while contemplating the apple. Still, it wasn't as though she were agreeing to join him in bed . . . only inside his carriage, where even now she had only to tip her head a bit in order to catch his delicious male scent, or lean slightly to one side to accidentally brush up against his long, athletic frame.

Worrying the edge of her lower lip between her teeth, she waged a silent battle, her heart warring viciously with her head. *Say no,* her conscience warned. Then he gave her a smile that turned her limbs to butter. "Yes, all right," she agreed in a rush. "How soon may we begin? Today?"

He laughed. "No, not today. It's too late in the afternoon to find any uncrowded streets, though I believe one of the parks might be the easiest location in which to begin. If you run a wheel off a lane there, the worst you'll do is crush a few flowers and tear out a bit of grass."

Up came her chin. "Who says I shall be running off the road? I suspect I will amaze you."

He grinned, tiny lines fanning out at the corners of his eyes. "I have no doubt that you will."

Pleasurable warmth washed over her skin, a sensation she knew had nothing to do with the late spring temperatures.

"What do you say to nine-thirty tomorrow morning?" he suggested. "Or is that too early?"

She shook her head. "I am an early riser, so that should prove a most excellent time."

"Ah, another intriguing morsel of information about your personal habits. I will think of you tomorrow morning as I bathe and dress, wondering if you are awake and doing the same."

She swallowed against the provocative images his words inspired. "I thought you had agreed to behave while we are having our lessons?"

"But we are not having a lesson. I said nothing of the times before and after."

Her heart thumped. "Then I see I shall have to be careful to avoid your company, except when I am being tutored."

Using barely perceptible movements on the reins, he slowed the phaeton and brought the vehicle to an easy halt. Shifting in the seat, he pressed his knee against her muslin-covered thigh. "You can certainly try, my dear Lily," he whispered. "In fact, I look forward to witnessing your attempts."

*God above, what have I gotten myself into?* she wondered.

"I will be here on the morrow to collect you," he murmured. "Try not to be tardy."

Only then did she realize they had arrived at her townhouse, and that her butler was holding open the front door to receive her. A footman came forward to assist her from the carriage, but the marquis jumped down first to do the honors. Instead of reaching up a single hand, though, he set his broad palms against her waist and lifted her from the carriage, cradling her against his body an extra second before placing her safely onto the ground. His hands lingered before he finally let her go. "Until tomorrow, madam."

With an elegant bow, he tipped his beaver top hat, then sprang once again into the phaeton. Taking up the reins, he drove away.

Steadying her wobbly legs, she forced herself to turn and walk inside.

Ethan arrived at Lily's townhouse the following morning at precisely nine-thirty to find her downstairs and ready to depart. All business, she offered him a polite smile as she pulled on a pair of dove-gray gloves that matched her fashionable carriage dress and sturdy kid half-boots. "Good morning, my lord. Shall we be on our way?"

With an indulgent grin, he swept an accommodating arm toward the door.

A small measure of her armor slipped once they were outside, her expression a bit nonplussed. "Oh, did you not bring the phaeton?"

He shook his head and extended a hand to help her inside his curricle. "Indeed no. A high-flyer phaeton is not the sort of vehicle on which a novice driver ought to learn. This equipage will be quite daring enough."

"It does not look *daring* at all," she murmured askance, as she eyed the elegant, yet far lower-slung, black carriage.

"Let us see if you still feel the same way once you are in control of the reins. Now, up you go."

Before she had time to remark further, he'd settled her in the carriage next to him and set the horses in motion. By the time they reached St. James's Park, her spirits were fully restored, excitement radiating visibly from her as he drove them through the entrance gates. He'd chosen this particular park in hopes of encountering few vehicles and even fewer members of the Ton. She would learn little if they were constantly stopping to chat. Besides, he rather hoped to keep her to himself—all to himself.

Locating an out-of-the-way stretch of road deep inside the park, he drew the carriage to a stop. "Here we are," he declared. "Time to commence our lesson."

"Oh, wonderful!" She straightened with undisguised anticipation. "So, what do I do first?"

"First, you listen," he said. "Now, the big fellow on your right, his name is Thunder, and you'll signal most of your cues through him. Lightning, the beauty on your left, is a good girl, who will always follow his lead."

"Thunder and Lightning, hmm?" she remarked, obvious humor in her voice. "Are they as volatile as their names?"

"Not a bit. I dare swear you would have trouble finding a more loyal, obedient team than these two. No, when it comes to being volatile, they leave that up to me." With a wink, he slid closer, letting his shoulder brush ever so lightly against her own.

Tossing him a look, she shifted deliberately away. "And what of your natural propensity for misbehavior? Are they conversant with that aspect of your personality as well?"

He laughed. "I'm sure they have a fair estimation of all my humors, though I do not believe they would view my actions as misbehavior. Horses, after all, are creatures of pleasure. Would that more humans took note and followed their lead."

Clearing her throat, she continued. "Speaking of leads, you were explaining how best to communicate with the team."

"Ah, yes, and so I was," he said with a grin. "Let us proceed."

Casting him a glance from underneath her lashes, Lily wondered if she had made a mistake agreeing to his lessons. So far his instructions had as much to do with seducing her as they did with driving. *But I can manage him,* she told herself, *at least I hope I can manage him.*

"Be gentle with the ribbons and learn to trust what your team tells you. Now, why don't we give things a try. Hold out your hands."

"My hands?" she repeated with skeptical caution.

"Yes. How else do you expect to learn to control the reins? Your voice and hands will always be your two best allies," he explained. "It's like making love. Whisper sweet things in their ears, keep your touch gentle and pleasurable, and you'll never go wrong."

She arched a reproving eyebrow.

He gave a slow, unrepentant grin. "Hands, please."

Despite her better judgment, she stretched out her palms.

A moment later, he slid close again and positioned himself so his hip was touching hers. Before she could object, he looped an arm around her shoulders, then reached down to cover both of her hands with his own. A helpless quiver unfurled deep within her, keenly aware of their unanticipated embrace. "My lord, what do you think you are doing?"

Apparent innocence shone from his eyes. "Merely instructing you, nothing more. How else are you to get the feel of things, if I do not show you? Now relax or you'll spook the team."

*Relax!* she scoffed. *How am I supposed to relax when I am practically sitting on his lap?* But she tried nonetheless, remaining quiescent as he pressed the reins into her hands and threaded the supple leather around and between her fingers.

"Stay loose and easy," he said, his mouth far too close to her ear. "Remain calm, yet always in control. Thunder and Lightning will read any hesitation or tension you are feeling and respond accordingly. To move them forward, flick the ribbons like so." Retaining his clasp, he matched his words to his actions, adding a low clicking sound with his tongue. The horses immediately eased into a quiet walk.

"Light pressure is all you need to signal direction. Softly, like this . . . ," he said, gently demonstrating the movement. "And a bit more for a turn, but we'll save that for later. Straight ahead is best for this first time out."

Keeping his hands curled over her own, he guided her

forward, flicking the reins again to subtly increase their speed. "And this," he said, after a couple more yards, "is how to bring them to a halt." Pulling back with effortless control, he eased the team to a perfect stop. "Everything clear?"

Willing her heart to quit hammering, she nodded, his instructions little more than a blur in her head.

"Good," he said. "Then, why don't you have a go on your own."

"All right." She arched her spine, quite pointedly inserting new inches between them. "I believe I should attempt this on my own. *All* on my own."

Grinning, he released her hands and withdrew his arm, then leaned back against the seat. A glance at his face reminded her of an expression she had once seen on Mouser's face right after he'd finished playing with a particularly lively mouse. *Well, I may be dressed in gray this morning,* she mused, *but I am no mouse.* Though at the moment, the marquis did bear a striking resemblance to a cat—a large, golden cat who took great pleasure in stalking his prey.

Drawing a deep breath, she forced such thoughts aside, then stared in consternation at the reins, struggling to recall what he'd shown her. Thunder chose that moment to shake his dark, equine head and snuffle softly through his nostrils, plainly aware of the change of drivers. Lightning followed suit, repeating the other horse's gestures, the pair of them apparently exchanging some sort of private communication.

"They're just testing you, wanting to know who you are," Ethan murmured. "Flick the ribbons like I showed you and let them know you are in charge."

Tossing him a sideways glance, she did as he instructed, moving the reins up and down in a light jingle.

Neither horse moved.

"A little harder than that," he encouraged with a barely concealed laugh.

Her lips thinned. *Harder, hmm?* Putting some strength behind her actions, she gave the reins a firm snap. This time the team lurched forward, sending the curricle into a jolting roll that slid both her and the marquis across the seat. But even as he reached out to help her, she eluded his hands, repositioning her hold more solidly on the reins. Arm muscles straining, she fought to control the more than one thousand pounds of horseflesh under her command, doing her utmost to guide the animals and the carriage in a straight line along the path. At her side, Ethan leaned back again in the seat, apparently willing to let her proceed for the time being.

The grass and trees flashed past at what seemed far too quick a pace, wheels whirring as the horse's hooves clop-clopped on the pavers. Her breath soughed in and out between her parted lips, her tongue growing dry, while the inside of her gloves dampened with perspiration. She waited for the marquis to attempt another intercession, but he remained relaxed and quiet.

And that is when a sudden realization dawned upon her. "I am doing it," she blurted. "I am driving!"

"Yes," he agreed with a smile in his voice. "You most certainly are."

Ahead of her, the path angled into a pair of easy curves. Holding steady, she guided the team around the first one and then the next, taking each as if she had been driving for years. A laugh burst from her throat, along with a simple, exuberant joy. Shooting Ethan a look, she met his gaze and read in his amber irises an enjoyment that mirrored her own. Dappled sunlight moved over his features, playing across his face and through his hair in a way that turned each short, thick lock a vibrant, gleaming gold.

Her pulse skipped like a stone. Turning her eyes forward, she fought the sensation, assuring herself it was a result of the moment and had nothing whatsoever to do with the man at her side.

*Liar.*

Suddenly another coach appeared, moving toward them at a brisk speed. Tugging at the reins, she pulled up too quickly and at too sharp an angle as she tried to maneuver out of the way. With a hard jolt, the right wheel bumped off the path and onto the grass, the team stopping as the other carriage rushed past.

"Had enough for one day?" the marquis inquired in a gentle voice.

Gathering a breath, she shook her head. "No."

He smiled, and helpless to stop herself, she smiled back.

A moment later, her arm muscles twinged hard, letting her know she might have spoken too soon. "Well, perhaps I could do with a tiny break." She cast a glance around. "Heavens, it seems I've pitched us into the boughs!"

"Not to worry. We'll be out in a thrice. You drove splendidly, by the way, for a first outing. Better than most."

"Most women, you mean."

"No, most people of either sex."

Warmth grew in her chest at his words of approbation.

"Would you care to steer us out?" he offered.

She mulled over the question for an instant, then handed him the reins. "Thank you, my lord, but for now, I shall leave such matters in your capable hands."

His gaze skimmed her face. "Ah, if only I could convince you to leave *everything* in my hands, we would have a fine time indeed."

"Enough of that, my lord," she admonished. "Or should I say *cousin*?"

A chuckle burst from his lips. "Distant cousin, remember? So, when shall we have our next lesson? Will the same time tomorrow morning suit?"

*Tomorrow!*

Even though she knew she should refuse, temptation beckoned. After all, how else was she supposed to learn to drive? "Yes, all right," she agreed. "Tomorrow morning it is."

His eyes alive with pleasure, he gave a soft click of his tongue, deftly righted the curricle, and set the team on its way.

# Chapter Ten

❧❧

$O$N A FINE, sunny June morning nearly two weeks later, Ethan stood bare-chested in front of his dressing-stand mirror. Wielding the well-sharpened edge of a straight razor, he scraped a last row of soap-covered whiskers off his left cheek, then set down the blade and splashed his face clean in a basin of warm water. As he straightened, a freshly laundered towel appeared within his line of sight. Taking it, he patted dry his smooth-shaven cheeks.

"Thank you, Welk," he said, passing the thick cloth back to his valet.

Crossing to the opposite side of his expansive dressing room, he donned the white shirt his valet had set out for him. Buttoning the garment, he tucked it into his dark-brown trousers, then added a dun-colored waistcoat before taking a position in front of the full-length mirror to tie his cravat. As plebeian as some aristocrats might find the habit, he preferred to dress himself rather than stand like a mannequin while his valet did all the work. Since the time he'd quit wearing short coats, he'd stopped needing help with anything other than the occasional tight-fitting coat or to remove his boots.

He'd just finished tightening a last knot when Welk reappeared in the doorway.

"Your pardon, my lord," the older man said, "but his Grace, the Duke of Wyvern, is here to see you."

"Show him up, of course."

"I'm up already," Tony called from the adjoining sitting room, having obviously overheard his and Welk's muted conversation.

The duke had ears as keen as a cat's, as Ethan had learned when they'd met all those many years ago as boys at Harrow. And very little escaped his notice, despite his often lazy-lidded gaze and outwardly relaxed façade.

Wyvern's blue eyes appeared keen and bright this morning, Ethan noticed as he strode out of his dressing room. "Hello, Tony. What brings you by so early?"

The duke planted a set of knuckles at his waist. "There's a prime stallion up for auction at Tattersall's this morning. I'm considering putting in a bid and was wondering if you'd care to accompany me."

That was another thing he well knew about Tony— that he was a bruising rider with an excellent eye for horseflesh. When an interesting animal came to his notice, he never hesitated to acquire the beast for his stables, which were generally regarded as among the finest in the country.

"Breakfast?" Ethan asked, crossing to a square mahogany table set beneath one of the room's three sun-filled windows. A footman was busy arranging plates of food on the linen-covered surface, the appetizing aroma of eggs, ham, and toast making Ethan's stomach rumble with hunger.

Taking a seat, he poured himself a cup of strong black tea, then a second for his friend. "There's plenty, if you'd like. Cook always makes more than I can possibly eat. Shall I have another plate brought up?"

"No, the tea will do fine, thank you." Tony slipped

into a chair on the opposite side. "So, what about the sale? Are you in or out?"

"Out, I'm afraid." Ethan cut a piece of ham and chewed, the smoky flavor bursting pleasantly on his tongue before he swallowed. "I am already otherwise engaged."

Wyvern arched a dark brow. "Really? You seem to be 'already otherwise engaged' a great deal lately. This assignation wouldn't happen to involve a certain red-headed widow, would it?"

Ethan ate a forkful of scrambled eggs, then bit off the crunchy corner of a buttered toast wedge. "Our meeting is not an assignation, it is a driving lesson."

"Oh, is *that* what they're calling such arrangements these days?" the duke asked in a teasing voice.

A scowl creased Ethan's forehead. "She is not my mistress, if that is what you are insinuating." *At least she isn't my mistress yet,* he mused. Of course he had plans to rectify the situation in the near future—the very near future.

Still, for reasons even he couldn't fully fathom, he had remained true to his word about keeping his and Lily's driving lessons strictly platonic. He might flirt and tease her, but beyond that he'd made no further overt advances. Of course, he'd seen her at a few balls, sharing a dance or a few minutes of light conversation over glasses of wine and punch. But in spite of his continued desire for her, he'd instigated no more meetings in midnight-dark gardens, and made no further serious attempts at seduction.

Truly, he could not account for his actions, leaving him to wonder if his reserve might stem from some strange sense of honor, a need to be finished with his promise regarding the lessons before his conscience would let him resume his quest to coax her into his bed. Whatever the cause, he wanted her with a desperation that was nothing short of painful. More than once, he'd awakened after a night of wild, concupiscent dreams about her to find his bedclothes twisted around his body, his skin damp, his male member aching and stiff as a pikestaff.

But his self-imposed need for restraint was about to end, perhaps as soon as today, since later this morning he would be giving Lily Smythe her final lesson.

Quick and exceptionally skilled, she had surprised him with her innate dexterity and aptitude. In tribute to her success, she would be driving them to Richmond Park, where he planned to celebrate with a picnic he was having specially prepared.

*After that,* he mused, *who knows what might occur.*

Nevertheless, he had no intention of sharing his expectations with Tony—longtime friend or not. He ate another bite of ham. "Tell me about this horse, then."

Lily held the reins steady and gave the horses their heads, letting the team increase their speed to an easy canter as they traveled along the turnpike toward Richmond. Beside her in the open curricle sat the marquis, his long, powerful body arranged in a lazy, all-male sprawl that would have drawn her full attention had she not been so solidly focused on her driving.

Late-morning sunshine filtered down from a nearly cloudless, azure-tinted sky, balmy air rushing past to tease her skin and tug at the carefully pinned strands of hair tucked beneath her short-brimmed bonnet. Her pale lavender gown matched her mood—buoyant excitement coupled with a sense of trepidation over an unknown future.

Today was her last official lesson in curricle driving. Or so Lord Vessey had informed her two days ago, when he'd suggested this outing as a dual final test and celebration of her success. He claimed she was as proficient as his tutelage could make her, and that she had no further need of him—only the inner confidence that continued practice would bring.

When they returned to London, he promised to aid her in purchasing her own equipage and team so she could drive around the city whenever and wherever she wished. The idea left her jittery but energized, longing for the freedom and power such a circumstance would bring.

To her consternation, she knew she would miss the marquis's daily company once this last lesson ended. Over the past two weeks she had come to enjoy his conversation and companionship, had come to anticipate their morning outings with an eagerness she ought to have found disquieting. She shouldn't wish for his company, she realized, but over the past several days she had made an alarming discovery: she liked Ethan Andarton. Yet she knew instinctively that he wasn't the sort of man with whom she could ever be friends, at least not strictly friends. He was far too bold, too masculine, too overtly sexual to ever be seen in anything but elemental terms.

*Not that I want him as a lover,* she hastened to assure herself, *because I do not. I don't want any lover.* Still, when it came to Lord Vessey, a woman would have to be made of granite to be immune to his appeal. Lily doubted any woman under the age of eighty could withstand the lure of his charm. He was practically a walking aphrodisiac!

Considering his behavior toward her of late, though, she wondered if his interest in her had waned. After that very first lesson, when he'd had her in his arms under the guise of teaching her, he'd made no further amorous attempts. He hadn't even tried to kiss her, behaving instead like a perfect gentleman—like a platonic cousin, exactly as he had promised.

Had his desire for her faded? she wondered. Did he

no longer want to be anything more to her than a friend? Her shoulders dipped at the idea. Foolish, she knew, since she ought to be relieved by the possibility rather than disappointed. From the corner of her eye, she noticed the leisurely smile that curved his attractive lips, and the twinkle in his golden-brown eyes—so compelling he set her skin atingle. Returning her eyes to the road, she continued to drive.

Coming upon a slow-moving farmer's wagon, topped tall and wide with a greenish-gold mound of hay, she signaled the team to go around. A pair of stalks sailed into the air, whirling briefly before landing—one on her skirt and the second on the small area of exposed flesh revealed just above her bodice. With her hands quite literally occupied managing the horses, she couldn't reach up to brush off the scratchy reeds. She wiggled slightly in hopes that one or both of them might fall off.

"Allow me," Vessey murmured. Leaning forward, he brushed the stalk off her skirt with a casual hand before reaching upward for the next. Her breath grew shallow, her heart bumping hard beneath her ribs as his fingers hovered just above her breasts. The warm backs of his knuckles brushed against her quivering flesh as he plucked away the slender reed. Shivers traveled through her body, rippling outward in gradually widening circles. *Mercy,* she thought, praying he would assume her trembling flesh was the result of the curricle's sway instead of her reaction to him.

"We're not far from Richmond," she stated in a sudden, desperate need for distraction.

"Assuming the last mile marker we passed is correct, we have less than two miles to go." Twirling the hay stalk between his fingertips, he leaned back again in the seat. "I thought we might stop in the park and enjoy nuncheon. I didn't mention it earlier, but I had Cook pack us a hamper. There is sure to be something inside to tempt your palate."

A picnic? She had assumed they would stop at an inn in Richmond where she and the marquis could enjoy a meal while the horses were watered and rested for the return journey to London. But a visit to the park sounded lovely, especially on such a fine, clement day. And surely there was a lake where Thunder and Lightning could partake of a drink.

"That sounds delightful," she answered with unfettered candor. "What a wonderful surprise!"

A grin creased his face. "I am relieved to know you approve." He twirled the hay again between his fingers. "With your last lesson all but officially over, I thought a special treat was in order."

"It does not have to be over—the lessons, I mean," she said before she had time to censor her words. "I've mastered the curricle, but you have yet to let me take a try at your phaeton. Or do you not think I am ready?"

An intense look came into his eyes. "Oh, you are ready, and I'll let you take a try at the rig one of these days. As for lessons, I believe we are done with those. Time both of us moved on to something new, do you not agree?"

She studied him for a long moment, wondering exactly what he meant by the statement. Shifting in the seat, his leg lolled daringly close to her own. Tossing her a rather wicked smile, he once again twirled the stalk of hay.

*Is he flirting with me?* She shot him a speculative glance, but by the time she looked again, his expression had cleared, leaving her to assume she was only imagining things.

An hour and a half later, as Lily sat on the lawn blanket Lord Vessey had gallantly spread over the grass beneath the shelter of several lavish old oak trees, she decided she wasn't imagining things, after all.

Their arrival at the park had begun harmlessly enough. Although in hindsight she realized the marquis had been the one to suggest she drive them to a lovely yet secluded area at the far edge of a glassy blue-green pond.

King Henry's Mound and the Queen's Ride were beautiful spots, he'd agreed, but they were also filled with clusters of noisy tourists. He would take her to see the views from those locations later, he promised, once they had enjoyed their nuncheon in privacy and in peace.

After arranging the lawn blanket, Vessey had seen to watering and feeding the horses while she unpacked the food and dishes from the hamper. He returned brief minutes later and dropped down onto the blanket, arranging his long, rugged form at an angle not far from her side.

He reached for a bottle of wine. With a few deft twists, he pulled the cork free, then located a pair of glasses and poured the Champagne.

"Congratulations on a most successful venture," he toasted. "Here's to you, Lily! The best driving student I have ever had."

"The *only* driving student you have ever had, I suspect," she said with a laugh. "But I thank you for the compliment nonetheless."

She drank, bubbles tickling the inside of her nose, the wine's cool, crisp flavor reminding her of the last time she'd drunk Champagne with Ethan Andarton. A frisson of sense-memory shimmered over her skin, a peculiar feeling of sameness despite the fact that this open, sun-filled venue was nothing like the darkened garden where they'd shared ice cream and Champagne weeks ago.

Such musings drifted away, however, when he passed her a china plate laden with a delectable array of foodstuffs—roast chicken with crisp, salty skin, fresh green pea and potato salad, pickled purple beets, and crusty slices of bread slathered with butter so fresh she suspected it had been churned that very morning.

One of the park's many deer—a red stag—wandered past, pausing to eye her and Vessey and the horses before meandering away, his great rack of antlers set at a regal tilt that clearly established they were on his territory.

"You've never told me where you grew up," the marquis murmured after the deer had gone.

"Have I not?" she replied, eating a forkful of salad. "I do not believe you've mentioned your childhood home either."

"Hmm, perhaps you are right. Most people don't have occasion to ask, since they are already acquainted with my family estate. Andarley, my home, lies on a beautiful stretch of land in Suffolk. Most of the estate is tillable farmland, but there are also woodlands, ponds, and a river that runs not far from the house. My steward and I are trying two new varieties of corn this year and we've reclaimed an old orchard that had fallen fallow, planting the property with a couple hundred apple, pear, and cherry trees."

"It sounds quite beautiful."

"It is." He chewed a bite of bread, then washed it down with wine. "So, what of you? I've shared all manner of details. Seems you are now honor-bound to do the same."

*Am I indeed?* In that moment, though, keeping all her secrets to herself didn't seem nearly as important as it might once have been. *What can it hurt if he knows a few particulars,* she mused, *so long as they are a very few?* After all, forever guarding her past did grow a bit wearisome at times.

"I'm from Cornwall," she divulged before she could think better of the impulse. "I grew up near the sea. Have you ever been there?"

Her stomach suddenly clenched, her nuncheon churning a little. *Heavens, what if he has visited there? What if he knows my home?* But Cornwall was a large place, she reminded herself, and she didn't have to reveal anything too specific.

A moment later, she discovered she need not have worried.

He shook his head. "No, I've always wanted to travel west, but the opportunity has never presented itself. I have heard it's a picturesque land, but rather harsh and unforgiving as well."

"The west country can be all those things," she agreed, "for there is no disputing that the land is both rugged and untamed. Most folk there eke out their livings in mining, fishing, and dairying, but the land has a special beauty that is quite unlike any other I have known." Relaxing, she let her thoughts drift. "On a clear afternoon, if you stand on top of the cliffs along the shoreline, you can see for miles. The wind whips off the ocean, the salt air as rich and sweet as the finest perfume. But when the storms come in, the world turns black, the water churns, and it seems as if hell itself has been unleashed.

"My mother used to be afraid of the storms, but I never was. I guess I took after my father in that regard. The wilder the better, he used to say. I loved those storms, the lightning and the thunder, the sound of the rain drumming in sheets against the roof. Storms can be a godsend sometimes. Storms can set you free."

She stopped, abruptly aware of what she'd been saying and the rapt expression of interest on Lord Vessey's handsome face. Silence fell, the trilling of a bird on a nearby branch unexpectedly loud.

"Heavens," she said, covering her discomfort with a laugh. "I do not know how we got to talking about all of that."

"You miss it," the marquis said, his words a statement and not a question.

She frowned, wishing she could take back the past five minutes. *I've said far more than I intended. I should never have let down my guard.* "Sometimes, I suppose."

She gave a shrug and forced herself to eat another mouthful of chicken. When she swallowed, the meat seemed to stick in her throat. Taking up her wineglass, she downed the rest of her Champagne.

A long moment later, she set her plate aside, then glanced up, her eyes colliding with Vessey's far-too-intelligent gaze. "London is my home now," she stated. "I have no wish to live anywhere else."

"Do you not?"

"No." Her words were emphatic.

"A city girl now, hmm?"

"Quite right."

"For a city girl," he mused aloud, "you seem awfully comfortable out here in the country."

"I am adaptable, my lord."

An unrestrained laugh rolled from his lips.

"Was that marchpane I saw inside the tin over there?" she asked, desperately in need of a change of subject.

He raised a single golden brow, then set aside his wineglass and plate in order to check. Leaning forward, he picked up the tin to which she referred. "This blue one, do you mean?" Springing open the lid, he looked inside. "Marchpane it is. Would you care for a piece?"

"Yes, please." Of all the sweetmeats available, she'd always had a weakness for candies fashioned from almond paste.

But instead of offering her the tin so that she might make her own selection, he chose a piece for her. Fashioned in the shape of a perfect, plump strawberry, the confection would have looked real had it not lacked the fruit's natural red color.

The marquis extended the treat. "Here," he murmured, "try a bite."

She stared. *Does he mean to have me eat from his fingers?* Glancing upward, she caught his gaze and saw that that was precisely what he intended. Her belly clenched again, but pleasurably this time as a syrupy heat spread through her limbs.

That's when she realized she hadn't been wrong earlier when she'd wondered if he was flirting with her. He wasn't only flirting with her, he was seducing her—and doing an excellent job of it as well.

"Go on, Lily," he coaxed in deep, mellifluous tones. "You know you want to."

Before she could stop herself, she sank her teeth into the soft, sugary confection. The intense flavor of almonds exploded in her mouth, delight flooding her senses as the sweet melted against her tongue.

Once the bite was gone, he urged her to take another. As if caught inside a spell, she obeyed, letting her eyelids drift shut as she chewed.

"And the last," he murmured after a long moment.

Her eyes popped open, her pulse hammering in a rhythm that warned her she was in danger. If she had any hope of resisting the marquis, she knew she needed to do it now, needed to put a halt to his provocative overtures while she still had the strength of will.

With that goal in mind, she shook her head in refusal.

*What a silly goose I am to have imagined, even for an instant, that he'd given up his pursuit of me! Has he merely been biding his time these past two weeks? Has he been waiting for our lessons to be done so that he might continue his campaign to lure me into his bed?*

She had but an instant to contemplate such an idea before he leaned closer. "If you won't have another taste," he said, "then I suppose I shall have to indulge in one myself."

But instead of eating the last bite of marchpane, he bent his head and captured her mouth with his own. Breath soughed in a rush from her lungs, her senses blazing hot, as if a match had been set to tinder. Without conscious thought, her mouth opened beneath the persuasion of his touch, his tongue delving inside to stroke and caress and explore.

"Umm, delicious," he murmured, drawing back just enough to speak. "Almonds and sugar and Lily, what better flavors could there be?"

*Your own,* she thought, loving the dark, masculine taste of him—divine as the richest chocolate, more savory than the finest, most buttery pastry ever made.

He hummed low in his throat and joined their lips again. A part of her knew she should pull away—or *push* him away, if need be. But even as she raised her hands to his shoulders to separate them, he deepened their kiss, bombarding her senses with a pleasure so intense she forgot all about her resolve.

Instead she found herself drawing him closer, her fingernails sinking into the fabric of his coat as if she needed to anchor him in place. But he was in no danger of ending their kiss, his tongue making passionate forays into her mouth that sent her mind spinning. A ragged shiver gripped her, tickling down her spine, and lower still, as her body turned hot, then cold, then hot again.

Her eyelashes fluttered closed, her tongue tangling with his in a caress that was as bold as it was blatant. Her toes pressed hard against the insides of her shoes, her senses awhirl as she let him take her deeper. Drawing back enough to capture her lower lip between his teeth, he bit gently, tormenting her with a teasing nip that he was quick to soothe with a tantalizing stroke of his tongue.

Shuddering, she met his next kiss with a breathless ardor, lost, in that moment, to everything but him. His hand moved upward then and caught hold of the ribbon beneath her chin, tugging loose the bow that held her bonnet in place. He was starting to lift her hat free when a buzzing sounded near her ear.

For a second the noise made no sense. Then the sound grew louder, closer, until suddenly she realized she was hearing a bee—a bee that was circling around her and the marquis.

Vessey paused and looked up, breaking their kiss long enough to wave the insect away. Turning back, he finished plucking the bonnet off her head, then resumed his embrace before she had a chance to regain more than a glimmer of her senses. His arms slid around her back and cradled her against his chest. Then he was plundering her lips once more, sweeping her under with a fresh wave of delight.

A sigh escaped her throat, along with a hum of satisfaction she couldn't deny. She answered his possession, following his exquisite touch everywhere he led.

Abruptly he stiffened, releasing his hold upon her as he jackknifed into an upright position. Catching herself to keep from falling backward, she saw him slap at his neck, then tear at his cravat. Unable to free the cloth from his throat fast enough, he dug his fingers inside, reaching between the linen and his skin.

He slapped again, then tightened his fingers as if he were crushing something. Drawing out his hand, he flung a vividly hued yellow jacket—now dead—away into the grass.

She jumped up onto her knees, ignoring her tangled

skirts. "Ethan, are you all right? How badly did that creature sting you?"

He rolled his neck. "Not badly. I'm fine." He rubbed a palm over his neck. "Blasted bee."

"Are you sure? You're hurt. Maybe you should let me see."

He shook his head. "My thanks, but there is no need. After all, it is only a little bee sting. Believe me, I have suffered much worse."

"Perhaps so, but still . . ."

"Do not worry, Lily. Five minutes from now, I'll have forgotten all about it." He took her hand and gently began to tug her close again. "Now," he mused, "where were we? Come here and refresh my memory."

This time, however, she resisted, leaning away as he tried to resume their embrace. The bee's attack had provided enough distraction to shake her loose from her earlier pleasure-induced haze. Since she and the marquis were inside the walls of a public park where anyone might happen by, she couldn't risk allowing him to resume their kisses, however intoxicating they might be. Even so, Lord Vessey had a way about him, a seductive magic in which a single touch seemed more than enough to enthrall her.

She did not dare let him touch her again.

Shuffling sideways on her knees, she held out a hand as though to ward him off. "There will be no refreshing of anything. No more kissing, my lord. I want you to stop."

"You don't mean that. After all, only a minute ago I was Ethan."

*Gracious, did I call him Ethan? Oh dear, I believe I did.*

More determined than ever to regain the upper hand, she reached for a dish and began to repack the hamper.

"Perhaps you were . . . are . . . but all my previous reasons for not becoming intimate with you still hold true."

"It seems to me we've been rather intimate as it is," he said, his words sounding slower than usual. "If you will remember . . . I am not your . . . brother."

She covered another dish and set it alongside the others, giving an ironic laugh. "Indeed you are not. Nevertheless, I think it is best if we remain friends. Only friends."

*Listen to me,* she thought, *telling him I want to be friends when that's the last thing I wish! But what else am I to say?*

He said nothing further as she packed away the last of the dishes. Glancing up, she was startled to find him seated with his eyes closed, a strange flush of blotchy white and red creeping up his cheeks.

"My lord? What is it?"

His eyes came open, his gaze intensely brown. "Nothing," he denied. "I'm fine . . . what did you say?"

"I asked if you are well." A little fist of concern formed beneath her breastbone. Gathering her skirts, she crossed to him and laid a hand against his skin, forgetting all about the promise to herself not to touch him again. "You seem warm."

"It's June and the sun is shining," he mumbled. "Of course I am warm."

"This has nothing to do with the temperature out-of-doors. Does your neck hurt?"

"No more than before."

"Take off your cravat."

He forced a smile. "Why, how forward of you, Mrs. Smythe."

When he made no effort to obey, she tsked and leaned near to yank at the knot holding his neckcloth closed. Quick and efficient, she unwound the strip of linen. A small gasp escaped her lips when she saw the angry red patch staining his throat.

"Oh heavens, your poor neck!"

"Maybe you should kiss it," he said, his words a little sluggish. "That . . . might help."

"Removing the stinger will help more, if it is still in there, as I suspect. Hold still."

Striving to be as gentle as possible, she drew the tips of her fingers over his abused skin, searching for the tiny, needle-like protrusion. She discovered it almost immediately, using the edges of her fingernails to catch hold of the stinger and draw it out.

"Perhaps you ought to see a physician," she suggested.

His expression turned mulish. "Don't need a physician. Had this happen to me once before as a boy . . . I'll get over it soon enough. Just a stupid bee sting, that's all."

His physical reaction suggested something rather more serious, yet his breathing was unlabored. What of his heart? Without giving herself time to consider, she unfastened the top few buttons on his waistcoat and slid her palm inside over his shirt.

"What are you doing?" he drawled.

"Just checking." Moving her hand slowly over the taut plain of his chest, she found what she sought, his heart beating at a strong, and reassuringly even, pace.

"Will I live?" he quipped.

"I believe so. Still, you do not look well."

"I only need . . . a few minutes to rest," he told her, his words continuing to sound slurred. "After that . . . I'll be right . . . as rain."

While she watched, his eyelids began to droop, creases lining his brow as though he was fighting to remain lucid.

*I cannot allow him to pass out,* she realized. *Not in*

*this park, anyway. If he falls into unconsciousness, I will*
*never be able to move him.*

Knowing she dare not lose a minute more, she
wrapped her arms around his wide shoulders and began
to coax him to his feet. "Come on, my lord. Let us get
you into the curricle so that I might drive you home."

He groaned. "Home? Home would be good. Or I
could . . . sleep here instead."

"No, no, sleeping here is a bad idea." She pushed at
him again. "There might be more bees. Come along
now."

"Lily," he stated in a firm voice, turning his head to
meet her gaze.

"What?"

"I am not an invalid, you know."

"No, of course you are not."

"Then release me. I can get to my feet and into the
curricle without your aid."

She hesitated, then withdrew her arms.

"Thank you."

Assuming an air of great dignity, he pushed himself
into a standing position, his stamina and determination
the only things keeping him erect as he walked across
the field to the vehicle and climbed inside. Exhaling, he
leaned his head back against the seat.

"Lily," he called in a low voice.

She came forward immediately, already nearby since
she had followed after him on his brief trek to the carriage. "Yes, what is it?"

His eyes remained closed. "I only wanted to say that
in the future, you may put your arms around me anytime you like."

She coughed to cover a laugh and shook her head at
his outrageous remark. "Yes, well, I shall keep that in
mind. In the meantime, why don't you relax while I
drive us home."

He nodded. "Good thing you know how to manage the team."

"Isn't it, though."

As rapidly as she could, she loaded the picnic hamper and lawn blanket into the carriage boot, then sprang into the curricle to take up the reins.

Well rested, Thunder and Lightning were eager to be on the road again, the horses settling into a quick but easy canter once they left the confines of the park.

Beside her, the marquis was quiet. *Too quiet,* she thought. With his cravat removed, she had no difficulty seeing the still blotchy red-and-white condition of his skin, nor the unhealthy pallor on his face.

She wondered again if he ought to see a doctor.

London was over an hour distant. What if both of them were mistaken about the seriousness of his reaction to the bee sting? What if she ignored his symptoms and he fell gravely ill during the time it took to reach the city? Her belly squeezed, worry sinking like a lead-shot ball.

Having already left Richmond behind, she was contemplating the prudence of turning the curricle around and going back when she spied a two-storied, ivy-covered inn a few yards ahead. As it was tidy and pleasant-looking, with a pair of busy ostlers in the yard, she had no hesitation about stopping. Of course, any inn would have done, she supposed, since Ethan's health took precedence over all else.

A porter came out of the hostelry only moments after she brought the curricle to a halt, the man offering a cheerful greeting.

"Are we here?" Vessey muttered, his lids opening, then closing again. "Have we reached London already?"

"No," she told him. "We are at an inn. I thought you

might prefer to stop and rest in greater comfort for a time."

He gave a soft grunt and a nod, but made no argument. In that moment, she knew her instincts had been correct.

Without waiting for assistance from the porter, she jumped down from the curricle and hurried around the vehicle.

A gray-haired man, who was clearly the innkeeper, bustled out the front entrance. "Good afternoon and welcome. How may I serve you?"

"His lordship is unwell and in need of a room, the very finest you have, please. We also require the services of a physician."

"Told you before . . . don't want a quack," Ethan complained, apparently coherent enough to follow the conversation.

"Hmm, so I remember. Why do we not get you to a room first; then we can discuss the matter."

Her words seemed to appease him. A bit wobbly, he stood and exited the carriage, stumbling only once. She feared he might insist on making his way up the staircase entirely on his own as well, but to her relief he let the innkeeper offer a steadying shoulder on which to lean. Another sign of how truly ill Vessey was feeling.

Once inside the room, he crossed quickly to the bed and collapsed full-length across the mattress. Closing his eyes, he released a weary exhalation.

She turned to the innkeeper, careful to lower her voice. "Call the physician, please."

The older man cast a concerned glance toward the marquis. "Yes, my lady."

She considered correcting him, since the man obviously assumed she was Ethan's wife. But in the next instant, she decided against it. There might be unwanted comment and disapproval were it known she and his lordship were not wed. *Besides, explaining the truth right now is simply too much trouble,* she reasoned.

Once the innkeeper departed, Lily hurried to Ethan's side. Leaning over him, she reached out a hand and gently brushed back his wind-tousled hair. Laying her palm across his forehead, she checked for fever but found his skin cool, though a little clammy. Needing to comfort him as well as herself, she stroked his hair once more. "Everything will be all right, Ethan," she whispered. "Everything will be fine."

The doctor arrived not many minutes later, trundling inside with a heavy, black leather case, and a pair of spectacles on his nose that made his eyes appear as round as an owl's. After a brief greeting, he set to examining the marquis, who roused enough to mutter a few words to the other man. Lily was afraid Ethan was going to refuse treatment, but he acquiesced instead, even reaching up to open the rest of the buttons on his waistcoat, then several on his shirt.

While the doctor listened to his heart and lungs, she tried not to look, struggling to keep her eyes off Ethan's bare chest and the thatch of gorgeous golden curls covering its firm expanse.

Continuing his examination, the older man inspected the marquis's ears and eyes before peering into his mouth. Finally, just as she was starting to grow a bit impatient, he turned his attentions to the wounds on Ethan's neck. Clucking his tongue a few times, he stepped back and began to rummage inside his bag.

She walked a few steps forward, hands linked at her waist. "Well, Doctor, how is he?"

"Oh, he's fine, my lady, or he will be with some rest."

"Is that not what I said?" Ethan murmured, not bothering to open his eyes.

She ignored the remark. "But his neck—"

"Aye, it looks bad now, but it'll heal soon enough.

Bees are capable of inflicting great pain and sickness with their venom, and sometimes the results can be grave. You were right to consult with me."

"Thank you, Doctor," she replied, feeling vindicated for her caution and concern.

Ethan said nothing, lying as though he were slumbering.

"Yes, yes," the physician continued as he pulled out a variety of small vials and packets, along with a mortar and pestle that he set up on a nearby table. "I watched a woman die once of bee stings—"

A quiet gasp escaped her lips.

"But she was a tiny female," the older man hastened to assure, "not a strapping fellow like your man here."

"He isn't my . . ." she began, only to break off.

The doctor crushed a thimbleful of seeds beneath his pestle, his concentration on his apothecary duties. "What's that?"

"He . . . um . . . I am relieved he will recover."

"Oh, he will." Pouring the pulverized seeds into a glass of water, he added a few drops of a clear liquid she suspected to be laudanum, then extracted a long-handled pewter spoon that he used to stir the mixture.

"Here, your lordship, drink this," he ordered softly.

Refusing the other man's offer of assistance, Ethan leaned up onto one elbow. His hand shook faintly as he accepted the glass. "What is it?" he questioned, eyeing the contents with a suspicious glare.

"It's medicine. Now, drink up."

Ethan hesitated another moment, then tossed down the concoction with a quick swallow. He grimaced, then thrust the glass back for the doctor to take before flopping unceremoniously back against the bed.

"That should help him rest, which is the best thing for him right now," the physician said, turning back to Lily.

"I'll put a poultice on the stings to take down the inflammation. Remove the remedy after an hour."

"Of course."

Lily crossed to the room's only chair and sank down upon it while the doctor completed his ministrations. By the time he was ready to depart, Ethan had fallen into a heavy slumber. The older man remained long enough to help her remove the marquis's boots and maneuver his large body under the blanket, and then he was gone.

Pulling the chair forward, Lily resumed her seat at Ethan's bedside. Visually, she traced the contours of his face, finding him even more handsome, boyish almost, with his features relaxed and utterly unguarded.

Curling her hand into a fist, she resisted the urge to touch him, to thread her fingers into his silky hair and stroke the length of his refined cheeks.

Once an hour had passed, she removed the poultice, grateful to see that the remedy had eased the worst of the discoloration and reduced the size of the welt so that it was hardly noticeable.

When darkness began to fall and Ethan slept on, she realized there would be no returning to London that evening.

Even as a "widow" propriety demanded she seek her own room, but she wasn't about to leave his side. He might need her in the night. Besides, the staff would most definitely question her and the marquis's relationship if she suddenly requested a separate accommodation.

Not long after, a gentle tap came at the door, a maidservant come to light candles in the room and ask if she would care for a bite of dinner. Until that moment, she hadn't realized she might be hungry, but at the mention of food, her stomach decided to convince her otherwise.

Clearly, Ethan would not be joining her, but he might

wake and crave something to fill his belly. She chose a bowl of hearty beef-and-vegetable soup for herself, plus enough bread, fruit, and cheese to satisfy them both should he wish to eat later.

Once the meal arrived, she ate. Later, after using the commode she discovered behind a privacy screen, she washed her face and hands, then brushed her teeth with a toothbrush and tooth powder the maid had procured for her use. Her ablutions done, she returned to Ethan's bedside to resume her vigil. Laying a palm against his forehead, she smiled to find his skin flushed with normal, healthy warmth.

*He really is going to be fine,* she cheered, coiled tension releasing like a great exhalation from her shoulders and back. Aware of the profound depth of her concern, she assured herself she would have felt the same for any injured person. But deep inside, she knew better.

As the minutes slipped past, the hands of a small mantel clock pointing toward midnight, she began to grow weary, the chair in which she'd sat for hours no longer comfortable.

She gazed at the empty half of the bed.

*Should I?*

*No,* she argued to herself, *I cannot share a bed with the marquis!*

Still, as the minutes ticked by and her eyelids began to droop, her resolve started to waver. *What would it hurt if I stretched out on top of the covers? He's sick and asleep. Chances are good he will sleep through the night.*

At one o'clock, weary beyond measure, she gave up the fight and crept over to the vacant side of the bed. Taking off her shoes, she climbed into bed and curled up with her back to him. Instantly, Lily fell asleep.

# Chapter Eleven

*ETHAN OPENED HIS* eyes to darkness.

A faint sliver of moonlight shone into the room through windows that were in the wrong position.

*Not in my bedroom,* he realized, *nor in my own bed,* the mattress under his back a bit lumpy. Groaning, he scrubbed his hands over his face and struggled to orient himself. Memories stole slowly over him, the pieces falling into place one by one.

*The inn. I'm at an inn somewhere on the road between Richmond and London.*

He sensed the hour was well past midnight and wondered how long he had been asleep. His last distinct memory was of drinking some foul-tasting brew the doctor had pressed upon him. At the time he'd hoped the potion contained only herbs and water, but the damn quack had added laudanum to the mix. He was sure of the addition, since his tongue was sticky with the sweet residue of the drug, his head muzzy as if his brain had been swaddled in cotton gauze.

At least the pain was gone from his neck, and the swelling as well, he discovered as he ran a palm over his flesh. He shifted, then stilled when his hip bumped against a soft shape huddled next to him.

*Lily.*

Despite the darkness and his less-than-peak physical

condition, he had no difficulty recognizing the person sleeping at his side. In fact, he suspected he would have known Lily even if he were blind and deaf.

Angling his head, he caught a hint of the sweet vanilla fragrance of her skin, keenly aware of her womanly figure and the exquisite feminine curves that lay so tantalizingly near. If only there weren't covers separating them, he would have slid closer so they could be touching. But Lily had chosen to lie on top of the blankets and leave him tucked safely and virtuously underneath.

*How ironic,* he mused, *to finally be in bed with her and feel too worn to do anything about it!*

He huffed out an inaudible sigh and lay unmoving for long moments. In that time he became aware of three things. He was hungry, thirsty, and needed to empty his bladder.

Deciding to take care of the most urgent matter first, he climbed from the bed and searched through the shadows for the commode. Once that bodily necessity was accomplished, he emerged from behind the privacy screen, taking care not to wake Lily.

When he found the food on the table, he sent up a silent prayer of thanks to Lily for her thoughtfulness. Tearing off a piece of bread, he added a wedge of cheese and made a small but satisfying meal. He ate a handful of fresh strawberries as well, then quenched his thirst with a glass of room-temperature lemonade. The repast had the added benefit of clearing a large measure of the lingering fog from his brain.

*Now, if I could only get this awful aftertaste of laudanum out of my mouth.*

He wasn't sure, but he thought he'd remembered seeing a toothbrush lying on the small dressing stand next to the commode. Returning there, he found the item, along with a tin of toothpowder that he hoped Lily wouldn't mind sharing.

Feeling noticeably refreshed after scrubbing his teeth and tongue and washing his hands and face, he padded back to the bed. He hesitated only a moment before stripping off his shirt and waistcoat, deciding he would refrain from taking off his trousers, since such an act might leave Lily scandalized come morning.

Turning, he set a knee on the mattress with every intention of lowering himself into the bed and going back to sleep. That's when he noticed the way Lily was huddled on her side, her arms wrapped close around herself as if she were cold.

*I can't leave her like that. Besides, it is ridiculous for us not to both share the covers.*

With only her comfort in mind, he began the tenuous process of tugging the blanket and sheet out from under her recumbent form. He was certain she would rouse at any moment, but she slept through the entire process, sighing aloud in pleasure when he draped the covers over her body.

He was stretching out on his side of the bed when a fresh thought occurred. *Is she sleeping in her stays?* She was still wearing her gown, so chances were good she had left her corset in place too, especially without her lady's maid to assist her as usual. He knew, from the remarks a few of his former bed partners had made over the years, that women tended to find the undergarment tolerable at best, always relieved to be rid of the stiff cloth-and-whalebone contraption at the end of a day.

With her back to him, finding the buttons on her dress proved a simple matter, even in the dark. In a thrice, he had them unfastened. With easy skill, he began to unlace the ties. Once those came loose, he slipped a hand around her front to pull the undergarment free. As he did, his hand brushed over one soft, pliant breast covered in nothing more than her thin lawn shift. Her nipple hardened instantly, the tight peak reaching out through the cloth as if begging for his touch.

His shaft sprang to attention with the quickness of a private saluting a general, snuggling its eager head against the graceful curve of her lower back. *So much for my maladies impeding my sexual appetites,* he thought. His head might not be crystal-clear yet and his body might still be in need of sleep, but his lower half was certainly alert and aware of what it wanted—aware of what it had been wanting all these long days and weeks.

He groaned quietly under his breath, telling himself to ease away and let her go. She was asleep and in no condition to make rational choices.

But even as he fought to end his ill-conceived embrace, his hand curled around her breast, cradling the supple roundness as his thumb began to stroke her of its own accord.

Her nipple tightened further, beading into a taut point while at her back his shaft began to throb with an almost unbearable ache.

*Oh, good God,* he cursed, *how am I going to stop?*

Caught in the grip of intense desire, he continued fondling her, slipping open the tie on her bodice so he could feel her warm, silky flesh against his palm.

Touching her bare breast only made matters worse, his fingers plucking gently at her nipple for a long moment before somehow he found the fortitude to break his contact with her.

His hands shook as he rolled away and flopped onto his back. Flinging an arm across his face, he lay in agony, his whole body on fire with a hunger to reach out and take her. But touching her that way would not be right, no matter how much misery he might currently be enduring.

*Go to sleep,* he ordered himself. *Hah, as if that is*

*going to happen,* he countered, *not with Lily lying here beside me.*

A minute later she stirred, rolling onto her back and then over once more so she lay facing him. Not close enough apparently, she snuggled against him, curving an arm across the naked skin of his chest.

His entire frame tightened, and then he shuddered.

He must have made some sort of noise as well, since she stirred this time, raising her head slightly.

"Ethan?" she murmured.

His erection jerked and pulsed at the low, sleepy timber of her voice. "Yes, it's me."

"Are you all right?"

*Lord, what a question.* He wanted to tell her that he would be dandy if only she'd throw a leg over his hips.

"I'm fine," he said instead, his answer coming out through clenched teeth.

She roused a little more. "You do not sound all right. You sound distressed. Here, let me see." Lifting a hand, she stroked her palm over his cheek.

He trembled, wanting to explode.

"You are a little warm."

*Hot. I am hot. Very, very hot.*

"Does your head hurt?"

*No, my shaft does,* he thought, a rude part of him wishing he would tell her to move her hand and wrap it around the portion of his flesh that really needed her touch.

"No," he grated out instead.

"Hmm, that's good," she murmured. "I was worried about you. So very worried."

"Were you?"

"Yes." She lowered her head to his shoulder and fell quiet, leaving him to wonder after a minute if she'd gone back to sleep. Then she spoke again, her fingers playing lightly over his collarbone. "Am I dreaming?"

He did his best to regulate his breathing, his blood thrumming beneath her touch. "No."

"Hmm. Because this seems like one of my dreams."

He stilled, intrigued. "Really?"

"Hmm hmm," she murmured. "Though usually you're kissing me."

He smiled. "Am I?"

"And touching me . . . like you did that night in the garden." She paused. "I liked that night in the garden."

"Did you?" he affirmed, his words sounding throaty and low-pitched, even to his own ears. "I liked it too. What about this? Do you like this?"

Curving an arm around her back, he slipped his hand inside her loosened dress. In a seductive glide, he traced the skin along the length of her backbone.

She arched, a kind of purring mewl coming from her lips.

"I'll take that as a yes."

Angling her closer, he bent his head and captured her lips in a fervent, yet unhurried kiss, her mouth tasting sweeter than wild raspberries and more decadent than brandied whipped cream.

Deciding to make another attempt at removing her stays, he lifted her upward ever so slightly, and never breaking their kiss, slowly eased the undergarment free. Victorious, he tossed the corset toward what he hoped was the foot of the bed. The garment hit and slid to the wood-planked floor with a muffled thud, instantly forgotten.

Threading his fingers into her hair, he began plucking out pins, her tresses tumbling downward in a silky cascade that framed their faces like a curtain, the coppery shade so vibrant he thought he could detect hints of color even in the moonlight. Closing his eyes, he deepened their kiss, tangling their tongues together in a riotous joining that left each of them gasping for breath.

She moaned as he stroked her back under her shift in

long, leisurely circles, his other hand roving lower in search of more bare skin. Catching the edge of her gown between his fingers, he inched the cloth upward until he found what he sought, his palm tingling as he curved it over the warm, satiny back of her knee just above her garter. Skimming upward, he roved over the sweet length of her thigh, then onward to settle across the lush curve of her delectable little buttocks.

Unable to restrain himself, he gave a gentle squeeze to one bare cheek.

She broke their kiss, a small cry falling from her lips. "Oh. You never did that in my dreams."

"Did I not?" he growled, squeezing her lightly again before caressing that portion of her flesh with another set of lazy circles. "How remiss of me. Shall we attempt it again?"

Down went his hand, drifting slowly over her thigh and knee before retracing his original path. A tremor raced through her frame, strong enough for him to feel.

"Ethan," she sighed on a near sob. "What are we doing?"

"What we should have been doing for weeks. What we were meant to do together." Taking her mouth, he kissed her with a kind of silent desperation. "Do not tell me you don't want this."

"I . . . do. But I should not."

"Why should you not? Does it not feel exquisite? Does it not feel right?"

Rotating his hand on her upper thigh, he moved his fingers around to trace the entrance to her inner feminine flesh. Without delving farther, he knew she was damp with desire.

Lily shuddered, her body in the grip of a driving need, a deep inward ache that begged to be assuaged—by Ethan.

*He is right,* she confessed. *His touch does feel exqui-*

site. So much so that she'd finally had to give up the illusion that she was caught up in some wonderful, half-waking dream. *But I am not dreaming at all. Ethan really, truly is touching me and merciful heaven, I like it. Love it, if truth be told.*

Nonetheless, she sensed that he would stop if she insisted. But did she really want to insist? And how could she possibly bear it if he did?

Calling upon all her old warnings and concerns, she waited for them to snap her out of her haze, to make her see reason and prudence. But her conscience stayed silent this time, refusing to lift so much as a finger in her defense.

Then Ethan caressed her again, stroking the trembling flesh no other man had ever touched.

Her mind grew dim.

"Yes," she murmured, unable to form another coherent word. "Yes." Leaning upward, she found his mouth with her own.

As if her willing response had unleashed some caged beast inside him, he growled low in his throat and began savaging her lips, her surrender apparently snapping the last tenuous hold he'd kept upon his restraint. Sliding his fingers into her hair, he cupped her head and angled her mouth so he could take her in deep, openmouthed kisses that made her mind spin and her body clamor.

Clasping her left thigh in his other hand, he drew her leg upward onto his stomach. Some thick, heavy protrusion strained upward as if struggling to burst free of his trousers, the flesh—his flesh—shifting in obvious eagerness as her knee rubbed across its length.

He groaned and kissed her harder.

*Is that him?* she wondered in amazement. *His . . . male member?*

A second later she had no time to think further as he slid a finger inside her. Shocked sensation broke like a fever through her body, her world narrowing abruptly down to his hand and the way he was stroking her with such incredible intimacy.

Slick and hot, her body welcomed his intrusion, the ache she'd felt earlier increasing threefold. Her hunger spiked again when he drew the finger out and returned with two.

Reacting without conscious thought, she bit his lower lip. He pulled back and paused before slowly licking the small wound. Then he was kissing her wildly again, while below his fingers glided in and out and in and out again.

She whimpered and broke away to bury her face against his neck, panting desperately for breath. But he wasn't content with that arrangement. Leaving his fingers in place inside her, he shifted her body upward, sliding her over him until she lay with her chest near his face. Using his other hand, he yanked aside her already loosened bodice and shift and fastened his mouth to one naked breast.

His fingers started moving inside her again the same instant his lips began to suckle—hot, wet pulls that seemed to connect directly to the flesh throbbing between her legs.

As though from a distance, she heard herself moan, her hands coming up to cup his face, her fingers laced into his hair while he feasted upon her, both inside and out.

He scraped his teeth against her nipple and sent her whole body shaking. Held completely in his thrall, she could do nothing but feel as he shifted his hand and did something quite extraordinary with his fingertips.

A jolt of pleasure exploded inside her, stealing her breath as she cried out against the sensation, each nerve ending sparking with delight, weeping with bliss.

For a long moment her mind went blank.

"I'll wager you never felt that with your husband," he said, his lips momentarily releasing her nipple.

"Who?"

A healthy, satisfied chuckle came from his belly. Cradling her in his arms, he rolled her to her back. "You'll never forget *me,* my dear Lily. Once we've made love, my name will be forever burned on your soul."

*It is already,* she realized, knowing she ought to be alarmed by the notion. Yet for now, all she could do was lie limp while he stripped off her dress and shift, leaving her naked except for her stockings and garters. Instead of removing those too, he sat up and thumbed free the buttons on his falls.

In the darkness she couldn't see precise details, but she made out enough to give her pause. Unless she was misreading the dim angles of moonlight and shadow in the room, Ethan was big—huge, in fact—his male member protruding like a long, thick, stiff rod from between his muscled thighs.

*How,* she wondered, *does he keep all that flesh tucked inside his trousers?* And why haven't I had the urge to stare at the area in the past? Her cheeks burned, and not from passion this time. Then a new thought occurred. *Surely, he doesn't intend to put that in me, does he? He'll rend me in two!*

But Ethan didn't seem at all concerned as he flung his trousers aside and crawled toward her again. Stretching out carefully so very little of his weight actually rested upon her, he crushed his mouth to hers.

Lily tried to relax, tried to focus on the undeniably mesmerizing beauty of his kiss, but that hard, hot part of him was pressing against her belly, twitching slightly, almost as if it had a mind of its own.

His lips skimmed her cheek and nose and temple before roving over her throat, down to her collarbone, where he paused to lave and suckle a patch of skin in a way she suspected would leave a mark. His broad palms glided over her skin, pausing to play with her breasts before flowing over her hips and thighs, then down to caress one silk-covered calf.

The ache flowered again between her legs, leaving her edgy and in need. Shifting restlessly, his shaft rubbed between their bodies, jerking strongly this time.

She tensed.

"What is it?" he murmured, catching an earlobe between his teeth. "Is anything wrong?"

Using the warm, wet edge of his tongue, he licked around her ear, then behind it, scattering kisses against a spot that made her toes arch, and her pulse stutter and jump.

"Nothing," she denied.

"Hmm, are you sure?" His warm breath flowed across her cheek. "Lovers can tell each other anything, you know."

*Can they? What a seductively dangerous idea! What would he think if I told him I am a virgin?* For a brief second she considered the idea, but decided she had better keep her secret to herself, since such a revelation might lead to explanations she would rather not make. *Still, what if he finds out without me saying? Can men tell things like that?* Hoping they couldn't, she held back her confidence. Her thoughts softened when he cupped a breast in one hand and idly circled his thumb around her areola.

"Go on," he coaxed, "tell me."

*Tell him what? Oh, that.* She supposed she could share that. "You're big," she whispered.

He paused and began to shift his weight. "Am I too heavy?"

"No," she said, reaching out to hold him in place. "You are fine, that way. It's just your . . . you know . . .

your—" *Lord, what should she call it?* "Your . . . *thing* is big. Huge."

"My thing? Oh," he murmured in sudden understanding. The *thing* responded, improbably stiffening even more. His lips curved. "I suppose I am amply endowed in that area. Ladies generally profess delight at the prospect, however." His hand stopped playing on her.

Lily swallowed and forced her fears past her lips. "If you must know, I do not think you will fit."

Ethan almost laughed, swallowing down the reaction before the sound could escape. A moment later, he was glad he had, realizing she was serious—and a little afraid, despite her instinctively passionate nature. For the past few minutes—ever since he'd discovered how small and tight she was inside—he'd deliberately been holding himself back, pacing his movements so she would be fully ready when he entered her.

From her reaction to his naked form, though, he could tell that her husband had not only been a tentative, unskilled lover, but had possessed a tiny penis as well. No wonder she hadn't been satisfied in the past.

"Do not worry," he promised in a low voice. "I will fit. You'll sheath me like a glove."

A faint gasp came from her throat.

"Would you like to touch me?"

"Where? There?"

"Yes."

"*No!*"

A silence fell.

"It is only me, you know," he explained, "a part of my body like any other."

*Well, not quite like any other,* he admitted, since his *thing* as she'd dubbed it was currently urging him to stop all the talking and bury itself inside the wet, pliant heat awaiting them both between her soft thighs. But he could control his urges and his needs—for a little while longer, anyway.

Just when he thought she was going to stand by her refusal, her hand moved up and brushed against him. He bit his lip to hold back a moan. The edges of her fingertips feathered over him, sending his heart kicking hard beneath his rib cage, his breath shallow in his lungs.

Forcing himself to hold still, he let her explore in that fashion for another minute. With her tentative touch driving him mad, he finally caught her hand and wrapped her soft little fingers fully around his shaft.

A low groan sang from his throat.

She stopped and started to pull back. Striving not to exert too much pressure on her hand, he held her in place. "Do not stop."

"Are you sure?"

"Yes," he grated out from between clenched teeth. "I'll let you know when you need to cease."

Emboldened, she caressed him, running her curled fingers up and down him in a velvety, gliding stroke.

"Oh," she sighed. "You're so hot and hard, but sleek."

"And you are hot and soft and sleek. Let's see if you're wet, too."

Without waiting for her consent, he parted her thighs, then slid a pair of fingers inside her again, testing the readiness of her response.

She moaned, her hand contracting on his flesh.

Gently easing out of her grasp, he stroked his fingers inside her, working in a rhythm designed to bring her maximum pleasure.

Her head rolled back against the pillow, her breath starting to come in tiny pants.

Wanting her as slick as possible, since penetrating her might not be as easy as he'd suggested, he closed his mouth around a breast and began to suck, using his tongue and teeth in a way he knew would bring her to the brink.

When she was literally writhing beneath him, her fists clenched into the bedclothes, her eyelids squeezed closed with wrenching desire, he pulled his hand and mouth away, then leaned up onto his knees.

Parting her, he settled himself between her splayed legs. Widening her more with his knees, he stretched her fully open so he could take her in a few deep, penetrating strokes.

Positioning himself, he thrust.

He frowned at the resistance he discovered. Thrusting again, he gained an inch, then another. She cried out, palpable tension returning to her body. Perspiration dampened his brow, his body engulfed in a profound hunger he could not stop or deny. He thrust twice more, seating himself only halfway. And that's when he realized the problem.

His eyes flashed wide to find hers in the dark, words rising to his lips. But then she moved again beneath him and he forgot everything else but the overpowering need to take her.

She shifted, bucking slightly as if she were trying to dislodge him; instead, her actions unknowingly helped him slide deeper. With a guttural groan, he curved his palms beneath her buttocks and angled her upward, urging her legs to lock around his waist. The change in position, and one last good thrust, drove him to the hilt.

A single tear slid down her cheek.

Softly, he kissed it away, then gave himself over to the moment as he began to move within her.

Lily clenched her teeth and fought the pain and the intrusion of his penetration. Biting her lip, she prayed his possession would be over quickly. For nearly a minute, he barely moved inside her, his strokes shallow as though he were allowing her to grow used to the sensation of him within her. As he did, something began to change; her inner muscles, which had only moments earlier been complaining of their abuse, softened and relaxed, clasping him tightly, as if she were indeed a glove.

An almost embarrassing wetness formed between her legs, the added lubrication allowing him to slide more easily back and forth. Desire unfurled like a fist low in her belly, gradually radiating upward until her whole body was consumed by flame.

Groaning, he thrust harder, faster, his motions taking him impossibly deeper. Holding on, she gave herself over to the ride, pleasure beating like a drum in her system, blurring her thoughts, leaving her with no anchor save one—Ethan.

She repeated his name in her head and on her lips, her mouth open as she struggled to find air. Clasping her arms around his sweat-slicked back, she surrendered herself to his hunger and found more of her own, drinking the sweet sensations in deep, greedy gulps.

As earlier, bliss flowed through her bloodstream. Yet this time, when she came, the rapture nearly broke her, a wail of glory literally singing from her mouth while ecstasy flooded her frame.

Shivering, her mind spun, Ethan pumping hard and fast, almost relentlessly until abruptly he stiffened above her. A harsh shout erupted from his throat as his body did the same.

Both of them fell still, struggling for breath and sanity, lying satiated and exhausted as the world slowly tumbled back. Pressing her face against his neck, she let herself drift.

At length, he slid out of her and rolled to lie at her side. She said nothing, content in the dark and the quiet, her eyelids beginning to droop with drowsiness. But apparently Ethan was not interested in sleep as he sat up, the mattress bouncing at his movements. Reaching out, he fumbled for a match on the night table and lighted a single candle.

Her eyes were wide open by the time he shifted back around to face her, his gaze no more than a degree above frosty. "So, Mrs. Smythe," he demanded in an implacable tone, "why don't you explain how you came to be a virgin."

## Chapter Twelve

✧⁓∾⁓✧

*L*ILY REACHED DOWN and drew the sheet up to cover her nakedness, as though the thin layer of material might offer her some vital source of protection.

*Damnation!* she cursed. *Apparently men can tell about these things*—or at least Ethan could. Lying back against the pillow, she forced herself not to panic.

"Well, have you nothing to say?" he pressed.

She smoothed her fingers over the top edge of the sheet. "What would you like me to say?"

His gaze bore into hers. "You might begin by mentioning the obvious. How is it you were married and yet never consummated your nuptials?"

*Count on Ethan,* she thought, *to go directly to the point.*

*So, what to say? I certainly cannot tell him the truth, not the real truth—that I never had a husband at all!*

Although she liked Ethan, even trusted him—obviously enough to have just given him her virginity—she knew she could not afford to risk confiding everything in him. She had no way of knowing how he might react to the news that her very existence was based on a fraud. Should he choose to do so, he would have the power to destroy the new life she had struggled so hard to secure. And that she could not permit. No, she must continue to maintain as much of her story as possible, even if it meant fabricating a new set of lies to placate him.

*So what to say? Think quickly, he's waiting!*

"There wasn't time," she said. "After our wedding ceremony, he was called away by his regiment and immediately embarked on the ship to Spain."

*There, that had sounded plausible, had it not?*

Ethan's golden brows drew close. "You married so quickly the two of you could not spend even a single night together?"

She shook her head. "He . . . um . . . asked me during his leave, and in the time it took for the banns to be read, he received his orders. We . . . married on that very last day and had time for no more than a few kisses."

Clutching the edge of the sheet with her fingers, she closed her eyes as she prepared to finish the deceit, a tight lump of guilt lodging beneath her breastbone. "We thought he would return in a few months, but before he could, he was killed."

After a moment, Ethan's large hand enfolded her own and gave a little squeeze. "I am sorry."

The pressure in her chest increased. She had lied to him before. Why was this troubling her so much now? Of course, before tonight she had not lain with him. Before now she had not known the full beauty of his touch, nor the great depths of his honesty.

*Lovers can tell each other anything.*

"Why did you not say?" he asked.

She opened her eyes. "Say what?"

"That you were a virgin. Did you not think I might wish to know? Might *need* to know?"

She shrugged to give herself an extra moment to consider. "It . . . um . . . seemed an awkward subject, not something one generally discusses."

Raising his hand, he stroked his palm across her cheek in a tender glide. "We have discussed a great many awkward topics this night, it seems. You ought to have confided that one as well." A fierce expression crossed his face. "God, Lily, I could have hurt you."

She turned her hand and entwined her fingers with his own. "But you did not—at least no more than could be helped given my untried state. I knew I was safe in your arms."

The last of the earlier coolness receded from his eyes, a flash of desire igniting deep in his amber gaze. Seconds later, however, the look was gone, replaced by something that appeared remarkably close to concern.

Sitting up, he scraped the fingers of one hand through his disheveled hair, then rubbed a thumb across his forehead.

"Does your head ache?" she inquired. "I suppose I forgot all about your illness while we were . . ." She broke off, strangely shy about saying the words. "So how is your neck? Does the sting still hurt?"

"No, I barely feel it. The doctor's remedy has proven surprisingly effective. And plainly I am well enough to have just made love to you." He fixed his eyes upon her, his brows low and troubled. "Lily, you truly ought to have told me."

"Told you . . . oh, you mean about my being a virgin. Well, I did not and the matter seems of little consequence now. It's done and cannot be changed."

Unless he wished it could be changed, and was even now regretting his impassioned haste in taking her innocence tonight, however unintentionally accomplished?

Her heart pumped out an uncertain beat. "Do not worry, it is fine."

The fierce look returned to Ethan's face. "Is it? I took something from you I had no right to take."

Her shoulders grew stiff. "You had the right I gave you when I consented to lie in your arms. You took nothing I did not freely give."

"You might believe that now, but I seduced you."

"From what I have observed, you have been seducing me for the past several weeks. You never before showed a bit of compunction in conducting your pursuit. Or were you only teasing about wanting me in your bed?"

"Did this evening appear as if I was teasing?" he questioned rhetorically.

"Well then, it would seem you achieved your aim. I should think you would be satisfied." She paused as a new idea suddenly occurred, a notion she had to force herself to voice aloud. "Or is that the difficulty? That I failed to please you and you are now searching for a graceful way to exit the situation?"

Keenly aware of her nakedness and a vulnerability she wished she did not suddenly feel, Lily sat up and reached for her shift. Keeping her eyes averted from his own, she slipped the garment over her head with as much speed as she could manage.

"Where do you come up with such absurdities?" he murmured. Clasping a hand around her arm, he exerted a gentle pressure to angle her toward him. When she refused to lift her eyes, he set a bent finger beneath her jaw and forced up her chin. "You pleased me greatly, very greatly. Never doubt that for an instant."

"Then—"

"I ruined you, Lily, and that I did not mean to do."

He grew silent for a long moment, as though weighing his next words. Drawing a deep breath of apparent resolve, he once more met her gaze. "Marry me. Let me give you back your honor."

Her lips parted on a stunned inhale. *Marry him!* Good heavens, of all the responses she'd considered that had not been one of them. A warm sensation spread inside her, a glow brought on by his gallantry, and yes, by the notion of being his wife. But just as quickly her emotions cooled, logic reminding her that his offer came not from any tender feelings on his part, but from a sense of duty and—lowering as the idea might be—guilt. Well, she needed none of that. Besides, she had no desire to be married. Not to Ethan. Not to any man.

"So you believe marriage will restore my honor?" she stated. "Now who is being absurd?"

His brows met on a sharp scowl. "I am trying to do the right thing."

*Yes, I know,* she thought, repressing a suddenly weary sigh. "And I am telling you there is no need. My honor is not ruined, not that I can see."

His jaw tightened. "I took your virginity."

"Yes, you most definitely did," she retorted, shifting against the slight soreness that was already making itself known within her delicate inner muscles. "But that doesn't mean we need to shackle ourselves to each other."

"You are not seeing this properly—"

She pulled out of his hold, then tossed up an arm. "No, you are the one who is not seeing matters properly. Did you ever think that maybe I do not wish to marry—"

"That is no longer an option."

"Of course it is. No one knows we are here together—"

He laughed in clear derision. "Oh no, no one except for your household staff, who saw us drive off together yesterday morning. My staff, who knew my destination, and any friends or acquaintances in whom we may have confided our day's schedule. No, no one at all."

Her lower lip slid out in a little pout. "You do not have to be nasty about it."

"Merely pointing out the facts."

Reaching behind him for his pillow, he drove a fist into the center, then slid down into the bed to settle his head into the dent. A sudden expression of tiredness crossed his face. "I will procure a special license when we get back to town. We'll be married by the end of the week."

*The end of the week!* Panic knitted a fuzzy lump inside her stomach. "No."

"Lie down, Lily, and get some sleep."

He closed his eyes as if the matter were settled.

"I will not marry you."

"You will change your mind come the morn."

"Maybe I should rephrase that. I do not *want* to marry you."

His eyes popped open, a gleam she thought might be hurt shining in his gaze before it vanished. "I had not realized marriage to me would present such a burden. Once you are a marchioness, I am sure your qualms will disappear."

"Pray do not fly up in the boughs. I don't mean that I do not wish to marry you personally. It is only that I do not wish to marry at all."

He quirked a brow. "Why not? Widows are generally eager for a new spouse."

"I am not one of them. Marriage is not for me."

"From the sounds of your first nuptials, you were hardly wed at all."

"I was wed enough to know I do not wish to be again," she bluffed. "And if you would think about this logically, you would see there is no reason for a union between us. A union, I will add, for which you have no more desire than I."

A long pause followed. "Who says I do not?"

"Your proposal does, since I would hardly call your earlier words an expression of undying affection and devotion."

"So you want love? If that is the cause of your refusal—"

"No, Ethan. I merely wish to stay as I am, single and

independent. And there is no reason I cannot. I am a . . . widow, and until tonight you thought I was a woman who had slept with at least one other man. The rest of the world assumes that as well and unless you plan to disabuse them of the notion, they will continue to see me as a woman of prior sexual experience."

"Yes, but—"

"No buts. Until you made your discovery that I was a virgin, you saw no problem in pursuing me. Or were you always planning to offer marriage once you'd claimed me for a bed partner?"

Fairly caught, he shot her a rueful look, then glanced away.

"Just as I suspected," she said. "Seems rather hypocritical to me that you feel honor-bound to wed me because I was a virgin, but were happy to enjoy my favors with impunity had I actually been experienced as you assumed."

"I never thought you were *experienced*; well, not in more than the basics, anyway."

She decided to ignore the observation. "Widows have affairs all the time, Ethan. You know that as well as I. Even if rumors start, no one will think much about it, especially if there is no direct evidence."

"You mean such as getting caught during a party shagging on the sofa in the host's library?" His lips quirked in a wry grin.

"Just so. And I do not want to know if you took that example from your own personal experience."

He showed his teeth in a grin. "Not mine. A friend's."

She wasn't sure she believed him, but it didn't matter. "Anyway, you see my point, which is that as kind and honorable as your offer may be, and however much I appreciate the intent, neither of us wishes to marry."

A peculiar distance shone in his gaze, a melancholy

she could not fathom. "No," he murmured, "you are right in that."

"Good. Let me say thank you, my lord, but no thank you, and leave it at that."

He did not reply for a long moment. "Very well, if you are sure."

"Yes, very sure."

But even as the tension eased from her frame, a wholly inexplicable sadness rushed in to fill the void. Ruthlessly, she brushed it away.

"So what next, then?" He stroked a hand over her bare arm.

*Yes, what next?*

She knew what she wanted and that was him. But continuing what they had started tonight would surely prove to be a mistake. *Would it not?*

"What is next is that we should get some sleep; then we will return to London come morning."

"And after that?"

"I do not think there should be anything after that. Tonight was lovely, more than lovely, but it ought to be left here at this inn."

His hand stopped and tightened against her skin. "What if I disagree?"

"Then I would ask you to change your mind."

Locking his gaze with hers, he stared. Suddenly, as if making up his mind, he leaned up and pulled her under him.

"Well," he growled. "If tonight is all I am to have of you, then I want to take the fullest advantage." Reaching down, he pulled off her shift, then cupped his hands around her breasts. "For now you are still mine."

Crushing her mouth beneath his own, he kissed her with a passion that demanded her complete surrender. Threading her fingers into his hair, she gave it eagerly.

\*      \*      \*

The following afternoon, Lily slid the tines of her nuncheon fork into a piece of perfectly poached salmon and lifted the bite to her lips.

"I called on you yesterday," Davina remarked from the other side of the Coateses' smaller dining-room table. The two women were alone in the family wing of the house, Lord Coates having departed hours ago for Parliament. "Your butler told me you had gone out driving. With the marquis again, I presume?"

Lily was glad she had already swallowed the food in her mouth or else she feared she might have choked. Reaching for her wineglass, she drank a slow, steadying amount. Taking her time, she returned the long-stemmed goblet to the linen-draped table. "Yes, another lesson. I thought I had mentioned I would be away."

Davina ate a forkful of scalloped potatoes, swallowing politely before she spoke. "You did. I merely assumed you would have returned by four in the afternoon. I had some pretty buttons I found at one of the Bond Street shops on which I wanted your opinion."

Inwardly, Lily winced. "I am sorry I had not yet arrived home. I should like to see the buttons. Why do you not show them to me now?"

"I will go get them as soon as we are finished with our repast."

Lily stabbed a slice of crisp cucumber, hoping Davina would take the hint and change the subject.

"So where did you go?"

Lily stabbed the cucumber again, leaving behind a series of tiny holes identical to those inflicted by her first bit of violence upon the vegetable. "When?"

"With the marquis, of course. Surely you did not spend all that time driving around the city."

She stabbed a piece of yellow tomato this time. "We went to Richmond."

Davina paused with her fork in midair, her eyes bright with interest. "Did you? How was the journey?"

"The journey went well. I drove."

"All that distance?"

She nodded. "My final lesson at curricle driving."

"Once you arrived, what then?"

*Then we spent the night at an inn, where I had my first real lesson at making love.*

Tamping down an invisible shiver, Lily struggled to put the memories aside, a difficult task since she had awakened in Ethan's arms only that morning. Already, those moments seemed so long ago, as though a lifetime had passed.

"We drove to Richmond Park."

"And?"

"And we had a lovely picnic, at least until the bee."

"There was a bee?"

*Blast my mouth!* Lily cursed, fearing she'd said too much.

"Yes, a yellow jacket," she offered. "The nasty creature crawled down the marquis's cravat and stung him. He had a reaction and fell ill."

Davina's eyes widened. "How dreadful! Is he all right?"

"Oh, yes, he is perfectly well now, though I am sure he would appreciate it if you were to say nothing of the incident."

"Not to worry, my lips are sealed. So you drove him straight back to town?"

Lily cut the tomato in half, then abandoned her fork on the plate. "No, we stopped at an inn, where a physician was called."

"My goodness. Well, that explains why you were so late returning," Davina concluded.

"Precisely." Lily crossed her fingers in her lap, praying her friend would not inquire about the exact hour of her arrival home, since Ethan had dropped her at her town-house just a few minutes after eight o'clock this morning.

"Well, what an adventure, I must say!" Davina commented, eating another bite of fish. "I suppose that is also why I did not see you at the Islings' soiree last night."

Lily lowered her gaze to her wineglass and studied the golden hue of the beverage, thinking again of Ethan. "Yes; it was a long day and I decided to stay in."

*Or rather at the inn,* she mused, cringing inwardly at the dreadful pun.

"I am not surprised. You must be tired."

"I am a bit," Lily admitted.

Weary and sore, to be honest. In fact, she'd almost canceled this afternoon's nuncheon with Davina, but had decided to follow through rather than have to make her excuses. Now, she wondered if begging off wouldn't have been easier, after all.

Her mind drifted back to this morning with the first rays of sun just breaking in the sky. She'd opened her eyes to find Ethan watching her, his hawkish gaze nearly unreadable except for the desire burning there like a barely banked fire.

"I suppose you are sore," he said in a tone that emerged as a growl.

Tentatively moving her limbs and feeling the twinge deep inside, she nodded, a wash of pink staining her cheeks to remember the cause.

After that first time, he'd taken her twice more, bringing her powerfully and satisfyingly to peak more times than she'd been able to count. He'd still been inside her that last time when she'd drifted off to sleep.

Realizing there would be no morning repetition of events, he sat up and tossed back the covers. "Get dressed, then. We will leave within the hour."

And so they had, Ethan driving this time, as he pointed the team toward London. He said barely a word during the return journey, and neither did she. What was there left to say after all that had been spoken of and debated last night?

When they arrived, there had been no good-bye kiss, not with Hodges and one of her footmen watching them with scarcely concealed interest. Ethan had stepped down long enough to escort her to the door, however, bowing over her hand as though they had done nothing more than return from an ordinary excursion. Then he was gone, flicking the reins so they made an audible snap, Thunder's and Lightning's hooves reverberating on the cobbled paving stones.

The servants, bless them, said little, offering words of pleasure at her return and asking in what way they could serve.

She'd called first for a bath—a hot soak in a deep copper tub that had done much to restore her, physically at least. Breakfast came next, then a couple of hours' sleep until noon, when she'd awakened to dress for her two o'clock nuncheon with Davina.

*Has he forgotten me already?* she wondered. *I gave him his freedom. Is he relieved now that he has escaped?*

Surely he must be.

*Was I a fool to cast him aside?*

She recognized that she'd been protecting herself. Yet were such precautions already too late? And if she could go back in time, would she choose to act differently?

Not about marriage, she decided; on that point she had not changed her mind. There were too many risks, too much potential for disappointment and heartache, particularly since he had offered marriage only out of guilt and a steadfast sense of honor.

*We would make each other miserable, wouldn't we?*

Yet she had been far from miserable last night, Ethan

bringing her the most extraordinary pleasure she had ever known. She could have continued to know his touch if only she had said yes to his offer to remain his lover.

But they were better off, she told herself. She didn't need Ethan Andarton mucking up her carefully laid plans, nor plaguing her with the cravings and desires stirred by the exquisite power of his touch.

*Easier to separate myself from him now than later, right?*

Sighing, she tore the small roll on her bread plate into a trio of pieces, making no effort to eat any of the three.

"Is something wrong?" Davina asked in a soft voice.

Lily glanced across at her friend, chagrined to realize she had drifted quite away in her thoughts. She forced down an incriminating blush.

"No, not at all. Only woolgathering."

Davina paused. "He is very handsome, is he not?"

"Who?"

"Your marquis."

"He is not *my* marquis. Whatever gave you that notion?" Taking up her fork again, she picked at her salmon. "No, yesterday's excursion was likely our last together. I rather doubt I will be seeing much of Lord Vessey from now on."

Her friend sent her a look, plainly unconvinced. "If you say."

"I do. Now, why don't you get those buttons you wanted to show me."

"Will there be anything else, my lord?"

Ethan glanced up from his book. "No, Welk, thank you. You may retire for the evening."

The manservant bowed. "Sleep well, your lordship."

"Good night."

Once his valet had withdrawn, Ethan returned to his

book, but read no more than three lines before he gave up the attempt. A glance at the blue Meissen clock on his bedroom fireplace mantel showed him the hour was well past one o'clock.

He yawned, his body also reminding him of the late hour and the fact that he'd had little rest the night before, not to mention having been bee-stung and subsequently drugged with laudanum. In a kind of rebellious defiance, however, he'd pushed himself through the day.

Upon his return home that morning, he'd bathed, changed clothes, and eaten a substantial breakfast. Afterward, he'd ignored his body's demand for sleep and instead spent a few hours reviewing correspondence and other business matters with his secretary.

A change into evening attire and he'd been out the door again, arriving at Brooks's Club for a drink and a few rounds of cards with Tony, Lord Howard, and another couple of his cronies. The group of them had gone to another St. James establishment for a hearty dinner of beefsteak and roast partridge pie. Soon after, Tony had departed for an assignation with his current paramour, while Ethan and the others decided to put in an appearance at a ball known for its wild goings-on and preponderance of demi-reps eager for a dance and a tumble.

He'd escorted a few of the women to the ballroom floor, their gowns blowsy and low-cut, their skin painted with kohl and rouge, the immoderate scent of their perfume lingering like decaying flowers in his nostrils.

Memories of fresh, vanilla-scented skin, cleanscrubbed cheeks, and bare pink lips tangled in his mind, his body longing for the untutored embrace of a young woman who knew nothing of sin and degradation, and who had no more in common with the females in this room than their gender.

Suddenly disgusted with both the demi-reps and himself, he left, driving back to his townhouse long before a gentleman of fashion would retire for the night.

Once again in his bedchamber, he'd washed himself from head to feet to rid himself of the women's stink, then slid into a clean dressing gown, tightening the belt at his waist. Selecting an edifying book from the shelf of literary works he kept in his adjoining sitting room, he'd poured a small glass of port and settled onto a chaise near the fireplace to read.

But he didn't get far, the letters and words running together in incomprehensible lines, meaningless symbols of black ink that meant nothing.

Only one word, one name, was clear in his mind.

*Lily.*

Just the thought of her made him stiff with desire, his body abruptly feverish and in need. If he'd thought she would welcome him, he would have dressed and ridden over to her house, then knocked on the door to demand entrance to her bed and her body.

But she'd made her wishes clear, casting him out, both as a prospective bridegroom and as a lover. Although it might seem a conceit, the truth was there wasn't a single woman of his acquaintance who would have refused him—only Lily. He couldn't count the number of women who'd cast out their lures toward him over the years, some wanting his body and his riches, others craving his ring.

Last night he'd been willing to give them all to Lily, ready to break his unofficial pledge to wed another in a union that would satisfy both his family and his legacy. Amelia was a much better choice for him all around; she was everything a marchioness should be. So why couldn't he even recall her face? And why, when he thought of her, did he feel as if he were betraying Lily?

Stupid, since Lily had decided to end their affair before it had truly even begun.

Even now he wasn't entirely sure why, since he knew she wanted him. No woman could fake the kind of unbridled passion and fiery response she'd given while in his arms, especially not a girl who had been a virgin until he'd take her innocence. If he'd had any doubt at all on that score—which he had not—seeing the spots of blood on the sheets this morning had proven her truthfulness.

So why deny him now that her chastity was gone? Had she loved her husband that much? Was her marriage to him so precious that she wanted to preserve the memory, even at the expense of her own happiness and pleasure?

As for himself, he should have been over her by this afternoon. The one night ought to have been enough, dimming his appetite at least enough for him to move on, to forget her as he searched for someone new.

Instead, taking her had only increased his longing, his hunger for her keener and more intense than ever. With a near growl, he closed the book and tossed the leatherbound volume aside.

*What I need is sleep.*

Striding toward his bed, he sat down on the sheets that had earlier been turned back in anticipation of his use. He was bending forward to blow out the candle when he noticed a single stalk of hay lying on the night table—the same windblown piece he'd plucked from Lily's breasts during their ride to Richmond. When he'd found it still inside his pocket this morning, he'd placed the stalk here beside his bed.

Pausing, he picked it up, twirling the slender reed between his fingers for a long moment. Lifting it to his nose, he inhaled the earthy scent, thinking of her and their time together.

Calling himself twice a fool, he nearly tossed the stalk

away. Instead, he placed it inside the night-table drawer, then snuffed out the light.

When he stretched out under the covers, he was certain he would be asleep instantly. In spite of his exhaustion, though, nearly an hour passed before slumber finally claimed him.

# Chapter Thirteen

*❦❦❦*

T HREE DAYS LATER, Lily left the house at nine o'clock in the morning to take a stroll around the square and through the nearby neighborhood streets, her maid trailing a few steps behind her for propriety and safety's sake.

Although the pastime might not be strictly fashionable, Lily still enjoyed taking a walk, and did so as her schedule allowed. After all, she had walked on a regular basis for nearly the whole of her life and saw no reason to stop simply because she now lived in the city.

True, there were no rugged, windblown cliffs, no rolling grassy fields or patchy, rock-strewn moors, but London provided a host of interesting sights nonetheless. In the mornings, milkmaids and orange girls called out their wares, while later in the day a variety of vendors would make their rounds, offering everything from fine inks and tea to fresh flowers and songbirds.

Lily would sometimes buy a few pence worth of flowers and had once been tempted to purchase a pair of beautiful yellow canaries. Ultimately she had decided against bringing the little birds into her home, though, for fear Mouser would take it in his head to stalk and eat them.

She could have gone to one of the parks, she supposed, and promenaded in fine style with the rest of the ladies and gentlemen. But she rather preferred being left to her own devises and musings without the need to pause every couple of minutes to engage in ten additional minutes of meaningless small talk.

This morning in particular she found herself in need of the exercise as well as the distraction. She had not slept well, her mind and body plagued by haunting, erotic dreams of Ethan that left her bleary-eyed and needy.

Last evening she had attended a rout and had seen him.

She'd been sipping a glass of sherry, waiting for her next partner to claim her for a dance, when she'd turned her head and found Ethan standing across the room. He'd been conversing with a ravishingly beautiful blond, smiling at whatever it was the other woman said.

Glancing up, his gaze had met her own, the smile falling from his countenance. For a long, almost painful moment, his eyes had lingered, his chin dipping in silent acknowledgment. Then he'd returned to his conversation and had not glanced at her again.

She'd waited for hours in a panic of anticipation, wondering how she would react when he sought her out. Would he ask her to dance? Would he try to lure her away to a private alcove or a shadowed garden to steal a few new kisses?

But as the evening wore on, he did none of those things, making no attempt to approach her. His response answered her earlier question about whether he'd forgotten her already. Apparently he had, his raw desire for her assuaged by their single night together at the inn. Her fault, she supposed, for having refused his offers.

Still . . .

When she'd called for her cloak, she'd vowed to be done with him, once and for all. But by the time she'd been tucked beneath the sheets, her eyelids lowered in sleep, the traitorous dreams had come.

Troubling her mind. Tormenting her body.

She'd awakened early, knowing she had to get up and out as soon as may be.

Turning her face to the sunlight now, she strode along, hoping each step would cleanse her spirit and drive away her distress. She was halfway around the square, nearing the Pendragons' townhouse, when the front door to the mansion opened.

The baroness emerged with her young son in her arms and a nursemaid trailing after. Behind them followed a tall, bald mountain of a man, an elegantly made wooden stroller held in his brawny arms. He carried it as though the contraption weighed no more than a matchstick. Negotiating the front steps with ease, he set down the little carriage on the sidewalk, then stood aside while the women tucked the toddler comfortably inside. The dark-haired child giggled, clapped, and kicked his small legs, clearly excited about the outing.

Beginning to feel a bit like an interloper, Lily decided she really ought to say something. "Good morning, my lady," she called, joining the group. "I see you are taking your boy for a stroll. Campbell, is it not?"

Julianna turned her head, her dark, faintly exotic beauty complimented by her indigo muslin day dress, the flowing skirt of the Empire-waist gown doing nothing to conceal the rounded shape of the new baby growing inside her.

A lively smile came to the baroness's mouth as she straightened to her full five feet one inch. "It is indeed. How do you do, Mrs. Smythe? Forgive me, but I only just noticed you. I hope you have not been standing there long."

Lily shook her head. "Only long enough to observe that you are very well occupied."

Lady Pendragon laughed in good-natured amusement. "Getting Cam and myself out of the house these days does tend to be an event."

"Cam!" the boy declared, thrusting his little arms into the air before bursting into a round of giggles, his vivid green eyes an exact replica of his father's.

Julianna's lips curved in an indulgent smile. "He is very taken with his name at the moment and uses it at every opportunity. His other favorite words are Mama, Papa, and Ben-Ben, who is his beloved stuffed bunny."

"Ben-Ben!" Cam repeated, the grin falling from his face a second later as he looked around, unable to locate the toy. "Ben-Ben. Ben-Ben."

"Some days I am not sure whom he loves more, Mama, Papa, or Ben-Ben," Julianna teased. Leaning over, she reached into the area of the stroller seat behind the child and extracted a floppy, brown velvet bunny with embroidered blue eyes and a pink nose and whiskers.

"Here he is, sweetheart," Julianna cooed, handing the well-worn toy to her son.

The boy hugged the bunny close. "Mama."

Lily laughed and leaned closer to waggle a set of fingers at the child.

Suddenly shy, he hid his face against the rabbit, peeking out at her from behind a set of long, floppy ears. His head popped up a second later, however, apparently recovered. "Cam!" he exclaimed.

*Adorable,* Lily mused. *What would it be like to have one of my own? I suppose I shall never know considering I do not plan to marry.*

An image of a child flashed inside her head, a tiny blond boy with hints of red in his hair, his face the image of Ethan.

*Good God!*

Her heart kicked, and she banished the fantasy.

"Well," she said, her voice strained. "I should let you continue on with your outing. I had no wish to intrude."

"Oh, you are not intruding at all. We are just going down the street. Are you headed in any particular direction?"

Lily shook her head. "No, I am merely taking a stroll."

"Then why do we not walk together, if you do not mind a slightly reduced pace? We are going to a confectioner's shop three blocks over. The proprietor sells the best caramels in London and lately I have been giving him a great deal of business." Julianna laid a palm over her protruding belly. "Terrible cravings, you see. Rafe advises me to send a footman 'round to purchase a fresh supply, but I fear I'll turn as round and ripe as a pear if I do not engage in a bit of exercise. And this way, I do not have to feel guilty when I eat the entire bag." She laughed.

Lily couldn't help but laugh with her, finding herself liking the other woman very much. Besides, company might help keep thoughts of Ethan at bay, which, considering her recent musings, would be a very good thing indeed.

"Yes, thank you," she agreed, "that would be lovely."

Julianna moved to take hold of the stroller bar so she could push her son, while Lily fell into step at her side. The maidservants walked behind, starting up a low-voiced conversation, while the huge bald man assumed a position at the rear of the group. Casting him a furtive glance, Lily repressed a shiver, his black eyes some of the most menacing she had ever seen.

Julianna apparently saw Lily's look. "Never mind Hannibal. He looks fearsome, but he's harmless. Well, mostly."

Having overheard, Hannibal scowled, his dark eyebrows boxing like a pair of pugilists on his forehead.

"Rafe feels better knowing I am accompanied," Lady Pendragon continued, "especially since I find myself with child again. It's easier to indulge him rather than squabble. Actually, when Rafe cannot accompany me, having Hannibal along can be very reassuring. There was a time . . . but that scarcely signifies now."

Pushing the stroller, the two of them continued onward.

"How do the lessons go, then? I heard Lord Vessey has been teaching you to drive."

*So much for forgetting about Ethan,* Lily mused.

"The lessons are finished, my lady. Lord Vessey has deemed me fit to drive on my own."

"Well, congratulations! What a liberating talent to possess! You shall have to take me up one of these days. Perhaps we can go shopping."

"That would be delightful, though I have not yet purchased my own rig and team."

"Oh, I am certain Ethan would be most happy to assist you in that endeavor."

Lily made a noncommittal noise in response and turned the conversation to more neutral topics.

The confectioner's shop proved diverting, and surprisingly busy considering the early hour. Replete with caramels for both herself and the baroness, their small party made the return walk in complete accord.

When they reached the townhouse, Julianna invited her inside. "Oh, do come in. It will only take me a few minutes to settle Cam in his room; then we shall have tea and eat these sweets."

Lily hesitated, thinking of the household accounts she ought to be reviewing at home. With an inner shrug, she decided she could do them later. "Thank you, yes, I will."

\*　　\*　　\*

"More tea?"

"Yes, please," Lily agreed, passing her cup to Lady Pendragon, or rather Julianna, as she now thought of her.

During the past two weeks, ever since she and Julianna had shared that first walk together, they had fallen into a pattern of sorts, strolling together in the mornings as often as their schedules permitted. Frequently little Cam and the rest of the entourage would accompany them. Afterward, Julianna always asked her in for tea, an invitation Lily accepted with alacrity.

Twice, Lord Pendragon had put aside his work to join them, charming Lily with his interesting conversation and intelligent observations. The way he treated his wife charmed her even more, his affection for Julianna unmistakable, his every gaze and gesture expressing the great depth of his love. And it was clear Julianna felt the same about him, her eyes gleaming with a happy inner light each time she so much as mentioned his name.

But more than love, Lily observed their commitment, saw the bond of loyalty, trust, and friendship that existed between them. Witnessing their happiness gave her pause, leaving her to wonder if she might have been too harsh in her former assessment of the marital state. Maybe all marriages were not the stuff of nightmare and misery such as she had observed growing up.

Still, Rafe and Julianna were an exception to the rule. Simply because they had been lucky enough to find lasting love did not mean such miracles happened to others. Finding real, genuine love was no more likely than being struck by lightning. Yet as improbable an occurrence as theirs might be, whenever she saw the Pendragons together, her thoughts eventually turned to Ethan, what-ifs drifting through her mind.

Though today she couldn't even use the couple as an excuse for her musings about him, since she and Julianna were on their own, Lord Pendragon apparently working in his study.

*Widgeon,* she chastised herself.

Obviously Lord Vessey had found it easy to relegate her to his past, and she would be wise to do the same with him. Perhaps he was one of those men who enjoyed a woman's favors once, then moved on to another, like a hummingbird flitting from flower to flower, never returning to the same one twice.

Her chest pinched tight at the idea of him making love to someone else, and for an instant she could not breathe.

*Stop it,* she warned. *He is not mine and never will be. Not that I want him to be, because I do not.*

"Lily?" Julianna's voice cut into her musings.

She glanced up and found Julianna holding out the teacup she'd passed her moments ago, tiny spirals of steam curling off the top of the refreshed beverage.

"Thank you," she said, accepting the saucer and cup. Careful not to scald her mouth, she drank a slow sip.

"What were you thinking about just now?" her friend inquired.

"Nothing of any importance." She flashed a smile. "So, you were telling me about your home in West Riding."

"You are right, I was," Julianna agreed. With a proud smile, she launched into a description of her and Rafe's country estate.

Twenty minutes later, they were trading a tidbit of gossip about Caro Lamb's latest indiscretion in her illicit pursuit of Lord Byron when a quick rap of knuckles sounded at the door. Seated in a wing chair whose tall back shielded her from the room's entrance, Lily couldn't see who approached.

A second later, she didn't need to.

"Good morning, Julianna. Rafe said you were here,"

Ethan stated in his rich, unmistakable voice, his footsteps quiet on the carpet as his long legs carried him deeper into the room. "I thought I would pop up and say hello before I— Oh, I didn't realize you had company."

Her shoulder muscles tightened, sensing him standing near. Too near.

"Pardon the intrusion, ma'am," he said as he strode around to face her. "I— Lily!"

Raising her head, she met his gaze, fighting to slow her suddenly erratic pulse. "My lord."

Straightening, he executed an elegant bow, his hair and eyes fiercely gold against the dark brown cloth of his coat. "Mrs. Smythe, how do you do?"

She angled her chin. "Quite well, thank you."

Lily didn't ask how he did. She could see that for herself. If possible, he was even more beautiful than she remembered. Ridiculous, considering that little more than a week had passed since she had seen him from a distance at yet another ball. Nevertheless, he was delectable enough to make an ice woman melt. Holding herself firm, she did her best not to drip.

Julianna glanced between them. "Come, come," she invited. "Sit and visit with us."

His brows drew tight, then smoothed again with a clearly conscious effort. "I was just visiting Rafe. I cannot stay long."

"Long enough surely to enjoy a cup of tea." Julianna poured, adding a spoonful of sugar before extending the beverage to him.

Politeness dictated he accept. After a small hesitation, he took the saucer and cup, then lowered himself onto the sofa. His position put him in a direct line of sight with Lily.

She lowered her gaze.

He stirred his tea.

Julianna cleared her throat. "So, of what were you men talking?"

Ethan set his silver teaspoon onto the saucer with a faint click. "The usual. Business, politics, the latest million Rafe just made on the Exchange."

"Ah," Julianna said with a smile. "That would be the usual. Rafe does have a unique talent for acquiring wealth."

"He has always been lucky that way. And now he is enjoying the same good fortune when it comes to love."

Lily glanced up, but instead of finding his eyes on Julianna, they were fixed upon her. A subtle quiver ran just beneath her skin. Curling her fingers together at her side, she hid them against the folds of her green-and-white-striped muslin day dress.

"How are you feeling, Julianna?" he asked, shifting his gaze back to the other woman. "You are positively blossoming."

She chuckled and laid a hand across her burgeoning belly. "What a nice way to say I have put on a few pounds, but Rafe assures me it is all baby. The sweetmeats in which I have been indulging convince me otherwise."

"Nonsense. You look gorgeous. And you are entitled to a few sweetmeats and cravings. After all, you are eating for two."

Julianna smiled, obviously pleased and reassured by his words.

Ethan turned his head. "And what of yourself, Mrs. Smythe? The Season seems to be agreeing with you."

"Yes, I believe it is."

"By all accounts, you are certainly never at a loss for a dance partner these days." He softened his statement with a smile, a gesture that didn't reach farther than his lips.

"One might say the same of you, my lord," she replied, "though I never suspected you had the time to bother noticing my activities."

"That Titian hair of yours is hard to miss. I believe you and Miss Mockingham are the only two redheads out in Society this year."

"Perhaps it is Miss Mockingham, then, whom you have been observing."

Slowly, he shook his head. "No. She is a full head shorter and tends to disappear in a crowd." He drank a swallow of tea. "I heard you went driving in Hyde Park Wednesday last."

She lifted a brow. "You have excellent sources, my lord, since you are quite correct. Lord Pedlam was good enough to take me up in his high-perch phaeton. He even let me try the reins so I could decide if I liked the high-flyer better than a curricle. I was just recently telling Julianna that I am still trying to decide between the two, was I not, Julianna?"

Julianna shot her a look, then glanced at Ethan, her expression one of unconcealed interest. When her eyes moved again to Lily, a tiny frown had settled between her brows. "Hmm, indeed yes, you did mention something of the sort."

"The curricle will do well for your purposes," Ethan pronounced in an authoritative tone. "A high-perch phaeton is in large measure a frivolous vehicle meant only for sport."

Arching her spine, she stood her ground, tipping her head in an act of unconscious flirtation. "And what makes you suppose I am not up for a bit of sport, my lord?"

*Dear heavens, did that come out sounding the way I think it sounded?* she wondered to herself.

He stared, an intense look darkening his eyes. "Well,"

he drawled, "I had recently been given cause to believe otherwise. Perhaps you have since changed your mind."

Her mouth grew dry, her heart turning over beneath her breast. *Why do I think we are not talking about carriages any longer?*

"Perhaps. Perhaps not," she hedged, deciding she had better steer the conversation back onto neutral ground. "Regardless, I have yet to choose a suitable carriage and team."

"I told you before I would be happy to assist you with such matters."

"Yes, but you have not been available of late."

"You have only to say the word, and I can rearrange my schedule."

"I would not want to put you to any bother," she said, deliberately adding a smile. "I am sure Lord Pedlam will be happy to help me."

His jaw turned to stone, a deadly gleam in his eyes. "I am sure Lord Pedlam would, but I must warn you that it is unlikely he would perform up to your expectations. You would be far better off allowing someone with the proper experience to guide you in such matters."

Just barely she held down the rush of blood that threatened to flood into her cheeks, refusing to glance over at Julianna to see if she was aware of the innuendoes whizzing like electric sparks through the room.

Suddenly in desperate need of retreat, Lily glanced toward the room's far wall and the casement clock with its face painted like a moon. "Oh, just look at the hour. Is it really half after eleven? I had not realized. Forgive me, Julianna, my lord, but I should be returning home."

She rose to her feet.

Ethan stood with her. "It is time I was departing as well. As I said upon my arrival, I cannot remain long."

Smooth as butter, he turned to Julianna and made her

a refined bow. "A delight as always. My thanks for the tea."

"Of course, Ethan."

He glanced toward Lily. "I shall escort you out."

"Oh, that is not necessary. I traveled by foot and as you know, the walk home is very brief."

"Nevertheless, a lady can always do with protection. I shall walk with you."

*Why didn't I bring my maid?* But taking Susan along had seemed superfluous at the time, since Lily knew she would be with Julianna and her servants, including the redoubtable Hannibal.

Recognizing the stubborn set to the marquis's mouth, though, she knew there was no further point in arguing. "Very well."

He strode toward the door to wait.

Lily crossed to hug Julianna, who had managed to gain her feet by that time. As she bent down, Julianna pulled her near.

"He's a good man, but have a care," the baroness whispered. "I do not want to see you get hurt."

"Don't worry. I won't." *If I could only be as sure of that as I sound,* she mused. "We are only walking home."

"Of course you are. Now, remember that we cannot meet tomorrow as I am engaged for a breakfast party. Unless you would like to accompany me, after all. Procuring an invitation for you would be no trouble in the least."

"You are most kind, but I have matters to which I really must attend. Until next we meet."

With a last good-bye, she walked across the room, then laid her hand on the sleeve of Ethan's extended forearm.

Once they'd departed the townhouse, she dropped her arm to her side. "You needn't walk me home, my lord. I can manage very well on my own. If you are concerned, you have only to stand here and watch until I arrive at my doorstep."

Reaching for her hand, he set her palm back onto his coat sleeve and held it there. "But then I would be too far away to aid you were you to meet with misfortune. This way, I will know you are safe."

"No harm will befall me in this neighborhood, as well you know."

"There are dangers besides thieves and villains. You might fall, for instance, and injure yourself."

She laughed. "That is highly unlikely, and were it to happen, I am sure I would manage to pick myself up just fine."

"But then you would be wounded, and that I would not like."

They walked for half a minute in silence.

"How have you been, Lily?"

"Quite well, my lord."

"Ethan. I was Ethan that last time we were together."

"We were many things the last time we were together," she said, her words quiet, "but all that is now in the past."

His hand tightened atop hers. "Is it? Are you sure?"

"Yes, completely."

"That is not how it sounded back in Julianna's sitting room."

Her eyes lifted to meet his. "Did it not? You must not have heard correctly."

"Oh, I heard just fine," he murmured, his gaze lowering to her lips.

Suddenly her lungs were straining for air. She blamed the deficiency on the exercise, relieved a few moments later when they reached her front door.

"Here we are," she chimed. "Good day to you, Lord

Vessey. I know you cannot stay, what with your prior commitments and need to hurry off."

She expected him to agree; instead, he set a foot on the first step to her townhouse. "Oh, I can spare a few minutes more. We can discuss a day and time when we may meet to find you that curricle and team."

"Phaeton," she shot back. "And I don't think my schedule will allow for such an outing, not in the near future."

"Why do we not go inside so you can consult your engagement calendar? My guess is you'll discover an available time."

Aware of her butler and footman standing at the open door, no doubt listening to every word, she gave a nod. Besides, she couldn't very well continue to argue with Ethan here on her front stoop. "All right, but only for a few minutes. I have an appointment this afternoon for which I must get ready."

He inclined his head. "A few minutes will do fine."

After handing his hat and gloves to the waiting servant, he followed her upstairs to her study. Once there she moved to her walnut desk, dawdling since she had no need to look in her engagement book. Her earlier statement had been nothing more than a ruse, one Ethan most likely already knew to be a falsehood.

The door shut at his back with a resounding click.

Startled, she glanced up. "What are you doing, my lord?"

He strode deeper into the room. "I thought we might need some privacy, so we might speak freely with no interruptions."

"You will not be here long enough to worry about interruptions." She stepped forward to confront him. "I have decided that I would prefer having someone else help me purchase a carriage."

He shook his head. "No, it has to be me. I am the only

one who will know what you want, what will gratify you and bring you pleasure. No other man will do."

Suddenly, once more, they were no longer talking about conveyances.

Her heart swooped like a sparrow winging from a branch. "Go away, Ethan. I do not want you."

He closed the space between them. "Don't you?"

"No," she declared.

Her eyes locked with his, Ethan's amber gaze hot and lambent, brimming with unconcealed desire. Her breath grew shallow, rushing in and out of her lungs as if there were not enough oxygen in the room. Blood throbbed in her temples, beating hard and fast at the base of her throat.

She couldn't look away.

One second passed, then two.

On the third, she flung herself forward while he did the same, catching her in a hard, crushing embrace that lifted her feet clear of the floor.

Clinging, she returned his ravishing kisses with wild ones of her own, each wet, tempestuous mating leading to another series of kisses that rocked her to her core. Greedy in a way that would once have shocked her, she locked her arms around his neck and gave free rein to her passion, returning each dark, velvety sweep of his tongue with a rich, heated suction of her own.

Growling deep in his throat, he caught her lower lip between his teeth and played upon her flesh, taking playful nibbles and teasing bites for a long, scintillating moment before pressing her mouth wide to take more of his kiss.

Eagerly, she returned his touch, sliding her fingers into the thick silk of his hair. Gliding her palms downward, she stroked over his cheeks and held him steady for her kiss, increasing the pressure with an ardent desire of her own. He rose to her challenge, making her senses whirl out of control.

On a whimper, she stroked her hands over him again, struck by the contrast between his clean-shaven cheeks and the ultra-smooth interior she found as she let her tongue explore the other side.

Stroking his hands over her back, he deepened their kiss even more, eliciting a full-body shiver as her nipples tightened into hard little points. With passion driving her hard, she hung on for the ride, the scent and taste and feel of him like an erotic elixir that swept everything from her mind but raw, primal need. Desperate, she raised her legs and looped them around his waist, uncaring of the way her skirts fell in a messy tangle between them.

Shifting his hands to her buttocks, he hoisted her higher, and settled the part of her that ached the most against the part of him that struggled to be free of his trousers. Mouths locked in a fervid dance, he carried her forward and placed her onto the desk. Using an arm, he swept a space clear on the surface, ledgers and papers and pens flying to the carpet below.

She should have been alarmed by the destruction, but all she cared about right now was him, and the need to have him inside her. With their mouths still fused, he slid her legs apart and stepped between.

Her nipples throbbed again, begging for his touch. As if he sensed her need, he went to work at the back of her gown, loosening her bodice and stays enough for her naked breasts to tumble free. Sliding his hands downward, he cupped her in his palms, holding her flesh while his fingers stroked her to devastating effect.

Her eyelids fluttered closed, a moan coming from her lips when he arched her back and closed his mouth around one breast. He suckled, the sweet, wet warmth making her literally shake in his arms. When he'd thoroughly appeased the first, he moved on to her other breast, feasting there with ravenous intent, scraping his teeth over her nipple before soothing it with his tongue.

After a time she reached down to urge him upward, but he dropped to his knees instead, pushing her skirts over her bare legs, then spreading her wide.

She had no notion of what he meant to do, her hips bucking involuntarily at the first brush of his lips against her nether flesh. Instinctively she tried to close her thighs, but he held her open, sliding her closer to the edge of the desk so she teetered there, trembling on the brink of madness.

Arching, she flattened her palms against the desk to keep herself from falling, gasping aloud in uncontrollable pants as he kissed her where she hadn't known a woman could be kissed. The pleasure nearly broke her, a brutal shudder raking through her body when his tongue played upon her before sliding inside.

She crashed hard, bliss gripping her as if she were caught in a blinding storm. But he wasn't done, driving her up until a single tear of emotion slid down her cheek, waves of ecstasy crashing through her to leave her gasping, a long moan keening from her throat.

Then he was on his feet, tearing open his falls to free his rampant erection. Lying her gently backward across the desk, he thrust into her with no further preamble. Not that he needed any, her body accepting his as if it had been fashioned for that purpose alone.

Unlike their first time together, there was no pain, no difficulty with his entrance, although his large shaft filled her completely. At his urging, she lifted her legs and linked them at his back, the angle allowing him to thrust deeper still.

Setting a rhythm that stole her breath, he pumped hard and fast, bracing his arms on either side of her head so he could kiss her again as he took her with him into a world where nothing existed but the stunning pleasure of his possession. She wondered if her heart might explode—the need so great, the delight so profound.

And then she was cresting again, a roaring rush sounding between her ears as if she were drowning, while an explosion of joy sent her flying skyward.

He captured her scream of release inside his mouth, muffling his own shout of completion against her lips moments later.

Panting, he collapsed briefly upon her, burying his face against the curve of her throat. Slowly, he removed his weight, levering himself up and away.

She lay with her eyes closed, too weary and replete to move, strangely afraid to look at him for fear of what she might see. But she discovered a few moments later that she need not have worried.

"Lily," he murmured. "I'm not letting you go again so do not even think of trying to get away. You don't wish to marry and that is fine, but I will not be kept from your bed again."

She peeked at him through half-raised lashes. "You are not in my bed."

"No, we used your desk, and that should show you quite a lot. Come, let me help you up before you grow impossibly stiff."

Glancing down, her eyes widened. "It would seem you are the one with that problem. How is that possible so soon?"

He shot her a smoldering look. "I've been without you for weeks. Long, impossible days that have left me with a powerful desire."

"There have been no others?"

"No. And there will not be, not until this passion between us subsides."

*What if it never does?* she worried.

A moment later, she decided to brush aside the question as well as the concern.

*Enjoy the now,* she thought, *and do not trouble about the future. There will be plenty of time later to face reality and all its sobering details.*

Gazing into the depths of his beautiful whisky-colored eyes, she smiled and accepted his hand.

## Chapter Fourteen

❦

*L*EANING BACK AGAINST a conveniently placed pillar, Ethan watched Lily glide around the ballroom floor in the arms of another man. Ordinarily he would have objected to the sight, but he kept his more primitive instincts at bay, reassured by the knowledge that he would be the one escorting her home, the one spending the night in her bed.

Three days had passed since he and Lily had made wild, impetuous love atop the desk in her study—an act that would forever change the way he viewed that particular piece of furniture, and desks in general.

On that first day, after she had finally agreed to become his lover, she'd led him to her bedchamber, confessing along the way that she had fibbed about having an afternoon commitment. Backing her against a wall, he'd pressed a torrid kiss to her mouth that left both of them gasping for air. Giving her his wickedest grin, he'd promised to keep her well occupied for the next several hours.

He had not disappointed.

Locking themselves inside her room, they'd stripped to the skin, then spent the rest of the day slaking their seemingly unquenchable passion for one another. More than once, just when he'd thought she'd finally wrung him dry, his hunger would reawaken like a ravenous tiger demanding to be fed. With great relish on both their parts, they'd done their best to appease the beast.

A few minutes before six o'clock that evening, he'd reluctantly pulled himself away from Lily. Tucking the covers around her, he'd dressed, leaving her in an exhausted sleep, a little smile curving her rosy mouth.

He'd sported a smile of his own, one that refused to be controlled, not even when he'd arrived at the Pendragon mews in order to collect his carriage. To his relief, Rafe and Julianna's servants were discreet, in no way indicating they found anything amiss in his more than six-hour absence.

Despite the naïveté of imagining he and Lily could hide their affair, he'd decided it would be best to at least make the attempt—thus his decision to go home instead of spending the night in her bed, as he would have preferred.

His good intentions didn't even last twenty-four hours, though, his aching member awakening him from a shallow sleep a little after one o'clock the next morning. Lying in the darkness, he'd fought his desire, telling himself to go back to sleep. But rest was impossible. In spite of the insanity of the act, he dressed, then left Andarton House to hail a hackney cab for the drive to her townhouse.

A night watchman called three o'clock just as he arrived on Lily's doorstep. Rather than waking her servants, he walked around the side and vaulted over the brick wall surrounding her small garden. Using a rather handy set of tools he had acquired years before from Rafe, he picked open the lock of her rear hallway door. Stealing silently up the stairs, he made a mental note to have new locks installed in her house and to obtain a key. Then he was inside her room, every thought but his need for Lily vanishing from his mind.

Removing his clothes, he eased into bed next to her.

Sensing her awakening, he clapped a hand over her mouth to silence her scream, placing his lips to her ear.

"It is I," he whispered. "Do not be afraid." When he felt her relax a moment later, he removed his hand.

"Good God, Ethan," she said, "you nearly scared me to death."

"My apologies."

"What are you doing here? What time is it?"

"Early. And I'm here because I could not sleep. I want you again."

She made a little sound that reminded him of a purr. "Heavens. How did you get in the house, anyway?"

"I'll tell you later."

Tired of talking, he slid his hands under the sheets and found her clothed in a nightgown. Impatiently, he pulled off the garment. "You might as well stop bothering with these for the next while. You'll only get tired of me taking them off you."

On a contented sigh, she threaded her fingers into his hair. "Will I?"

"Yes," he promised, covering her body with his.

"Good."

Seconds later, nothing else mattered but the divine beauty of Lily's touch and the potent blessing of her kiss.

Even now as he watched her dance, he could remember the sensation of her little hands on his skin, the burgeoning skill of her still untutored caresses. She was proving to be a quick learner, and he had a lot he wanted to teach her. But first he had to get through the next three hours; then, discretion be damned, he would be taking her home.

Besides, they needed to be up early tomorrow so he could escort her to a sale where he planned to find her an excellent team of horses. Afterward, they would shop for a carriage.

He smiled, looking forward to the outing.

His smile lingered, remembering their conversation last night when she'd informed him she wanted a phaeton painted the cerulean blue of a perfect June sky.

"A curricle, you mean," he said.

"No, a phaeton. A beautiful bright-blue phaeton."

He'd laughed, deciding to tease her a little over choosing such a purely feminine shade. "That would be unique. I'm not even sure carriage paint comes in that color. You'll probably have to settle for a darker hue, such as navy."

Her nose wrinkled. "I do not care for navy, not for myself, anyway."

"Or black. Now that's a color you'll have no difficulty finding."

"Ugh, no black. It's cerulean I want. Surely the carriage-maker can procure the proper colors to mix such a shade?"

"Well, we shall have to see. I am not certain it will be possible."

Framing his face with her palms, she gave him a sweet, lingering kiss. "It will be," she whispered. "We shall find a way."

In that moment, gazing down into her eager face, he'd vowed she would have her sky-blue carriage, even if he had to hire a landscape artist to do the painting.

Now, in the ballroom, the dancing ended, the music falling silent as the gathered couples made their way from the floor. As she crossed on the arm of her partner, Lily's eyes darted toward Ethan, gliding over him with a shy yet lingering caress.

An eruption of heat burned low in his belly, desire striking hard and fast. He stared for another long moment, then broke eye contact, his hands turning to fists at his side as he fought to compose himself.

*Damnation,* he cursed, *this is going to be a very long evening.*

He fixed his gaze upon her again, where she was now standing in conversation with her friend Davina Coates.

*On the other hand, the evening doesn't necessarily have to be long.*

Striding out of the ballroom, he located a pen and paper, then dashed off a note. Finding a footman, Ethan passed him the folded missive, along with a coin to ensure prompt delivery. He waited only a moment more, then turned and made his way outside.

Half an hour later, Lily glided down the front steps of the townhouse and crossed to the closed coach waiting not far away. A footman opened the door and assisted her inside.

From out of the waiting darkness emerged a hand, reaching out to enfold her own. The door closed just as she was tugged forward, the vehicle springing into motion as she tumbled onto a pair of powerful, masculine thighs.

The evocative scent and sensation of the man on whose lap she sat reassured her even as being in his arms increased the speed of her racing heartbeat.

"Ethan," she murmured. "What do you think you're doing?"

Without preamble, he gathered the skirt of her lilac silk evening gown in his hands. Sliding the material upward, he stroked the bare flesh of her legs in a tantalizing caress.

"What does it feel like I am doing?" Bending forward, he placed his lips against her neck and nuzzled her with a skill that made her arch in instinctive delight. "I am making love to you."

"Is that why you sent that note? I thought perhaps something was wrong."

Leaning back, his gaze locked with hers. "Something *is* wrong. I have need of you."

"Carnal need, you mean. But surely we can wait. The party will be over soon."

"Not soon enough. I want you now," he said on a near growl.

"Are you going to turn autocratic on me?"

"About this, yes. You are my mistress and I will have you. Wherever and whenever the both of us please."

Claiming her mouth, he swept her into a realm of passion and possession, his kiss demanding her surrender as well as her unbounded response. Not for an instant did she think to resist, his every touch perfection, his embrace branding her with a sizzling passion that made her melt and moan. Only when she lay trembling against him, breath soughing from her lips in little gasping pants, did he ease away.

But not for long. His broad palms slipped higher on her skin so that her gown bunched around her waist. Shifting her, he positioned her astride his lap, her legs settling naturally on either side of his hips, her stocking-clad knees pressing into the plush, velvet-covered seat.

Reaching between them, he opened the falls of his black silk evening breeches. His flesh sprang free, thick and more than ready.

"But we're in your coach," she whispered, half-scandalized, half-excited.

"We were here once before, if you will recall, but we were interrupted that time. I've been waiting for a second chance ever since."

"But surely we can't—"

His teeth flashed in the dark. "Of course we can. My driver will circle the park until I tell him otherwise. Hold on, love, I promise you'll enjoy the ride."

Spreading his thighs apart, he widened her in a way that left her fully exposed to him. Wet heat coiled low within her, a quiver tingling through her extremities. She barely had time to react to the sensations before he grasped her hips, raised her upward, and brought her down onto his straining shaft.

She cried out, his length seeming to fill her even more than usual, if that was possible. Holding on, she met his vigorous thrusts with ones of her own, the sway and bump of the coach heightening every stroke.

Needing his kiss, she tunneled her fingers in his hair and captured his lips in a torrid, tumultuous joining. He groaned and plunged higher and harder, burying himself even deeper inside her as he increased the pace of his thrusts.

Teetering on the edge, she knew she needed only the slightest push to topple her over into oblivion. A moment later, the coach hit a rut, the shock bouncing both of them up, then down hard on the seat.

The motion drove him deeper still, the joyous friction shooting a climax through her that literally stole her breath. Pressing her face against his neck, she let herself shake, joy pumping like a drug in her veins, ecstasy leaving her floating as if buoyed atop a cloud.

Sliding his strong arms across her back, Ethan arched her slightly away and quickened his rhythm, plunging harder, deeper, faster. Then he was shaking too, his release long and satisfying for them both.

Collapsing against the seat, he cradled her in his embrace, stroking her back as he trailed his lips across the hot, flushed skin of her cheek. Long minutes elapsed before he lifted her up so she curled against him on the seat, his arm cradling her to his hip.

"If you want," he murmured, "there's probably still an hour of the party left. I could take you back."

"In this wrinkled gown? If I did return, I fear everyone would know what we've just been doing." Leaning up, she kissed him. "Let us go home to bed, Ethan. It's the only place I want to be."

\*      \*      \*

"Ooh, he's a pretty boy," Lily declared the following morning as she and Ethan strolled the stable yard at an estate not far from London. The former owner had recently passed away and his son—a lord known more for his love of gaming than of horses—was auctioning off the animals to the highest bidder.

Ethan sent her an indulgent glance. "That gelding may be 'pretty,' but I suspect he will not be well-suited as a carriage horse. I am given to understand there are a few teams available, including a pair of matched grays."

"That sounds promising, and I must admit that gray would go well with the sky-blue phaeton I am going to buy," she suggested, flashing him a wide smile.

A laugh burst from his lips. "Indeed it would, but as you well know, there is far more to a horse than his color. Once we ascertain the conformation and temperament of the available steeds, then we shall consider how well their color will match your new black curricle."

She swatted him on the shoulder as punishment for his continued teasing, a harmless blow that elicited yet another robust chuckle. Laughing still, Ethan captured her hand, tucked her gloved palm securely into the crook of his elbow, and led her forward.

Thirty minutes later, they'd narrowed their selection down to two teams: a pair of bay high-steppers with beautiful black points and the grays, their soft dappled coats as gentle as their spirits. Not wanting to broadcast interest in either team, and possibly drive up the price, she and Ethan were circumspect in their comments, whispering between themselves while taking care not to openly praise either set of animals.

They had moved on and were standing not far from a pair of jet-black geldings whose regal lines and bearing were drawing significant interest when a tall, aristocratic gentleman sauntered up.

"Hello there, and how goes the horse hunting?" The

Duke of Wyvern stopped and executed an elegant bow. "Vessey. Mrs. Smythe, a pleasure."

Lily gazed up at the duke, struck as always by the saturnine beauty of his countenance and the sex appeal that radiated off the man like an intoxicating cologne. Of course she preferred Ethan's golden good looks and tawny eyes, a mere glance from him having the power to send her heart careening in a crazy zigzag inside her breast. Nonetheless, that did not mean she wasn't capable of recognizing and appreciating another devastatingly handsome man when she saw him, even if her interest might be of an empirical nature.

She and the duke were virtual strangers in spite of having been introduced during the course of the Season. Nevertheless, she was aware that he and Ethan were close friends. Until today she had not given much thought to Ethan's associations. Now, as she found herself under the public scrutiny of the duke, she wondered what, if anything, Ethan might have revealed to the other man about her. Had he told the duke she was now his mistress? She stiffened slightly at the notion.

Obviously aware of her unease, Ethan laid his hand over her own to keep it in place on his arm. Moments later, though, she met Wyvern's gaze, relaxing when she found nothing more than warm cordiality in his smile.

"I assume you've narrowed the field to the bays and the dappled gray pair at the far end of the stalls," the duke remarked in a voice lowered so it would not carry.

"What makes you think that, Your Grace?" she asked, wondering if she and Ethan had unwittingly signaled their preferences, after all.

He quirked a raven brow. "They are the best of the lot, and Ethan knows a silk purse from a sow's ear when he sees it. None of the other teams are worth having, and pairing individual horses can be a precarious endeavor at best. Sometimes the grouping works and sometimes it does not. When it does not, your two horses can suddenly turn into an investment of three or four animals, and I doubt you are looking to lay out those sorts of funds, even if you could resell them later on."

She blinked, never having considered such a thing.

"Personally, I'd go with the grays if I were you, ma'am. A brother-and-sister team out of Pegasus, a horse of exceptional lineage," Wyvern volunteered. "Either pair would do, however."

A smile limned Ethan's mouth. "Lily has already expressed a preference for the grays. She says their color will complement her new carriage."

The duke grinned.

"They all seem like fine steeds, whatever their color," she defended. "I have yet to decide."

But they all knew she wanted the grays.

Had the duke noticed Ethan's use of her given name? she wondered. If he had, he offered no reaction. From the way Ethan was holding her hand cradled beneath his own, though, everyone seeing them had to suspect an intimate relationship.

*And if people did guess the truth?*

Then and there, Lily decided she would quit fretting over the matter. She had no wish to sneak around, trying to hide her liaison with Ethan. She wanted to be with him, and so she would be. Society considered her a widow, and as such would turn a blind eye to the affair, even if there might be an occasional whisper behind her back.

Word must already be spreading, she assumed, since he'd spent the night at her house again, staying to share breakfast with her this morning before leaving to attend the sale. The damage, as it were, was already done.

"And which horse has captured your eye, Your Grace?" she inquired.

"Oh, one or two." He said nothing more, obviously preferring not to reveal his hand. "Shall we adjourn to the auction block? I believe the bidding is about to commence."

Flanked on either side by the handsomest men at the auction—and likely in all of England—she strolled forward.

Two hours later, Lily was smiling from ear to ear, the team of matched grays now hers, bought at a price Ethan and Wyvern both agreed to be more than fair. The duke had bid on and won three horses, including one of the black geldings she'd been admiring earlier in the day, along with a pair of broodmares he believed would add greatly to his breeding program at Rosemeade's stable.

As for Ethan, he'd surprised her by bidding on the team of bays, jumping in at the end to take them for a fraction of their true value. After the auctioneer declared Ethan the winner, she tossed him an inquiring look, to which he shrugged.

"Seemed a shame to let good horses like those go to someone else," he remarked. "If you decide you prefer them to the grays, you have only to let me know."

His eyes met her own, his sensuous mouth sliding upward into an easy, intimate smile.

Warmth spread through her center, radiating outward like a glowing sun, her limbs turning soft. Leaning imperceptibly closer, she watched his amber irises heat with an expression she was beginning to know well, and despite being in public, she knew she would not have turned away his kiss. But he was a true gentleman, contenting himself with nothing more than a gentle squeeze of her hand.

Soon after, Wyvern excused himself, moving away to take care of his purchases.

Adopting a more leisurely pace, she and Ethan ambled arm in arm across the yard.

"If you've the energy," he commented, "shall we visit the carriage-maker and pick out that curricle for you?"

She narrowed her eyes, enjoying their game. "Yes indeed. Let us go choose my new *phaeton*."

"Good. Then afterward you can give me a ride."

"But surely the carriage won't be ready so quickly."

"I wasn't talking about that kind of ride."

Her eyes widened. "Ethan!"

A hearty laugh burst from his mouth.

"Has anyone ever told you, Lily, that you are a prize?"

The glow spread again inside her belly. Pulse jittering, she tamped down her sudden anticipation, realizing the days ahead with Ethan were going to be unlike any she'd ever known.

With a new smile on her lips, she let him lead her forward.

# Chapter Fifteen

❦

THREE MONTHS LATER, Ethan sat at his desk in Andarton House, dark ink flowing as he drew his quill pen in a hasty scrawl across the paper in front of him. Finishing one letter, he sanded the missive and handed it to the young man who served as his secretary. Efficient and well educated, Cooksey sealed the paper with wax, then applied the address and the Vessey frank, leaving Ethan free to move on to the next piece of business correspondence.

Eager to be done, Ethan was rushing through his work, anxious to finish the duties and demands required by his title so he could return to the pleasure of being with Lily.

Without quite realizing when or how, the pair of them had drifted into a comfortable routine ever since they had become lovers. At first, he'd tried to restrict himself to spending a few hours of the evening in her company, acting as her escort to a ball or dinner party where they would usually separate for a time so as not to invite too much comment. Afterward, he would take her home, often accompanying her inside and upstairs to her bedchamber. Later, he would force himself to leave, making the journey to his townhouse in the early hours of the morning when no one but weary lamplighters and the occasional overeager milkmaid was about.

But as July came to an end, so too did the Season, most of Society leaving the heat of the city behind to retreat to the comfort of their country estates. And once Parliament recessed in early August, even more of the Ton withdrew, London growing thin of aristocratic company.

Even Rafe and Julianna, who spent a great deal of their year in the city, removed the knocker from their door, packed up their servants and little Cam, and made the journey to West Riding, where they would spend the rest of the fall. Rafe had told him they might even remain in the north through the spring since Julianna's confinement was drawing near, the baby now due in little more than a month.

As for Tony, he often traveled to and from Rosemeade—the three-hour trip to Town an easy one. But although Tony made an occasional appearance in London, Ethan didn't expect to see much of him, the duke having already accepted two separate invitations to country-house parties with other friends.

Ethan had been invited as well, but had refused, preferring to stay in the city so he could continue seeing Lily. She'd been given the opportunity to depart as well, Davina Coates asking her to spend the rest of the summer in Middlesex. Lily had declined, however, waving good-bye to her friend several weeks ago.

With the city quiet, he and Lily had taken to spending more and more time together until he rarely left her side. Today, in fact, was the first time in a week he'd been to Andarton House, returning to collect a fresh supply of clothing and toiletries, and to see to several pressing matters of business—such as the stack of correspondence he was currently answering.

His steward, with whom he would normally have met at Andarley weeks ago, had written for instructions on everything from the purchase of new bed linens for the servants to his agreement to plant a new variety of winter wheat in the northwest fields. Moving rapidly through all the queries, Ethan finished his reply, sanded the paper, and once again passed it to his secretary to prepare for the post.

Soon after, the younger man stood and began a concise recitation of each remaining letter, making notes of Ethan's answers so he could compose appropriate responses. Ethan swallowed a sigh, knowing that he would have to return again soon to sign all the letters drafted by his secretary.

He tried not to give much thought to the fact that never in his life had he wanted to spend so much of his time with a woman. Certainly, he'd never before stayed in Town through the summer for one of his mistresses. Though Lily was far more than a mistress; she was also his friend.

Honestly, he'd expected the fire between them to have burned out long ago, roaring hot and quick before dying a natural death. But as the weeks passed, his desire for her had only deepened.

Amazing as it might seem, he hungered for her more now than he had when he'd first been pursuing her, making love to her with a pleasured intensity he hadn't imagined possible. As far as he could tell, she seemed to feel the same, trembling with delight in his arms and smiling dreamily afterward.

Beyond physical desire, though, was the simple enjoyment of being with her—a fact that should probably alarm him, but strangely enough did not. In bed and out, she never failed to charm him, her smile alone enough to brighten even the gloomiest of days.

He still remembered weeks ago when her cerulean-blue phaeton arrived. Exuberant as a child on Christmas morning, she'd pulled him out to share her first ride, seemingly oblivious to the eye-popping sight they must have made with her perched high in the driver's seat, him at her side, while she drove them around the city.

The outing had created a minor scandal of sorts, the tale repeated in tones laced with equal shares amusement and admiration. There were many men incapable of handling such a precarious equipage; for a woman to do so, well, that was truly outstanding. But more than her accomplishment was the way she handled herself, her manner displaying an easy grace and style that set her apart from all the rest. He'd been proud of her, as he continued to be, content to let her shine and to revel in her reflected light. In his whole life, he'd never known another woman like Lily. Thinking again of her now, he knew he never would.

Returning from his mental wanderings, he noticed his secretary waiting, his pen at the ready in case Ethan had any further commands to relay.

"I believe that will conclude our business for today, Cooksey," he stated, "unless there is something else that requires my immediate attention."

The younger man laid down his pen. "No, my lord, nothing urgent. The afternoon post just arrived." He stood and handed Ethan a letter. "I took the liberty of glancing through the rest, mostly business correspondence and bills, but this one appears to be a letter from the dowager marchioness."

Shifting his gaze, Ethan stared at the cream-colored vellum bearing the Vessey crest, his London address written clearly in his mother's pale, flowery hand. After a long moment, he reached out to accept the missive.

Cooksey returned to his desk.

*So Mama has written, has she?* Ethan mused. *No doubt she is wondering why I am not at Andarley, or at least attending some house party in the countryside.*

He'd had a similar letter from her previously. At the time, he'd penned a brief note, informing her that he had decided to remain in Town for a few weeks.

That had been a few weeks ago.

He supposed he ought to write her again and let her know he would be remaining in London for the remainder of the fall. As for winter, well, he guessed he would have to go home for Christmas. As head of the family, his presence was expected for the holiday.

A frown settled over his forehead, the idea of leaving London, leaving Lily, causing an uncomfortable knot to form in his chest. *Perhaps I could invite her? And introduce her as what? My friend?* Only family came to Andarley for Christmas, and Lily was not family.

*She would be if she were my wife.*

He paused at the thought, then just as quickly brushed the notion aside like a pesky speck of lint. Lily had already made her wishes clear on that subject, and she had given no indication since that she might have changed her mind. Besides, they were only having fun, enjoying themselves until the passionate spell they were under finally dissolved, as such whims were sure to do.

By next month, he and Lily might be heartily sick of each other. By November, they would probably be bored and mutually eager to part ways, leaving him free to journey home for Christmas, their affair nothing more than a pleasant interlude whose memory would grow more distant by the day.

A frown collected on his brow, his hand curling into a fist on his desk. Forcing himself to be calm, he steadied his emotions. His suppositions were exactly that, possibilities that might or might not occur. For now, Lily was his, and so she would remain until the day he no longer wanted her in his life.

As for what to tell his mother . . . he would say that

he planned to stay in London a while longer. After all, he was no more obligated to discuss the reasons for his behavior with his mother than he was required to share the specifics of his sex life with her.

Thinking of his sex life made him think of Lily and the fact that he'd been here at Andarton House since early this morning. Eager to be back in her company, he set the letter aside. He would read his mother's missive later.

Shoving back his chair, he got to his feet. "Well, if we are done, then I'm off. I shall see you in a couple of days."

If his secretary had any opinion about his employer's recent absences from home, or where Ethan was spending his nights, he gave no indication. "Good day, my lord. I will have today's correspondence ready for your review upon your return."

With a nod, Ethan strode through the door.

The actors' voices boomed on the stage two nights later, their recitation of *A Midsummer Night's Dream* carrying clearly through the theater, even upward to the private boxes set aloft.

As Pan quipped and cavorted in his impish garb, Lily shifted her attention away from the action unfolding below to gaze at the man seated at her side. Possessed of his own special kind of magic that more than rivaled that of the characters on stage, Ethan held himself with elegant aplomb. His golden hair glinted even in the low light of the darkened theater, the angles and planes of his chiseled features so magnificent they literally stole her breath.

As if aware of her scrutiny, he shifted his gaze and caught her looking. Eyes twinkling, his lips turned upward in a slow, easy smile, an intimate, exclusive smile he shared only with her. The blood in her veins rushed faster, her body tingling with a familiar pleasurable hum that flowed to the ends of her fingers and tips of her toes. Had she and Ethan not been in full public view, she knew he would have kissed her. Or else she would have kissed him.

Since coming to his bed, she had blossomed under his expert tutelage, no longer reticent about expressing her physical desires, whatever those needs and wants might be. He'd told her once that there should be no secrets between lovers, and when she was inside his arms there were none, every touch honestly given and joyously received. He'd taught her that when it came to making love, nothing should be forbidden, not if the act brought both parties pleasure. And in his embrace, she had discovered she always found pleasure. Lately, he didn't even have to touch her to evoke a response—a mere glance enough to leave her aching for his possession.

He worked his spell upon her now, lowering his gaze to trace her lips in a way that made her mouth throb as if he really had kissed her.

Then he returned his attention to the stage, watching and listening to the actors as they danced and pranced and made amusing fools of themselves. The audience laughed. Ethan chuckled, enjoying whatever jest had just been told.

Knowing she ought to be watching the play as well, she fixed her gaze upon the players. Less than a minute later, though, her interest had turned once again to Ethan. Needing his touch, even a simple one, she laid her hand over his where it rested on his thigh.

Without shifting his eyes from the play, he turned his hand over and linked his fingers with hers, cradling her palm inside his own in a snug yet infinitely tender clasp.

She relaxed, secure in the embrace.

*I should not feel this way,* she thought. *I should not like being with him so much, but heavens, I do. In my entire life, I have never before been so content . . . and yes, I might as well admit it—so happy.*

Months ago when they had begun their affair, she hadn't expected their liaison to last more than a few weeks at most. He was a man of experience, and she was by no means the first woman to share his bed. She'd assumed he would grow weary of her, and she of him.

But that had not happened. Quite the opposite, in fact. Instead of familiarity breeding contempt, their time together had only drawn them closer; the more they learned about each other, the more they found to like. At least, that was how she felt.

Her favorite time of day was morning, when she would awaken to find his arms around her, both of them warm and cozy beneath the sheets. Later, she would lie on her stomach in bed and watch him shave, adoring the masculine ritual as he scraped the overnight whiskers from his cheeks with a confident skill she found amazing.

During the past couple of weeks, they had taken to having breakfast together, talking over plates of eggs and toast like an old married couple. Only they were not wed, and not likely to be.

*How long will this last?* she wondered. *How long do I want it to last?*

A little voice whispered *forever,* but ruthlessly she pushed it aside.

*I do not love him. I will not let myself.*

Her mother had loved her father, and look where the emotion had led her. Not that Ethan was anything like her father. For one thing, she had glimpsed in his behavior no tendencies toward an insatiable lust to wander. *As for insatiable lust . . . well, I cannot complain of that,* she mused with a little inner smile. Nonetheless, Ethan and her father were both men, and men, in general, had a habit of disappointing women. Lily did not wish to be disappointed, nor had she any desire to be left with a broken heart.

If she had any sense, she would break things off between them. Already, she was pushing the boundaries of common sense, continually risking the possibility of finding herself with child. Not long after losing her virginity, she'd worried about the ramifications of the act. When her monthly had arrived on time, she knew she had been lucky. Of course that hadn't stopped her from letting Ethan seduce her again, nor kept her from agreeing to become his lover. Afterward, however, she had known she must take precautions.

She had considered going to Davina to ask for advice, but couldn't imagine discussing such an intimate topic, not even with her friend. Next, she'd thought of Julianna, but quickly discarded the idea, feeling uneasy at the idea of discussing contraceptive options with a pregnant woman, especially since Ethan was a Pendragon family friend.

In the end she'd decided to go to the source, so to speak, and broach the matter with Ethan. After all, he was the one who might get her with child, so it seemed only reasonable he should be involved in keeping her from doing so.

He'd taken in her blushing query with calm composure, apologizing for not bringing up the issue himself. French letters, he said, were mostly useless since, as the saying went, they were nothing more than a barrier to pleasure and a cobweb against pregnancy. As for early withdrawal, he knew of two fellows who claimed to have practiced the method religiously and ended up begetting more than one unplanned child. An herbal preventative would be best, he decided, along with a bit of caution between them on certain days of the month.

Two afternoons later, he arrived with the promised remedy—a bitter tincture that was to be taken every morning without fail. Brewed by an elderly woman with a knowledge of ancient herbal draughts and potions, the concoction was purported to be all but foolproof.

So far, the claim had proven true.

Nevertheless, Lily's affair with Ethan was a risk, and not just because of pregnancy. Although they continued the pretense of maintaining separate lives, in reality Ethan was practically living with her. He stopped at Andarton House only to deal with business concerns, tending to ignore his clubs in favor of spending his evenings with her. He claimed company was sparse these days at Brooks's and White's, but she knew he preferred being with her.

This week alone they had attended the opera and a lecture on ornithology he thought she would enjoy, and tonight they were here at the theater.

She had loved them all, but she loved even more knowing that she and Ethan would be going home afterward, where they would spend the night in each other's arms whether they decided to make love or not.

Seated beside him now with her hand tucked comfortably inside his, she wondered again what it was she thought she was doing.

*Falling in love?*

And that was what terrified her the most, the very real possibility that she might lose her heart to him. If she were truthful, she was halfway there already.

*But I shall not fall all the way,* she assured herself. *Ethan and I are only having a bit of fun with each other, a few weeks' delight before the interlude ends.*

And when the affair was over?

Air left her lungs as though she'd taken a little punch to the chest, a small, involuntary gasp escaping her lips.

Ethan turned to her and lifted an inquiring brow. "Is everything all right?" he whispered.

Meeting his gaze, she forced herself to smile. "Everything is wonderful."

*And it is,* she thought, *at least for now.*

# Chapter Sixteen

❦ ❧

OUTSIDE LILY'S BREAKFAST-ROOM window, a pair of rust-colored fall leaves raced each other through the clear, cold mid-October sky. Focused on his morning meal, Ethan paid no mind to which leaf landed first as he bit into a triangle of crisp, golden toast smeared with strawberry preserves. Across from him at the dining table, Lily broke the red wax seal on a letter that had been delivered only moments ago.

"Oh, what happy news!" she declared. "Rafe writes to say that Julianna has had the baby, a girl, just as she had hoped." She paused for a moment, a smile forming on her pretty lips. "The delivery went smoothly, much easier than the first, and both baby and mother are in fine health."

"That *is* wonderful," Ethan agreed, taking up his knife and fork to cut a piece of the ham on his plate. "So what have they named her?"

She shook her head. "Nothing as of yet, it would seem. They are still deciding and have narrowed the choices down to three."

"Well, so long as it is not Harriet, I shall have no complaint." Underneath the table, Mouser rubbed against his trouser leg. Glancing down, Ethan met a pair of eager green feline eyes, the animal's small, brick-pink nose and black whiskers twitching at the enticing aromas of ham and bacon. Cutting a tiny wedge of ham, Ethan dropped the meat onto the carpet and was quickly rewarded with a series of loud purrs.

"What in the world is wrong with Harriet?" Lily questioned, setting the letter next to her plate.

"Harriet is the name of a cousin who used to torment me as a child," he explained. "Every time she paid a visit she would force me to wear some ridiculous cap she had embroidered. One year she stitched May flowers on the thing." He rolled his eyes. "I ask you, is that any sort of present for an eight-year-old boy? The only saving grace was the fact that my brothers had to wear caps of their own."

A slow grin appeared as he remembered. "Arthur, in particular, hated it, since he said the hats ruined his dignity as the heir. Mother would never hear a word of argument though, making him, and the rest of us, wear those accursed caps so as not to abuse Cousin Harriet's tender feelings. What about our tender feelings? Personally I think she sewed the blasted things just to watch us squirm."

"I am sure she did not," Lily countered with a chuckle in her voice. "She likely spent a vast amount of time making the caps and was prodigiously proud of her efforts. My guess is she would have been devastated to think you did not like them."

"Oh, she knew. The old harridan enjoyed watching us suffer," he finished, only half-teasing in his analysis.

Lily raised her teacup to her mouth and covered a smile.

A beseeching meow floated upward. After a slight pause, Ethan cut another smidgen of ham. Lily shot him a reproachful look. "You are only spoiling him, you know. If you keep that up, he'll stop hunting mice altogether."

"And give up his favorite sport? Never. But you are right, Mouser is rather overindulged."

When she reached for the honey pot, Ethan used the distraction to slip the cat one last bite. Glancing up, he caught Lily watching.

She shook her head, but made no comment about the infraction. "You know, I should love to have seen one of those caps."

Ethan cut the last of his ham in two and ate half. "Surprisingly enough you probably still can. I believe Mama has kept everything we children ever owned or wore. When Arthur and Frederick died, she had all their belongings stored, though for what possible purpose I do not know. A waste, if you ask me."

Reaching out, she covered his hand with her own and gave a comforting squeeze. "You miss them a great deal."

Her words were a statement and a sympathy shared. Why should they not be, since she understood the pain and emptiness of loss? Growing still, he laid his fork aside. "They were my brothers. Of course I miss them. Just as you miss your parents and your husband."

Her lashes swept down, a tiny frown marring the smooth line of her brow. "Of course."

Drawing her hand away, she paused for a moment before reapplying herself to her breakfast, nibbling on a small bite of bacon and a forkful of scrambled eggs that must surely have gone cold by now.

Following suit, he ate the rest of his preserve-laden toast and waited while he chewed to see if she would make any further comment.

She ate in near silence, flashing him a little half-smile before she reached out and lifted the teapot. Taking care, she refilled both of their cups.

"You never talk about him," he said, voicing aloud

the thought that had been prodding him like a sore tooth over the last few weeks.

The teapot wavered in her hand before she placed the china safely inside its cozy. "Who?"

"Your husband. If you think I mind you discussing him, you need not worry. I understand that he was a part of your life, just as my brothers were a part of mine. You may speak of him without fear of discomfiting me."

Her gaze lowered toward the tablecloth. At length, she picked up her teacup and took a long, contemplative swallow before setting the china onto its matching saucer with a faint tap.

He tried to read her expression but could not, her features composed and uncharacteristically enigmatic.

"Thank you, Ethan," she murmured, "that is most kind of you."

He waited to see if she might open up at last, but she ate another bite of toast instead, then patted her napkin to her lips.

A footman entered the room a minute later and at Lily's signal, began to clear.

Ethan considered questioning her further, suddenly needing to understand more about this man who figured so prominently in her life. Until recently, he'd been largely content to live without much discussion about either of their pasts, and yet the specter of her dead husband lay between them, the memory of him unspoken yet present nonetheless.

He was familiar with the man's name—John Smythe—and was aware Smythe had been an infantry officer who had lost his life in service to his country during the Battle of Vittoria. Beyond that, Ethan knew virtually nothing about his ghostly rival, not what he'd looked like, how tall he'd been, where he'd been raised, his likes and dislikes, nor how he'd come to meet and marry Lily.

He assumed she had loved the man and yet she never mentioned him, not even by so much as a casual reference. Why?

Was it because those days with John Smythe had been so brief and fleeting, their details already beginning to grow dim and fade? Or was it because the pain of his loss was still too sharp to be borne, buried too deep to be brought forth without cracking the barrier she wore around herself like a snug-fitting cloak?

And she did keep a barrier between them—a thin, nearly transparent wall, like a piece of glass through which he could see but not touch. She might give him her body, but her mind and innermost emotions remained her own. Perhaps it was selfish of him, but he wanted more. Wanted her. All of her.

Mind, body, and soul.

*What is she hiding, and why will she not tell me?*

If shaking her would have done the trick, he might have tried the maneuver. But Lily was the most independent-minded female he'd ever encountered, and nothing would force her to reveal things she did not wish to share. So he would have to employ alternate means. What those were, he would need to ponder.

For now, he wanted her thoughts off John Smythe and focused on him.

The footman departed, along with Mouser, who followed the man out on a quick dash, in hopes no doubt of being invited to share a dish of interesting morsels in the kitchen.

As soon as they had gone, Lily stood. He knew that she was planning to do a bit of shopping this noontime and would therefore need to change from her morning gown into a day dress before leaving the house.

She was about to excuse herself when Ethan pushed back his chair and reached forward, curling his fingers gently around her wrist. "Come here," he murmured.

"Ethan," she exclaimed. "What are you doing?"

He grinned and tugged her forward, tumbling her across his lap. "I just want a kiss."

"Is that all you want?" She gave him a smile that was as much a tease as it was a scold, then leaned close to press a quick peck to his lips. "There. You've been kissed."

He locked his arms around her back. "That was no kiss. You will have to do better."

"Will I indeed?"

"Hmm, quite definitely. Kiss me, and don't stint on the tongue."

Her eyes flashed wide, then she laughed. "You are wicked."

"And you love it."

She snuggled against him, casting a glance toward the door. "What about the servants? Someone might come in."

"If they do, they'll leave again soon enough. I think by now your staff has an idea that the two of us kiss. Now quit talking and get to it." With the flat of his hand, he gave her a light swat on the behind.

She inhaled on a sharp breath, then relaxed and sidled closer, locking her arms around his neck. A moment later, her mouth met his own, plundering in a way that turned his body hard and ready.

Closing his eyes, he gave himself over to the pleasure, her lips as savory and intoxicating as wine. Plying her nimble tongue to devastating effect, she more than satisfied his earlier command, his blood flowing like a swift, fierce current inside his veins.

At length he pulled back, senses on fire. Meeting her gaze, he noted the dreamy glaze of desire shimmering in her emerald eyes, the delicate smile riding her rosy mouth, her cheeks brushed with a similar heightened hue.

He considered taking her right there, and was of half a mind to do so in spite of their location, when she leaned close and skimmed her mouth over his cheek, pressing a kiss behind his ear.

A blissful shiver radiated along his spine.

"Take me to our bed, Ethan," she whispered. "Love me where we can be alone."

At her words, something shifted in the vicinity of his heart, a sensation that had nothing at all to do with passion. *Love her?* The question elicited equal parts anxiety and elation.

*Do I love Lily?*

In that moment, he realized he could love her if he let himself, with a fierceness he feared would either lift him to impossible heights or send him crashing into black despair.

*And if she does not—or worse, cannot—love me?*

He would think of neither possibility for now, he warned himself, shaking off the thoughts. What he and Lily shared was good, almost too good. Why sully the waters with troublesome quandaries and questions?

*Enjoy the now. Relish having her here in my arms, asking to be taken to her bed—our bed.*

"Yes," he said, placing her onto her feet. "Let's go where we shall be alone, just us two."

With his arm around her waist, they walked out of the room.

Ethan dipped his head to keep from hitting the lintel as he strode through a London tavern's low entrance two days later. Pausing on the threshold, he scanned the array of diners—common clerks and government officials who were congregated to enjoy their afternoon nuncheon break before returning to their duties.

The room was dim, illuminated only by the sunlight streaming through the vinegar-streaked windowpanes in a way that created alternating pools of shadow and sunshine. Scanning a bit farther, he located the object of his search, a sandy-haired man not much older than himself. Tucked into a far corner, the slim fellow sat at a small, wooden dining table, a leather-bound book open near his elbow. Ethan watched as his old friend ate a bite of what appeared to be a meat pie before turning a page and continuing to read.

On silent shoes, Ethan slid into the chair opposite. "You are not an easy man to find, do you know that?"

The sandy-haired man startled and glanced up. With a small thunk, he laid his fork onto his pewter plate. "Blue blazes, Vessey, you shouldn't sneak up on a fellow like that, especially not when he's eating. I'll probably go home with dyspepsia tonight because of you."

"Hallo to you too, Ross. And if you have indigestion this evening, blame it on the beef pie and that tankard of ale you are consuming."

"Pigeon pie," Ross corrected, "and I always said you should have let me put you into service as a reconnaissance man during the war. A waste of those quiet, catlike skills, if you ask me."

"I performed a few interesting tasks over the years as I recall, without the necessity of joining up. As you well know, I had the title and couldn't risk shaking hands with the sharp side of a bayonet or a shiv. My mother had lost two sons already; she didn't need to worry about losing a third."

Ross waved a hand and ate a forkful of pie. "True, true." Lifting his tankard, he drank deeply, then set it down, lifting a napkin to wipe his lips dry. "Well then, what brings you to this side of Whitehall? For that matter, what are you doing in London at all? Shouldn't you be off hunting pheasants or some such by now?"

"I could say the same of you, but I suppose Foreign Office business takes precedence."

"Indeed it does. So, what do you want?" Ross leaned his chair back against a worn spot on the tavern wall.

"Do I have to want something?" Ethan asked in feigned innocence.

Ross released a guffaw. "If you did not, you'd have sent a note 'round inviting me to dinner. Let's have it."

Smiling, Ethan leaned forward. "There's a man, an army officer, about whom I'd like some information. I was hoping you could help."

"Why don't you just go to Regimental Headquarters and ask yourself?"

"The man in question is dead. I figured you would have easier access to his records." Ethan rubbed a thumb over one of the gold buttons on his waistcoat. "Plus, it is a matter of personal interest that I would rather keep private. You are a man I know I can trust."

"Buttering me up now, are you?"

"Yes, if you require the greasing."

A deep-throated laugh burst from Ross's mouth as he tipped his chair forward. "Doesn't sound like a terribly difficult assignment; I shall see what I can do." Reaching inside his coat, he withdrew a thin silver case containing paper and a small pencil. "So what is the fellow's name?"

"John Smythe," Ethan said, reciting the proper spelling so there would be no mistakes.

"Rank?"

Ethan frowned, realizing he didn't know. "I am not certain, lieutenant or captain would be my guess."

"Regiment?"

"He was in the infantry, killed in the Battle of Vittoria. Beyond that, I do not know. His widow comes from Cornwall, so perhaps the 32nd Foot, though it is entirely possible he purchased a commission wherever one was available."

Ross paused in his note-taking, an intrigued gleam in

his gray eyes. "I understand you have taken up with a rather comely young widow of late. She wouldn't have been this fellow's wife, now, would she?"

"Just find out what you can with my thanks." Ethan extended a palm.

Ross accepted and the two men shook hands.

"Well, I shall leave you to your book and your meal," Ethan said, rising to his feet. "And we will have to meet for that dinner you mentioned one of these evenings."

"I look forward to the occasion."

With a nod, Ethan turned his back and made his way out into the street and the midafternoon crowd.

# Chapter Seventeen

❧❧❧

LILY WAS SMILING several days later as she and Ethan strolled arm in arm through the throng gathered for a fair being held a few miles north of London. As if a small city had sprung full-grown from the earth, scores of farmers, tradesmen, and vendors lined the makeshift lanes to offer their wares, while musicians played, jugglers and mimes amused, and barkers called out in an effort to entice the curious and unwary alike. The enlivening scents of herbs and apples clashed with the heavy aromas of sizzling meat, yeasty ale, and quite a number of unwashed bodies. For Lily, the panoply was all part of the excitement and vitality of the event.

Knowing herself safe in Ethan's care, she paid scant heed to the clusters of half-drunken men they passed, nor did she notice the occasional hard-eyed ruffian who slithered through the crowd in hopes of liberating coins and watches from their unsuspecting owners. She knew Ethan would do an excellent job of avoiding any unsavory types.

"Have a comfit," she suggested, extending the small brown paper sack of sugared almonds Ethan had purchased for her. "They are utterly delicious."

"They must be," he teased, "considering the number of them that you have already consumed."

"If you are going to make comments like that, I may

decide not to share, after all," she replied in feigned affront.

With a wink of apology, he dug a hand into the sack and popped a couple in his mouth. "They are quite tasty," he agreed, reaching again for the sack.

Playfully, she held it away. "Say please. Otherwise they are all mine."

"Going to make me beg, are you?" He met her gaze. "Very well, then. *Please,* may I have some more?"

She blinked, a bit surprised at his easy acquiescence. "Of course, since you asked so nicely."

Instead of reaching inside the sack, however, he slid his arm around her waist and pressed her close against his hip, his mouth lowering to her ear. "You realize I shall now require you to return the favor."

"What do you mean?" she murmured.

"Only that I will have to make sure you beg a boon from me," he stated on a husky growl. "Perhaps I shall do so tonight. In bed, I believe. It shall be my very great pleasure to keep you teetering on the edge of desire until you are literally pleading with me to satisfy you. I can hear you now, crying out—*please, Ethan, please!*"

A hot fist curled low in her belly, warmth spreading through her that had nothing to do with the sun, infusing her cheeks with betraying color. "You wouldn't."

He sent her another wink, a naughty one this time, that promised he would be doing exactly as he'd said.

Her mouth grew dry and her body moist at the idea.

Laughing, he removed his hand from her waist and linked their arms together again. Reaching into her bag of comfits, he drew out a fresh helping, then urged her to continue their leisurely stroll among the revelers.

As they walked, Lily fought to restore her composure, peeking upward through her eyelashes to find Ethan calmly eating his sugared almonds as though he hadn't just been whispering lustful suggestions in her ear. Her equanimity, and her pulse rate, had finally calmed by the time she and Ethan stopped to watch one of the animal acts.

A trio of small dogs wearing orange-and-red-checkered harlequin hats and tiny matching capes danced on their hind feet, spinning slowly as they barked and jumped to the enthusiastic commands of their owner. She and Ethan laughed and clapped along with the crowd, delighted by their antics. Next came a quartet of cats, each of whom could walk across a tightrope and leap through suspended rings of fire. Cheers rang out when the act concluded, Ethan tossing several coins into the performer's cap.

Afterward, she and Ethan wandered the grounds, stopping to buy warm beef pasties and cups of cool cider. Once their meal was finished, they took seats on one of the wooden benches set up in front of the acting troupe's tent, and settled in to watch an exaggerated yet lively comedic farce that made some rather pointed jests at the church and government, including a few at the Prince Regent himself. Ethan, she noticed, took no offense, laughing at a number of the jokes, which she had to confess were very amusing.

The tableau was nearing its end when a sudden flash of light caught her eye, the glint like that of metal reflecting off the sun. Glancing over, she noticed a man standing in front of a nearby vendor's cart, his back turned toward her. Thick-necked and stocky, he had the build of a bull, his ill-trimmed black hair crushed under a beaver hat, the cut of his clothing marking him as a member of the gentry.

A shiver chased under her skin, something about him seeming familiar. He reminded her of . . . Edgar Faylor.

Abruptly, her mouth grew dry, her heart pounding so hard she could hear the quick beats echoing between her ears. Surely it was not him. Surely the man she saw was not Faylor, but another who shared no more than a faint resemblance to the crude brute her stepfather had once wanted her to marry.

Shrinking down in her seat, she huddled closer to Ethan, closing her eyes as she tried to take comfort from his reassuring warmth and strength, her body suddenly gone cold.

*He is not Faylor,* she assured herself. *The real Faylor is hundreds of miles away in Cornwall, not here at this impromptu fair on the outskirts of London. It is not him. Oh God, please let it not be him.*

Long seconds passed before she could gather the courage to look again. Slowly, careful to keep as much of her face shielded by her bonnet brim as possible, she finally forced herself to look. And saw only the vendor's cart.

The thick-set man was gone.

Hurriedly she glanced through the nearby crowd, searching for him, but there was no one even remotely similar. Whoever he was, it was as though the man had vanished.

*Perhaps I only imagined the man looked like the squire,* she thought. Regardless, at least he had not turned, had not seen her. She was still safe.

Turning back, her gaze collided with Ethan's, his eyes filled with concern. "Lily, what is wrong? Your cheeks are pale as powder."

"I am f-fine. I—"

She wanted to tell him, but she could not. To reveal her concern over Edgar Faylor would be to reveal everything—all her secrets, all her lies. How would Ethan react if he knew the truth?

He clasped her hands, chaffing them. "Your fingers are like ice. You aren't coming down ill, are you?"

Knowing she needed some explanation for her behavior, she seized on the excuse. "I am sorry, but I think perhaps I am. I believe I would like to go home now."

"Of course. We'll leave immediately. Are you all right to walk?"

*Goodness,* she thought, realizing he would carry her if she wished. Her heart turned over in her breast, warmth bursting at his kindness, his caring. Another emotion shifted inside her as well, one she knew she dare not acknowledge.

"I can walk," she murmured. "Let us go, Ethan. Take me home."

Lily's "illness" did not last long—a warm bath, a light meal, and a night spent wrapped inside the protective comfort of Ethan's embrace doing a great deal to drive away the worst of her fears.

By breakfast the following morning, she had convinced herself she must have been mistaken about the man's identity. He had resembled Faylor, true, but nothing more than that. There must be any number of stocky, dark-haired, bull-necked men in England, she argued to herself; Faylor was but one. She had jumped to conclusions, she decided, and let her anxiety overrule her good sense. The man at the fair had been no more than a stranger, and she would do well to put the incident out of her mind.

For the remainder of the day she did exactly that, allowing Ethan, who was still concerned that she might be coming down with a cold, to cosset her. At his suggestion, she agreed to stay at home and relax on the sofa for the day. When she refused to take a midday nap, he produced a deck of cards and the pair of them indulged in a lively game of piquet. She won, though she suspected Ethan might have let her take a few extra points here and there.

He stayed to share an early dinner of roast chicken,

buttered parsnips, and tender, golden-orange carrots. Cook fixed a toothsome apple cobbler for dessert, which was served with an utterly decadent brandied whipped cream.

Afterward, they retired to her sitting room, where they settled together into a wide, cozy chair in front of the fireplace. Having already chosen a book, Ethan read to her, his deep, melodious voice lulling her into a state of drowsy relaxation.

She was drifting, her eyes half-closed, when he set the book aside and carried her to bed. He stripped her, then himself, toasty as a stove as he climbed in next to her, and tucked them both inside the sheets.

Her eyes opened hours later to find the bedchamber swathed in darkness, a last few embers glowing red in the fireplace. She turned and snuggled closer against Ethan, adoring the sensation of his naked flesh sliding against her own. Breathing in his clean, musky scent, she rubbed her cheek against his chest, then laid her lips on the spot, kissing his shoulder before moving upward to drop lazy kisses against his collarbone, neck, and the whisker-rough skin of his cheek.

He came awake moments later, his palm sliding reflexively over her bare back. "Hmm," he murmured, "are you feeling all right? Why are you awake?"

"I don't know. I just awakened. As to the other, I'm feeling lovely." *More than lovely,* she thought, brushing her mouth over his jaw. She sensed the passion rise in him, as it had already risen inside her.

Threading his fingers into her hair, he cupped her head and captured her mouth in a claiming that was warm and slow and tantalizingly delicious. A hum of pleasure sighed from her lips, followed by a whimper when he drew slightly away.

"No headache?" he asked, massaging her scalp where his hand still cradled her head.

"None," she said, her answer as light as a whisper.

"No sniffles?"

She smiled and waggled her head from side to side. "Not even a sniff."

"Well then, if you are recovered . . ."

Reaching down, he caught her hips in his strong palms and gently lifted her on top of him. Without preliminaries, he parted her legs so they fell naturally around his waist; then, with a supple glide, he slid inside her.

She bit her lip at the splendid fullness, her body growing instantly wet and ready for his possession. But he kept their lovemaking unhurried, taking her with a tenderness that was a rapture in itself. She didn't even know her peak was near until the climax came upon her, joy exploding, then spreading outward—hot and sweet as honey, her limbs turning waxen and weak.

On a quavering sigh, she held him close, rocking with him until he found his own ease. His gasp of pleasure made her smile, his obvious exultation a balm to her ears. Lying bonelessly against him, she knew there was no place she would rather be than inside his arms. No other man with whom she wanted to be. Not now. Not ever.

Love burst inside her heart—a love she should not feel, a love she did not want, and yet could no longer deny. Closing her eyes, she burrowed against him, tucking her face into the warm, resilient curve of his neck.

"What is it?" he murmured after a long moment.

Words tumbled into her mouth but stuck there, her tongue unable, or perhaps unwilling, to say aloud what she had only just discovered.

*I love you,* she thought. *And I do not know what to do.*

Shaking her head, she remained silent, kissing his neck and cheek before once again lying still.

"Sleep," he said, running his hand over her hair in long, soothing strokes.

Giving in to his command, she did exactly that.

Ethan strode into Andarton House the following afternoon, planning to meet with his secretary and deal with several matters of business. Once all essential items were resolved, he intended to go upstairs to his rooms and change into suitable evening attire, since he and Lily would be attending the opera tonight.

Lily had been unusually quiet over breakfast this morning, enough so that he had suggested they cancel and remain at home again. But her smile and reassurances had soon persuaded him otherwise.

"I will not hear of missing tonight's performance," she'd said, sending him an even brighter smile than her first.

Still, he wondered at her mercurial mood. Something untoward had happened at the fair, though he couldn't for the life of him imagine what that something might be considering she had never left his side.

At first, he'd assumed she was coming down ill. Later, though, he began to wonder if her reaction might stem from some other cause. A few times yesterday he'd gently tried to probe for answers, but she'd brushed his efforts aside. Deciding she needed rest more than a confrontation, he let the matter drop. Perhaps she was only a bit under the weather as he had originally assumed, and he was just imagining trouble where none actually existed.

Now, after greeting White, his butler, he handed his hat and greatcoat to the other man, then started across the marble foyer toward the hallway that led to his office. He'd only taken a few steps when the older man spoke, stopping him in his tracks.

"My lord," White called. "If I might have an additional word, I thought I should mention that the dowager marchioness is in residence."

Ethan swung around. "My mother is here? How long ago did she arrive?"

"Two evenings since, my lord. We had expected you yesterday, which is why I sent no note."

As Ethan recalled, he had mentioned stopping by the house yesterday, but when Lily came down ill he had changed his mind.

"Not to worry, White. Where is she now?"

"*She* is in the drawing room," replied a quiet, well-modulated feminine voice from the second-story hallway.

Turning, Ethan tipped back his head and looked up, meeting his mother's blue-eyed gaze where she stood on the landing above. "Hello, Mama."

She smiled down. "Hello, dear. I thought I heard you and came to investigate. It would seem I was right. I have been enjoying a cup of tea in the family drawing room. Why do you not come upstairs and join me?"

Ethan paused for a moment, then, deciding he could spare a few minutes, crossed to the stairs. If he watched his time, he should be able to visit with his mother, meet with his secretary, change his attire, and still not be late for his evening with Lily.

"More tea, if you would be so good, White," she called down to the butler. "And a few of those crumpets and the lemon curd his lordship prefers."

"Right away, my lady." The butler bowed, then departed to carry out her request.

When Ethan reached the landing, his mother threw open her arms for an embrace. "Come and give me a kiss."

Crossing to her, he bent and pressed his lips against one lavender-scented cheek, noticing in passing that she had a few more strands of white in her sophisticated blond coiffure and a new set of creases at the edge of her mouth. Still, despite having passed middle age a few years before, the dowager marchioness remained a very attractive woman—slender and elegant, her eyes as shrewd and intelligent as ever.

"You should have let me know you were coming to Town, Mama," he said, as they strolled down the hallway and into the drawing room. "I would have taken care to be here to greet you."

"And I would have written had I known you might not be at home when I arrived." Her words were pleasant, but he had no difficulty catching the underlying censure.

Taking a seat opposite him, she reached for a cup and poured his tea. A moment later, a light tap came at the door. "Ah, here are the crumpets now," she declared.

After the maid set down a laden silver tray and closed the door behind her, his mother prepared a plate for him. "As we were saying," she continued, passing him the offering, "I was surprised to find you not in residence. Have you perhaps been traveling, after all? Grown tired of the city, since you missed coming to Andarley this summer?"

Deciding not to play games, he set his untouched plate aside. "No, I am not at all tired of the city and have not been traveling, as I am sure you already know."

She lifted her gaze to meet his own. "Yes. To be perfectly candid, I have been hearing rumors, even as far as the wilds of Suffolk."

He refrained from mentioning that Suffolk was hardly anyone's idea of a wilderness. "Oh?" he drawled. "And what are they saying?"

Her pale brows narrowed on her forehead. "That you are living with a widow here in the city, some redheaded creature who has apparently beguiled you."

His jaw tightened, his voice turning hard. "Lily is not

a 'creature,' and you will never refer to her as such again."

His mother laid a hand against her chest as if he had wounded her. "Is that her name? Lily? I had clung to a tiny shred of hope that the rumors were false, but I see you make no effort to deny them. Though it pains me to say this, Ethan, you are a fair way to making a disgrace of yourself."

"Am I indeed?" he said in a chill voice, tapping his index finger against the arm of his chair. "I hardly think my private affairs are anyone's business but my own."

"Ordinarily I would agree, and I dislike even bringing up the topic." Glancing down, she hesitated for a long moment. "I understand that men keep mistresses, and on that I will say nothing further. However, most gentlemen are scrupulously circumspect in their dealings with such women. They do not ignore convention by moving out of their family residence and spending all their time in some love nest."

"Mrs. Smythe's townhouse is quite respectable, hardly a love nest. And though I am not here as often as I used to be, I have not moved out of Andarton House."

*For all intents and purposes, have I not, though?* he admitted to himself. He rarely stopped home anymore, and then only to oversee household and business matters. In fact, he could not recall the last time he'd slept in his own bed. Given his absence and the fact that his mother had spent the last two nights in the townhouse alone, he could see why she might assume he had moved out. He could also see how his defection might be viewed by Society at large. His fingers curled into a fist on his thigh. *Society be damned,* he thought. *I want to be with Lily, and with Lily I shall be.*

Yet what of *her* reputation? Was he harming her standing, ruining her good name? She was a virtuous woman—*my God,* he thought, *she's been with no man but me.* Though, of course, no one except the two of them knew that. Still, he could not let his mother continue to think the worst.

"Lily Smythe is a fine woman, a true lady, and not as you obviously believe her to be," he said. "She is bright and beautiful, with an independent spirit that is nothing short of admirable. I believe you would like her if the two of you were to meet."

His mother gave him an arch look, then unbent enough to relax her rigidly erect posture. "Perhaps I would, but what do you know of her? Who is her family, Ethan? What of her lineage? From what I am given to understand, no one really seems to know much about her except that she is a wealthy widow who apparently hails from Cornwall. What more has she told you of herself?"

*Not a great deal,* he realized. He knew her—the person, the woman, the lover—knew how she took her tea in the morning, that her favorite color was blue, and that she preferred comedic plays to any of the tragedies. But as for tangible details about her background . . . well, the specifics largely remained a mystery, even now. Even to him.

He saw his mother watching him with expectant eyes, waiting for his answer. "I know that she comes from good family," he asserted. "One can see that in each of her movements, in every word she speaks. She is educated and well-mannered, but more importantly, she is sweet and kind and generous to a fault. I also know that she is a very private person, who has suffered much grief in her short life. As for her lineage, we have not really discussed it, since such issues matter not."

"No, I would guess they don't, considering your circumstances. But that is the point—how your association with this woman appears to the world, no matter how sweet and good she may be. The two of you are living together, and that can hardly be seen in a beneficial light."

"Perhaps I do not care how it is seen."

"Does she feel the same? And what of Lord Sutleigh and Lady Amelia? I suspect they will be distressed should news of this reach their ears. After all, you have an engagement to consider, in case you had forgotten."

He had not forgotten, at least not completely. Then again, he had given his long-ago understanding with Sutleigh's daughter little thought, especially of late.

"I am *not* engaged, Mama," he stated, the edge returning to his tone. "I may have spoken to Sutleigh in regard to marrying his daughter, but nothing has been settled, nothing made public. There is no fixed arrangement between us at all, and what has been said hardly constitutes an engagement."

Her mouth dropped open, a faint gasp escaping her lips. "But Amelia Dodd is the perfect girl to be your marchioness. Surely you do not mean to renege on your decision to wed her?"

He paused. "I am no longer certain."

"This is because of *her,* because of this Lily Smythe. Dear heavens, you aren't going to marry her, are you?"

*Marry Lily?*

He had asked her once to be his wife and she had refused. At the time, he hadn't regretted her answer, since his proposal had originated from of a sense of honor and obligation over having taken her virginity. But now . . .

*Do I love her?*

*Yes,* he realized, with a sort of dawning certainty. He would marry Lily in a minute if she would have him. But would she? After all these months together, she showed no signs of having changed her mind on the subject of marriage, seemingly content to go along exactly as they had been doing.

*What if I propose again? What if she says no again?*

He swallowed against the crushing rush of emotion the idea evoked. He had yet to hear back from Ross on his findings about John Smythe. If Ethan hoped to battle a ghost—especially one as important to Lily as her deceased husband—he would do well not to proceed without first knowing everything he could about the man.

"So?" the dowager prompted, deep concern showing on her attractive face.

"I have no plans to marry Lily Smythe." *At least no immediate plans,* he thought.

His mother released an audible sigh. "Well then, that is good. You will not have to dash Lady Amelia's hopes."

"Mama, I did not say—"

She held up a palm. "Yes, I know, but take a bit of time. Do not rush into any decisions right now. Promise me you will say nothing to Sutleigh or Lady Amelia for the present, whatever your ultimate decision might be."

He did not wish to marry Amelia Dodd. He knew that now, knew as well how deluded he'd been to ever consider tying himself to a girl he did not, and never would, love. But he supposed he could placate his mother a while longer. At least until he made some permanent decisions about his future with Lily.

"Very well, Mama, I promise to say nothing to Sutleigh for a few weeks more, if that is what you wish."

She sent him a pleased smile. "It is." Leaning over, she patted his hand. "Thank you, dear."

On a nod, he returned her smile.

"Now," she pronounced. "Since you are here at home, why do we not have dinner together tonight? I am sure Cook can make at least one of your favorite dishes. Roast beef, perhaps?"

"As delightful as that sounds, I am afraid I've already

made other plans. I have business to see to with my secretary, and then I am going out to the opera."

"With her, I suppose," she said, the smile disappearing from her face.

"Yes. With Lily." He paused, then took a chance despite the mild impropriety of the suggestion. "You are welcome to accompany us, if you would like."

She shook her head. "Thank you, but no. Come to that, Ethan, I shall be removing to the dower house tomorrow."

"You do not need—"

"But I do. I have decided to remain in Town until Christmas. The Little Season is starting and I should like to enjoy a bit of company. That said, I will be more comfortable in my own residence. I only came here to Andarton House because I was having my sitting room redone. The work should be finished by the morrow."

"Very well, Mama. I shall look forward to sharing dinner with you on another occasion." Glancing at the clock, he noted that more time had passed than he'd imagined. "I really must be going."

"You are busy. I understand."

Leaning down, he kissed her cheek. "Do not worry, Mama. All will be well."

An odd little smile curved her mouth. "I know you are right. All *will* be well, Ethan. Now, do run along."

He studied her for a moment, wondering at her last remark. Generally, his mother was a calm, reasonable woman, who lived her life and let others do the same without interference. When it came to family, though, she did not always abide by that rule. In her estimation, if a loved one needed "protecting," even from himself, then no remedy was too extreme.

Once, years ago, she'd publicly boxed the ears of one of his sister's suitors when she had overheard the man making a mildly suggestive remark to her. With half of

London looking on, the dowager had cuffed the young lord, then literally hauled him out by the ear, ignoring the guests' laughter and the yelping, stumbling young man.

Ethan frowned, and thought again of his mother's desire to see him wed to Amelia Dodd. *But what can she do?* he reasoned. *It's not as if she can make me marry the girl.* Deciding he had nothing over which to worry, he murmured his good-byes. By the time he reached his study, the matter had vanished from his mind.

## Chapter Eighteen

❦

THE LAST DAYS of October drifted by like falling autumn leaves, November ushering in a new session of Parliament, and along with it the return of Society to London. Although the Ton's numbers remained thin in comparison to all those who would flood the city for the full Season come spring, there were enough aristocrats assembled to throw an exciting entertainment or two.

Lily and Ethan were among those selected to receive invitations—although there was the occasional high stickler who decided to drop Lily from her guest list as a sign of disapproval of her current "wanton misbehavior." In general, however, the aristocracy loved titillating bits of gossip, and what could be more fascinating than watching the public byplay between lovers? Especially lovers whose affair was so passionate the couple could scarcely be parted from each other—not even, it was whispered, for so much as a night.

Still, Lily was only partially aware of the speculative interest she and Ethan were generating, too focused on her own inner musings to worry about the curiosity of others. Ever since the night she'd realized she loved Ethan, she had been in a quandary, one that continued to plague her now as she sat in her study attempting to reconcile her book of household accounts. Ethan had gone out for a few hours, providing her the opportunity to see to the necessary task. Unfortunately, she wasn't making much progress, her pen drooping in her hand, the ledger and a small stack of bills forgotten near her elbow.

*Should I tell him how I feel or not?*

That was the question that seemed to revolve like some steadily spinning planet inside her mind. Far too often these days she found herself dwelling upon the topic, growing silent, then having to cover the lapse with one sort of excuse or another. Sometimes she even dreamed about the question, imagining herself saying the words to Ethan—*I love you*—then gazing into his handsome face to await a response the phantom Ethan never gave. And therein lay another dilemma.

*What if he does not feel the same way about me?*

Despite their time together and their undeniable closeness, she wasn't certain his interest in her went much deeper than friendship. He liked her, of that she had little doubt. But love? Commitment? Family? Would he want those things with her? More confusing, did she want them with him?

When she had staged her death and run away from home, changing her name and her identity in an effort to sever all ties with her past, she had been so sure she would never wish to marry. Marriage was a prison, after all, a cage set to lure women inside, then leave them weeping and regretful once their freedom had been taken away. But lately she found herself questioning that assumption. Her mother had endured two unions that had brought her little more than pain. Yet was her mother's lot necessarily destined to be her own?

Over the past several weeks, she and Ethan had been virtually living together. They took their meals together. They spent long hours of every day in each other's company. They went out together in the evenings to attend a party or see a play. At night, they shared a bed, making love with an intensity that never failed to leave her satisfied. And on the occasional night when they did nothing but sleep, they spooned together under the blankets in a blissful contentment, one she'd never imagined she might enjoy. And enjoy Ethan she did—each day at his side a new adventure, each night in his arms an exquisite delight.

But what of the future? Did they even have one together, or was she simply spinning fancies she would be better off crushing in their infancy? To say nothing of her circumstances and the fact that her present life was based on a lie.

How would Ethan take the news, should she decide to share the truth of her past? For such a revelation, once uttered, could never again be recalled. *Dare I take the chance?* she pondered. *Dare I open myself and my life up to such risk? Dare I trust Ethan with everything, including my heart?*

Yet ultimately what choice did she have? As much as she wished it might be otherwise, she and Ethan could not continue on with their current arrangement forever. The two of them did not live in a cocoon, tucked away from reality; she knew wild talk and speculation about them was beginning to spread through the Ton. At some point she and Ethan would need to make a decision. *Either we must end our affair and stop seeing each other,* she thought—her chest constricting with a tightness that verged on pain—*or continue on to the next step. And the only possible next step is marriage.*

*But do I want to be his wife?*

The answer that whispered in her head surprised her, the pen rolling from her grasp. *I do,* she realized, *I do want to be his wife. But will he have me?*

She'd refused him once, brutally honest in her dismissal of his suit. At the time, they had both been relieved to remain free of the parson's noose. But what about now? Did Ethan still feel as he had then, or might he, too, have had a change of mind and heart?

*Oh, if only I knew!*

Withdrawing a handkerchief from her pocket, she dried her suddenly perspiring palms, balling the cloth inside one fist. She would have to tell him, she realized, not only of her feelings, but the truth about herself as well. For good or ill, at least then she would know.

*So when? When shall I take the plunge?*

She knew she should tell him right away—tonight, in fact. But he was promised for dinner with the Duke of Wyvern, who had just returned to Town, while she had agreed to accompany Davina to a lecture, her friend also having only recently arrived from the country. She could always tell him in bed, she supposed, but she hesitated to do so. What if everything did not go as she hoped? No, she needed a day when they had no other fixed engagements and could stay home.

The Mossgroves were throwing a ball in three days' time, after which she and Ethan had decided to sleep late and spend the remaining afternoon and evening at home. Following the ball should be perfect, and the extra time between then and now should give her enough leeway to decide how to share the truth with him.

*After the Mossgroves' ball,* she thought, *that will be the day I tell him.*

Her mind made up, she retrieved her pen and began to copy numbers.

The air was draped in an almost wintry chill as Ethan reached out a hand to help Lily step down from his carriage three nights later. He took in the scene, noise and excitement whirling like snowflakes around the entrance to Lord and Lady Mossgrove's townhouse, satin- and velvet-clad guests making their way inside to participate in the festivities. Light burst from every door and window, the scent of melting candle wax, wine, and perfume mingling with the honeyed aroma that emanated from the large vases of hothouse roses arranged throughout the house.

Less than ten minutes after their arrival, an acquaintance approached, a young lord with whom he occasionally talked politics. The other man made an effort to be pleasant, pausing first to offer Lily a gracious compliment on her very becoming lilac satin gown before moving on to a discussion of Parliament's latest legislative actions. Obviously he was hoping to encourage Ethan's support on an issue of importance to him. When Davina Coates arrived, Ethan traded smiles with Lily as she excused herself to visit with her friend. He would see her again soon enough, he knew.

After hearing out the budding politician without making any unwanted promises, Ethan strode in Lily's direction. As he walked, however, he found himself stopping often to exchange a few words with friends and trade greetings with acquaintances. Nearly an hour passed before he managed to locate Lily again. She was dancing, he discovered, looking utterly vivacious as she whirled in the arms of one of her old admirers. Restraining the urge to cut in and give the gossipmongers additional grist, he contented himself by simply observing.

He had no cause to be jealous, especially considering her response to their lovemaking last night. His blood warmed even now to remember the breathless little gasps and ragged moans she'd made as he'd brought her to completion over and over again. They'd both been exhausted and indescribably satiated before he'd let sleep claim them. And this morning when she awakened, a smile had been riding her sultry lips as though begging for another kiss. Before rising to dress, he'd given in to temptation one last time, claiming her mouth—and a bit more—much to their mutual satisfaction.

Later, however, she'd seemed strangely nervous, worrying the tip of her fingernail between her teeth when she thought he wouldn't notice. He'd nearly asked her if anything was amiss, but then he'd glanced at the clock and known he must leave immediately if he didn't wish to be late for a nuncheon date with his mother.

As though the thought of his mother had brought her to his side, he watched the dowager marchioness cross to him. He schooled his features to mask his surprise, since he hadn't realized she planned to attend tonight's entertainment.

"Ethan dear," she said, leaning up to brush a kiss across his cheek. Dutifully, he bent down to receive her touch. "I knew I would find you eventually," she continued. "Such a crowd there is here tonight! Lady Mossgrove must be delighted at the attendance, particularly considering the time of year."

"People are always in want of a party, no matter what season it may be," he murmured. "You should have told me, Mama, that you planned to attend tonight. I would have greeted you earlier."

Perhaps she had not wanted to meet Lily, he thought, nor be put to the difficulty of refusing to share the carriage had he decided to ask her to accompany them. And mayhap he was expecting too much, since Lily was his mistress and men did not generally effect introductions between their paramour and their mother. But Lily was a lady, not a common courtesan, and if all went as he hoped, one day she would be his wife. But until that time arrived, he supposed matters might go more smoothly if he did not push the two women together. Mama would likely think him insensitive, and Lily might be made uncomfortable, even embarrassed, especially if Mama was less than warm to her.

"I was not certain I planned to attend this evening," she said, continuing their conversation. "But then the most delightful thing happened. Only look who has come unexpectedly to Town."

Turning to the side, she motioned a hand to usher forward two people he hadn't noticed standing in the crush. The Earl of Sutleigh he knew immediately, and at the older man's side was a slender nymph of a girl, her cheeks even paler than her ashen blond curls.

*Amelia Dodd. Lord above, what is she doing here now?*

A scowl lowered across his forehead.

"Is this not a wonderful surprise, Ethan?" his mother declared. "Lord Sutleigh and Lady Amelia arrived only yesterday and called upon me this afternoon, not many minutes after you had gone. I convinced them to come to the ball tonight so you might be reacquainted."

Forcing his frown lines to ease, he set a pleasant expression on his face and executed a respectful bow. "My lord. Lady Amelia. How good to see you both."

Sutleigh thrust out a gloved palm, which he accepted for a firm handshake. The girl meanwhile sent him a quick, skittering glance before returning her gaze to her white evening slippers.

*Good heavens,* he thought, *she looks petrified. Surely she is not scared of me? But apparently she is. And to think I once planned to wed this child.*

Tomorrow, he decided, he would speak with Lord Sutleigh about ending the proposed engagement. Even if he had never met Lily, Ethan knew he and this frail waif would never have suited each other. More relieved by his narrow escape than he cared to admit, he did his best to be gracious over the next several minutes, going out of his way to be kind to the nearly mute Miss Dodd.

He was attempting to extricate himself from the pair, hoping to finally reunite with Lily, when his mother said something that stopped him in his tracks. "Ethan, why do you not take Lady Amelia in to supper? I am sure you two young people would have a lovely time conversing without her father and me there to listen to every word."

Amelia's pale blue eyes darted up, grew huge as plates, then fell once more upon her toes, her hands clasped tightly at her waist.

Ethan shot his mother a narrowed look, but recovered his manners with no more than a second's hesitation. "Why, of course. I would be honored." Having been neatly maneuvered, he did as politeness required and extended his arm.

Obviously trapped as well, Amelia laid her little palm on his sleeve, her trembling noticeable even through the cloth.

*A couple of hours,* he assured himself, *and I can go home with Lily. A couple of hours and this girl and I can be quit of each other for good.*

*Who is that chit with Ethan?* Lily wondered from across the room. *And why is he taking her in to supper?* The child looked barely old enough to be out of the schoolroom, let alone socializing with a man of Ethan's age and reputation. And if Lily did not misread the situation, the girl appeared half-terrified to boot. A cousin perhaps, she speculated, noticing the middle-aged couple strolling just behind Ethan and the child, the older woman quite obviously Ethan's mother.

The family resemblance between the two of them was plain to see. The shape of their eyes was the same, as was the graceful sweep of their noses, one nearly a match for the other, size and gender being the only distinctions. *Yes,* she mused, *that elegant older lady is*

*Ethan's mama.* He had made no effort to introduce her to his mother, she noted, though given her current relationship with Ethan, she admitted such a meeting might prove awkward. And yet if all went well tomorrow, perhaps that situation would soon change.

A small fist squeezed inside her chest, anxiety battling with anticipation. Tomorrow she planned to tell him everything. *Though maybe if I can work up the nerve, I should tell him tonight that I love him and wish us never to be parted.*

*Does he love me? Surely he does.* After all, how could a man make the kind of intense, tender love Ethan made to her if his heart was not engaged? How could he spend his days and nights at her side, sharing the very fabric of their lives, if he harbored no genuine attachment to her?

And once she knew for certain that he did love her, then she would reveal the truth about how she had come to London and why she had become war widow Lily Smythe. He would be angry at first, she assumed, but after he'd had a chance to consider the untenable nature of her circumstances at home, he would understand why she had acted as she had.

*At least I hope he will.*

Letting her gaze drift over him as he and the girl waited to enter the supper room, emotion swelled inside her like a cresting wave. *Life would surely be easier if I did not, but heavens, I do love him!*

"P-pardon me, Mrs. Smythe, but I was wondering if I might have the honor of escorting you in to supper?"

The question shattered her thoughts. Glancing up, she discovered Lord Ottwell at her side, an optimistic expression on his pleasant face. Having expected Ethan to take her in, she had already turned down two other gentlemen who had offered to share the supper interval with her. But since Ethan was apparently otherwise occupied—she scowled again, wondering at the identity of the girl—she supposed she would do well to accept Lord Ottwell. At least he wasn't a bad sort, neither a lecher nor a bore, and since no carriage-driving would be involved at the supper table, she supposed she would be safe enough.

Giving him a gracious smile, she nodded and took his arm. "Thank you, my lord, that would be most welcome."

His own smile widened, then he led her forward. After a short silence, he cleared his throat. "I . . . um . . . see that Lord Vessey has taken Miss Dodd in tonight."

She stiffened briefly, willing her muscles to relax. *So that is her name, is it?* Lily mused. *Miss Dodd!*

"Though perhaps I should not have said," he continued.

"No," she forced herself to reply. "That is entirely all right. You know the young lady, then?"

"Oh no, not personally. But I am slightly acquainted with her father, the Earl of Sutleigh. He and Vessey both have extensive holdings in Suffolk. Their families are old friends, I believe."

*Old friends, are they, and not cousins?* Perhaps the girl was only visiting Town and Ethan was being kind in order to please his mother. That would account for the child's nervous demeanor at least.

Walking into the crowded supper room, her gaze flew straight toward Ethan where he sat alone with Miss Dodd. Her free hand curled into a fist at her side. Making her fingers relax, she allowed Lord Ottwell to lead her to an unoccupied table and assist her into a chair.

"I shall procure plates for us both and be back in a thrice," he declared.

Forgetting him almost as soon as he'd departed, she glanced again at Ethan, then away. Releasing a sigh, she realized this was going to be a very long evening.

\*     \*     \*

*Lord save me,* Ethan thought, *will this night never end?*

He'd just spent the last hour enduring young Miss Dodd's nearly silent company, the girl barely able to say much above "thank you," "no, thank you," and "yes, the quail is excellent."

Now that the meal was finished, manners required that he escort Amelia to her father. Once that duty was done, he would then be free to seek out Lily. He could only imagine what she must be thinking. Hopefully she wasn't too angry. Regardless, he promised himself he would make things up to her once they were alone.

Locating Lord Sutleigh should have been a simple matter, but he found himself and Lady Amelia waylaid by more than one acquaintance who wished to chat. The strains of the first country dance were fading into silence by the time he spotted the earl. The older man was easily visible now, standing on the ballroom steps so that he was a full head above the crowd. At his side stood the dowager marchioness. Ethan frowned and wondered what the two of them were doing there.

Just then, his mother lifted her hands to call for silence. "Everyone," she said in a carrying voice, "your attention and a moment of your time, if you please."

At once, the entire room grew quiet, all eyes turning in her direction.

"This evening is a very special occasion," she began, "one a mother only enjoys a very few times in her life, if she is so blessed."

*What is she saying?* Ethan wondered, his pulse beginning to beat at an increased pace.

"As some of you may know, the Earl of Sutleigh and I have long been friends. His late wife was my dearest companion and confidante before she was taken from us at far too young an age."

A buzzing started between his ears, air harder to draw into his lungs.

"Yet from the day she and I became mothers, we knew one thing—that our families were one day destined to be joined."

*Bloody hell, she isn't,* Ethan thought. *She couldn't. I have to stop her. Now!*

Yet even as he shook off Amelia's hand so he could race forward, his mother continued to speak.

"Which is why it is my great joy and delight," the dowager said, "to announce the engagement of my son, Ethan, to my friend, the Earl of Sutleigh's beautiful young daughter, Amelia."

Gasps resounded throughout the room. If his mother had taken one of the carving knives from the supper table and stabbed the blade through his chest, he could not have been more shocked. Or felt more furious.

"Felicitations to my son and my future daughter!" The dowager and the earl smiled widely, raising their hands to clap. "Oh, and the official notice will be in the *Morning Post* tomorrow," she called as a final parting shot.

*A true fait accompli,* he thought, grinding his teeth together so hard it was a wonder his jaw didn't crack. His mother, it would appear, had thought of everything to catch him neatly in her trap.

A rash of comments and congratulations broke out around him, people coming forward to shake his hand and pat him on the back. Nearby, Amelia was receiving similar attention, looking a bit like a feather caught up in a windstorm. But he didn't care about her; his thoughts were all for Lily. Turning his head, he scanned the crowd for her, the words of the people around him coalescing into a dull, garbled hum.

And suddenly there she was, standing on the far side of the ballroom, looking lost and alone. She held a hand clutched at the base of her throat as though she could not breathe properly, her face as stark and white as a first winter snow. Even her lips had lost their color.

Their gazes met and held, a moist sheen of unshed tears making her eyes gleam like glass, anguish and disbelief swimming in their vivid green depths. Abruptly she whirled, hurrying across the room as rapidly as her feet would carry her.

Damning politeness and not caring how his actions might appear, he started forward, only to be stopped when his mother curled a hand around his arm. "Ethan, where do you think you are going?" she demanded in a low voice. "You cannot abandon your bride. People are staring."

He glared down at her, his gaze frigid. "Let them stare. And she isn't my bride yet, despite your best attempts to make it so. Now release me."

She trembled but held her place. "I only did what was best. What needed to be done to secure your happiness."

"If you cared a jot about my happiness you would never have interfered. You may well have ruined my life, madam, and right now, I can scarcely stand to look at you."

On a soft gasp, she let him go.

Stalking forward, he cut through the crowd, ignoring the few individuals who were either brave enough or foolish enough to attempt to get in his way. Bolting down the hallway, he sped out the front door and down the steps. For a long moment he thought she was gone, but then he caught a glimpse of lilac satin fluttering in the chill wind. She hadn't stopped to retrieve her cloak, and as he walked closer he could see that she was shivering, her arms crossed at her waist.

"Lily, thank heavens you haven't left! What just happened back there in the ballroom, it is not what you think."

Refusing to acknowledge him, she stared straight ahead.

"You're freezing. Come back inside where it's warm and we'll talk." He reached out to take her arm.

"Don't touch me!" she said, jerking away from his grasp.

He drew a breath, striving for patience. "I know you're upset, but if you will just let me explain—"

She turned on him. "Explain what? That you are secretly engaged, and obviously have been for some while? How long, Ethan? How long have you been using and deceiving me?"

His shoulders drew back, a muscle ticking near his eye. "I have done neither. Making that announcement tonight was my mother's idea."

"And you, of course, had no part in it," she said.

"No, I did not," he told her, enunciating each word. "Give me a chance—"

"A chance to what? Concoct more lies and excuses? Well, I, for one, have no wish to listen to them. Now, hadn't you best hurry back inside before you are missed by your little fiancée?"

A set of fingers curled at his hip. "We're going to talk about this."

"No, we are not. Go away, Ethan, and . . ." her voice broke, ". . . and leave me alone." Her lower lip trembled as she dashed a hand across one eye. When a hackney rolled to a stop at the curb, she moved toward it.

He caught her elbow. "Surely you are not planning to ride in that? Let me call for my coach so we can go home and discuss this."

"I do not want your coach. In fact, I want nothing further from you. And if by 'home' you mean my townhouse, you are no longer welcome there. Go to Andarton House, Ethan. That is where you live." Yanking out of his hold, she stepped inside the hackney. Seconds later, she slammed the door shut and the vehicle set off.

"Lily!" he shouted. "Lily come back here!" But even as the words left his mouth, he knew it was too late, the hack hurrying down the street before rounding a corner and disappearing from view.

*Damn and blast,* he cursed, smacking a fist against his thigh. He considered following her, ordering the fastest horse available so he could chase her down. After all, she needed to listen to reason, had to be made to understand the truth. But what was the truth now, since, like it or not, he was an engaged man in the eyes of Society? Until he could figure a way free of that entanglement, the best he could offer Lily were his explanations and his word.

The knowledge that she had so little faith galled him, but he supposed she had just cause considering his mother's outrageous maneuverings tonight. As much as he longed to storm over to Lily's townhouse and make her hear him out, he knew she was in no mood to be coerced or cajoled. Perhaps he ought to give her a small bit of time, he decided, a few hours in which to calm down before he approached her again.

Raking his fingers through his hair, he cursed under his breath. Resigned to what was sure to be a lonely, frustrating night, he strode forward and called for his coach to go home.

# Chapter Nineteen

❧❦❧

$L$ILY THOUGHT SHE would cry, imagining she would burst into a torrent of tears the instant she was alone. But the tears stayed locked inside her, the wound too deep to be relieved by such a simple balm.

She had no recollection of the journey home, arriving shivering but safe, only to be led inside by a concerned-looking Hodges. Her lady's maid took her in hand next, leading her upstairs for a dish of hot tea and a change into her warmest woolen nightgown and robe. Susan asked only once if his lordship would be arriving later.

"No," Lily said in a flat tone that sounded odd even to her own ears. "His lordship will not be arriving at all."

*He will never be here again.*

After brushing Lily's hair and putting away her jewels, Susan murmured good night and let herself out of the room.

Huddled beneath the covers, Lily tried to sleep, but rest eluded her, the bed far too big and far too empty. Mouser joined her, his purrs soothing in the dark and quiet. Sliding her fingers into his fur, she stroked him, rubbing her cheek against his silky coat, grateful for his comfort.

Hours passed, memories replaying in her mind—Ethan with Amelia Dodd, the two of them sharing supper and dancing. His mother calling everyone together, a wide smile on her face as she made her dreadful announcement.

*Engaged. Ethan and that girl are to be married.*

*Just how long has he been planning this?* she wondered. Had he pledged his troth to another, even while he was sleeping with her? Or was this arrangement of a far longer duration? One made in his infancy, perhaps, before Amelia Dodd had ever been conceived? Was that why he had thought nothing of it? Why he had not been expecting his mother to announce the engagement tonight?

*And what of his long-ago marriage proposal to me?*

Lies. All of it lies. He'd wanted her in his bed and he'd done what it took to get her there. He'd probably even offered to wed her, knowing how she felt about marriage, confident she would turn him down. Maybe he'd used the ploy to convince her how "honorable" he was, so she would lower her guard.

And lower her guard she had, opening her heart in a way she had never thought she would for any man. Tucking her fisted hands tight against her breasts, she stared into the darkness.

When the first rays of dawn light peeked inside the room, she rose to open the curtains. Pulling on a robe, she went to her dressing room to locate an empty hatbox. Container in hand, she returned to the bedroom, crossed to the stand Ethan had been using as a dressing table, and began tossing in items.

His straight razor went first, then his leather strop. Next landed his shaving brush and soap, his carved ivory comb, and a pair of round, silver-backed hairbrushes with his initials, *EEA,* engraved upon them. A spare calling-card case—empty of cards—joined the collection, along with his toothbrush, tooth powder, and a watch fob and watch key. A handful of coins clinked their way to the bottom of the box, rattling as she laid a small case containing two jeweled cravat pins on top. A length of sealing wax and a matchbox joined the cache.

Toiletries finished, she stalked to the highboy and yanked open a drawer. Taking up a stack of neatly laundered cravats, she shoved them into the box. Handkerchiefs, stockings, and a pair of shoe buckles came next. Three pair of gloves were squashed into a convenient spot, followed by a nightshirt she had never once seen him wear. With the container now overflowing, she set it aside and began tossing clothing onto her bed.

The bedroom door opened as she was laying down a stack of lightweight woolen drawers.

"Are you awake, ma'am?" her maid inquired in a soft voice, a floorboard giving a tiny squeak as she stole slowly into the room. "I heard noises and thought I would check . . . mercy me!"

Lily flicked a quick glance over her shoulder as she crossed back for an armful of shirts. "Oh, good, I'm glad you are here. You can help me finish packing all of this up. From the look of it, we shall need another box or two at least to do the job." Closing one drawer, she pulled open another, discovering two coats and three pairs of trousers folded neatly inside. Grabbing them up, she flung them on top of the growing pile of garments littering the bed.

Staring in plain astonishment, her maid stood unmoving in the center of the room.

"Boxes, if you please, Susan."

Lily's quiet admonishment produced the desired effect, the girl bobbing a curtsey before springing into action. She returned a short while later bearing a pair of large, rectangular bandboxes well suited for garments.

During her absence, more items had joined the pile, Lily having added two silk-lined beaver top hats, a pair of evening pumps, and an ebony cane set with a gold handle in the shape of a roaring lion.

She had once commented to Ethan about this cane, telling him she thought it an excellent symbol for him to carry, since he was her strong, beautiful golden lion. Lips tight, she gave the cane a dismissive shove, then spun and went to scour the room for any items that might have escaped her notice.

Twenty minutes later, the bed stood empty once again, all of Ethan's belongings packed away. Even the original overflowing hatbox had been rearranged, since Susan had been unable to fit the lid on top otherwise.

"What shall I do with his lordship's things, ma'am?" her maid inquired.

Lily wanted to tell the girl to fling them out the window, or better yet take them to the Thames and let the river claim them. But then, she need not have seen his clothes and other belongings boxed up had she wished to have them destroyed. Besides, she reasoned, indulging in such overly dramatic behavior would only prove to Ethan how deeply wounded she was by his treachery. She would not give him the satisfaction. The return of his belongings without any fanfare would send a far better, more eloquent message.

"Have one of the footmen take the dog cart and drive all of this over to Lord Vessey's townhouse."

"Yes, ma'am."

"And ask Hodges to attend me, if you would."

After Susan departed, Lily traded her robe for a dressing gown, moving into her sitting room while two footmen carried the boxes out of the bedroom and down the stairs.

A brief knock came at the door, her butler standing on the threshold. "You wished to see me, ma'am?"

Looking across from where she stood at the window, she gave a nod. "I did. I want you to send for a locksmith. Tell him if he can have all the doors reset and re-keyed by this evening, there will be an extra amount added to his wage."

The servant's eyes widened faintly, but to his credit he showed no other reaction to her request. "Of course, ma'am. I shall see to it immediately."

Once he'd left, she started toward her bedroom, and that was when she saw it—a leather-bound book resting on the end table near the fireplace. Ethan had been reading the work only two nights ago, relaxed in the accompanying wing chair, a glass of port close at hand.

She'd gone to him and snuggled against his side, asking him to read a few paragraphs to her out loud. He'd done so, his rich voice reciting the story, until her wandering hand distracted him and he'd set the book aside. He'd taken her to bed where they'd made love. Little had she realized that coupling would be their last.

Grabbing up the book, she spun, intending to catch the footman before he left. But after only three steps, she drew to a halt, unable to continue. Slowly, she raised the book to her breasts and cradled it there, realizing suddenly this was all she had left of Ethan.

A harsh sob escaped her lips. Her shoulders shaking, she began to cry.

Ethan tossed back the covers after a sleepless night, rising early to shave and dress. He wanted no breakfast, not even tea, before he strode downstairs to his study. Seated at his desk, he penned a note to Amelia Dodd, asking permission to call upon her as soon as may be. Even if she did not wish to see him, she *would* grant him an interview. Once there, he would demand to see her alone so that he could convince her to end this farce of an engagement. After his behavior last night— deserting her only moments after the announcement had been made in order to chase after his mistress—his request to be released from his promise should certainly come as no surprise. And given her trembling diffidence in his presence, he assumed she would send him packing with profound relief.

The Ton was abuzz, of course, but he didn't care, far too concerned about repairing the damage that had been done to his relationship with Lily. Good lord, he couldn't get the sight of her face out of his mind—the shock and the horror, the misery gleaming in her eyes. As soon as he'd spoken to Amelia, he would go to Lily to make amends. That way, at least, he would be able to give her the good news that the engagement was off before he begged her forgiveness. Surely once he explained what had happened, she would understand and welcome him back.

A tap came at the door. He glanced up to find his butler there, a peculiar expression on the man's usually emotionless face.

"Yes, what is it, White?" Ethan asked, setting down his pen.

"Pardon me, my lord, but a footman has arrived with some boxes."

He raised a brow. "What sort of boxes?"

"Bandboxes, my lord. I am given to understand they contain your . . . um . . . personal effects. Clothing and such, from . . . um . . . your recent habitation in Bloomsbury."

*Bloomsbury!*

*Christ, she has sent back my things.*

Which meant that Lily had decided to cut him out without even granting him a hearing. Though perhaps to her way of thinking their brief conversation last night had already served that purpose.

His hand curled into a fist, a fresh wave of fury and frustration rising inside him. Silently, he cursed his mother again for her outrageous, high-handed interference. If strangling her would do any good, he would march over to her townhouse right now to do the deed. But violence was useless—though if the time came when he could once more stand to be in the same room with his mother, she would likely find herself on the sharp side of a good tongue-lashing. Still, the nightmare events of last evening had occurred and nothing could change that fact. All that remained was to repair the damage as best he could.

Standing, he moved past his butler and strode out of the room and down the hall. In the foyer, he found a small hillock of boxes. Lifting the lid off one, he stared down at his belongings, catching a glimpse of his razor and comb, along with a few stray pence and shillings that winked up at him in a kind of taunting derision.

A muscle ticked near his eye, a growl working its way into his throat. He swallowed the sound as a single, daunting realization set in. *Not only is winning Lily back going to be hard,* he thought, *it's going to be hell.*

Truer words had never been spoken, Ethan realized later that afternoon as he paced across the Sutleigh townhouse drawing room, Amelia Dodd seated on the nearby sofa, garbed in demure white.

"What do you mean you won't break the engagement!"

Amelia cringed, her pale face growing paler. "Oh, please do not yell at me."

"I am not yelling at you," he blasted back, realizing that perhaps he was bellowing a bit. Closing his eyes for a brief moment, he drew a breath and willed himself to be calm. "My apologies if I raised my voice," he continued in an even tone. "Miss Dodd . . . Amelia . . . I understand that all of this is very distressing for you. Frankly, the situation is distressing for me as well, since neither one of us had agreed to the unexpected announcement that my mother made last night. I assume you were as stunned as I."

Her lashes lowered over her eyes, a faintly guilty expression pinching her pretty features. Apparently she had known something about his mother's plans. Perhaps that was why she had been so nervous in his company last night.

"Papa said you offered for me months ago," she explained in a breathless rush. "That last night was a mere formality."

"I told your father that I was *considering* offering for you," he stated. "But that nothing was settled as of yet. I planned to pay my addresses to you this spring to see if we would suit. Did you not find it odd that I would supposedly consent to an engagement without even speaking to you about the matter first? Without actually proposing to you in person?"

She said nothing, her chin lowered as she stared at her clasped hands.

He walked a few steps forward, then back, stopping in front of her. "Amelia, let us speak honestly. What happened last night was a mistake, something my mother, and apparently your father, concocted in order to force us together. I am truly sorry for any embarrassment and pain this debacle has caused you. However, it is not too late to undo the damage."

She released a small sigh.

He seized upon the sound, taking it as encouragement to continue. "You and I are not married yet, and we do not ever need to be. But you must be the one to end things between us. You can break this engagement; you have that prerogative. As a gentleman, I do not."

She shook her head. "But we are publicly pledged now."

"We do not have to be," he urged. "Have you not been listening? All you need do is jilt me."

Her mouth parted on a faint gasp. "I cannot."

"Why not? Dear lord, we barely know each other, so there can be no possibility that feelings are involved. Surely you do not truly wish to wed me?"

"My papa wishes me to wed you," she said, finally looking up to meet his gaze. "I cannot disobey him. He will be frightfully angry if I do."

"And I shall be frightfully angry if you do not."

Her eyes widened at that, but despite a slight tremble, she held her ground. "I am sorry, my lord, but I have given Papa my word. I cannot go back on it."

Ethan began pacing again, thumping a fist against the side of his thigh. If simple reasoning would not work, maybe a more direct method would have some effect.

"So you care nothing for the fact that I am in love with another woman?"

Her shoulders tightened, followed by a long pause. "Your mistress, you mean? The one they say you followed outside last night."

"Yes, the woman I want to make my wife. I ask you not to stand between that, for all of our sakes."

"Papa says all men have mistresses."

He swallowed the growl that rose into his throat. "Your papa says a lot of things, does he not? And what has he to say of you and your own happiness? Or haven't you a right to find pleasure and contentment in your life? Haven't you the right to find love?"

Her face crumpled at his words, her lower lip quivering before she could prevent the reaction.

"Ah," he said, moving to sink down next to her on the sofa. "So there is someone else already. Who is he?"

She shook her head. "No one. I should not have said."

"You did not. Your face did the talking for you. Is he a neighbor?"

Her eyes darted upward, her surprise clear. "How did you know?"

*You are seventeen and have lived all your life at home. Who else could it be?* he reasoned. Instead of voicing his thoughts aloud, he shrugged. "Lucky guess. What is his name?"

"Robert," she admitted, her tone warming as she spoke the obviously beloved name. "Robert Hocksby. He is the local vicar's son and only two years my senior. He and I used to take our lessons together at the vicarage when we were children."

A smile moved over her mouth, the color back in her face. "We talked of so many things," she said, "sharing our dearest wishes and most daring dreams. Robert wants to be a physician and has apprenticed with our own village doctor. He would like to attend medical college, then afterward conduct his own research in order to investigate more of the science behind disease. But Papa says—" She broke off, as if suddenly realizing how much she was revealing.

"Yes?" he asked in a soft voice. "What does your father say?"

"He says that physicians, even trained ones, are nothing but quacks and charlatans destined to prey on others for a meager stipend. Robert may have been born a gentleman, but he is an impoverished one and impoverished young men do not marry earl's daughters, no matter whether feelings are involved or not."

Looking up, she met his gaze, her expression one of sad resignation. "I am sorry, my lord, but I cannot go against my father. You and I must marry whether we wish to do so or not." She ran her fingers over a ribbon on her dress. "You may keep her, though, if you wish—

your mistress, that is. I understand and will not interfere."

*So she understands, does she?* He didn't think Lily would be quite so generous in her attitude. He could only imagine her explosive reaction were he to suggest such an arrangement. If she didn't skewer him first, she would most certainly kick him out on his ass. Which, come to think of it, she had already done in a sense, considering the return of his clothes and grooming essentials. No, Lily was not the sort of woman who would be content to share—no more than he would be easy with the notion of her taking another man to her bed. Besides, he didn't want Amelia Dodd for his wife, even if she didn't mind him "keeping" Lily.

The muscle ticked near his eye, keen vexation smoldering like a barely cooled ember in his chest. He wanted to reach out and give Amelia a good shake, yell at her a bit more until she saw reason and agreed to free him from his obligation. But he could see such coercion would have little effect.

He could always jilt her, he realized. But such a course would not only brand him as a cad, the act would sully Amelia's reputation forever. Antiquated as the notion might seem, he knew many still considered an engagement almost as binding as having taken marriage vows. If he were to reject Amelia, her social standing would be permanently damaged, her chances of making a good marriage cruelly diminished. He could not do that to her—or at least he was not ready to do that to her unless such a drastic step proved to be the only solution. Surely there had to be another way out of this disaster, some means of convincing Amelia to defy her father and refuse to marry him. Yet until that time arrived, he supposed he would have to remain engaged to her, whether he wished to be or not.

And what of Lily?

When he arrived here this afternoon, he'd planned to depart a free man. He had intended to go to Lily and explain everything, then afterward, drop down onto a single knee and ask her to be his wife. But obviously that plan would no longer work. He couldn't very well ask one woman to marry him while still engaged to another! He supposed only the truth would do. Surely once he explained the situation to Lily, she would forgive him and be willing to wait. Gazing again at his "fiancée," he decided to give persuasion one more try.

"Amelia," he said. "I cannot believe your father will refuse to let you end this engagement, if you explain to him that is what you truly wish. Say you cannot stand the sight of me and that after last night you think I am a beast. He'll huff and puff a bit, but then he will adjust. And by the time the full Season arrives this spring, this incident will have faded from everyone's minds, leaving you free to seek another worthy beau."

She gave him a pitying look. "My lord, you obviously do not know my father as well as you think. Ever since you approached him a few months ago, he has talked of little else but our impending nuptials."

A scowl furrowed his brow. "I asked him to say nothing to you on the subject."

"Well, he did. You may not realize this, but he has been anticipating a marriage between our families quite literally for years. You and I are his only hope of achieving that aim, and now that a wedding is arranged between us, he is not about to let me call it off because I have taken a supposed dislike to you. I am afraid such an idea will not serve." She sighed. "I am sorry, my lord."

*But not sorry enough!* he raged silently. *Not sorry enough to end this dreadful misalliance by calling it off.*

"Very well, Miss Dodd. I see I must at present accept your refusal." *At least until I can think of a way out.*

Standing, he executed a clipped bow. "Good day to you, my lady."

"Good day, my lord."

Fists set at his side, he strode from the room.

## Chapter Twenty

*L*ILY PUSHED ASIDE her uneaten nuncheon, together with the cup of tea that sat on the tray, both the food and beverage having long since grown cold. She knew she should force herself to do something, anything other than continue to sit idle here in the chair in her sitting room, staring into the fire. If only she could somehow find the will.

*Later,* she decided. *I will busy myself with an activity later, but not right now. Sleep is an activity, though, is it not?* She could do with a long afternoon nap. After all, she had not slept last night. The rest would do her good. More important, sleep would let her escape, let her forget her present misery as she curled up inside a warm cocoon of oblivion.

Climbing out of her chair, she started toward her bedroom, but before she'd taken more than a few steps a knock came at the sitting-room door. Hoping whoever it was would go away, she said nothing. When the door opened despite a lack of invitation, she expelled a sigh and turned to face the intruder.

"Pardon the interruption, ma'am," said her butler, an apologetic expression on his face, "but Lord Vessey is here. I know you gave explicit instructions that he not be received, but he insists upon seeing you."

Her tiredness disappeared, her spine straightening as

though she had been whipped by a lash. "I assume you told him that I am not at home."

"Yes, ma'am. He . . . um . . . he says he can tell when I am prevaricating and, um—how did he put it?—I am to inform you that he isn't going away until the two of you have talked."

*Isn't going away, is he?* she fumed. *Well, he can wait downstairs until snowflakes start to fall in Egypt.*

"Pray advise his lordship that anything he has to say can be addressed to me by letter." *Which I will cheerfully burn upon its arrival,* she promised herself. "Then inform him that he can either leave this house voluntarily or be thrown out. You and the footmen should be up to the task."

Alarm lines carved themselves deep in Hodges's brow. "Oh, ma'am, I do not think that would be wise. He won't go easily and the marquis is a lord, after all. Laying hands upon a member of the nobility can land a man in gaol."

She tsked and shook her head. "Lord Vessey is not going to have you tossed in prison. Besides, he'll know you were only doing my bidding."

"She's right," remarked a resonant voice from the threshold. "I would not sic the law upon you, Hodges, though I might beat you and the footmen senseless first. I am rather handy with my fives, and I expect you would have a devil of a time wrestling me past the threshold."

Lily glared at Ethan. "*You* are supposed to be downstairs."

He quirked a defiant brow and strolled into the room. "*I* came up."

"Well, you can go back down." She thrust a finger toward the door. "Be gone, my lord. I have nothing to say to you."

"Good. Perhaps then you'll keep silent long enough

to listen to me this time." He cast a meaningful glance at the waiting servant. "That will be all, Hodges."

She set her fists on her hips. "Do not order my servants around. You have no right. Particularly since you are no longer welcome in this residence."

A muscle on the underside of Ethan's jaw flexed tight. "One of the many things we need to discuss." He strode farther into the room and took up a position near the fireplace. Crossing his arms, he met her gaze, his expression reflecting the same stubborn defiance that was visible in his posture.

Lily restrained the urge to stamp one of her feet in frustration. Short of having him tossed bodily out of the house—which her manservants were apparently too pusillanimous to attempt—there would be no getting rid of him. At least not until she listened to whatever he'd come to say. "Hodges," she stated in a quiet voice. "You may withdraw."

The butler darted a glance between her and Ethan. "Yes, ma'am." Retreating into the hallway, he shut the door behind himself and left them alone.

"Well then, speak," she commanded. "And be quick about it, so you may depart with equal haste."

He dropped his arms to his sides. "Must we be at daggers drawn?"

She shot him a look that was hot enough to weld iron. "Yes, I believe we must and you have only yourself to blame. I suppose that is what comes of being manipulated and deceived."

"I did not deceive nor manipulate you," he stated through clenched teeth.

She drew in an audible breath. "Hah! And I suppose you are going to tell me I imagined seeing your engagement notice in this morning's paper. You *are* affianced to that girl, are you not?"

His lips thinned. "At the moment, yes, but I'm—"

"Then I have heard everything I need to hear." Bile burned under her sternum, threatening to leave a hole in its wake. "The door is there. Shut it on your way out."

He growled low in his throat. "I'm not leaving until you let me have my say. Why are you so determined to deny me?"

*Because I can't risk letting go of my anger and possibly letting you in again, not when the wound you've already inflicted has cut so deep.* "Because I don't care to listen to more of your excuses and prevarications!" she said aloud. "How many times must I say it?"

With fury boiling in her blood, she looked around, her gaze alighting on a small porcelain figurine of a shepherdess and a lamb. Without thinking, she picked it up and hurled the china full force at his head. He ducked, the figurine shattering into a dozen pieces against the fireplace surround. Tears stung her eyes, appalled by what she'd done. Blinking fast, she refused to weep, determined not to let him see the extent of her distress.

"Last night was not my idea," he defended, plainly braced to dodge anything else she planned to throw in his direction. "I had no idea my mother was going to do what she did. If I had, I would have stopped her."

"And what difference would that have made? Obviously, you were secretly engaged, even if it had not been announced yet."

"I was not engaged. It's true that I spoke to Amelia Dodd's father several months ago before I had even met you. But there was no marriage agreement, and no engagement between Lady Amelia and myself."

"Your mother and the earl obviously believed there to be."

His fingers drew taut at his sides. "The earl believes what he wants to in order to satisfy his own objectives. As for my mother . . . well, she knows better and pro-

ceeded regardless in order to force my hand. Sutleigh
and Mama have been dynasty-building in their heads for
decades. One of my brothers was supposed to do the
honor of joining the families by marriage, but after
Arthur's and Frederick's deaths, the task fell to me. I
should never have even entertained the notion of acced-
ing to their plans—"

"But you did," she accused.

He met her gaze. "I wasn't going to marry her. I had
already decided to speak with Lord Sutleigh and tell him
I would not be offering for his daughter, after all. I
would have talked to him before the ball had I realized
he was in town."

"Oh, and all these weeks before, you had no access to
pen and ink?"

He raked his fingers through his hair, sending the
golden strands into a disarray that only made him more
appealing. Lily cursed herself for noticing, and for being
susceptible to his magnetism even now. *The strength to
resist him will come with time,* she assured herself, des-
olation sweeping through her like a bitter January wind.

"Frankly, I had all but forgotten about my overtures
in that direction," he said. "Nothing was settled between us, or so I thought, and I was far too wrapped up
in you to pay the matter any heed."

"So now I am to blame for your inability to remember
being engaged."

"How many times do I have to tell you, I was not engaged!" he roared.

"Perhaps not then, but you are now," she said in a
quiet voice. *Oh God, he is to marry another and the
knowledge is tearing me apart!* She held her arms close
to her chest and struggled against the need to tremble.

He tossed up a hand. "Yes, all right, fine, I am engaged. But it is only temporary. You have to believe that
I do not want to marry her."

In that, she could see he was being honest. Releasing a sigh, she lowered her arms to her sides. "Even if I do believe you, it changes nothing. You are engaged to . . ." She swallowed and tried to say the name, but the appellation refused to travel past her lips. ". . . th-that girl, and the matter cannot be undone."

"Yes, it can," he stated, striding forward. "And it will. I'll find a way."

"What way, Ethan? Not counting the seventy-five or so people who heard the announcement last night, there is the notice in *The Morning Post* to consider. There is no taking this back. You are pledged to her." She paused and drew a shaky breath. "Unless she is foolish enough to change her mind and release you from your promise, the engagement will stand."

He narrowed the space between them. "It will not. I will see this travesty ended one way or the other. Right now, she is refusing to call off the engagement, but I will find a way to convince her otherwise."

"So you've spoken with her already?"

"Yes. I came here directly from meeting with her. I couldn't let another minute go by without talking to you. I tried to explain all this last night, if you will recall, but you were too upset to listen. Now, you are finally hearing me out." He wrapped his hands around her arms. "Lily, you are the one I want—not her, never her. Give me time to straighten this out; trust me enough to make things right again."

"But how can I when you lied to me? How can I trust anything you say when you deceived me from the start?"

"Because I love you."

Her heart turned over in her chest. *Loves me?* she wondered. *Does he truly?*

A need rose inside her, so sharp it was very nearly painful. Lord, how she wanted to believe him. How she longed to put aside her hurt and anger and accept his declaration without the necessity for questions or doubt. What a relief it would be to set aside all this discord between them and simply go on as before. To once again be held within the sheltering strength of his arms, secure in the knowledge that he loved her as she loved him. Yet as much as she ached to give in—and heaven knew she did—something continued to hold her back.

"If you do love me," she challenged, "you certainly have an odd way of showing it."

He gazed into her eyes for a long, intense moment. "Maybe this will better demonstrate my feelings," he murmured. Before she could object, his mouth lowered to hers as he swept her into an embrace she found herself powerless to deny.

Seductive and sensual, the thrill of his kiss blazed through her with the quick, raging heat of a summer fire. Yielding, she let him take her deep, drawing her into their own private world where nothing existed but lush need and boundless pleasure. Softening, she returned his kiss, matching his passion with her own. Breath ragged, she savored the intoxicating scent of his skin, opening her lips wider to capture the dark, luscious flavors that lingered like honey on his tongue.

He pressed her tightly against him, making no effort to conceal the unmistakable evidence of his growing arousal. Turning his head, he claimed her lips from a different angle, gliding his hand down her back, and past her waist, to stroke over the curves of her buttocks.

The sensation awakened a dormant corner of her mind, reminding her what came next. If she let their lovemaking proceed, he would soon be whisking her up into his arms and carrying her into the bedroom. Once that happened, the battle would be lost.

*She* would be lost.

Ethan said he loved her, but did he really? Or were his

promises nothing more than a clever means of worming his way back into her bed? Before yesterday, she had believed in him implicitly, thinking him to be everything that was honorable and good. Last night had shattered her faith, ripped the blinders of delusion from her eyes.

*What if he is lying to me again?* she wondered. *What if he only wants a convenient bed partner for the time being—all the while intending to marry that girl to please his family and further his noble lineage?* The idea had the same shocking effect as a dunk in an icy river, waking her up, making her think. Suddenly she realized she had to free herself, that at all costs, she must protect what remained of her heart.

"No!" she cried, breaking their kiss. "No, stop." On a harsh gasp, she wrenched herself from his arms.

"Lily, what—" He reached for her again, but she took several faltering steps backward.

"No, don't touch me. So long as you are engaged to her, do not so much as come near me. I want you out!"

"You don't mean that. You are not being reasonable—"

"Am I not?" she charged. "I am not the one who lied about his intentions. The one who has promised himself to another and is no longer free. I may have been your lover, Ethan, but by God, I will not be your whore!"

His head went back as if she had struck him, his skin paling. "I am not asking you to be."

"Aren't you? Because I'll be no better than one if I agree to let you back into my life. And I will have nothing but your promise that you will not wed her. What am I to do when the day comes and you cannot break the engagement? What will I be left to think when you walk down the aisle with another woman?"

Anger flashed in his eyes, his hands balling into fists. "I won't be walking down the aisle with any other woman. The only one I want is *you,* and I would ask you to marry me today if I were free to do so." He paced a pair of steps. "Damn and blast, I am not lying!"

Her breath hitched in her throat, hope welling upward like a glittering spring at the thought of being his wife. But just as quickly, she remembered his engagement. Her shoulders slumped. In the past, she had wished for things, prayed for them with a steadfast faith, only to be disappointed. If she let herself believe and he betrayed her, she didn't know how she would be able to go on.

With a shake of her head, she quashed her longing. "No. You need to go away. I cannot let myself trust you. I know far too much about broken promises and easy deceptions. My father spent his life telling one tale after another to us, spinning his stories in order to convince my mother and me that he would stay, that next time would be different. Until he lied again. Until he left again. I won't let you do that to me."

"Dear God, Lily, you're refusing to trust me because of your father? In case you have forgotten, he and I are not the same man."

"No, but you are both men," she declared, too wound up to consider her words. "Timothy Bainbridge was a selfish wanderer, who hurt people with his carelessness and neglect. And my stepfather . . . well, he is a vile serpent disguised in a pretty skin. But you, Ethan, in your own way, you are worse than both of them because you made me think there could be something more, made me believe we could have something pure and good and real. But that's not possible, not anymore."

*So why do I still love him? Why does the thought of sending him away make me want to rage and cry?* Furious at her own weakness, she straightened her shoulders. "I want you out. Now! And just in case you decide to try sneaking in one night, I must inform you, your house key will no longer work. I have had the locks changed, on every door and window."

His cheekbones tightened, fury snapping like a whip in his eyes, along with what appeared to be pain. When he spoke, his words were like ice. "I assure you, madam, should I choose to sneak in here one night, your trifling efforts to prevent me will have no effect. But rest assured, I shall not importune your favors without your prior express consent.

"Be aware, however, that this is far from over between us and I will be back. When I return, it will be as a free man, no longer engaged to any woman. On that day, I will expect a suitable recompense from you for your marked lack of faith. So, madam, I suggest you use the intervening time to consider how you plan to beg for my forgiveness. If you do it well enough, I might decide to take you back, though it may be as nothing more than my mistress."

Her lips parted on a silent gasp.

"I bid you good day, Mrs. Smythe." Executing a sharp bow, he turned on his heel and strode from the room.

Agony blossomed beneath her breasts, a pain that lodged like a stone near her heart. *Did I misjudge him?* she wondered. *Was I wrong to send him away? Oh God, what have I done? And if he truly does love me, has that love now turned to hate?*

Trembling, she sank into a nearby chair and pressed her knuckles to her lips. A tear slid down her cheek, hot against her cold skin before it dripped onto her bodice. More tears joined the first as she buried her face in her hands and began to cry.

Long hours later, Ethan swirled the brandy in his snifter, watching the translucent spirit run in clinging rivulets inside the glass, the liquid winking as its depths refracted in the candlelight. Abruptly losing interest, he drank down the whole, then raised a pair of fingers to signal one of the White's Club waiters to bring him another.

As the servant left to do his bidding, a new figure arrived and lowered himself into the chair opposite with an insouciant grace that only a full-blooded duke could carry off.

"Haven't you had enough?" Wyvern remarked, nodding toward the empty snifter—the fifth Ethan had downed since arriving at the club.

Ethan's lip curled. "I would have to say no, since I am still capable of carrying on a conversation with you. If you've come to bully me, you can take yourself off again."

"Me? Bully a man who is so obviously blue-deviled? What sort of friend would I be if I did that?"

"The kind who's come to gloat, no doubt. Go on, say it. I was an idiot for aligning myself to that girl, to that child that I will never love, and to whom I may yet find myself leg-shackled. Quite against my will, I might add."

Wyvern gave a sympathetic shrug. "Well, I will admit I did warn you, but you are miserable enough without me rubbing more salt into your wounds."

Ethan beat a fist against the padded arm of his chair. "I've got to do something, Tony. Amelia Dodd has to be made to see reason and agree to call off this travesty."

"Is that why you are so low?"

Meeting his friend's gaze, he shook his head. "Lily has cast me out."

"Ah. I had wondered how she was taking the news."

"Not well. She has convinced herself that I am lying about my real intentions toward Lady Amelia. She thinks I only want to continue having my way with her, and that I plan to marry Amelia regardless of my promises otherwise."

"And what *do* you want from her?"

"Everything," he said, his voice softening. "I love her, Tony. Furious as I am with Lily for not trusting me, my feelings for her are stronger than ever. If only she could see that. If only she would believe me and give me time to figure a way out of this mess. Blast my mother for her meddling!"

"You'll get no arguments from me on that subject."

No, he would not, Ethan knew, well aware of Tony's history with his own mother.

The waiter arrived, setting down a tumbler of Scotch for Wyvern and a fresh brandy for him. The duke waited until the man departed before proffering a comment. "Regretful as it is to say, what can you do if Lady Amelia insists on proceeding with the wedding?"

Ethan scrubbed a hand over his face. "I'm not certain, short of jilting her. But there has to be some other means of convincing her to call off the engagement."

"And if there is not? Are you prepared to repudiate her and face the scandal that will inevitably follow? Many will view such an act as unpardonable, especially your family and hers."

*So long as Lily will have me, I do not care what anyone else thinks. But will she welcome me back? Or am I only assuming the depths of her feelings for me?*

Despite her obvious anger over his perfidy, she had never actually said she loved him. Given her opinions about the steadfastness of men, he was no longer certain such feelings would matter. He had wounded her badly by lying, he realized, even if that lie had been one of omission instead of outright deceit. When the time came, he would have to work hard to win back her trust. But would she let him, or would she bar him forever from her heart and her life?

"I will do whatever is required not to marry Amelia," he said, "on that I am resolved." Lifting his glass, he tossed back a long draught, enjoying the fiery tang the alcohol left in his mouth. "And it is not as if she really even wishes to wed me. Apparently, Lady Amelia is in love with the local vicar's son, some impoverished fellow whose suit the earl will not entertain. If only I could convince her to run off with him, my problems would be solved." He froze, suddenly aware of what he'd just said. "My God, that's it!"

"What's it?"

"I need to get Amelia and her would-be beau alone together in the same room, then put the idea of an elopement into their heads. Surely, if she loves him as much as she claims, she won't be able to resist running off to marry him, despite the threat of her father's ire."

Tony gave a faint snort. "Which is sure to be formidable indeed, were such an event to occur."

Ethan ignored Wyvern's remark and set his glass aside. Leaning forward in his chair, he smiled, hope buoying his spirits for the first time since this matrimonial disaster had begun. Concentrating, he felt frown lines take shape on his forehead. "Now I just have to remember his name," he murmured aloud. "What was it? Robert something . . . Robert . . . Robert what?" He trailed off for a moment, then snapped his fingers. "Hocksby! Robert Hocksby. And considering that he is the vicar's son and an apprentice physician, he should not be too hard to locate."

The duke met his gaze, one of his dark brows taking wing. "Oh, no—"

"Oh, yes. Tony, how would you like to take a little trip?"

## Chapter Twenty-one

LILY TRIED TO focus on the printed words in front of her, but every time she returned to the story, her thoughts would drift away, invariably settling upon Ethan.

With a sigh, she gave up the attempt at reading and set her book aside. More than a week had passed since he had walked into this very room, demanding that she listen to his side of the circumstances that had led to "the engagement," as she had taken to calling it. Well, she had listened; then she had turned him away. Despite her edict, a part of her had expected—perhaps even hoped—that he would once again attempt to contact her.

But nothing.

His silence was absolute, as though there had never been any kind of relationship between them at all. And perhaps for him their affair really was done. He'd said what existed between them was not finished, that he would be back to prove his word and reclaim her as his own. And yet if the society pages were to be believed, he was having no difficulty forgetting her. Reports mentioned him out and about—Lord Vessey attending one party after another, Lady Amelia often seen on his arm.

This morning when she'd read about him dancing with his fiancée last night, she'd ripped the column from the paper and fed the crumpled page to the fire. For a moment, she'd derived a measure of perverse satisfaction in seeing the newsprint burn, but once the paper had turned to flying bits of blackened ash, a familiar melancholy returned.

She had stopped crying and was forcing herself to climb out of bed each morning, to wash and dress and eat breakfast exactly as she had always done. Yet nothing was right anymore, most especially her.

She missed Ethan more than she had realized was possible. In her weak moments, she even imagined herself going to him and agreeing to be his mistress again if he would have her. But pride held her steady, her sense of self-worth keeping her from making an utter cake of herself. Which is why she had stayed at home this past week, refusing callers—even Davina, who had stopped twice to inquire about her welfare. She was having Hodges give out the tale that she had come down ill with a cold, but of course, anyone with a brain could guess the real reason for her malaise.

At first she had wondered if she truly was ill, so tired and listless she'd barely managed to leave her bed long enough to take a meal. For a brief while she had wondered if she might be with child, but one morning soon after, she had awakened to a familiar cramping ache and had known there was no baby.

She ought to have been relieved, since heaven knows the last thing she needed was to find herself carrying Ethan's out-of-wedlock child. But perversely the knowledge only brought on a fresh bout of tears, as though the discovery placed an even greater distance between her and Ethan.

Sighing again now, she gazed out the window at the cool but sunny November day. Generally, she would have been outside enjoying the city on such a fine afternoon. *And regardless of my humor,* she realized, *that is precisely what I ought to do.*

Moping was not like her. In the past, she had always met life's difficulties with action and fortitude. This time should be no different, in spite of the recent blow to her heart. After all, even if she wished it, she could not hide away forever.

*Life goes on, and so must I.*

Resolved, she rose from her chair and walked out of the room then down the hallway. Vaguely she heard voices, but she was too wrapped up in her own thoughts to pay them much heed. Rounding the top of the stairs, she started down. "Hodges," she called, "please have my phaeton made ready. I wish to go out."

"By God, it *is* you!" remarked a silky voice that hid a core of menace. "For a dead woman, I must say you look remarkably fit."

Lily's feet slipped on the wool staircase runner, a quick grab at the railing all that saved her from a fall. As she clung, she gazed down at a face she'd hoped never to see again, her heart pounding like death drums in her ears.

*Gordon Chaulk.* And beside him, Edgar Faylor, an expression of triumph glittering in his cruel black eyes.

"I told you it was her," Faylor said.

"Indeed, you did, Edgar," replied her stepfather, his polished good looks as much in ironic juxtaposition to his reptilian character as ever.

"I am sorry, ma'am. I told them you were not receiving," Hodges declared from his place next to the door. And she could not blame him for letting them in. From the position of the door, she could tell that he had obviously been in the process of forcing the two men out when she had unwittingly rushed onto the scene.

Saliva dried on her tongue, the metallic taste of fear rising into her throat. If running would have done her any good, she would have sprinted away. But escape, she knew, was already too late.

*Oh God, they have found me!*

The following afternoon, Ethan grinned and gave himself a silent pat on the back as he stood in his study and reread the urgent note he had just received from the Earl of Sutleigh. In it, the earl was pained to share the "dreadful" news that late last night his daughter, Amelia, had run away with Mr. Robert Hocksby, an unsuitable boy with whom she fancied herself in love. Even now, the earl was in his coach on the Great North Road hoping to catch the wayward pair before they reached Gretna Green.

What the earl did not know was that the lovers were traveling in one of Ethan's fastest unmarked coaches, and that arrangements had been made so that they would have a quick and easy change of horses at each coaching stop along the way. If the pair continued on with no overnight stops, they should arrive in Scotland well ahead of the earl and be married by the time he discovered them—most likely the following day. Should matters somehow work out otherwise, Ethan knew he need not worry since Amelia would have been well and truly compromised by that time, leaving the earl no choice but to let his daughter marry her beloved Robert.

When Tony had arrived two days ago with Hocksby in tow, however, Ethan had not at first been sure his plan would succeed. Intelligent and earnest, with a pair of discerning gray eyes, Hocksby had initially been suspicious of Ethan's suggestion of an elopement. He had also been offended at what he saw as nothing short of a bribe.

"I cannot accept twenty thousand pounds from you," Hocksby declared, his shoulders squared with outraged pride. "I would appear no better than a fortune hunter."

"But do you love her?"

Something shifted in Robert's young face, a longing that was plain to see. "Of course I love her, more than you will ever know."

"Then you surely want her happiness, which is why you must do as I suggest. If Amelia and I wed, she will never be happy, and she most definitely will never be yours."

Sadness shone in Hocksby's gaze, a misery Ethan could well understand since his own recent separation from Lily.

"As for the money," Ethan continued, "I am not offering you a lump sum outright. I would be granting you a living on my lands in Suffolk, caring for those in the surrounding village and town. We have need of a skilled medical practitioner, but first I would expect you to attend and graduate from medical college. I understand you have an interest in that field."

"Yes, I do." Hocksby appeared mildly stunned, but the fresh glow of interest was clear in his eyes. "So let me understand this rightly. I could study medicine, have a practice after I earn my degree, and possess the financial means to marry Amelia too? Why? Why would you do this for me?"

"I am not doing it for you. There is someone I love as well. Elope with Amelia, so that all of us might be happy."

Moments later, Hocksby was pumping Ethan's hand in gratitude and saying yes, demanding to know how soon he might speak with his beloved.

Convincing Amelia to defy her father had taken a bit of doing as well, but once she heard about Ethan's offer, and stood inside the circle of Robert's loving arms, she couldn't bring herself to refuse the chance to be his wife.

After that, Ethan and Tony had made all the arrangements, even helping the lovers flee in the dark of night.

The plan had proceeded without difficulty, in part because Ethan had been careful all the previous week to act the dutiful fiancé. He'd wanted no possibility of suspicion, especially on Sutleigh's part, that he was planning to do anything other than proceed with his engagement to Amelia.

With that problem now resolved, he was once again free to return to Lily and show her he'd meant what he said. First he would have to convince her to trust him again. Once she did, he would persuade her to put aside her fears and agree to be his bride. He'd already known that he loved her, but these past few days apart had only intensified his feelings, showing him that nothing less than a lifetime of loving her would do.

Setting the letter on his desk, he turned to go upstairs to refresh his attire so he might depart to see Lily. Glancing up, he discovered his butler standing on the threshold.

"A Mr. Ross is here to see you, my lord," the older man announced.

*Ross! Good heavens.* In all the recent upheaval, he'd completely forgotten about the request he'd made of the other man. Well, Ross's timing could not have been better, since Ethan would be able to learn something of Lily's husband before he returned to plead his case. Surely, the extra knowledge could only do him good.

"By all means, show him in."

Ross strode into the study less than a minute later, looking harried and disheveled, as usual.

Ethan moved to shake his hand and offer a warm greeting. "I was not expecting you, but very glad you have come. Have a seat and let me get you a drink."

"No time for drinks, Vessey," Ross said as he sank down into the chair.

Ethan leaned a hip against his desk. "Well then, what news have you for me?"

"Some of the rather unexpected kind, I believe you will agree. Actually, the search took me a great deal longer than planned."

"Oh," Ethan said, lifting a brow. "And why is that?"

"Principally because this fellow you sent me to look for—this John Smythe—well, the long and short of it is that he does not exist."

"What? But that is impossible. There must be some mistake."

"And so I thought initially. But after checking the records and coming up empty-handed, I took the initiative to write to all the commanding officers who lost men at Vittoria. To a man, not one of them ever served with a 'John Smythe.' "

Ethan felt his mouth drop open. *How is that possible?* he questioned. It made no sense. Yet his friend Ross was sharp and meticulous in his work, and not the sort who was prone to making mistakes. If he said there was no John Smythe, then there was no John Smythe.

"Are you positive of the name?" Ross inquired.

"Yes, of course, I am positive. Lily has mentioned him any number of times."

And yet, when he really considered the matter, she had always been strangely reticent to talk about her husband, providing scant details about his background and her time with him. She'd never even said how they met, come to think of it. In the past, he had always attributed her silence to grief, resisting the urge to press for specifics. But what if her reserve stemmed from an entirely different cause?

*No, it could not be,* he told himself. Thoughts tumbled through his brain like rough stones, the edges being smoothed and polished as ideas and suppositions fell into place. A single, niggling fact presented itself, one he'd convinced himself to dismiss long ago, but which

had never really made sense. Lily Smythe was a widow,
and yet she had come to his bed a virgin.

An odd tingle ran over his spine like a mocking laugh.

*Lord, it could not be, could it?* Even considering such
an idea seemed preposterous, and yet the notion suddenly made perfect sense. She'd told him her marriage
hadn't been consummated because there had not been
the time. But what if there had been no consummation
because there was no groom! The more he considered
the possibility, the more the wild idea began to make
sense.

*Devil take me, but I think widow Lily Smythe is no
widow at all!* And if she is not, then . . .

Fury spread through him like drops of ink splashed
onto a blank page, bleeding outward in ever-widening
circles until all that remained was black. Eyes narrowed,
he fisted his hands at his sides. *What a dupe I've been!*
he raged. *What a cretin!* And to think how easily he'd
fallen for her stories of tragedy and grief, her tales of
love lost and how she couldn't bear to ever wed again,
when in truth she'd had no husband and no man to
mourn. Later he might be glad to know her heart had
never belonged to anyone else, but right now, he was too
irate to care. *Why, the little conniver! When I next lay
hands upon her, she might do well to run,* he fumed inwardly, ideas of paddling her backside black-and-blue
dancing in his brain.

"Vessey, are you well?" Ross asked, an inquiring
frown on his brow.

Ethan startled and looked across at the other man,
having forgotten Ross was even in the room. "I am
fine."

As for Lily, he couldn't vouch for how she would be
once he'd finished with her.

*        *        *

Ethan was in a rare lather by the time he rapped on the front-door knocker of Lily's Bloomsbury townhouse. Nearly two hours had passed since Ross had arrived at Andarton House and shattered every assumption he'd ever held about Lily. If his suspicions proved correct—and he was convinced they would—then she had a great deal of explaining to do, along with an enormous amount of groveling and begging for forgiveness.

To think she had the nerve to castigate him for lying! What he'd done was minuscule compared to the extent of her own apparent falsehoods, and at least his omissions had not been done with the deliberate intention of deceiving. Whatever her reason for masquerading as a bereaved widow, it had better be a good one. He was just waiting to hear, and hear he would, since he meant to have things out with her. As for the paddling, he was still debating that. Whatever occurred, once their confrontation was finished, all the lies between them would be over—for good.

As soon as the door opened, he stepped inside without waiting for Hodges to invite him to enter. But instead of the butler's usual polite greeting, he saw what looked like alarm on his face.

"Oh, my lord," Hodges said in a rush, "I am so glad you have come. Perhaps it is not my place, but Mrs. Smythe . . . she . . . she . . ."

Part of Ethan's ire fell away, a trickle of uneasiness replacing the emotion. "Yes? She what? Where is Lily?"

"Gone, my lord. She departed yesterday afternoon with a pair of men, who arrived quite unexpectedly."

The trickle of disquiet became a surge, his throat squeezing tight. "What pair of men? And why would she leave with them?"

"The one said he is her stepfather and that he had come to take her home."

With difficulty, Ethan forced himself to stay calm. "And the other one?"

Hodges glanced away, obviously reluctant to meet his gaze. "He claimed to be her fiancé. Madam did not appear to agree, but said little on the subject. I got the distinct impression that she disliked the man quite a lot. I don't believe she much liked her stepfather either."

Ethan did not doubt that, although until recently, he hadn't even realized she had a stepfather. What had she called him? A vile serpent disguised in a pretty skin? And what was this about a fiancé? Preposterous!

"And she went willingly?" he demanded.

The other man glanced away again. "She left, although ever since she departed, I have wondered if it was of her own free will. She did not even take her lady's maid."

"What were their names, these men? Do you remember?"

"Her stepfather announced himself as Chaulk. Yes, that was it. Gordon Chaulk. As for the other man, I only heard his first name. Edgar, Chaulk called him. Big fellow, he was, reminded me of an ox."

A big scary ox and his reptilian associate, who had terrified Lily enough to force her from her home.

"Oh, and he said something curious, my lord."

Ethan glanced at the servant. "Yes? And what was that?"

"Chaulk remarked that she looked awfully fit for a dead woman. What could he have meant by that?"

Yes indeed, what had he meant? Had Lily been playing a corpse? Had she pretended to be dead for the same reason she had assumed the identity of a widow? *Good heavens, in what sort of danger is she? And how am I going to get her out of it?*

"She left yesterday, you said?"

Hodges nodded. "In the early afternoon. Mrs. Smythe

went upstairs with her stepfather and returned carrying a portmanteau. Susan wanted to accompany them, but she was refused."

Ethan's gut clenched. Had Lily been threatened? Is that why she had left without a struggle? "Did they say where they were headed?" he asked.

"She did, and rather distinctly, as if she were anxious for me to remember, now that I think upon it. She said she would be traveling to Bainbridge Manor near Penzance, and that if any of her friends should call for her, I was to tell them to come visit her very soon. Her stepfather gave her a fearsome glare; then the three of them were out the door, driving away in his coach."

*A cry for help,* Ethan thought, *if I ever heard one. Good for you, Lily.* But why had she not tried to contact him? Perhaps, given their recent troubles, she had thought she could not. If only he had resolved matters with Amelia a day earlier, maybe he could have prevented Lily from being forced to leave London. Well, he was going after her now, and he would not return without her.

At that same moment, many miles distant, Lily picked at her dinner of boiled beef and cabbage, the precarious nature of her situation leaving her very little appetite. Chaulk and Faylor suffered from no such difficulties, contentedly eating the meal provided to them by the proprietors of the coaching inn where they had stopped for a change of horses and a bite of dinner.

Situated on the main road that led west from London, the inn was similar to many others along the route, the cramped common room bustling with noisy patrons, a pungent mixture of beer, onions, and tobacco smoke scenting the air. On their arrival, the innkeeper had offered them the quiet comfort of a private parlor, but Chaulk resented paying for anything he considered an unnecessary expense—and "expensive private parlors" fell into that category. To be honest, though, Lily was just as glad to be among a crowd, worn already by the hours she had spent closed inside the coach with the two men.

"Eat up," Chaulk advised, gesturing with his fork toward the uneaten portion on her plate. "We'll not be stopping again for food until daybreak. Should you find yourself hungry, it shall be your own fault for being too stubborn and choosy."

*Choosy, am I? Nauseated, actually. Or has he no conception of how thoroughly I detest him and his unctuous cohort?*

Agreeing to leave London with them had been a huge mistake, she realized now, but at the time her options had seemed extremely limited. Particularly when Chaulk told her he would summon the authorities and have her arrested for thievery. As her legal guardian, he had sole discretion over not only her person, but her wealth. Galling as the reality might be, as an unmarried female, she had no right to spend her inheritance without her stepfather's express consent. And not only had she staged her own death and run away—probably crimes in their own right—but she had been living under a false identity during her time in London. Even worse, she had been doing so as a married woman. She knew that Chaulk was by no means exaggerating when he said the law would take his side should he decide to file an official complaint. In the eyes of the court, she belonged to him.

She'd been stunned when she had come down her townhouse stairs to find him and Faylor standing in her front hall. All she could think in those first few moments was that the bullnecked man at the fair those many weeks ago really had been Faylor. Still reeling, she

had allowed herself to be bullied into doing as Chaulk
ordered—at the time seeing no other means of escape,
not with him literally dogging her every step. She'd con-
soled herself with ideas of fleeing later, but the farther
she traveled from London, the more unlikely such an
opportunity appeared.

*Oh, God,* she bemoaned, *what if he succeeds in forcing me to return home? Worse still, what if he manages
to marry me off to Faylor?*

Her stomach literally churned at the idea, a shiver
raising goose pimples on her skin when she glanced up
to find Faylor leering at her breasts. Slowly lifting his
gaze to hers, he licked a glossy bit of beef fat off his thick
lips as if he were imagining tasting her instead. When
she visibly shuddered, he laughed, then ate another forkful of his dinner.

"Enough of that for now, Edgar," her stepfather admonished in an even tone. "You'll have plenty of time to
woo my daughter once the pair of you are wed."

"I would as soon marry a goat!" she said, unable to
contain the words.

Chaulk's handsome face grew hard and without so
much as a glimmer of warning, he reached across the
table and brought his palm down hard across her cheek.

She gasped, her ears ringing while a fiery blaze of pain
engulfed the entire left side of her face. Trembling, she
lifted her hand to cover the wound, sniffing back the
tears that rose automatically to her eyes.

"There'll be worse than that if you do not behave,"
Chaulk told her in a voice made all the more menacing
by its restraint. As though he had not just struck her in
plain view of an entire room of people—people who she
noticed were doing nothing to help her—Chaulk patted
his lips on his napkin, folded the cloth neatly, and set it
aside. He fixed a pair of gimlet eyes on her untouched

meal. "If you are finished, we should be continuing on our way."

*I cannot just leave,* she realized. *There must be something I can do, some way to save myself even now. No matter the danger, I have to try.*

"V-very well," she said, deliberately casting her eyes downward in a show of obeisance. "But first, I need to use the necessary."

He sighed. "Yes, all right. I shall accompany you."

"To the ladies' water closet? How indiscreet!" She once more lowered her gaze to emphasize her supposed embarrassment.

Her stepfather said nothing for a long moment, then leaned back and chuckled. "Such delicate sensibilities! Go on, then, but if you aren't back in five minutes, Edgar and I will come looking for you and you won't like it."

"I will return," she promised, giving him a compliant little smile.

Gripping her reticule, which by some miracle they had allowed her to keep, Lily made her way out of the common room and down the hall to the ladies' necessary. In case one of the men had followed her and was watching, she went inside and latched the door. But instead of tending to the call of nature, she opened her handbag and drew out a small, silver-cased writing tablet and pencil. Thinking fast, she composed a message, one she'd had no time nor opportunity to write before leaving home.

*Ethan,*
*I am in trouble and beseech your help. Come without delay to Bainbridge Manor near Penzance. I promise to explain everything later.*
*Anxiously awaiting your arrival,*
*Lily*

Folding the paper in half, she quickly inscribed Ethan's name and address on the outside. She'd made a point of telling Hodges where she could be reached, but she had little hope that Ethan would call at her London town-house anytime soon. And despite her request for a "visit" from her friends, she was doubtful any of them would realize she needed their assistance, especially considering that none of them knew of her present distress.

Palming a guinea coin, together with the note, she cracked open the door and peered out. With no evidence of Chaulk or Faylor in sight, she eased out of the room. Her palms grew moist, her heart beating in her throat as she hurried along the hallway in hopes of locating one of the inn's staff. She would have to be quick though, or else risk being missed by her stepfather.

Just then, a maid emerged from the kitchen. Lily raced toward her. "Please," she murmured in a hushed undertone, "you must help me. I am in terrible difficulty. Pray see that this note is delivered with utmost speed. Here, take this note and say you will see it on its way."

Eyes wide, the servant girl stared. "A-all right, miss, but is there naught I can do?"

Lily shook her head. "No. Say nothing to anyone. Please just promise you will make certain this missive is sent at the first opportunity."

When the girl nodded her agreement, Lily reached out to press the paper and coin into her palm. Before the exchange could be completed, though, a large male hand descended like a claw and snatched the note from her grasp. The gold guinea popped free as well, bouncing and spinning across the wooden floor.

"And what have we here?" Chaulk demanded.

A shiver stole through her as she glanced up and met her stepfather's cold blue gaze. Opening the note, he gave the message a quick perusal, then folded the paper again. With apparent calm, he tore the page into little strips, then crushed the whole inside his palm. "You will have to excuse my daughter," he said, turning to the servant girl to give her his most charming smile. "She is rather prone to hysterics."

Lily's heart sank as she watched the young woman respond to his handsome countenance and practiced guile, the girl casting her an uncertain glance. If only she realized that his seemingly pleasant exterior hid a core of malevolence and deceit!

"She is always imagining things," Chaulk continued, "making up stories of danger and mayhem where none exist at all." Striding across the hallway, he bent to retrieve the coin. "Here," he said, holding it out to the servant. "Take this and let us forget all about the incident. I do my best to care for my dear daughter, you know, but some days she can be a trial."

When the serving girl looked at her again, her gaze was filled with pity and derision.

"Come along, Lily," he said, taking her arm in a bruising grip, "we should be on our way." Turning her, he marched her toward the front door.

But she refused to fall in line, digging in her heels as she tried to break free of his grasp. "He's lying!" she called to the girl. "Please, you must believe me." Ignoring the pain in her arm as Chaulk hauled her forward, she called out again. "Contact the Marquis of Vessey in Mayfair, London! Tell him Lily Smythe needs him. He can find me near Penzan—"

"Enough," Chaulk hissed in her ear as he forced her outside into the coaching yard. "Lily Smythe indeed. Has your lover any idea who you really are? No matter, since he isn't going to come to your aid. From what I hear, he has already washed his hands of you in favor of an earl's daughter."

*Ethan would help me,* she assured herself, *if he knew I needed him.* Whatever their recent difficulties, he wasn't the sort of man to stand idle while an injustice was done—and forcing her to return home and marry against her will was most definitely an injustice. Still, what would he think if he knew that she had lied about her identity? How angry would he be? Angry enough to turn his back on her? Then again, she would probably never know, since Chaulk had thwarted her attempt to contact him.

Her stepfather forced her onward. "Considering what a trollop you've become since your 'death,' you ought to be grateful Faylor is still willing to marry you. Frankly, I'd give you to him without a wedding ceremony, but then he would be under no obligation to cut me in for half of his mining interests, and I want those mines. Luckily, he doesn't mind enjoying soiled goods." He gave her a shake. "Do you know what a great deal of trouble and expense you have put me to, searching for you? If Edgar hadn't seen you at that fair, parading around on your protector's arm, you might well have left us in ignorance of your deception. Think you're clever, do you? Well, we'll see how clever you are now. Here is the coach; get in."

Shifting her weight, she tried to break free, though where she hoped to run, she had no idea. She cried out, pain jabbing like a knife through her arm as Chaulk's hand tightened so fiercely she was surprised the bone didn't snap. Unshed tears burned her eyes.

"You'd best behave." He glared down at her. "Any more tricks from you, and you may well find yourself traveling in the luggage boot."

Lily trembled, knowing his threats were never idle ones. She ceased her struggles.

"Good choice," Chaulk murmured. Turning his head, he nodded as Faylor approached. "If you are ready, Edgar, shall we depart?"

"Yes, let us be on our way. I am most anxious to reach

home." Climbing inside, he settled his solid frame, then leaned over and patted the seat beside him. "Miss Lily can sit by me," he invited with a lecherous grin.

Chaulk gave her a small shove. "You heard your fiancé. Step in and keep him company. We have a long ride ahead."

She steeled herself for the ordeal to come, then climbed inside. A shudder raked her frame when Faylor reached over and clasped her hand.

Acting on instinct, she yanked her palm free. "Don't touch me!" She prepared herself to suffer a blow— another slap, or worse. Instead, Faylor tossed back his big head and released a booming laugh. "Play your little games for now, missy," he said, waving Chaulk into his seat opposite. "There'll be plenty of time for touching once we're wed in a few days' time." He gave her a wink.

Bile rose into her throat, and in that moment, she vowed that she would never marry this man. *Somehow I will find a way out,* she thought. She couldn't afford to consider the alternative.

# Chapter Twenty-two

❧

$T$RAVEL-WORN AND WEARY, with cold, wet mud caking his boots and the hem of his many-caped greatcoat, Ethan strode into a small tavern on the outskirts of Penzance. After five days of hard riding he was in need of rest, but he couldn't allow himself to pause for more than a few minutes, just long enough to inquire about Bainbridge Manor and be on his way again. Finding Lily was imperative, even more so after the disturbing report he'd heard at one of the coaching stops along the way.

He'd been asking the innkeeper if he'd seen a young woman matching Lily's description when a serving girl interrupted.

"I seen her," she volunteered. "She were with two men. A handsome bloke, who said he was her father, and another one, a stocky, thick-necked sort."

Ethan turned toward her. "Yes? Go on."

The girl cast a quick glance at her employer, who gave her a nod to proceed. Tucking her hands in her apron, she continued. "The lady, she wanted me to send a note fer her. Gave me the coin and everythin', but then her father stopped her. Told me she were knocked queer in the head and to nevermind what she says. But since then I've wondered . . ."

"Wondered what?" Ethan encouraged.

"If she might have been telling the truth after all. Said she were in trouble and needed to contact a man. Some marquis in London."

"Vessey. Was the man's name Vessey?"

Her eyes grew round. "Aye, that's it exactly. How did ye know?"

"Because I am Vessey. Now, start again at the beginning and do not leave out a detail."

Since then, he'd been riding as fast as he could, stopping only to change horses, eat a quick meal, and catch an occasional couple of hours' sleep. But even though he made up time, Lily's coach stayed ahead, her stepfather maintaining an equally grueling pace, as if aware he was being pursued.

Now, having journeyed to the very end of England, Ethan was nearly at his destination. Walking up to the tavern's long, wooden bar, he took a seat.

"What'll ye have?" asked a grizzled old man with a missing pair of front teeth.

"Whatever is hot and strong and fast."

"One mulled wine, it'll be." The man turned and approached a kettle on the nearby grate, returning a moment later with a steaming mug.

Ethan slid a coin across the bar—more than was needed to pay for the drink. He took a sip, finding the brew surprisingly tasty. "I'm looking for Bainbridge Manor. I was wondering if you could provide me with directions."

The man frowned. "Got business with Chaulk, have ye?" he said, practically spitting out the words.

"No, I have come to see a young woman. Lily Smythe."

"Don't know no Lily Smythe. You must mean Lily Bainbridge." The barkeeper's eyes turned sad. "Terrible thing that, but then you must not know."

"Know what?"

"About poor Miss Lily. Last spring she were drowned at sea. Her stepfather put out word that she'd gone swimming and met with an accident. But Lily Bainbridge was the nearest thing to a mermaid these shores have ever had. Her father taught her to swim when she were just a wee tyke. No, her death weren't no accident, even if there was a bad storm that day."

"What do you mean?" he ventured.

"I mean she swam out in a gale and let the sea take her rather than marry that brute Faylor. Everybody knows he had the eye for her and she'd turned him down. Heard rumors her stepfather wouldn't take no for an answer, and ordered her to wed the man. She drowned mysterious-like a few days after."

Lily swam out to sea in a storm? How had she survived? "Was a body found?" Ethan asked in a thick voice, already knowing the answer.

"Never. But then many go straight down to the bottom, and never turn up again."

"You say she died rather than wed this man, Faylor. Was she married before?"

"Miss Lily? No. She lived at home her whole life. Took care of her mum until Mrs. Bainbridge—I mean Mrs. Chaulk—died last winter. Mayhap that's why the girl did herself in, too much grief for so short a life."

Ethan drank more wine, beginning to believe he understood. Once he had Lily back, she could explain the rest. "My thanks," he said, "but I am still in need of those directions."

Morning sunlight streamed through the windows of Lily's bedroom—or rather her prison now, since Chaulk had forced her upstairs and inside the room last night after their arrival at Bainbridge Manor. Until Lily married Faylor, he'd told her, she was to remain captive.

Exhausted from long days spent in the coach, she had

stripped off her travel-stained clothes and had taken a sponge bath with the warm water one of the maids brought up to her. The servant—a new girl with whom she was not familiar—had also brought her a meal. Dressed in her shift and a woolen robe, Lily had drunk a cup of hot tea and eaten a couple of bites of roast chicken and mashed potatoes. On the verge of falling asleep, she had soon given up on her meal, choosing instead to stretch out beneath the sheets, her once familiar bed feeling strange beneath her body. Soon enough, however, she had been fast asleep, too tired even for dreams.

Awakening now, she found herself momentarily disoriented. But a quick glimpse of her old blue-and-white-striped wallpaper reminded her precisely where she was—and what day this was supposed to be.

*Her wedding day to Squire Faylor.*

A shudder raked her frame, followed by a sudden burst of determination. Tossing back the covers, she pulled on her robe and shoes, then crossed to the door to give it another try. Locked, just as she had assumed, the metal knob rattling in a fixed position. Whirling around, she moved to the window in search of another means of escape. Admittedly, climbing out the window would be a risky choice given the lengthy drop from her second-story bedroom to the chilly ground below. But if that was the only way to be free, then she would take the chance. Yet when she tried to push open the window, it refused to budge. Straining harder, she tried again, only then taking the time to study the wooden sill.

*Nailed shut!*

Heaving out a breath, she stopped. *Why, that villain!* she thought, silently cursing her stepfather. Before he'd even left for London, he must have ordered her windows sealed. She'd eluded his control once before, and obviously, he was determined she would not be successful at doing so again.

Scanning the room, she spied the utensils from last night's dinner. Scooping them up in her hand, she set to work. Twenty minutes later, the cutlery was bent into a trio of scarred, badly distorted shapes. As for the nails, they had not budged by so much as a fraction of an inch. Next, she tried the fireplace poker, but found the tool too thick to be anything but useless. The bases of two different candlesticks worked no better.

She had just snapped off the tip of her silver letter opener when she heard the sound of a key scraping in the lock. Her muscles stiffened as she prepared herself for a possible confrontation with her stepfather.

Tension flowed out of her when she saw the visitor was only the maid, fresh towels draped over her arm, a pitcher of wash water in her hand. A little gasp escaped the girl's lips as she surveyed the damage Lily had wrought. "Oh my!"

Aware of the door standing open at the servant's back, Lily abruptly knew she could not lose this chance. Ignoring the fact that she was dressed in nothing more than her shift and a robe, she dashed forward.

Brushing past the girl, she wrenched the door wide and raced out into the passageway that led to the main staircase. With any luck the servants would be busy elsewhere, as would her stepfather, who usually spent his mornings inside his study. Her feet flew down the stairs, her heart beating like a set of primal drums. With no footmen in the front foyer, her hope grew stronger, potential freedom only footsteps away. But just as she reached out her hand to open the front door, the knob turned, and there in the doorway stood Faylor and Chaulk.

Dashing sideways, she sprinted toward the rear hallway, hoping somehow she could outrun them both long enough to still get away. But like a fox being hunted by a pack of merciless hounds, she soon found herself cornered. A scream echoed from her throat when Chaulk's hard arms curved around her waist and brought her to a halt.

Spinning her toward him, his hand came up and cuffed her across the face—hard. Pain exploded in her head, her ears ringing like church bells. "What did I say about disobeying me?" he bellowed.

Despite her misery, she refused to cringe before him. *Let him do his worst,* she thought. *Let him beat me to death, since I would prefer it to the abuse I will suffer at Faylor's vile hands.*

But her hopes were dashed yet again when Chaulk lowered his hand to his side. "I knew you'd try something. But it didn't work, did it? Back upstairs with you until the ceremony. After all, you know what they say about it being bad luck for the groom to see the bride before the wedding." He displayed his teeth in a feral grin.

Faylor smiled as well, lustful anticipation gleaming in his dark gaze. He raked his eyes over her body in a way that left her feeling violated.

Caught in her stepfather's steely grip, she was marched back up to her room. She thought he would shove her inside and lock the door, but to her further horror, he dismissed the serving girl and had a pair of his most trusted footmen come in to scour the room for anything she might use as a weapon, or as a further means of escape. When the room had been stripped bare, including the sheets and blankets on the bed, they left, imprisoning her inside.

Sinking onto the naked mattress, she hugged her arms around herself and wondered how she was possibly going to survive the ordeal to come.

\*    \*    \*

An hour later, Ethan rode his horse up the lane toward the entrance of Bainbridge Manor. A large house, the dwelling was constructed of solid Cornish stone, rising heavy and gray against the rugged, rocky landscape and wide, blue sky. Cold and strong, the wind whipped his hair and exposed skin, the scent of brine filling his nostrils—an indication of just how close he was to the sea.

*So this is where Lily was raised,* he mused, knowing suddenly how much the wild, uncompromising territory suited her. An environment such as this demanded strength, and his beautiful Lily had that and so much more.

Now he was here to save her, and claim her as his own at the same time. Swinging down from his mount, he ignored the stares of a pair of servants as he mounted the front steps. Lifting the knocker, he gave a powerful rap.

The broad wooden door creaked faintly as it swung open, a somewhat grizzled middle-aged man pinning him with an inquisitive gaze. "Aye? Who's calling?"

Ethan raised an eyebrow. "The Marquis of Vessey. I am here to see Miss Lily."

The man's eyes rounded like those of an owl, his mouth taking on a similar hooting shape. "M-Miss Lily ain't here. Everybody knows that. She drowned last spring."

"I believe she just unexpectedly returned from the dead, did she not?" he stated in an unequivocal tone, watching an awareness of the truth flash in the older man's gaze. "Now, let me inside."

The servant—obviously under orders to keep out strangers—tried to block Ethan's entrance. Larger, stronger, and far more fit, Ethan had no difficulty forcing open the door and stepping into the entry hall.

"You aren't welcome here," the butler complained. "The master isn't going to like this."

Ethan ignored the warning. "Inform Mrs. . . . Miss Bainbridge, that she has a caller."

"Who the devil are you?" demanded a new voice, one that was silky yet full of menace.

Turning, Ethan glanced across the hall as a handsome, dark-haired man strode out of a nearby room. *Ah, this must be the stepfather,* he mused. "As I already informed your man, I am the Marquis of Vessey and I have come for Lily."

Chaulk blinked, shifting easily into a lie. "You have me at a loss, since my stepdaughter is not here."

"Of course she is here. You came to London and forced her out of her townhouse, coercing her with some threat, I'm sure. I've been tracking you for days, hearing some very interesting reports along the way about two men and the redheaded young woman accompanying them. I also know she attempted to contact me and you prevented her from sending the note. Now tell me where she is."

A sneer turned up the edges of Chaulk's mouth. "Her present location is none of your concern, my lord. Apparently you want her back in your bed, but she has made other plans. My stepdaughter is to be married this very afternoon to the local squire to whom she was promised many months ago. Last spring, she had a few reservations and ran away. She has since had a change of heart, has she not, Faylor?"

Just then, another man—the squire, he presumed—stepped out of a nearby room. Brawny, with rough-hewn features, he reminded Ethan of one of the oxen his tenants sometimes used to plow the fields—though to give Faylor some credit, he did not appear to be quite as lacking in intelligence as the animals. Folding his arms over his heavy chest, Faylor glared, hostility radiating from his stance and gaze. "Be gone," he spat.

Ethan stood his ground. He'd dealt with bullies before and knew the type. Despite being outweighed by several stone, his fighting skills were well up to the challenge should matters come to that. "Oh, I shall leave and gladly, as soon as I have Lily with me."

Striding quickly forward, he headed for the staircase. But Faylor moved just as fast and blocked his way. "You are not going anywhere."

"I would advise you to stand aside, if you do not wish to suffer an injury."

Faylor shared an amused glance with Chaulk. "An injury, is it? I'd like to see you try. Otherwise, slink away and leave my woman to me."

"She is not your woman. Lily is, and always will be, mine," Ethan replied in a deadly quiet tone that would have been warning enough for most.

Instead the squire smirked. "Is that right? Well, we'll see who she ends up spreading her legs for tonight." Sharing another jovial look with Chaulk, Faylor threw back his head and laughed.

He hadn't quite finished the guffaw when Ethan ended it for him by driving his fist hard into the big ox's belly. The squire wheezed out a harsh, gasping breath, bending double in pain. Rather than give him so much as a second to recover, Ethan shifted angles and threw his strength behind a powerful uppercut to the jaw, then another blow in the opposite direction.

The squire staggered slightly but maintained his footing. Red droplets leaked out of his nose, splattering downward to stain the white linen of his neckcloth. Swiping a hand over the top of his lip to clear away the blood, he gazed at the damage in obvious shock. Up came his head, his facial muscles tight with outrage, fury burning like coals in his gaze.

Just then, Ethan heard rushing footsteps on the landing above and glanced up to see a welcome sight. "Lily! Thank God, are you all right?"

"I am now," she called down, gripping the banister. "Whatever they've told you about me, it's a lie. I'm here against my will and don't want to marry him," she said pointing a finger at the squire. "Please, Ethan, please take me away."

"Gladly. It's why I've come."

"The hell she's going with you," roared Faylor.

Ethan heard Lily scream, the sound echoing around the entry hall at the same instant the squire launched himself forward. Moving fast, Ethan leapt back to elude him but was too late. Suddenly pinned inside Faylor's bearlike grip, he wrestled with him for a long moment before they crashed together to the floor, the squire's massive bulk landing on top. Pain ricocheted through his ribs and back, but Ethan ignored it and brought up his fists to pound them into the other man's head. But the squire didn't resemble an ox for nothing, easily shaking off the punishing blows.

Dimly, Ethan heard Lily cry out his name. He wanted to respond, but found his world narrowing fast as Faylor's heavy hand wrapped around his throat and began to squeeze. Sucking in a desperate breath, Ethan struggled, realizing that the man's hold was cutting off his air. Curling his fingers around the brute's grasp, he pried and pulled to break his hold. A loud humming rang out in his ears, spots dancing before his eyes, his consciousness wavering fast. Acting on instinct, he reached up and clasped the squire's face between his palms. Without mercy, he dug his thumbs hard into his opponent's eyes.

Faylor screamed and let go, reeling back in agony.

Shaking off his breathlessness and pain, Ethan rose and pushed the squire completely off him. Bringing up his fists, he landed another blow, this one connecting with a jolt that reverberated all the way up his arm. Faylor blinked and groaned, weaving where he sat. Panting, Ethan stood, waiting to see if the other man had more fight in him. But Faylor was through, his eyes rolling backward in his head seconds before he toppled over in an unconscious sprawl across the floor.

Fists still clenched, Ethan whirled to find Lily.

The hem of her robe billowed around her ankles as she raced down the stairs. As she ran full tilt toward him, neither of them noticed Chaulk. Quick as a cobra, her stepfather reached forward and grabbed her tightly around the waist. Ethan watched, fury rising as she cried out and struggled to break Chaulk's grip without success.

"Let her go, Chaulk," he demanded. "Or would you prefer to end up like your friend?"

Chaulk cast a quick glance at Faylor's prostrate form, then back up to meet Ethan's gaze. "You're not taking her. She is my ticket to a tidy sum of money, and I don't intend to be cheated out of it."

"Don't give him a thing," Lily said, continuing to fight against her stepfather's hold. "He's a bully and a cad, and deserves nothing."

"You're right on both scores, my dear," Ethan said. "But as for money, I would pay any amount to set you free. To me, you are more priceless than rubies and pearls."

Chaulk smiled. "A wise man, your lover. Well then, how much for her?"

"No, Ethan. He's a vulture. If you give him a pence, he'll be back for a pound."

Chaulk gave her a shake. "Shut up, or have you no

sense at all? And how in the blazes did you get free of your room? I thought we had you locked up tight."

Her lips curled back in a fearless smile. "I found a hairpin on the floor and worked the lock. You think yourself smart, but you're nothing but a cowardly, dull-witted conniver."

Chaulk's lips thinned at the insult, his arms tightening enough to make her whimper in pain.

Ethan stalked forward, intending to put an end to the situation. At the same instant, Lily raised her foot and gave a backward kick worthy of a mule. Her stepfather bellowed and loosened his hold, enough for Lily to wrench free.

Chaulk straightened just in time to meet the business end of Ethan's fist, which struck him square in the jaw. Like the squire before him, Chaulk swayed for a long moment, his eyes glazing over, before he crashed to the floor in an unconscious heap.

Lily stared at her stepfather in shock and relief, trying to take in the fact that he was truly vanquished. Turning, she launched herself into Ethan's arms. With a reassuring murmur, he caught her close and lifted her off her feet to cradle her against his body. Burying her face against his neck, she breathed in his warmth and strength. "Ethan, you're here, you saved me. I didn't think you would come," she said, tears dampening her cheeks. "I didn't think you knew."

"I knew," he murmured, stroking a hand over her back. "Though too late to stop Chaulk and Faylor, and for that I am sorry. So sorry."

"It doesn't matter, not anymore. You've dealt with them admirably. Just take me home with you; that's the only place I want to be."

"That's where you belong. But first there is something I must do."

"And what is that?"

With infinite tenderness, he touched his lips to hers and showed her exactly what he meant.

An hour later, dressed in a gown and cloak, Lily leaned back against the worn leather squabs of the coach that was taking her and Ethan toward London. Although the hired vehicle was not nearly as fine as any of Ethan's own coaches, she was nonetheless grateful for use of the conveyance. When one of the wheels hit a rough patch of road, though, and bounced her up—then down—hard against the seat, she wondered whether she had been too generous in her initial appreciation. Rubbing a hand against her hip, she caught Ethan's gaze.

"Are you all right?" he asked, concern, and some much deeper emotion, gleaming in his amber eyes.

"It was only a rut. The roads are always muddy this time of year."

"That is not what I meant," he said, his voice as rich and velvety as a dish of morning chocolate.

The sound curled inside her, warming her from the inside out.

"What I meant," he continued, "is are you all right? How badly did they hurt you, Lily? Did Faylor touch you?"

She shook her head. "No, he never came near, at least not in the way you mean. Other than some bruises, I suffered no lasting damage."

Tension eased visibly from his frame before he shifted closer to her on the seat. "That's good, because otherwise I would need to go back and do more than knock him senseless."

She smiled inwardly, remembering the small jolt of satisfaction she'd experienced when she and Ethan had come back downstairs, after going to her room so she could change clothes and gather her meager possessions, to find Faylor and her stepfather still lying insensible on the entry-hall floor. The servants had given Ethan looks of respect as she and Ethan walked from the house.

Gently, he laid his palm against the uninjured side of her face and slowly stroked a thumb over her cheek. "I swear that no one will ever hurt you again. In that I make you my most solemn vow."

She trembled, a rush of emotion welling up within her. "Oh God, Ethan, I was so scared. I thought I could handle things, but the more time that passed, the worse everything became."

"Shh," he hushed, brushing his lips against hers before moving to draw her into his arms. "It's over now," he reassured her, "and you are to do everything in your power to put these last few days out of your mind. All will be well again, you will see."

*Will it?* she wondered. So much still lay unresolved between them, including the falsehoods she had told him about herself. Despite her reservations, she knew that matters had come too far for her to conceal the truth from him any longer. After everything he had done to find her, to save her, she owed him that and more. But even as she prepared herself to confess, she hesitated, a queasy, fluttering sensation beating like a pair of tiny wings in her chest. Leaning back slightly in his arms, she finally forced herself to speak. "Ethan, there is something I have to tell you."

"Whatever it is, Lily, you don't need—"

"But I do," she interrupted, determined to proceed now that she had begun. "There is a great deal I have to say, so much I *should* have said long ago. My only excuse, I suppose, is that I was afraid of what you would think, what you would do."

"Lily—"

"Please, let me have my say."

After a small pause, he inclined his head. "As you wish."

She scooted back, putting another inch between them before she continued. "I have not always been completely truthful with you about myself. My name is . . . my real name is Lily Bainbridge, not Smythe."

"I know."

Her lashes lifted, her gaze flashing upward. Oh, well, of course he knew that, she supposed, given that he'd tracked her home to Cornwall. But as for the rest . . .

"No," she went on. "You do not understand. When I say my name is not Smythe, I mean it was *never* Smythe. Ethan . . . I . . ." She drew an unsteady breath, then pushed out the words. "I was never married."

She braced herself, waiting for an explosion, an exclamation of shock and confusion, even anger. Instead he gazed at her out of calm, steady, completely unsurprised eyes.

"Yes, I know," he said again.

The jolt she'd thought he would feel went through her. "What do you mean, *you know*!"

"Exactly that. Although I didn't piece together your deception until quite recently, I did figure it out."

"But how?" she sputtered.

"Because the military keeps records, my love. No officer by the name of John Smythe fought at Vittoria, let alone died."

She swallowed, incapable of forming a coherent response while she digested the unexpected turn of events. Of all the possibilities, she had never once considered that he might check on the military service of her make-believe husband. *And here I always considered myself so careful and so clever. Not so clever lately.* Then a new thought occurred.

"And you aren't angry?" she asked, studying his face for signs of his true feelings.

He raised a golden eyebrow, remonstrating her with its curve. "I was initially. In fact, I was furious when I first realized that you had lied to me, particularly given you had just accused me of having done the same. But . . . ," he said with a significant pause.

"Yes?"

"Finding out that you were gone, and that I might lose you, well, the reality of that put everything in a different perspective. I admit that I have not completely forgiven you yet for your elaborate fiction and the ease with which you perpetrated it upon me—"

"Deceiving you was never easy," she interjected.

"—But I know you had reasons for doing what you did, reasons I have recently come to understand more and more. My word, Lily, did you really stage your own death? The story in Penzance is that you swam out to sea and drowned. How much of that is true?"

"A great deal of it—actually, everything except the dying part. When Chaulk demanded that I marry Faylor, I refused, but he would have seen me wed despite my refusal. I knew I could never submit to such degradation, such utter misery, and that I would rather risk my life than spend it tied to a brute like the squire. So I swam out during a storm and let everyone assume I had perished."

"You played a dangerous game that could really have cost you your life. How exactly did you survive?"

Taking a breath, she told him her story—how she had run away to London and met him en route, about claiming her inheritance and her decision to turn herself into a widow. Wanting no secrets between them, she was careful to leave nothing out.

When she finished, he leaned back against the seat. "You went to such extremes, then, so you would never have to marry?" he remarked in a contemplative tone. "So you could remain free and independent of men?"

She rubbed a palm over her skirt. "Yes, that is what I intended."

He remained silent for a long moment. "And do you still hold those same opinions now?"

*No,* she thought, the answer rushing upon her. Once she had viewed marriage as a trap, a miserable prison into which women were tricked, then left to suffer. But her days living with Ethan had proven her wrong on that score, and despite her earlier hurt feelings and sense of betrayal, she knew she wanted nothing more than the chance to share her life with him. So long as it was Ethan who asked her to marry him, then her answer would be an unequivocal "yes."

But he hadn't asked her, she realized, crumbling a little inside as she remembered his fiancée in London. Still, she was made of sterner stuff, was she not? If she truly loved Ethan—and she did—then she owed it to herself to fight for him.

"No," she said aloud, pressing herself against his chest. "I do not feel the same. I know that girl . . . Lady Amelia, stands between us, but I do not want her to. I love you, Ethan, and whatever you decide, whatever you tell me, I will believe you this time. I only want us to be together."

He reached up a hand and stroked her hair. "Do you? And if I tell you I want you as my mistress again?"

Disappointment washed through her, but she ruthlessly pushed it aside. "Then that is what I will be."

Sliding a finger beneath her chin, he urged her face upward so that she was looking into his eyes. "That is a very generous offer, but entirely unnecessary."

"What?"

"I didn't ask you my question about marriage so you could become my mistress. I asked you so you could become my wife. Marry me, Lily. And this time, I will accept nothing other than a 'yes.' "

"But what about Lady Amelia?"

"Mrs. Hocksby by now, I would expect," he corrected. "About the same time you left London, Amelia eloped to Gretna Green with a young man she loves. I assume the pair are now husband and wife, leaving me free to plight my troth where I will. So, tell me you will be my wife."

For a moment she couldn't breathe, joy bursting like fireworks through her veins. "Oh, yes, yes, my love."

Mouth curved in a wide smile, she tossed her arms around his neck and drew his head down to hers. Humming low in her throat as he responded, she took the lead, plundering his mouth with a thoroughness that made her burn from head to toe. Wishing they were closer, she murmured her delight when he lifted her off the seat and onto his lap, settling her where both of them could claim an even deeper level of intimacy.

As their kisses continued, she lost awareness of her surroundings, threading her fingers into his hair while he played upon her desires with a series of long, heated kisses, interspersed by quicker, shorter nips and licks. Her lips were swollen, her body aching, by the time they broke apart to take a full breath of air.

"Good Lord," he exclaimed. "I don't know how I've done without *that* for all these many days."

"I've missed you too." She smiled.

"Don't look at me like that or I may decide to take you here and now, after all."

"Then why do you not?" she encouraged, brushing her fingers against his cheeks and temple.

"Mostly because of the condition of these coach springs. I fear if we try anything, we might both emerge as cripples."

A laugh escaped her at the image.

He bounced her playfully atop his thighs. "But that does not mean I plan to wait long."

"You do not have to wait at all. It isn't as if we have not been intimate already."

"True, but as much as I am dying to return to your bed—and believe me, I am—I was thinking we might have a traditional wedding with a reading of the banns and all the requisite trappings. I am proud to make you my bride and I want everyone to know it. By the time we wed, no one will doubt we are marrying for anything other than love."

A tremulous smile spread over her lips, warmth glowing inside her like a summer sun.

"What would you think of being wed at Andarley?" he continued. "The family chapel is small and would not hold above twenty guests, but it is a pretty enough little building. I believe you would like it."

"The chapel sounds divine. Though I would marry you anywhere, even if it were in a hut."

Pleasure burnished his gaze, followed by a humorous twinkle. "A hut, hmm? Well, I can do a bit better than that for the ceremony, though we might be able to locate a hut for the honeymoon, if you are set on such an accommodation."

She laughed. "Wherever you like, my lord, so long as we are together," she pledged. "I love you, Ethan."

His face turned serious. Bending his head, he brushed his lips over hers. "I love you too. Now and forever."

# Chapter Twenty-three

*"O*H, YOU LOOK absolutely beautiful!" Davina declared five weeks later as she stood back to survey the final touches made to Lily's wedding ensemble. Gowned in winter-white velvet with elbow-length sleeves and a square-cut bodice, Lily had to confess that she did feel a little like a princess. Only minutes before, her maid had finished arranging her hair into a fashionable riot of curls before pinning an ankle-length veil of the finest Brussels lace onto her head. Her hands tingled, her heart beating at a wildly erratic pace. In all her life she had never felt so nervous, yet so ebullient. There were moments when she wondered if her white, pearl-encrusted slippers were still touching the floor.

"Davina is right," Julianna agreed from where she stood with them in one of the guest bedrooms at Andarley. "I cannot recall ever seeing a more radiant bride."

Lily gazed at her two friends, wanting to hug them both, but afraid she might ruin everyone's hard work of the past two hours if she did so. "If I do look as well as you both say," she replied, "it is only because I am so happy. Thank you for being here with me today and standing as my matrons of honor."

"I would not have missed your wedding for the world," Julianna said. "How could I, when it means seeing two of my best friends joined?"

Despite having only recently finished her lying-in, Julianna had declared herself healthy enough to make the journey from West Riding. Of course, Rafe, Cam, and baby Stephanie had accompanied her.

"You could not have kept me away either," Davina stated. "And I must say, I was pleased to see that the dowager marchioness is attending. It is always good to have peace within a family."

"Yes," Lily replied, restraining the urge to elaborate on the subject. "Very good."

She still wasn't sure what Ethan had said to his mother to make her change her initial refusal to attend the ceremony, but she had to give her future mother-in-law credit for at least appearing to welcome her into the family. With time she hoped the older woman would put aside her disappointment in seeing her matrimonial plans for Ethan foiled. Maybe they would never be as close as mother and daughter, but perhaps they could at least be friends.

"Oh, look at the hour," Davina remarked. "Nearly ten o'clock and time to leave for the chapel. Let us help you into your cloak."

With great care, Julianna and Davina assisted Lily into her matching, fur-trimmed white wool cloak, a necessity on such a cold Christmas Eve. Yet the morning sun was shining, making the blanket of snow covering the land wink and sparkle like diamonds, as if nature had decided to celebrate with her and Ethan.

"There, you are ready," Julianna pronounced. "Why do you not take a last quiet moment to yourself? Davina and I will be back in just a couple of minutes; then we shall be off to the chapel."

Lily sent both women a smile and a small wave, but once they departed, she found she could not relax enough to sit—though not out of fear, she knew, but anticipation. Since agreeing to become Ethan's wife, she had experienced not a single qualm, nor so much as an instant of doubt. Contrary to her earlier worries, she knew that nothing in her life had ever felt as right as her decision to marry Ethan. Whatever the future might bring, all would be well because they were together.

When the door clicked open behind her, she turned, expecting to find Julianna or Davina returned to help her down to the coach for the short ride to the chapel. Instead, Ethan stood in the doorway.

Her pulse jittered at the sight of him, wondering how he could possibly be more handsome, and yet somehow he had managed the trick. Dressed in traditional wedding attire, a blue tailcoat emphasized the breadth of his shoulders, his firm chest garbed in a white shirt and gray waistcoat, while tight-fitting pale gray breeches hugged his thighs. Above, his starched white linen cravat was tied in a perfect mathematical, while below, black stockings hugged the muscled contours of his calves, polished black shoes gracing his long, elegant feet.

"Oh, don't you look magnificent!" she sighed aloud.

He smiled and shut the door behind him. "I was thinking the same thing about you. Good God, love, you fair take my breath you are so gorgeous, and I haven't even seen what's underneath that cloak of yours."

"Nor shall you until the ceremony begins," she chided with mock reproof. "You shouldn't even be here, you know. Julianna and Davina would have a fit if they knew you had snuck in."

"Well, it shall be our little secret," he said with a wink as he strode forward. "I have something for you and I didn't want to wait to give it to you."

"You could have sent it up."

He shook his head, stopping in front of her. "No, not this. I had to give this to you in person. I would have done so last night, but the package only just now arrived by special messenger from London." Reaching into his coat, he withdrew a long jeweler's box covered in black velvet.

"Oh, you didn't have to get me another wedding gift," she declared. "You already gave me this exquisite diamond necklace and earrings." Untying the ribbon at her throat, she opened her cloak just enough to reveal the gemstones. "See, I am wearing them now."

"Those are Andarton family jewels, and yours, by right, as my bride. And as undeniably lovely as they are on you, what I have here is a special gift meant only for you. I hope you will like it."

"I like everything you give me," she murmured. But a moment later, a gasp caught in her throat as he opened the box to reveal the jewelry inside. Simply designed yet stunning all the same, the necklace was fashioned of round, perfectly matched diamonds set in gold. At its base lay a large, oval gemstone of the purest, most luminous blue she had ever seen.

"I know that cerulean is your favorite color," he murmured, "so I had Rundell and Bridge search for a sapphire that most closely matches the sky on a brilliant, sunny day. They found this one. What do you think?"

Reaching out a trembling hand, she brushed one fingertip over the stone, finding the surface smooth and surprisingly warm. "It's breathtaking."

"I wanted you to have this," he continued, "so you can take a little piece of the sky with you wherever you go."

"Oh, Ethan." Forgetting all about her wedding finery, she flung her arms around him and pressed her lips to his.

He kissed her back, smiling against her mouth. "So you like it?"

"I love it," she sighed. "But not half as much as I love you."

"And I adore you. I promise to make you happy."

"And I promise the same."

"Here," he said, moving a step back. "Let's put this on you." Reaching around, he unfastened the clasp of the necklace she was wearing and set it on a dressing table. Lifting his gift from its velvet bed, he placed the sapphire and diamonds around her throat, then hooked the clasp. "There," he pronounced. "Glorious." The gemstone winked, its rich shade truly resembling a piece of sunny sky.

Moving closer, she kissed him, pouring all her love into the embrace.

"I cannot wait until tonight," he murmured against her mouth.

"Even though you snuck into my room last night? That was very naughty of you, you know. What if we'd been caught?"

He grinned. "We weren't. And after weeks without you, I couldn't stay in my room, knowing you were only just down the hall."

"I stopped taking the contraceptive herbs," she confided. "I might already be with child."

His arms tightened at her waist. "If you are not enceinte now, I'll take great pleasure making sure you are soon."

She laughed, until he silenced her again with another lengthy kiss. Her eyes were closed and she was floating on a surfeit of pleasure when a sharp exclamation broke the quiet.

"*Aah!* What do you two think you're doing?" demanded Davina in obviously shocked tones as she rushed into the room. "You can't kiss before the ceremony!"

Ethan lifted his head and grinned. "As you can see, we already are."

"What I mean is that you are not allowed to be together," Davina said, her outrage plain. "*Shoo*, my lord! *Shoo, shoo.*"

Ethan straightened, lifting a brow as if he had never before been told to *shoo*.

Julianna entered the fray. "Yes, Ethan, let her go and take yourself off. Rafe and Tony are waiting for you below, checking their watches every half-minute and grumbling about being late. It's really quite bad of you, stealing in here to see Lily when you ought to be at the chapel."

Lily eased out of Ethan's arms and turned, pointing a finger at her new necklace. "He came to give me this."

The other women moved forward for a look, letting out cries of delight. "It's fabulous!"

"Stunning!"

"I know," Lily said, smiling widely. "It's my own little piece of sky."

Davina recovered first. "As beautiful as your necklace may be, we are all late now. What are you still doing here, my lord? Do you not know it is bad luck to see the bride before the wedding?"

Ethan paused for a moment, then met Lily's gaze. "I don't hold with such superstitions. Besides, with Lily by my side, I have all the luck I will ever need, and all the love, as well."

Read on for a sneak peek
at

# *His Favorite Mistress*

Tracy Anne Warren

Coming from Ballantine Books
Available wherever books are sold

$A$LL IT WILL *take is a single bullet straight through the heart,* Gabriella St. George told herself as she clutched the pistol in her hand.

She was a good shot and had confidence in her skills. After all, she'd been taught by the best—the Great Moncrief himself, who was billed in entertainment circles as the finest sharpshooter known to the civilized world. Her biggest concern was finding the courage to hold fast to her resolve and carry through with her plan—that and keeping her arm from shaking so violently that she fouled her aim.

She supposed she had good reason for her jitters, despite the fact that this wouldn't be the first time she had taken a life. True, all those she had killed before had been animals—rabbits and birds that she'd hunted for food as she'd traveled across England. She'd even been known to poach a deer on occasion in order to hold starvation at bay. But tonight would be different.

For tonight she planned to kill a man.

Easing deeper into the late evening shadows that painted the walls and corners of the study black, she waited, knowing that eventually he would come. She'd been observing him this past week and knew his habits, knew that he always stopped in this room for a few minutes each night before retiring upstairs.

Thanks to a maid who didn't mind chatting with a friendly stranger while out completing her errands, Gabriella had learned that, except for the servants, he was alone here in this immense townhouse. His wife and young children, so she had been told, were at his estate in the north of England.

The information had come as a relief, since she had no desire to involve innocents. After all, his crimes were his alone; he was the only one deserving of retribution. Even so, she couldn't completely set aside the guilt that nibbled at her, aware that her actions tonight would bring grief to others. But she pushed aside her qualms, reassuring herself once again that he deserved the judgment she planned to mete out.

*One life,* she argued, *in recompense for another.*

When she'd slipped through a convenient window a couple of hours ago, she'd heard the low rhythm of male conversation, punctuated by sporadic bursts of laughter. He'd invited friends over, a small group of men gathered to share dinner, then drinks while they played a few rounds of cards. Having long ago learned the art of patience, she'd settled into a corner, gun in hand, and allowed time to pass.

At length, the house had grown quiet as his guests said their farewells and departed, the servants retreating to make their way to their beds. Only the steady tick-tock of the room's finely-crafted satinwood casement clock broke the silence, together with the gentle crackling of the fire she'd watched a maid refresh about an hour earlier. *Not long now,* she judged, *and he will be here.* Shifting slightly, she worked to ease the stiffness and pent-up tension that had gathered in her muscles and joints.

Another five minutes elapsed before she finally heard footsteps. Pressing her back flat against the wall, she sank deeper into the concealing shadows and watched him stride into the room.

From the moment he entered the study he dominated the space, commanding his surroundings with not only his impressive size and athletic grace, but with the innate forcefulness of his personality. Despite the tenebrous light, she recognized the arrogance in his gait, along with an unmistakable air of noble authority she would have assumed was bred into him from birth had she not known otherwise. Before tonight, she'd only viewed him from a distance, yet he seemed taller up close, his hair darker, so deep a brown as to be nearly black. A trick of the late evening shadows, she assumed.

Shivering, a tingle whispered along her backbone, her heart pounding with the force of a hammer striking an anvil; a reaction she had never before experienced while observing the man. Likely the sensation was a product of the tension she felt, well aware the moment she had been preparing for was now nearly upon her. Gathering her nerve, she tightened her grip on the gun and let him come farther into the room.

Reaching the desk, he searched for a match and candle. Light flared to life moments later, illumination spreading in a comfortable yellow glow over the space. She forced herself not to tremble, holding her position as he stepped toward a nearby bookshelf and began to peruse the titles.

She moved forward, the pistol held straight out before her. "Rafe Pendragon," she declared in a clear, unwavering voice. "Prepare to pay for your crimes."

His shoulders stiffened before he slowly turned to face her.

Only then did she see him fully, her gaze riveted to his impossibly handsome face. Classically hewn cheekbones framed a long patrician nose, his forehead strong, his jaw and chin cleaved from a heritage of ancient aristocratic stock. His lips were blatantly seductive, as if nature had designed them to entice a woman into wanting to commit any number of earthly sins. Then there was his complexion—swarthy instead of pale, with a delicious evening's growth of whiskers that only enhanced his aura of masculine sensuality. Yet of all his attractive qualities—and they were legion—his most compelling physical feature was his eyes. Rich and deep-set, they were a pure, almost velvety blue, dark as midnight yet brilliant as a summer sea. Right now those eyes were gazing at her, full of keen observation and powerful intellect. *He is studying me,* she realized, *just as I am studying him.*

A soft gasp escaped her lips, but she held herself and the gun steady. "You're not Pendragon!" she accused.

The stranger arched a dark eyebrow. "Indeed no, I am not. I trust you won't shoot me for disappointing you, Miss . . ." He let the sentence trail off. "You are a miss, are you not, despite your present choice of masculine attire?"

Earlier this evening she'd decided to dress as a boy. After all, sneaking into a townhouse to kill a man was not easily accomplished while wearing a gown, stays, and petticoat.

She ignored his query. "Where is he?"

"Rafe, I assume you mean. Well, I am not likely to aid you by revealing his whereabouts. Why do you want to harm him anyway? Is it money you're after?"

Her shoulders tightened. "I am no thief. If I were, I could have liberated a king's ransom from this room while the lot of you were having dinner. Yes," she offered when he tipped his head in inquiry, "I have been here for some while, waiting unobserved."

"A regular little cat, are you? Tiptoeing in on silent feet. A useful ability for any person, I will admit."

"I have many useful abilities, but I am not here to engage in a round of banter with you, whoever you might be."

"Ah, forgive my lack of manners," he drawled. "Wyvern at your service. I would make you a bow were I sure you wouldn't put a bullet in me while I attempted the move."

"I won't shoot unless you give me cause," she stated, inching the pistol higher. "In the interest of safety, however, I suggest you take a seat over there." She nodded toward an armchair that faced the desk.

"Thank you, no. I am perfectly comfortable standing."

"Comfortable or not, pray be seated."

At a height of more than six feet, he towered over her. Aware she needed every possible advantage in a situation that was suddenly not going at all as she'd planned, she knew he would pose far less of a threat were he ensconced in a chair. Despite his apparent affability, she didn't trust him for a second.

He met her gaze, then shrugged. "Very well, if you insist. After all, you are the one with the weapon. But first, tell me what grievance you have against my friend. He doesn't generally engender such a violent reaction, especially among the fairer sex."

Her breasts rose and fell beneath her threadbare linen shirt, a cold lump wedged deep within her chest. "He harmed me and mine, and that is all you need to know. Believe me, I have just cause for despising the man."

"Did your family fall upon hard times, then? Did you lose your home and decide to lay the blame at Rafe's doorstep?"

"Believe me, whatever blame I cast belongs at *no other* doorstep but his."

Wyvern crossed his arms over his chest and leaned a hip against the desk. "How old are you? You look little more than a girl."

She drew herself up. "I am a woman grown. Seventeen, if you must know, though I fail to see what difference it makes."

"Oh, it doesn't, not really. It strikes me, however, that most young women your age would be tucked up tight inside their houses, far too afraid to venture out on their own, let alone go about dressed in male attire, and brandishing a pistol."

"You will find that I am not like most young women."

The edge of his mouth tipped upward, a twinkle glittering in his brilliant blue gaze. "Yes, so I am beginning to see."

A fresh tingle inched down her spine as if he had reached out and stroked a hand over her skin, the sensation having nothing to do with the peril of the situation, and everything to do with her awareness of the man himself. *Indisputably, he is the most breathtaking man I had ever encountered. But I have no business noticing such things,* she scolded herself, *particularly not now when I have come on a mission of vengeance. A mission I cannot afford to delay.*

"Now, Mr. Wyvern," she said, determined to move matters forward. "If your curiosity has been satisfied, I suggest you take that seat."

"It's Wyvern. Just Wyvern."

"Fine, *Wyvern*—"

"As for my curiosity," he continued, "you have done nothing but further whet my appetite. You haven't even told me your name."

"No, I have not," she stated emphatically.

He inclined his head. "As you prefer, then. Now, which seat is it that I am to take?"

Mildly surprised by the question, she hesitated, relaxing her stance a bit as she gestured toward the correct chair. "That one. Just there."

"Here?" He pointed, stretching out a hand.

She frowned, wondering if he might be hard of hearing. "Yes, there."

Quick as a flash, he reached out and seized hold of her wrist, yanking her off balance. She gasped, unable to recover from his trick before he wrested the gun from her grip and imprisoned her inside his arms. In the blink of an eye, she found the tables turned, going suddenly from captor to captive.

"Ooh!" she cried, wiggling inside his hold. "Let me go!"

He tightened his arms, her body pressed firmly against his own. "Tut, tut. Quit your squirming, girl."

She stomped on his foot, wincing as a rebounding pain jolted along her instep.

"Quit that, too," he admonished, a spark of amused annoyance gleaming in his eyes. "You're only causing yourself harm, since I have no intention of releasing you before I am ready to do so. In case you had not noticed, I am bigger and stronger and you are now entirely at my mercy."

Grasping her so tightly the air wheezed out of her lungs, he leaned back and set the gun atop the desk. Turning around, he moved the two of them a few steps away—too far for her to have any chance of recovering the weapon. Only then did he ease his hold enough to let her breathe normally again. On a sharp inhale, she filled her lungs with air, the movement pressing her breasts against the solid wall of his chest.

Gazing downward, he quirked a brow. "I must admit I have to agree with your assessment."

"My assessment of what?" she demanded in a winded voice.

"That you are a woman full-grown." He snuggled her closer, and stroked a hand over her back and across her hip. "You may be young, but you are curved in all the right places. Considering our current proximity, you really ought to tell me your name, you know."

She squirmed against him. "Release me!"

He chuckled softly. "So you would rather have me use persuasion, would you, to force out the answer?" His gaze lowered to her mouth, his tone dropping to a husky drawl. "You will find I have a rare talent for persuasion."

"And you will find that I am well used to the blandishments of smooth-talkers and confidence tricksters. I doubt your efforts will prove any more successful than theirs."

"A challenge, is it? I like challenges, especially ones issued by pretty little minxes like you."

Before she knew what he meant to do, his lips came down on hers. At first she stiffened inside his embrace, straining to be free despite the futility of the action. But even as she struggled, a part of her brain registered the captivating pleasure of his mouth moving against her own, the breath she'd barely managed to regulate becoming fast and shallow once more.

Still, with a last ounce of determination, she gave another wiggling push. To her dismay, however, her attempt did nothing but encourage him to reach down and secure her wrists behind her back, before he slowly bent her body into his own, leaving her front plastered breast to chest, stomach to thigh, against him.

She barely had a chance to adjust before he slanted his mouth and kissed her harder, compelling a response from her that she was helpless to resist. For in spite of having previously fended off unwanted advances from men, this was the first time she'd ever been caught by one.

The first time she had ever been kissed.

*And what a kiss it is,* she had to confess, her limbs turning warm and waxen as if they had a will of their own. Her brain might argue that she didn't want this—want him—but her body most decidedly did not agree. Ragged heat washed over her, a shiver following as he coaxed her lips to part.

Using his tongue, he painted her mouth with the lightest of strokes, a move that sent her heart racing at breakneck speed. Trembling from the almost shocking carnality of the act, she let him continue, let him delve inside her mouth to play there with a finesse that quite literally made her whimper.

Then, as suddenly as it had begun, the kiss ended, Wyvern lifting his head to peer down into her eyes. His own gaze was lambent, eyelids half-lowered as if he too was trying to recover from an unexpected surfeit of pleasure. Yet he didn't release her from his hold, obviously not so far gone as to forget why she had come into his possession in the first place.

"Have you had enough," he asked roughly, "or shall we try for another?"

Seeing his expression that was half-challenge, half-anticipation—as if he knew he would win no matter her answer—she decided it might be wise to acquiesce to his original demand. "It's Gabriella," she murmured. "My name is Gabriella."

His lips turned up in a smile. "It suits you. A pleasure to meet you"—pausing, he shifted so their bodies rubbed together—"Gabriella."